Iain and Marion

When we are as one, everything in my world is right and perfect.

When a Laird Loves a Lady

Highlander Vows: Entangled Hearts,
Book One

by
Julie Johnstone

The best way to stay in touch is to subscribe to my newsletter. Go to www.juliejohnstoneauthor.com and subscribe in the box at the top of the page that says Newsletter. If you don't hear from me once a month, please check your spam filter and set up your email to allow my messages through to you so you don't miss the opportunity to win great prizes or hear about appearances.

Dedication

For my editor Danielle Rose Poiesz who constantly challenges me to reach greater heights on the mountain of publication by daring me to dig into my arsenal of tools and use them to reach the summit. Thank you. You never blink an eye at what I throw your way, and you are unfailingly supportive.

I'd like to give special thanks to Chrissie MacRae with Stòrlann Scots Gaelic and Brian Wilton with the Scottish Tartan Authority for their assistance on answering my questions regarding Gaelic, plaids, and tartans.

I'd also like to give a heartfelt thanks to Eliza Knight and Kathryn Le Veque for answering my many messages about random medieval and Scottish questions. Their generosity deeply moved me!

Author's Note

Dear Readers,

I have taken great pains to make sure the words I used in writing this story were as historically accurate as possible. However, given that I am writing to a modern audience, there are some instances when I chose to use a word that was not in existence in the fourteenth century, as they simply did not have a word at that time to correctly convey the meaning of the sentence.

If you're interested in when my books go on sale, or want to be one of the first to know about my new releases, please follow me on BookBub! You'll get quick book notifications every time there's a new pre-order, book on sale, or new release with an easy click of your mouse to follow me. You can follow me on BookBub here: www.bookbub.com/authors/julie-johnstone

All the best,
Julie

One

England, 1357

Faking her death would be simple. It was escaping her home that would be difficult. Marion de Lacy stared hard into the slowly darkening sky, thinking about the plan she intended to put into action tomorrow—if all went well—but growing uneasiness tightened her belly. From where she stood in the bailey, she counted the guards up in the tower. It was not her imagination: Father had tripled the knights keeping guard at all times, as if he was expecting trouble.

Taking a deep breath of the damp air, she pulled her mother's cloak tighter around her to ward off the twilight chill. A lump lodged in her throat as the wool scratched her neck. In the many years since her mother had been gone, Marion had both hated and loved this cloak for the death and life it represented. Her mother's freesia scent had long since faded from the garment, yet simply calling up a memory of her mother wearing it gave Marion comfort.

She rubbed her fingers against the rough material. When she fled, she couldn't chance taking anything with her but the clothes on her body and this cloak. Her death had to appear accidental, and the cloak that everyone knew she prized would ensure her freedom. Finding it tangled in the branches at the edge of the sea cliff ought to be just the thing to convince her father and William Froste that she'd drowned. After all, neither man thought she could swim. They didn't truly care about her anyway. Her marriage to the blackhearted knight was only about what her hand could give the two men. Her father, Baron de Lacy, wanted more power, and Froste wanted her family's prized land. A match made in Heaven, if only the match didn't involve her...but it did.

Father would set the hounds of Hell themselves to track her down if he had the slightest suspicion that she was still alive. She was an inestimable possession to be given to secure Froste's unwavering allegiance and, therefore, that of the renowned ferocious knights who served him. Whatever small sliver of hope she had that her father would grant her mercy and not marry her to Froste had been destroyed by the lashing she'd received when she'd pleaded for him to do so.

The moon crested above the watchtower, reminding her why she was out here so close to mealtime: to meet Angus. The Scotsman may have been her father's stable master, but he was *her* ally, and when he'd proposed she flee England for Scotland, she'd readily consented.

Marion looked to the west, the direction from which Angus would return from Newcastle. He should be back any minute now from meeting his cousin and clansman Neil, who was to escort her to Scotland. She prayed all was set and that Angus's kin was ready to depart. With her wedding to Froste to take place in six days, she wanted to be far away before there was even the slightest chance he'd be making his way here. And since he was set to arrive the night before the wedding, leaving tomorrow promised she'd not encounter him.

A sense of urgency enveloped her, and Marion forced

herself to stroll across the bailey toward the gatehouse that led to the tunnel preceding the drawbridge. She couldn't risk raising suspicion from the tower guards. At the gatehouse, she nodded to Albert, one of the knights who operated the drawbridge mechanism. He was young and rarely questioned her excursions to pick flowers or find herbs.

"Off to get some medicine?" he inquired.

"Yes," she lied with a smile and a little pang of guilt. But this was survival, she reminded herself as she entered the tunnel. When she exited the heavy wooden door that led to freedom, she wasn't surprised to find Peter and Andrew not yet up in the twin towers that flanked the entrance to the drawbridge. It was, after all, time for the changing of the guard.

They smiled at her as they put on their helmets and demi-gauntlets. They were an imposing presence to any who crossed the drawbridge and dared to approach the castle gate. Both men were tall and looked particularly daunting in their full armor, which Father insisted upon at all times. The men were certainly a fortress in their own right.

She nodded to them. "I'll not be long. I want to gather some more flowers for the supper table." Her voice didn't even wobble with the lie.

Peter grinned at her, his kind brown eyes crinkling at the edges. "Will you pick me one of those pale winter flowers for my wife again, Marion?"

She returned his smile. "It took away her anger as I said it would, didn't it?"

"It did," he replied. "You always know just how to help with her."

"I'll get a pink one if I can find it. The colors are becoming scarcer as the weather cools."

Andrew, the younger of the two knights, smiled, displaying a set of straight teeth. He held up his covered arm. "My cut is almost healed."

Marion nodded. "I told you! Now maybe you'll listen to me sooner next time you're wounded in training."

He gave a soft laugh. "I will. Should I put more of your paste on tonight?"

"Yes, keep using it. I'll have to gather some more yarrow, if I can find any, and mix up another batch of the medicine for you." And she'd have to do it before she escaped. "I better get going if I'm going to find those things." She knew she should not have agreed to search for the flowers and offered to find the yarrow when she still had to speak to Angus and return to the castle in time for supper, but both men had been kind to her when many had not. It was her way of thanking them.

After Peter lowered the bridge and opened the door, she departed the castle grounds, considering her plan once more. Had she forgotten anything? She didn't think so. She was simply going to walk straight out of her father's castle and never come back. Tomorrow, she'd announce she was going out to collect more winter blooms, and then, instead, she would go down to the edge of the cliff overlooking the sea. She would slip off her cloak and leave it for a search party to find. Her breath caught deep in her chest at the simple yet dangerous plot. The last detail to see to was Angus.

She stared down the long dirt path that led to the sea and stilled, listening for hoofbeats. A slight vibration of the ground tingled her feet, and her heart sped in hopeful anticipation that it was Angus coming down the dirt road on his horse. When the crafty stable master appeared with a grin spread across his face, the worry that was squeezing her heart loosened. For the first time since he had ridden out that morning, she took a proper breath. He stopped his stallion alongside her and dismounted.

She tilted her head back to look up at him as he towered over her. An errant thought struck. "Angus, are all Scots as tall as you?"

"Nay, but ye ken Scots are bigger than all the wee Englishmen." Suppressed laughter filled his deep voice. "So even the ones nae as tall as me are giants compared te the scrawny men here."

"You're teasing me," she replied, even as she arched her eyebrows in uncertainty.

"A wee bit," he agreed and tousled her hair. The laughter vanished from his eyes as he rubbed a hand over his square jaw and then stared down his bumpy nose at her, fixing what he called his "lecturing look" on her. "We've nae much time. Neil is in Newcastle just as he's supposed te be, but there's been a slight change."

She frowned. "For the last month, every time I wanted to simply make haste and flee, you refused my suggestion, and now you say there's a slight change?"

His ruddy complexion darkened. She'd pricked that MacLeod temper her mother had always said Angus's clan was known for throughout the Isle of Skye, where they lived in the farthest reaches of Scotland. Marion could remember her mother chuckling and teasing Angus about how no one knew the MacLeod temperament better than their neighboring clan, the MacDonalds of Sleat, to which her mother had been born. The two clans had a history of feuding.

Angus cleared his throat and recaptured Marion's attention. Without warning, his hand closed over her shoulder, and he squeezed gently. "I'm sorry te say it so plain, but ye must die at once."

Her eyes widened as dread settled in the pit of her stomach. "What? Why?" The sudden fear she felt was unreasonable. She knew he didn't mean she was really going to die, but her palms were sweating and her lungs had tightened all the same. She sucked in air and wiped her damp hands down the length of her cotton skirts. Suddenly, the idea of going to a foreign land and living with her mother's clan, people she'd never met, made her apprehensive.

She didn't even know if the MacDonalds—her uncle, in particular, who was now the laird—would accept her or not. She was half-English, after all, and Angus had told her that when a Scot considered her English bloodline and the fact that she'd been raised there, they would most likely brand her fully English, which was not a good thing in a Scottish mind. And if her uncle was anything like her grandfather had been, the man was not going to be very reasonable. But she didn't have any other family to turn to who would dare defy her father, and Angus hadn't offered for her to go to his clan, so she'd not asked. He likely didn't want to bring trouble to his clan's doorstep, and she didn't blame him.

Panic bubbled inside her. She needed more time, even if it was only the day she'd thought she had, to gather her courage.

"Why must I flee tonight? I was to teach Eustice how to dress a wound. She might serve as a maid, but then she will be able to help the knights when I'm gone. And her little brother, Bernard, needs a few more lessons before he's mastered writing his name and reading. And Eustice's youngest sister has begged me to speak to Father about allowing her to visit her mother next week."

"Ye kinnae watch out for everyone here anymore, Marion."

She placed her hand over his on her shoulder. "Neither can you."

Their gazes locked in understanding and disagreement.

He slipped his hand from her shoulder, and then crossed his arms over his chest in a gesture that screamed stubborn, unyielding protector. "If I leave at the same time ye feign yer death," he said, changing the subject, "it could stir yer father's suspicion and make him ask questions when none need te be asked. I'll be going home te Scotland soon after ye." Angus reached into a satchel attached to his horse and pulled out a dagger, which he slipped to her. "I had this made for ye."

Marion took the weapon and turned it over, her heart pounding. "It's beautiful." She held it by its black handle while withdrawing it from the sheath and examining it. "It's much sharper than the one I have."

"Aye," he said grimly. "It is. Dunnae forget that just because I taught ye te wield a dagger does nae mean ye can defend yerself from *all* harm. Listen te my cousin and do as he says. Follow his lead."

She gave a tight nod. "I will. But why must I leave now and not tomorrow?"

Concern filled Angus's eyes. "Because I ran into Froste's brother in town and he told me that Froste sent word that he would be arriving in two days."

Marion gasped. "That's earlier than expected."

"Aye," Angus said and took her arm with gentle authority. "So ye must go now. I'd rather be trying te trick only yer father than yer father, Froste, and his savage knights. I want ye long gone and yer death accepted when

Froste arrives."

She shivered as her mind began to race with all that could go wrong.

"I see the worry darkening yer green eyes," Angus said, interrupting her thoughts. He whipped off his hat and his hair, still shockingly red in spite of his years, fell down around his shoulders. He only ever wore it that way when he was riding. He said the wind in his hair reminded him of riding his own horse when he was in Scotland. "I was going to talk to ye tonight, but now that I kinnae…" He shifted from foot to foot, as if uncomfortable. "I want te offer ye something. I'd have proposed it sooner, but I did nae want ye te feel ye had te take my offer so as nae te hurt me, but I kinnae hold my tongue, even so."

She furrowed her brow. "What is it?"

"I'd be proud if ye wanted te stay with the MacLeod clan instead of going te the MacDonalds. Then ye'd nae have te leave everyone ye ken behind. Ye'd have me."

A surge of relief filled her. She threw her arms around Angus, and he returned her hug quick and hard before setting her away. Her eyes misted at once. "I had hoped you would ask me," she admitted.

For a moment, he looked astonished, but then he spoke. "Yer mother risked her life te come into MacLeod territory at a time when we were fighting terrible with the MacDonalds, as ye well ken."

Marion nodded. She knew the story of how Angus had ended up here. He'd told her many times. Her mother had been somewhat of a renowned healer from a young age, and when Angus's wife had a hard birthing, her mother had gone to help. The knowledge that his wife and child had died anyway still made Marion want to cry.

"I pledged my life te keep yer mother safe for the kind-

ness she'd done me, which brought me here, but, lass, long
ago ye became like a daughter te me, and I pledge the rest
of my miserable life te defending ye."

She gripped Angus's hand. "I wish you were my father."

He gave her a proud yet smug look, one she was used
to seeing. She chortled to herself. The man did have a
terrible streak of pride. She'd have to give Father John
another coin for penance for Angus, since the Scot refused
to take up the custom himself.

Angus hooked his thumb in his gray tunic. "Ye'll make
a fine MacLeod because ye already ken we're the best clan
in Scotland."

Mentally, she added another coin to her dues. "Do you
think they'll let me become a MacLeod, though, since my
mother was the daughter of the previous MacDonald laird
and I've an English father?"

"They will," he answered without hesitation, but she
heard the slight catch in his voice.

"Angus." She narrowed her eyes. "You said you would
never lie to me."

His brows dipped together, and he gave her a long,
disgruntled look. "They may be a bit wary," he finally
admitted. "But I'll nae let them turn ye away. Dunnae
worry," he finished, his Scottish brogue becoming thick
with emotion.

She bit her lip. "Yes, but you won't be with me when I
first get there. What should I do to make certain that they
will let me stay?"

He quirked his mouth as he considered her question.
"Ye must first get the laird te like ye. Tell Neil te take ye
directly te the MacLeod te get his consent for ye te live
there. I kinnae vouch for the man myself as I've never met

him, but Neil says he's verra honorable, fierce in battle, patient, and reasonable." Angus cocked his head as if in thought. "Now that I think about it, I'm sure the MacLeod can get ye a husband, and then the clan will more readily accept ye. Aye." He nodded. "Get in the laird's good graces as soon as ye meet him and ask him te find ye a husband." A scowl twisted his lips. "Preferably one who will accept yer acting like a man sometimes."

She frowned at him. "*You* are the one who taught me how to ride bareback, wield a dagger, and shoot an arrow true."

"Aye." He nodded. "I did. But when I started teaching ye, I thought yer mama would be around te add her woman's touch. I did nae ken at the time that she'd pass when ye'd only seen eight summers in yer life."

"You're lying again," Marion said. "You continued those lessons long after Mama's death. You weren't a bit worried how I'd turn out."

"I sure was!" he objected, even as a guilty look crossed his face. "But what could I do? Ye insisted on hunting for the widows so they'd have food in the winter, and ye insisted on going out in the dark te help injured knights when I could nae go with ye. I had te teach ye te hunt and defend yerself. Plus, you were a sad, lonely thing, and I could nae verra well overlook ye when ye came te the stables and asked me te teach ye things."

"Oh, you could have," she replied. "Father overlooked me all the time, but your heart is too big to treat someone like that." She patted him on the chest. "I think you taught me the best things in the world, and it seems to me any man would want his woman to be able to defend herself."

"Shows how much ye ken about men," Angus muttered with a shake of his head. "Men like te think a woman needs *them*."

"I dunnae need a man," she said in her best Scottish accent.

He threw up his hands. "Ye do. Ye're just afeared."

The fear was true enough. Part of her longed for love, to feel as if she belonged to a family. For so long she'd wanted those things from her father, but she had never gotten them, no matter what she did. It was difficult to believe it would be any different in the future. She'd rather not be disappointed.

Angus tilted his head, looking at her uncertainly. "Ye want a wee bairn some day, dunnae ye?"

"Well, yes," she admitted and peered down at the ground, feeling foolish.

"Then ye need a man," he crowed.

She drew her gaze up to his. "Not just any man. I want a man who will truly love me."

He waved a hand dismissively. Marriages of convenience were a part of life, she knew, but she would not marry unless she was in love and her potential husband loved her in return. She would support herself if she needed to.

"The other big problem with a husband for ye," he continued, purposely avoiding, she suspected, her mention of the word *love*, "as I see it, is yer tender heart."

"What's wrong with a tender heart?" She raised her brow in question.

"'Tis more likely te get broken, aye?" His response was matter-of-fact.

"Nay. 'Tis more likely to have compassion," she replied with a grin.

"We're both right," he announced. "Yer mama had a tender heart like ye. 'Tis why yer father's black heart hurt her so. I dunnae care te watch the light dim in ye as it did yer mother."

"I don't wish for that fate, either," she replied, trying hard not to think about how sad and distant her mother had often seemed. "Which is why I will only marry for love. And why I need to get out of England."

"I ken that, lass, truly I do, but ye kinnae go through life alone."

"I don't wish to," she defended. "But if I have to, I have you, so I'll not be alone." With a shudder, her heart denied the possibility that she may never find love, but she squared her shoulders.

"'Tis nae the same as a husband," he said. "I'm old. Ye need a younger man who has the power te defend ye. And if Sir Frosty Pants ever comes after ye, you're going te need a strong man te go against him."

Marion snorted to cover the worry that was creeping in.

Angus moved his mouth to speak, but his reply was drowned by the sound of the supper horn blowing. "God's bones!" Angus muttered when the sound died. "I've flapped my jaw too long. Ye must go now. I'll head te the stables and start the fire as we intended. It'll draw Andrew and Peter away if they are watching ye too closely."

Marion looked over her shoulder at the knights, her stomach turning. She had known the plan since the day they had formed it, but now the reality of it scared her into a cold sweat. She turned back to Angus and gripped her dagger hard. "I'm afraid."

Determination filled his expression, as if his will for her to stay out of harm would make it so. "Ye will stay safe," he commanded. "Make yer way through the path in the woods that I showed ye, straight te Newcastle. I left ye a bag of coins under the first tree ye come te, the one with the rope tied te it. Neil will be waiting for ye by Pilgrim Gate on Pilgrim Street. The two of ye will depart from there."

She worried her lip but nodded all the same.

"Neil has become friends with a friar who can get the two of ye out," Angus went on. "Dunnae talk te anyone, especially any men. Ye should go unnoticed, as ye've never been there and won't likely see anyone ye've ever come in contact with here."

Fear tightened her lungs, but she swallowed. "I didn't even bid anyone farewell." Not that she really could have, nor did she think anyone would miss her other than Angus, and she would be seeing him again. Peter and Andrew *had* been kind to her, but they were her father's men, and she knew it well. She had been taken to the dungeon by the knights several times for punishment for transgressions that ranged from her tone not pleasing her father to his thinking she gave him a disrespectful look. Other times, they'd carried out the duty of tying her to the post for a thrashing when she'd angered her father. They had begged her forgiveness profusely but done their duties all the same. They would likely be somewhat glad they did not have to contend with such things anymore.

Eustice was both kind *and* thankful for Marion teaching her brother how to read, but Eustice lost all color any time someone mentioned the maid going with Marion to Froste's home after Marion was married. She suspected the woman was afraid to go to the home of the infamous "Merciless Knight." Eustice would likely be relieved when Marion disappeared. Not that Marion blamed her.

A small lump lodged in her throat. Would her father even mourn her loss? It wasn't likely, and her stomach knotted at the thought.

"You'll come as soon as you can?" she asked Angus.

"Aye. Dunnae fash yerself."

She forced a smile. "You are already sounding like you're back in Scotland. Don't forget to curb that when speaking with Father."

"I'll remember. Now, make haste te the cliff te leave yer cloak, then head straight for Newcastle."

"I don't want to leave you," she said, ashamed at the sudden rise of cowardliness in her chest and at the way her eyes stung with unshed tears.

"Gather yer courage, lass. I'll be seeing ye soon, and Neil will keep ye safe."

She sniffed. "I'll do the same for Neil."

"I've nay doubt ye'll try," Angus said, sounding proud and wary at the same time.

"I'm not afraid for myself," she told him in a shaky voice. "You're taking a great risk for me. How will I ever make it up to you?"

"Ye already have," Angus said hastily, glancing around and directing a worried look toward the drawbridge. "Ye want te live with my clan, which means I can go te my dying day treating ye as my daughter. Now, dunnae cry when I walk away. I ken how sorely ye'll miss me," he boasted with a wink. "I'll miss ye just as much."

With that, he swung up onto his mount. He had just given the signal for his beast to go when Marion realized she didn't know what Neil looked like.

"Angus!"

He pulled back on the reins and turned toward her. "Aye?"

"I need Neil's description."

Angus's eyes widened. "I'm getting old," he grumbled.

"I dunnae believe I forgot such a detail. He's got hair redder than mine, and wears it tied back always. Oh, and he's missing his right ear, thanks te Froste. Took it when Neil came through these parts te see me last year."

"What?" She gaped at him. "You never told me that!"

"I did nae because I knew ye would try te go after Neil and patch him up, and that surely would have cost ye another beating if ye were caught." His gaze bore into her. "Ye're verra courageous. I reckon I had a hand in that 'cause I knew ye needed te be strong te withstand yer father. But dunnae be mindless. Courageous men and women who are mindless get killed. Ye ken?"

She nodded.

"Tread carefully," he warned.

"You too." She said the words to his back, for he was already turned and headed toward the drawbridge.

She made her way slowly to the edge of the steep embankment as tears filled her eyes. She wasn't upset because she was leaving her father—she'd certainly need to say a prayer of forgiveness for that sin tonight—but she couldn't shake the feeling that she'd never see Angus again. It was silly; everything would go as they had planned. Before she could fret further, the blast of the fire horn jerked her into motion. There was no time for any thoughts but those of escape.

Two

Iain MacLeod strode out of Odiham Castle and toward the stables without a backward glance. He was in a foul mood. He'd been in England for a fortnight, and it was a fortnight too long. And now he had to make a stop along the way home to marry some Sassenach he'd never met. And for a man who had no desire to ever marry again, the impending wedding did not instill any warmness in his gut.

He stalked past King Edward's guards, who still gaped every time they saw him, in spite of the fact that he'd been here several days trying to work out the terms of David II, King of Scot's release. Iain scowled at the sacrifice it required, as marrying once more was indeed a sacrifice for him. But he'd do it for David, as they were longtime friends. The last guard flinched, then his eyes widened as Iain strode past. He wasn't sure what fascinated the young guards more, his size or the size of his sword. Either way, he was tired of being stared at, weary of bland English food, and annoyed with the politics between David and King Edward.

He continued walking, paying no mind to their stares, until he reached the stable, where he found Rory Mac—his friend, companion on this trip, and council member of his clan—napping in the hay by their horses. Iain shook his head. He'd not had a decent night's sleep since David's missive had arrived at Iain's home, Dunvegan Castle, over a fortnight prior. The letter had implored him to depart at once for England, and since the letter had been unclear and simply stated that David needed Iain's help to persuade King Edward to negotiate his release, Iain's mind had not allowed him to rest. There had been many possibilities of what the letter might signify—war, murder, an attempted escape, though unlikely given the impossibility of an escape without attack. Of all the possibilities, however, Iain had never once considered that the way he was to help was by marrying a Sassenach.

Rory Mac snored loudly, and Iain stared down at him with annoyance. The man seemed to be able to sleep anywhere at any time, unlike Iain. Of course, that was not Rory Mac's fault. Iain nudged his friend in the leg to wake him.

Rory Mac slowly opened his eyes and grimaced, then stretched his arms above his head and rolled his shoulders. "I'd hoped to be home today. Alanna will be angry that we've been gone so long."

Iain nodded his understanding. Rory Mac's wife, Alanna, had not wanted him to come to England because she'd had a feeling that something terrible would happen. She'd thought that bad fortune would befall her husband, but with the predicament Iain now found himself in, he wondered if the bad fortune she'd feared was not his.

"I wish to be home, as well," Iain said. "I miss Dunvegan."

Rory Mac stood up and dusted the stray hay from his braies. "What do ye miss most?"

Iain thought about it. He missed bathing in the cold seawater, even if it did make his bollocks curl painfully tight. He'd not say that, of course. "I miss grievances of the clan," he said, knowing it would surprise Rory Mac, given how irritated Iain always got when he had to spend hours on end listening to complaints.

Rory Mac cocked his eyebrow as they walked to the horses to ready them to depart. "I dunnae believe ye."

Iain laughed, understanding why, yet it was an awareness of their clan's ways that he appreciated even more now, having been here among the English for so long. "It's true. We air our grievances unlike the English. It's tiresome but honest. The English dunnae do that, and I dunnae trust King Edward does, either."

"Nor does David, which is why he summoned ye, I think."

Iain nodded and made a derisive noise from his throat. "Of course David does nae trust Edward, but David knows he can trust me." Iain stared at his friend. "Dunnae mistake Edward to be weak. David would have never been able to summon me if it did nae suit Edward's purposes."

Rory Mac nodded. "I'll nae forget. Tell me of the talks today. I suppose an agreement was made for David's release?"

Iain motioned to the stable door to imply that he'd speak when they were alone. Once they were outside, had mounted their horses, and were a respectable distance from the castle, Iain answered Rory Mac's question. "A date was set to come back to the table to discuss and set the official terms of David's release, but it's still a long way off."

Rory Mac grimaced. "Why must ye come back? Why could they nae set the terms of David's release while ye're here?"

He slowed his destrier and looked at his friend. "King

Edward has a provision that must be met before he will consent to talk officially of releasing David." The muscles in Iain's neck tensed at the thought of marrying again.

"What is it?" Rory Mac demanded, his eyes narrowing with obvious wariness.

Iain wondered if that's how he had looked when David had told him what King Edward wanted. It was likely. He took a deep breath. "I have to marry some Englishwoman—the daughter of Baron de Lacy," he muttered, trying to keep the ire out of his voice, but he knew immediately that he'd failed when he saw the look of pity on Rory Mac's face.

"Marry a Sassenach?" his friend cried out in surprise. "Ye?"

"Aye," Iain said on a long, irritated sigh. An image of his late wife, Catriona, filled his mind, making his chest ache. He clamped his emotions down as quickly as they had arisen. "The king of England suspects Baron de Lacy and William Froste of plotting to take the throne."

Rory Mac pressed his lips into a thin line, his nostrils flaring. "Are ye speaking of the knight who cut off Neil's ear? The tourney knight?"

Iain's jaw clenched thinking of Froste. The man was as renowned for his skills in battle and on the tourney field as his cruelty. Iain didn't normally pay any heed to rumors but Froste had proven himself hard-hearted when he'd cut the ear off one of Iain's clansman for a crime Froste knew damn well the man had not committed. Iain had a score to settle with Froste, and he welcomed the opportunity.

"Well?" Rory Mac demanded, bringing Iain's attention back to him.

"Aye, the one and the same," Iain growled. The men locked gazes and spit toward the ground at once to signify what they thought of a man with no honor. "It seems the king got word that Froste is to marry de Lacy's daughter, and it's a match the king intends to stop. Froste wanted land from the king and the title of baron, which King Edward refused, and de Lacy..." Iain shrugged. "The king believes de Lacy wants the throne, and if he and Froste join forces, the two would have enough knights, money, and allies that the king is nervous." Iain rolled his shoulders, which now throbbed with pressure, as Rory Mac stared intently at him.

Taking a deep breath, Iain continued. "The king is savvy. He is using the fact that he has David imprisoned to weaken de Lacy and Froste's scheme. He intends to strip de Lacy of the land that is currently in his control, which the king knows Froste wants, and give it to me upon my marriage to de Lacy's daughter. In return, I had to pledge that if de Lacy and Froste should rise against the king, our clan would fight beside King Edward."

"But of course they'll rise against him!" Rory Mac cried out, his lip curled back.

"Aye," Iain agreed, holding his friend's outraged gaze. "The king kens it, too. And he understands that David and I ken it, but King Edward would nae say as much out loud. I'm the perfect solution. He can quell the rebellion without sacrificing any English blood, except of course de Lacy's and Froste's."

"Why did David nae ask Gowan's son to marry the lass to gain his freedom instead of ye? Gowan is laird of the MacDonald clan and the lass *is* his niece, so surely they should make the sacrifice and nae ye?"

Iain had asked David that same question. "Because he does nae trust Gowan to become a possible ally with the King of England. David only trusts me."

Rory Mac shook his head. "I ken he's your friend, but ye could say nay. He asks too much of ye."

The thought of marrying again made Iain clench his teeth, but he forced himself to relax his jaw. "He is my friend and my king, and he needs my help so I'll give it. I'd have done the same if I'd been imprisoned in England without word of when I'd be released. David knows I'd never turn against him and join forces with Edward, but he does nae ken that of Gowan. The laird is cunning, much like the King of England himself." Iain stared at the dusty road ahead, hoping the conversation was over. While his own reaction to his upcoming alliance was negative, he did not want to instill dislike of the Sassenach in his clan.

But Rory Mac pressed on. "Do ye think Gowan knew of King Edward's demand?"

"I imagine David told him. Gowan is Lord of the Isles, and as ye said before, the lass is his niece, though I dunnae think he's ever met her."

Rory Mac scratched at his chin, a contemplative look coming to his face. "Ye ken, Gowan likely didn't argue David's plot to ask ye to sacrifice yerself 'cause Gowan thinks binding ye in marriage with his niece will make ye feel a certain fealty to him."

Iain had thought the same thing, and if it was true, Gowan was partially right. Once he was married to the MacDonald's niece, Iain would join forces with the laird to defend the MacDonalds *if* the need arose, but the old laird was a clot-heid if he thought that would make Iain any less wary of the cunning laird trying to steal MacLeod lands.

"What do ye ken of the lass?"

"Nae verra much. Her name is Marion." He turned the name of the faceless woman over in his mind. He felt nothing, except the inevitableness of the marriage. Perhaps

David had done him a favor. Iain had no wish to marry, but he did have a duty as laird of the MacLeod clan to produce an heir. He'd tried to forget the duty, but David had pointedly reminded him. So now he'd marry some pale, pampered Sassenach who he'd not really like. At least he'd not make the same error again and fall in love with his wife. Loving and losing Catriona had nearly destroyed him. He had no wish to love like that again.

A Sassenach would never take the place of the beautiful, delicate wife, whom he'd vowed to keep from harm and had failed. He was safe from being bewitched by de Lacy's daughter, but he'd treat the woman well, which was a great deal more than she could have expected from Froste. The thought made Iain grin.

"I may take no pleasure in remarrying," he said, "but I take a sinful amount of pleasure in the fact that I'll be relieving Froste of the woman he wants—or rather, the land and title he wants. The man deserves more for what he did to Neil, but this is a good start. Come, let's pick up the pace. The quicker we collect my soon-to-be bride from her home, the faster we can be on our way to Scotland."

‧⸰⸱✦⸱⸰‧

As they rode through the day and into the night, Iain steeled himself for the likely tears from the Sassenach when she learned she was to marry a stranger, and a Scot at that, as well as the anger from de Lacy when he either realized or suspected that his king had checkmated him. It would be a boon if Froste was at de Lacy's home when they arrived, and Iain could tell the knight to his face that he wouldn't be getting his coveted land or a title.

By the time the castle came into view, Iain felt prepared for anything. Yet his lips parted in surprise at the thick, smoke-filled air that swirled around the castle, which stood high on a hill. The smell of burning wood drifted in the air from the bailey, from whence large flames flickered. The drawbridge from the bailey to the land beyond was down, and knights and servants swarmed across the length of the bridge and in front of the bailey. Torches of orange light peppered the darkness surrounding the source of the fire.

Iain stared at Rory Mac, who had already unhooked his sword from where it had been strapped on his mount. "Be ready," Iain commanded, "but hold for my word. I'd rather nae fight my future wife's father just yet, unless it's absolutely necessary."

"As ye wish," Rory Mac said, in spite of his scowl. He was clearly itching for a fight, as he often was. He did not have a temper, but he certainly wasn't afraid to yield when challenged, and that was one of the reasons he was so useful to Iain. The man would listen when told to hold, but he'd also fight to the death when ordered.

Rory Mac muttered under his breath, indicating he had more to say on the subject. "I say it's best to have our weapons drawn. If King Edward is right in his suspicions, de Lacy and Froste may decide to kill us both to prevent their king from outmaneuvering them."

Iain nodded, reaching for his own sword to make sure it was where it should be. It was, of course. "I dunnae think we need be worried at the moment. Openly defying King Edward's orders would be akin to declaring war, and since they've no notice of this and, therefore, have been unable to make any preparations, I dunnae think they are foolish enough to do that. They'll want, at the very least, to appear as if they are going to obey until they can gather their knights. Besides"—Iain flashed Rory Mac a grin—"the king gave us leave to kill either man if they try to kill us."

Rory Mac scowled at Iain. "Ye might have said so."

Iain chuckled. "I just did."

"What other details should I ken?" Rory Mac asked, his tone impatient but amused.

"Well," Iain said, drawing the word out just to annoy his friend, "we're to make it seem as if King Edward did nae ken anything about the future marriage of de Lacy's daughter and Froste, and that the king simply offered the woman to me as a sign of trust that he means to continue talks of David's release."

Rory Mac snorted. "We're to lie?"

"Aye," Iain scoffed. "Just like Englishmen."

Both men laughed at that and spit toward the ground at the same time.

As they neared the first group of what appeared to be servants and a young page, a warning horn blasted from high above the hill where the lookout tower stood. Iain assumed the horn had sounded to signal their approach, and his hand automatically returned to the hilt of his sword. As the men drew closer, Iain quickly assessed them and concluded they were indeed likely servants. For one, they were weaponless, and for another, their dress was simple, as a servant's would be. They wore woolen hose, hats, and thick, unadorned woolen coats. There was a woman, dressed in a plain skirt and cloak of the same material as the men. She was also weaponless. The woman's wide eyes locked on him. Beside her stood a boy—no, a page—likely no more than a young lad by his slight build and hairless face. The cloth of his clothes was finer than the others', and he had a dagger sheathed at his side, which he withdrew as he lifted his chin and squared his shoulders.

The woman grabbed for the boy's arm, making his graceless attempt to quickly withdraw his weapon even more graceless. He shrugged off the woman's hand. "Halt, Scot!" he demanded as two older men flanked his sides.

Iain bit back the laughter in his throat. "Sheathe yer weapon, ye young fool, before ye get yerself killed. I'm steady as a slow-trickling stream, but my companion is a nervous sort." He tilted his head toward Rory Mac, who was clutching the hilt of his sword.

The boy's eyes, brightened by the torches, moved from Rory Mac to Iain and finally settled there. "You really are a Scot!" the boy exclaimed, as if he thought his eyes might have deceived him. Hearing Iain's thick brogue must have confirmed the poor lad's fears.

It was an accusation, to be sure. Iain released the chuckle he'd been holding back. His merriment pierced the momentary silence around them. "Aye. I'm Iain MacLeod, laird of the MacLeod clan, and I'm here on business from yer king. Are the Baron de Lacy and his daughter in residence tonight?"

The boy's face fell, and the older woman, who stood a few feet behind him now, burst into tears. The boy reached for the woman's hand and clung to it as he glanced over his shoulder. When he turned back, worry pinched his young face. "The baron is approaching."

Iain stared in the direction the lad had looked and heard the thundering of horses' hooves as a line of knights came galloping across the bridge. Iain tensed, and he and Rory Mac exchanged a look of shared understanding—*be prepared.*

Twelve knights formed a V shape headed by a man of about fifty, Iain judged from his graying hair and weathered face. He rode a white mount, and his surcoat was adorned with a gold, fire-breathing dragon. The man Iain assumed to be the baron appeared to be expecting a battle by his dress. Either the king was correct in his suspicions or de Lacy was a man who liked to be ready for the unexpected at all times.

He pulled his destrier to a halt a handbreadth from Iain. The men behind him did the same. He swept his narrowed eyes over Iain, lingering on his sword. "I'm Baron de Lacy. What business have you here?"

"I'm here by the order of your king and mine to marry your daughter, Marion de Lacy. It's a marriage of good faith between the kings to begin the process of negotiations for David's release. I'm Iain MacLeod, chief of the MacLeod clan."

"If you are the chief, where are your clansmen to defend you?" the baron demanded, his face showing no hint of how he felt about what Iain had just told him.

"I dunnae need defending when I travel, Baron. That is the sign of a weak man," he added, disliking the baron more with each of the man's words.

"A man surrounded by skilled knights is the sign of a *strong lord*," the baron countered.

Iain was about to refute the man's comment but thought better of it. His time was best spent on the road home, not being drawn into an argument. He shrugged. "We're simply nae in accordance." He withdrew the scroll sealed by King Edward and held it out. "This is for ye."

The baron took the scroll, studied the seal, and opened it with the tip of a dagger he had produced. When he finished reading, he offered Iain a cold smile. "I'm afraid you've traveled here in vain."

"Ye mean to defy yer king, then?" Iain asked, cutting

his eyes to Rory Mac, who gave him an almost unnoticeable nod that he was ready to fight if needed.

"Of course not," de Lacy replied, his words smooth—too smooth. They sounded measured to Iain. He studied the man and noted his hands gripping his horse's reins so tightly that de Lacy's knuckles were white. The man was angry, very angry, and very good at hiding it.

Baron de Lacy offered a thin-lipped smile. "I must admit King Edward's decree does come as a surprise."

Iain shrugged. "I'm afraid ye'll have to take that matter up with yer king. But I strongly suggest ye produce yer daughter."

Baron de Lacy's mouth twisted wryly. "If you care to grab a torch and help search the sea for her body, I'll be happy to let you take her back to Scotland with you."

Iain stared at the baron for a minute before he responded. He was sure the man was telling him—without the slightest hint of sorrow—that his daughter had drowned, which explained the confusion in the outer keep, the torches, the people who looked as if they were searching for someone, and the woman's tears of moments ago. What he didn't know was whether her death was an accident or not. If not, then whoever had killed Marion de Lacy was now his sworn enemy. In spite of the fact that he'd never met her, she would have been his wife. The moment she had become his future wife, she was his to keep safe. If she had been murdered, it made no difference if the person had not known she was Iain's. Ignorance changed nothing. He didn't ever intend to fail to keep a woman that was his safe again. He didn't care what Father Murdock kept telling him about Catriona's death. It mattered not that he knew she'd been wracked with sickness all her life. His heart told him he should have been able to save her from anything—including herself.

He flicked his gaze to the inner bailey where smoke still rose up in the distance, and another possibility struck him. Had a fire been set to distract the knights so the Sassenach could be captured and whisked away? He would keep the thought to himself for a time. "Are ye thinking she was murdered?"

"No," the baron replied, his voice indifferent. "There's no Englishman fool enough to cross me."

Iain didn't miss the way the baron tapped the king's scroll against his leg. The implication that there was one unnamed fool was apparent.

"Marion couldn't swim," de Lacy continued. "And the dim girl seems to have gotten too close to the sea cliff and fell over." He drove a fist into the palm of his hand, then stilled, seeming to realize he was showing emotion. "Andrew there"—he pointed at a knight who hung his head in what appeared to be shame—"found her cloak, but he didn't manage to find her. Did you, Andrew?"

The knight slowly looked up, his gaze settling on Iain. "I did not. I failed to keep her from all dangers." His voice was hoarse and full of sorrow, and made Iain wonder if there had been something between this knight and the baron's daughter.

Not that it mattered a great deal if she was dead.

"What makes ye sure she drowned?" Iain asked.

"Her cloak was found tangled in the tree brambles by the cliff's edge. She was always a foolish girl. And now she has ruined—" He stopped and scrubbed a hand across his mouth. "Forgive me. I am simply distraught."

The stiff words rang false. The man was not upset at all. Iain felt sure de Lacy was angry that he no longer had his daughter to entice Froste to join him in overthrowing the king. Iain also didn't doubt that de Lacy would secure Froste's allegiance some other way. He could still offer to make Froste a baron, and if de Lacy became king, he could easily grant Froste land. There would still be war between the king of England and de Lacy. Iain was sure. What he didn't know was what new requirements King Edward would demand before he'd talk further of David's release. Iain was certain his sword arm, and those of his men, would still be needed.

Iain eyed the baron for a long moment. The man sickened him. No loyalty meant no honor. And not loving your own child meant the man had a black heart. "I'm sorry for yer loss," Iain managed to choke out through the offense compelling him to tell the baron what he thought of him.

"Yes, it's a pity," the man answered with no trace of sadness. "Her marriage to William Froste would have allied me with a great many knights. And of course," he added, "her marriage to you would have pleased my king, and I always aim to please Edward." Sarcasm rang through each word.

The man's callousness further kindled Iain's ire. The woman was dead, the marriage off. It was time to head for home. He'd been ordered by King Edward to send confirmation of the marriage through one of the king's knights stationed with the Dominican Friars in Newcastle. Iain would abide by that plan, as he and David had talked of what to do if the marriage did not occur for some reason. David wished for Iain to go to Skye and speak with Gowan about securing funds to offer King Edward to come to the table of negotiations.

"We'll be going now," Iain said, "since ye'll nae need our help searching for yer daughter's body."

"Do stay. I'm sure as a beastly Scot you enjoy a good

beating, and I have several to deliver," the baron said with a smirk.

"I dunnae enjoy the discipline of any man," Iain replied through clenched teeth. Sometimes it was necessary but never pleasurable.

Beside him, Rory Mac, who had surprisingly held his tongue thus far, made a derisive noise from deep in his throat, implying without words what he thought of de Lacy.

"That's a shame," de Lacy replied, flicking his gaze to Rory Mac and then back to Iain. "The first one will be a good one. The man is stout as a tree. I would guess it will take twenty licks to attain a response. The idiot set fire to my stables."

Iain frowned. "Purposely?"

"He says not, but he's the stable master. He should know to be careful. If you care to stay, I'll even let you have the first turn punishing him." An odd smile pulled at de Lacy's lips.

Iain knew plenty of leaders who enjoyed punishing their men, but he wasn't one of them. With a nod of farewell to the baron, Iain tapped his horse gently and motioned Rory Mac to follow. Once they were a good distance from the baron and his men, Rory Mac spoke.

"We'll be going to war," he grumbled.

"Aye," Iain agreed, stress already vibrating through his veins. "I do believe Edward was correct about de Lacy and Froste, and I dunnae have a doubt the man will still demand we fight for him before he will release David."

"Are we going back to speak to David?" Rory Mac asked. His tone didn't display the misery the idea brought him, but his grimace did.

Iain laughed. "Nay. David told me to go home and

speak to Gowan about raising money if the marriage did nae proceed."

Rory Mac blew out a sigh. "That's good to hear. Are ye glad that ye'll nae have to marry?"

"Aye," Iain admitted. "And I feel terrible about it. I would never wish ill on anyone, nor death."

Rory Mac nodded. "Still, ye likely would have had to kill de Lacy in the future, and then yer wife would have hated ye."

"Perhaps," Iain said, wondering for the first time what sort of woman Marion de Lacy had been. Having met her cold father, he suspected she was a quiet sort that started at her own shadow. Or maybe she leaped to her own death to avoid marrying Froste. Either way, he felt sorry for her.

Without a cloak, the cold night air cut through Marion's gown and chilled her to the bone. As she shifted from foot to foot—as much from impatience to leave Newcastle as from the cold—Marion wrapped her arms around her middle and watched warily as Neil bickered with the captain of the birlinn. It seemed the man had changed his mind about leaving tonight as the air felt damp, and he thought a storm was brewing. Yet, while a storm may be coming at sea, she'd chance the voyage rather than stay so close, where she could easily be dragged back to her father if her deceit was discovered.

"Ye listen to me," Neil shouted at the captain. The Scot had obviously lost his temper, and Marion had lost hers, as well. She was finished with waiting around for Neil to solve the problem. She could solve her own problems. This needed the soft touch of a woman, or money at the very least. She strode toward them, not caring that Neil had commanded she stay put. She was done with men commanding her. As she neared Neil and the captain, both men turned to look at her.

She straightened her spine, preparing for battle. It was dark and quiet on Pilgrim Street. She'd seen no sign of anyone other than the guard that had let her into Newcastle, yet her nerves tingled as if something bad was coming—or more like someone was coming to get her. Surely it was her imagination, but the feeling was there all the same, stirring the sense of urgency she felt to stormy proportions.

"Gentlemen," she said in a sweet voice.

Neil raised his red eyebrows as a scowl turned down his lips.

The captain was less subtle. "What do ye want?" he demanded, in a tone that told her what he thought of a woman interrupting.

She looked the captain straight in his dark, narrowed eyes. "I will pay you more to depart tonight."

A greedy grin lit the captain's face. "How much?"

Marion opened the bag of coins Angus had left for her and withdrew eight of them. She dropped them one by one into the captain's outstretched hand. Each time a coin clinked against another, her gut clenched tighter. She was giving away the only money she had.

The captain nodded. "We'll leave directly. Let's go down to the birlinn. It won't take long to—"

Marion frowned as the captain's speech came to an abrupt halt. He looked past her, his eyes searching the darkness. Her heart suddenly shuddered, as the ground beneath her feet vibrated with the familiar sensation of horses approaching. Without thought, she withdrew the dagger Angus had given her, even as she saw Neil unsheathe his sword.

She turned to face the direction the captain was looking. At first, she saw nothing, only shadows dancing, but then the flickering of torches appeared as dots in the distance.

"Let's go!" she demanded, unreasonable fear racing through her veins. It could not be someone coming for her. It was impossible. Her plan had been solid. And yet... She tugged on Neil's arm. "Please. Let's go down to the birlinn."

Neil nodded as the sound of galloping horses grew louder. She turned, nearly slamming into the captain, who stood motionless. "Lead the way," she ordered.

His eyes narrowed on Neil and then on her. "Why are you acting so fearful? As if you've done something wrong. Your husband"—he motioned to Neil—"told me you wanted to leave tonight to get back home to your dying father. But seems to me like you're running from something. I don't want trouble. I have a wife and children to see to."

"Here." She thrust the bag of coins at him as the sound of men's voices filled the night. Their laughter floated toward her. She peeked over her shoulder, her breath catching as she counted five men approaching, their cloaks billowing behind them in the wind. If they had surcoats on, she could not make them out. She swiveled around to the captain. She didn't have time to convince him with just words. "Take all my money. I vow to you I've done nothing wrong."

He took the money, and as he did, he grabbed her wrist and pulled her near. She whipped her dagger toward his throat as he pointed one at hers, the coins he'd been holding clattering to the ground. They stood, each with a weapon at the other's throat. Marion's blood pounded in her ears. Out of the corner of her eye, she could see Neil creeping toward them.

The captain tightened his grip on her wrist, increasing the pressure tenfold, and she winced in pain. He didn't take his eyes from her as he spoke to Neil. "I would not try it, if I were you. You might wound me before I can wound your wife. You might not. All I want to do is verify that you are telling the truth. If you are, then we will be on our way."

Directly behind her, Marion heard the neighing of horses as the hoofbeats slowed. The voices of the men died, and she caught another glimpse of Neil, whose gaze moved from her to the captain to the men.

"What have we here?" a cruel voice demanded.

Marion's knees went weak. She would know that voice anywhere.

The hiss of swords being unsheathed pierced the air. No! She refused to simply go willingly.

"You!" Froste bellowed. "Let the woman go and come here."

Relief rushed through Marion as the captain released her. The second he did, she cut her eyes at Neil. He caught her gaze and nodded in understanding as she looked from him to the stairs that led down to the water. The birlinn they were to take was somewhere below them, and their only chance was to reach it.

"Turn around, woman," Froste commanded.

Marion swallowed the fear rising in her throat. If she turned around, he'd know for certain it was her, and even if she did escape, she knew he'd come after her. They had to chance it.

Now, she mouthed to Neil before she took off in blind

desperation. Shouts broke out behind her, but she reached the stairs, nearly tumbling down them in her haste. When her feet hit the bottom step, she turned to ask Neil which way it was to the birlinn. The question died on her lips. She was alone, and above her, Neil's scream of agony filled the night.

Marion's heart pounded in terror, knowing she had to go back and help him. She could not leave him to Froste's mercy, for the man had none, but maybe, just possibly, he'd grant it this once, as a wedding present to her. She'd only taken two steps up when Froste himself loomed at the top of the stairs, his angular face lit by the torch he held. He stared down at her for a long time before he closed the distance between them and jerked her to his chest. His hand went to her chin in a painful, iron grip. He turned her face to the left and the right before yanking it back toward his gaze.

"I'm sorry, Marion," he offered in pitiless voice. "I'm simply surprised to see you have risen from the dead. I've just come from your father's and he had informed me that you had drowned. What have you to say for yourself?"

Marion tried to beat back the panic rising in her chest. If Neil had not been captured, she'd try to stab Froste and flee, yet she had to think of Angus's cousin. "I was taken," she said, tears of fright coming to her eyes. "That man up there, the Scot, was going to bring me home to Father."

A smirk came to Froste's lips. "Odd. The captain claims you were trying to flee England with the Scot. Come, let us cut out the man's tongue for disparaging you."

Froste eyed the dagger she still clutched in her hand. "Sheathe your weapon, my dear. I'd hate for you to cut yourself trying to use it."

With little choice at the moment but to obey and fearful if she didn't he'd take the blade from her, she sheathed it as he dragged her up the stairs. When they reached the top, she gasped at the sight of Neil swaying on his feet, clutching the left side of his head. Blood streamed from beneath his fingers. He saw her and paled further. "I'm sorry, lass," he murmured, right before he fell to his knees and then face forward onto the ground.

She moved to go to him but was pulled swiftly backward into Froste. "Leave him," he ordered.

"What did you do?" she cried out.

"I cut off the man's ear. He's a thief, and that is the consequence. He was trying to steal from me."

"What do you think he was trying to steal from you?" she demanded, her fury making her spit the words.

"Why, you, of course. You are mine."

She stared at Neil's still form and prayed the man was alive. "He was trying to help me!"

"Yes," Froste bit out. "Escape England."

"No, I told you—"

"Ah, yes," Froste interrupted as he spun her around to face him. "You claim the captain is lying. Well, then forgive me for my error," he offered in a cold tone as he gripped her by the arm and dragged her over to the captain, who stood silently looking fearful.

"What are you going to do?" she demanded, digging in her heels uselessly.

Froste stared at her, indifferent. "The captain is a liar, so I'll cut out his tongue."

"No!" she shouted at the same time the captain did, but Froste didn't listen, and with a sharp nod, she found herself being taken by two knights. Each gripped her by an arm.

Froste grabbed the captain by the throat and lifted his dagger to the whimpering man's face. "Open your mouth."

"No!" Marion cried again, struggling to be released to no avail. She could not let him cut out the man's tongue, even though the truth would seal her fate. "I lied. The captain is telling the truth."

Froste turned toward her as he flicked a hand at the captain. "Out of my sight."

Marion watched with a sinking feeling as the captain, all too readily, abandoned her. Froste stepped toward her, gesturing to the knights to release her. He moved closer, towering over her, and tangled his hands in her hair.

"I'm going to have to punish you, Marion."

After locating King Edward's man and delivering the news of Marion de Lacy's death, Iain and Rory Mac made their way out of the friary and then mounted their horses to ride north to Pilgrim Street. Silence lay thick as a highland fog over Newcastle at this late hour, and each time their horses' hooves struck the stone street, the sound seemed deafening. Though inns crowded both sides of the streets, all had their doors shut and most were dark, the tenants abed for the night. It made no difference, though. They were headed to the northwest in the direction of yet another friary. There was a priest there by name of Father Thomas, who was an old friend of the MacLeod clan, and he had offered to bed them down for the night on their return trip to Scotland. Iain only wanted a few hours of sleep before departing.

The sound of neighing horses reached his ears over the clopping of his horse Olaf's hooves, followed forthwith by the hum of voices. Low voices. Male voices. As they neared the end of Pilgrim Street, torches lit the night near the gate.

A group of four men seemed to have formed a semicircle. As Iain and Rory Mac drew closer to the group, he caught a glimpse of one of the men's surcoats—burgundy and gold with a gold snake on the front—Froste's personal arms that he and his followers wore. Iain had seen the man fight in tournaments, so he knew the coat of arms.

Iain led his horse off the street so they would not be seen. "Froste," Iain said under his breath as he quickly dismounted and tethered his horse.

"Aye," Rory Mac answered, doing the same. "I saw the snake. What do ye want to do?"

Iain scratched his stubble. Froste needed to suffer for what he had done to Neil. The question was, how best to get retribution. Before he could decide, a woman's scream filled the night. He scrambled toward the shadows of the side street and motioned for Rory Mac to follow. He stopped near enough to see but not be seen or heard. A lass with hair pale as the moon, a face sculpted in determination, and a beautiful body wrapped in a gown that fit her form rather than hung loose like those the highland lasses wore, gripped a dagger with her slender fingers. She held it steady and pointed it at Froste. Behind her, a man lay with his back to the sky. The man on the ground groaned.

When Froste began to advance toward the woman and man, the fair-haired Sassenach held her dagger higher. "Do not come a step closer."

Iain started, then quickly shed his shock like snake skin. He smiled in grim satisfaction as he readied his sword to aid the woman and seek revenge on Froste. It was a stroke of good fortune that he'd come upon the knight.

"Should we help now?" Rory Mac asked in a low tone.

"Hold for one moment. We will use the distraction the woman is sure to provide to our benefit."

Rory Mac frowned. "Why do ye think—"

"You wouldn't dare stab me," Froste snarled at the woman, cutting off Rory Mac's question.

"I most certainly *will* stab you in the heart if you come closer," she snapped. "I'm offended that you believe I would lie."

Iain gave Rory Mac a triumphant smile while biting back a burst of laughter at how outrageous the woman's comment, given her situation. The Sassenach looked as though she meant it true enough to Iain.

Froste offered her a bored look, and when he did, the Sassenach, to Iain's astonishment, turned the dagger on herself and held it to her throat. "If you or any of your men move again without giving me your solemn vow that you will not kill this man"—she motioned to the man on the ground—"I will slit my throat, and you'll not get what you most want."

Now this was a most curious plan. Iain exchanged an amazed look with Rory Mac. With the bold claim she'd just made, he hoped the woman knew what she was doing.

"And what is it I most desire?" Froste asked.

"Me," she answered promptly and without a trace of boastfulness. "And you want me alive, to be sure. It certainly makes it easier to acquire the land you covet from my father if I'm alive, now doesn't it?"

Iain felt himself gape. Marion de Lacy was alive? And she was no cold, proper Sassenach after all, and she most certainly was not weak. His wonder vanished with his next breath. She was alive, and she would soon be his wife.

"Iain, is—"

"Aye, that's my bride," Iain answered, fierce anger now flowing through his veins as he determined how to most effectively attack Froste while ensuring Marion would not be harmed. Marion waved her dagger in the air, stealing Iain's attention for a moment.

"I'll have your vow to let the Scot go," she demanded in a voice of steel, as she tilted her head toward the form on the ground.

As Rory Mac hissed in disbelief beside him, Iain found his gaze drawn briefly to where the man lay. He was dressed in a plain wool cloak, and whoever the man was, he'd taken pains not to be noticed. Was he here for Marion? Had she planned to escape marrying Froste? Iain found he hoped so.

As one of the knights moved his hand to his weapon, Iain's thoughts raced forward, establishing a plan in his mind. He nudged Rory Mac. "Ye take the two men farthest from us. I'll get Marion and take out Froste and the other knight."

Rory Mac nodded.

"Now!" he said in a fierce whisper as the knight closest to Marion lunged toward her.

Iain surged forward, withdrawing his sword and closing the distance between himself and the knight who had grabbed Marion. Her eyes widened in shock at the sight of him, and her dagger flashed upward, then hovered as if she wasn't sure who was the greater threat. In a rush, her lips pressed grimly together, and she plunged her dagger into the knight's arm. The man roared, drawing his sword up to counter. Iain knocked the sword away with his own, then brought his blade down to finish the knight. He fell to the ground in a heap.

Iain glanced over at Rory Mac, who had already felled one knight and was engaged with the other. Iain looked away just in time to see Froste launching toward him. Behind Iain, Marion screamed. Iain raised his sword once more and his weapon met Froste's in midair, the sound of metal against metal echoing in the night. They withdrew, circled each other again, and met once more in midair, but Iain spun, brought his sword down quickly, and struck a blow to Froste's back.

He stumbled and cursed, but straightened. He stared hard at Iain, as if he only just realized who Iain was. The knight wiped a hand across his face and moved his sword from one hand to the other, his gaze moving from Iain to behind him where Iain could feel Marion hovering near his feet. He had no idea what she was doing until suddenly she moved to his side, her bloody dagger in her hand. He barely knew the woman, but he already respected her courage.

"What are you doing in England, MacLeod?" Froste thundered.

"I came to speak to yer king regarding David's release, and now I'm here to collect my bride, Lady Marion, by orders of yer king."

Beside him, Marion stiffened, but he could not chance looking at her to see her face and being distracted.

"You sniveling, lying swine," Froste bellowed. "I'll see you dead before I let you take Marion anywhere."

"And I'll see ye quiet," Iain growled. He rushed forward as Rory Mac came at Froste from the side. Rory Mac knocked the sword out of the unsuspecting knight's hands, and Iain shoved his open palm into the man's throat. Froste doubled over, gasping. Iain pulled Marion to him, shifted her behind him, and kicked his foot into Froste's stomach to send him sprawling onto his back. Iain placed his boot on the man's heaving chest and his sword at the knight's throat.

"I've a good mind to kill ye," Iain said.

Suddenly, a very soft, warm body pressed against his back. "You mustn't kill unless your life is at stake," Marion scolded. "He's no threat presently."

Marion's warm breath tickled the back of his neck and made him shudder. No woman other than his late wife had ever made him react so. He frowned, as much at his response to her as to the fact that she was right about sparing Froste. He could ensure the knight did not follow them, if Froste was intent upon doing so, without killing him.

"Put him to sleep," Iain told Rory Mac, who grinned in answer.

Froste jerked, as if to stop whatever was coming, but Iain simply reminded him of his deadly situation by pressing his sword against the man's windpipe. Froste stilled, glaring at Iain, but when Rory Mac hit him on the side of the head with the hilt of his sword and Froste's head lolled sideways, the glare vanished, much to Iain's satisfaction. Iain removed his foot from Froste's chest and looked around him. Rory Mac had felled two of the man's knights, and Iain had dispatched the other.

Behind Marion, the Scot on the ground still lay motionless. "Who is that?" Iain demanded, pointing at the man.

Marion narrowed her eyes, which were as green as the lush rolling hills of the Highlands in the summer. "Who are you to make demands of me?"

"I already told ye, I'm to wed ye by orders of yer king."

"You did not tell *me*," she bit out. "You bellowed it at Froste. And forgive me if I don't readily believe you. I need proof."

Iain produced the decree stamped by King Edward's ring and signature. Her eyes widened considerably as she read it. "But why? Does this have to do with the negotiations you mentioned?" She sounded angry. He supposed he couldn't blame her, being traded from one man to another as she had been.

"Because," he said gently, considering how much he should tell her and deciding to be as truthful as he could. He would tell her the remainder when he knew he could trust her. At the moment, he didn't even know how she had arrived here. Had she feigned her drowning? It seemed likely. "King Edward wants to seal a bargain between himself, David, and me."

Her brows dipped together. "What sort of bargain involves me?" she asked obstinately.

He sighed. "I'll tell ye all when we are safely on the way to Scotland."

"I'm not moving until you tell me," she said, crossing her arms over her chest.

Iain shared a look with Rory Mac, who gave a nod of understanding. With one swift motion, Iain picked Marion up, snatched her bloody dagger out of her hands, and slung her over his shoulder. His future wife bellowed as she beat her fists against his back. Iain took a long approving look at her perfectly formed bottom. He may not want a wife with his head or heart, but his body certainly responded to Marion's. He ground his teeth and caught Rory Mac studying him. Iain glared at his friend while handing the dagger to him. "Keep this until the Sassenach does nae want to use it on me."

Rory Mac grunted. "I may have it forever, then," the Scot teased as he strode toward the man who'd been lying on the ground, his face in the dirt, but was now struggling to sit up.

"Put me down," Marion shouted.

Iain ignored her for a minute as he stared at the man

who was now standing with Rory Mac's help. The man wobbled, but Rory Mac steadied him, and then the man looked at Iain. For the second time since coming to Newcastle, Iain stared in shock at Neil MacLeod. He strode, with Marion still cursing and hitting him, toward his clansmen.

"Neil," he growled, then quickly softened his tone when he realized Neil had blood on the left side of his face.

Neil moved his hand toward his ear and winced. "Froste, the clot-heid, took my other ear and my sword." He groaned and swayed again.

"Put me down!" Marion demanded again. "I can help him."

Iain set her on her feet. "Be quick about it," he ordered, wanting to be gone from this place.

Marion pulled up her skirt, displaying her slender ankles, which Iain found himself staring at until he felt her stare on him. He pulled his gaze to her face. "How can I help?"

She held the edge of her skirt out to him. "Tear this. I need to dress his ear."

Iain complied, then handed the strip of material to her.

She took it from him with wary eyes. "Do you have any spirits?"

"Aye. For cleansing the wound?" he asked.

"Yes."

Iain took Neil's arm and nodded to Rory Mac. "Fetch it."

Rory Mac tipped his head and rushed off. Iain turned to Neil. "What are ye doing here? Ye did nae mention a word of coming. How do ye ken Lady Marion?" As he waited for Neil to answer, Marion rushed over to the knight Iain had felled. Beside the man was Neil's sword. As she struggled to lift it, Neil spoke.

"I dunnae, nae truly," he said, giving Marion a disgruntled look. "My cousin Angus has been her father's stable master for years, and he recently sent word to me asking me to bring her back to Scotland to the MacDonald clan. It was nae till I got here that he told me the whole of it, that she was to marry Froste against her wishes. He begged me to take her to safety, and I could nae refuse."

"I'm so sorry," Marion cried to Neil, dragging the sword behind her as she moved toward them.

Iain turned to help her, but the murderous look she gave him told him she wished to get the sword to Neil on her own. And she did. Her fortitude impressed Iain as she heaved and huffed and finally lifted the sword toward Neil. "I'm sorry you lost your other ear because of me."

Neil tried to take the sword, but he faltered, and Iain quickly snatched it from Marion. Neil frowned but nodded. "It was nae your fault," the Scot said to Marion. "It is Froste's fault. He's wicked." They all glanced at Froste, who still lay in a swoon. Neil's gaze locked on Iain. "May I borrow your dagger?"

Iain knew the man wanted retribution, and rightly so. He handed his dagger to the Scot, and then helped him hobble over to Froste, releasing Neil when he seemed steady. Marion made haste behind them.

"What are you going to do?" she whispered, her voice filled with fear. Did she think Neil would kill a man who could not defend himself?

Neil paused and glanced back at her. "I'm going to take out his tongue so the man can spew no more evil orders."

When Marion swayed, Iain reached out with his free hand and seized her arm to keep her upright.

"Ye should look away so ye dunnae faint," Neil commented.

"I assure you I do not faint," she said, sounding irritated, yet the fingers she had lifted to her temple trembled. "Neil." Her voice had taken on the soft tone that Iain recognized at once as one of persuasion. "It seems a bit much, almost evil, to take his tongue. Is there not another way to get your retribution?"

Neil tilted his head in thought and then finally said, "I suppose."

As Neil bent down, Rory Mac approached and gave Iain a questioning look, which Iain answered with a shrug. Suddenly, Neil plunged Iain's dagger deep into Froste's favored fighting arm. Froste flinched and howled, and Iain silenced him with a quick punch to the face. Froste fell silent once again, and Marion gasped, turning quickly away. When Neil stood, the three men exchanged a look of understanding and spit as one at Froste's feet. The man was without honor, and now he was defenseless, at least temporarily.

Silently, Marion turned, took the spirits from Rory Mac, and cleaned Neil's wounds. He hissed and moaned until the dressing was wrapped around his head. Then he slumped against Rory Mac.

Iain caught Rory Mac's eye. "I need a minute."

Rory Mac nodded and led Neil a short distance away. Uncertainty glimmered in Marion's eyes as he moved close to her so they could speak privately. Immediately, her feminine freesia scent surrounded him. He forced himself to keep his attention on his task.

"How did ye end up here?" he asked, though he'd meant to wait until they were away to have this discussion.

She wrapped her arms tightly around herself, looking so vulnerable that he suddenly yearned to enfold her in his embrace. She notched her chin up as if to tell him she was not sad, or maybe not afraid. "My father is a blackhearted devil who thought to marry me to Froste for the man's allied knights. To avoid the marriage, I feigned my death and then made my way here. Neil already told you of our meeting." Her gaze grew flinty. "But you, sir, will be stunned if you think my father will be happy that we are to be married."

Iain nodded, relieved there could be truth between them. "I ken he'll nae be happy. Marion, yer king suspects yer father of plotting to overthrow him."

"What?" she gasped. "Did King Edward tell you this himself?"

"Aye. He suspects that Froste and your father are allying to attempt to take the crown. He wants me to marry ye in hopes Froste will abandon their plot if he cannot have land presently."

"And what is the benefit to you?" she asked, her tone wounded.

"Edward will talk with the Scots to discuss David's release."

Her gaze burned into him. "Marriage to a woman you do not love is a steep price."

"Aye," he agreed, his voice gentle as he could make it. "It is, but David is my friend and he needs me."

She sighed, a long, tired sound. "I was coming to you," she said. "Isn't that odd?" Her voice had taken on a brittle, almost shaky quality. He suspected she was on the verge of unraveling under the strain of the day.

"Why were ye coming to me? I thought ye sought a place in yer uncle's clan." There was no need to tell her that her uncle would turn her away and bind her in marriage to Iain anyway so that Iain would be bound to the

MacDonalds.

"Angus, *my* friend, asked me to join your clan. He was certain you'd allow it, and might even find me a husband." She laughed, the gentle rumble tinged with the high notes of hysteria. "I suppose there is no need for you to find me a husband now." Marion tilted her head back so that her thick pale hair fell over her delicate shoulders.

Long-dormant desire sparked within him, and he had the urge to brush her hair off her neck and let his fingers graze her skin to see if it was as smooth as it appeared. He knew it was not wrong to hunger for a woman who was to be his wife. It did not wipe away his past. Simple lust never could replace what he'd felt for Catriona, yet guilt filled his belly. "So ye've decided nae to defy yer king and marry me?"

She scowled at him. "I do not have a choice! If I stay here, my father will simply force me to marry Froste, and then I would be the wife of an evil, cruel man who is also intent to overthrow the king!" She looked at him dubiously, as if judging how much to say. "I do not think our marriage will stop them."

Iain nodded. "I dunnae think so, either."

Her mouth parted at his admission. "So what then? Will King Edward require more of you if my father and Froste continue with their plot?"

"Aye. Edward will require my men to fight to bring down yer father if it comes to that."

She sucked her bottom lip between her teeth. "I was afraid of something like that." He expected her to weep at the unfairness of it all; instead, she drew herself up and unwrapped her arms from around her waist. "I'll marry you on one condition."

He refrained from pointing out that she was in no

position to have conditions. It was kinder to let her state them. "What is it?" he asked, motioning for her to follow him. He led her to Rory Mac and Neil, and the men fell into step behind him as the four of them moved down the street toward the horses.

"We must rescue Angus from my father," she finally said.

"I would never leave a man of mine behind, Marion," he said, irritated that she'd think he might.

She set her hands on her hips. "What about a woman of yours?"

"It depends on the woman," he replied, just to see what Marion looked like when outraged. And he wasn't disappointed. Her eyes glittered in the moonlit night, and her full lips parted as she huffed in a breath that made her chest rise enticingly. Suddenly, all he could think of was what she might be like to join with. Guilt shoved at him, but he shoved back. Lust was not love.

Marion pursed her lips. "Angus is a good man."

"Of course he is. He's a MacLeod," Iain boasted, "and I'll nae leave him to the likes of yer father. I went to yer home to get ye, and yer father was set to beat him for accidentally starting a fire."

"What?" she gasped and grabbed Iain's hand. "We must make haste! When my father gets in a temper, he can become excessive with his violence."

Iain had a sudden sneaking suspicion. "Did he ever do that with ye?" he asked casually.

"Sometimes," she said with a shrug that belied the hurt that crossed her face. She lowered her head as they rushed on, and fierce anger burned a hole in Iain's gut. Death was too good for a man who would beat his daughter. But Iain would not kill de Lacy unless to defend himself or Marion.

The king had commanded as much, and Iain would not risk hindering David's release.

After he secured the weapons onto his horse and then untethered Olaf, Iain helped Marion onto his mount. He swung into the saddle behind her and pulled her between his thighs and against his chest to protect her. She started to wiggle her very soft bottom, but he put a staying hand on her hip. "Dunnae do that," he demanded through clenched teeth. Lust had taken hold of him, and riding would be painful if he did not gain control.

She stilled immediately. "Please hurry. I must save Angus."

He was glad the Sassenach was facing forward and could not see him gaping at her. *She must save Angus?* Her loyalty to Angus pleased him, as did her courage, but God's truth such courage concerned him, as well. If she was too courageous, she was more likely to do something foolish and get herself killed.

"I'll rescue Angus and ye'll remain with Rory Mac and Neil," Iain said, clicking his tongue to get Olaf to go once Rory Mac and Neil had settled on Rory Mac's horse. They moved down the street toward the gate that would lead them out of Newcastle and back to Marion's home.

As they rode toward the same gate through which they'd entered earlier, Iain turned to Neil to ask him of Angus, but Neil was slumped forward in the saddle with Rory Mac holding the man around his waist to keep him upright. Iain had a vague memory of hearing something about Angus, but the recollections were not clear.

He stared at Marion for a moment before speaking. "Why did Angus come to England to work for yer father?"

She turned her head slightly, presenting him with her perfect profile. Her nose wrinkled and then smoothed. "He came with my mother when she was forced to marry my father. Angus felt he owed her a debt. He was to come to Scotland soon after I departed, yet he had to wait a short while to avoid my father becoming suspicious."

He glanced at Rory Mac to see if he knew of Angus's past, but Rory Mac shook his head. "I dunnae ken much about Angus MacLeod. Neil never speaks of him, but I do remember my father talking years ago about his friend Angus leaving Scotland for England."

They rode in silence for a few minutes, but when the iron gates of Newcastle came into view, Marion spoke. "When we get to my father's home, you must let me go into the castle to save Angus. I am afraid Father will try to kill you and make it seem an accident. He'll not want me dead, at least not until he has his knights."

Iain gaped at Marion and noticed Rory Mac was doing the same thing. Rory Mac shook his head, a bewildered expression on his face. Iain scowled at the top of Marion's head. She needed to understand a few things. "Ye offend me by implying I kinnae keep myself and ye safe." He slid an arm around her stomach and tightened his hold as they neared the gate. If there was to be trouble, he wanted to have a firm grip on her if he needed to gallop away.

She stiffened under his touch. "You implied I couldn't defend myself by commanding me to remain behind when we get to my father's!"

He frowned. "Ye're a woman." No more explanation was needed. "I dunnae ken how it was before, but now, ye'll let me keep ye from danger. Ye will do as I say."

"Are you always this arrogant?" she demanded, trying to scoot forward on the horse.

Iain pulled her back to him and grinned. "Aye. It's good of ye to praise me so."

"That was not praise," she grumbled. "I fear we will not fare well at all."

He chuckled. "As long as ye obey me we'll fare nicely."

He didn't hear her response, having shifted his attention to the guards, but whatever she was saying, her tone was sullen and it made him want to laugh again. Taming the Sassenach was going to be fun, and it had been a long time since he'd had any fun.

Three

*A*s they came to the guards of the gate out of Newcastle, the Scot pressed his lips close to Marion's ear, sending an odd tingle through her body.

"Dunnae speak," he commanded.

Normally, she would have protested his command, but she decided it would not do to create any trouble when they were in a hurry.

"We need to depart Newcastle," Iain told the approaching guard.

The man looked up at Marion and Iain. "When you came in, you said you were leaving England. The letter you bring from King Edward grants you permission to leave, not enter." The guard withdrew his sword and braced his legs. Marion stiffened in alarm, but behind her Iain didn't move.

"That's true enough," Iain replied with an exaggerated sigh. "But King Edward also bade me to marry Lady Marion de Lacy, who ye see sitting in front of me. When I went to her home, her father, Baron de Lacy, was very distraught because she was missing. It seems the lass did nae want to marry an ugly Scot such as myself, so she ran off. I found her here and must now, by orders of your king, take her back to her father to marry her."

The lie was so smooth that Marion's stress lessened,

and she exhaled a breath she hadn't even known she was holding.

The knight laughed at Iain's explanation, but then he seemed to sober. "How do I know King Edward ordered you to marry Baron de Lacy's daughter?"

Behind her, Iain moved around for a minute and then leaned down and held out King Edward's written order. "Ye'll see the decree is signed and sealed by yer king," Iain said with ease.

As the knight read, Marion considered what was about to occur. She was going to marry a man she did not know, and certainly did not love. It was exactly the sort of marriage she had not wanted, one born not of love but necessity. She didn't even know Iain well enough to decide if she thought he was a man she could possibly love in time, yet she had no choice but to marry the stranger pressed hot and hard against her back. The blue-eyed, black-haired chief apparently had no need for a wife with an opinion or a backbone. She turned to eye Iain MacLeod, laird of the MacLeod clan, and he didn't even shift his gaze toward her, simply kept it unmoving and steely on the guard.

She studied him for a moment. He was not handsome in the style of a traditional Englishman. His dark hair grazed his shoulders and a shadow of stubble covered his square jaw. He did not look a bit refined, but rather tough and sinewy, as if he could kill a man with one blow. And his looks were not deceiving: he was a warrior, as she'd seen with her own two eyes.

Angus was the tallest man she'd ever known, but Iain was taller—and certainly leaner. Angus liked his ale, and as he was an expert brewer, he drank plenty of it and had a bit of a gut. By the feel of Iain's hard stomach against her back, he must not drink much ale. She faced forward once more. God's truth, leaning against Iain was like leaning against a boulder. The thickly corded arm wrapped around her middle made her feel alternately safe and trapped. And his large hands... She stole a glance as he spoke to the guards. His hand was spread flat on her belly, which suddenly fluttered as her cheeks heated. It was indecent the way he was holding her, yet she did think he might have been trying to protect her; however, if they were going to be married, she'd have to make him understand she could protect herself. Angus had taught her to, after all.

The sudden groaning of the Newcastle gates as they opened jerked her thoughts back to the present. As soon as they passed through and were far enough away from the guards, Rory Mac startled her when he moved his horse up beside her and Iain, and addressed her. "How does a privileged baron's daughter ken anything about the healing arts?"

The question didn't anger her, even if it was a little offensive that the Scot thought her pampered and spoiled. She could see why it would seem odd to him, though. "My mother knew the art of healing and taught me a small bit before she died. The rest I learned from an older woman who lives just outside my golden castle walls." She couldn't help but add the last part.

Behind her, she could hear Iain's low laugh, which filled her with gladness. So her future husband had a sense of humor. That was a good start. Encouraged, she continued. "When I got weary of being pampered by my loving father, I decided to help others he loved to pamper with regular beatings." She raised her eyebrows at Rory Mac, certain she had made herself clear and daring him to ask her more.

"Ye're bold for a Sassenach." His tone carried just a hint of surprise.

"Well, I am half-Scottish, so maybe my boldness comes from that bloodline," she offered as a sort of olive branch of friendship.

"Aye." He beamed. "I'm sure ye're correct." With that, Rory Mac moved the horse carrying Neil and him ahead of her and Iain.

Iain's hand moved against her belly, his fingers brushing perilously close to the underside of her breasts. Her body shuddered. "Ye did good, Marion."

Heat consumed her chest and belly and made her shift as it spread through her. Was the need for his respect making her feel so strange? "Thank you," she murmured.

"Ye're welcome. Now, quit yer wiggling," he demanded, his warm breath fanning her earlobe.

The pleasure of seconds ago disappeared. He barked orders much as her father always had. "Then loosen your hold," she snapped.

"Why?" he teased gently. "Does my touch light a fire of want within ye?"

"A fire?" she asked, her voice shaking. 'Twas true that the way the man went from cold to hot in his tone made her thoughts tumble over one another. And his fingers… They brushed back and forth over her ribs, making her heart pound so fast she was having trouble controlling her breathing. Suddenly, his fingers stilled and pressed into her flesh once again.

"Desire." His words came out low and husky.

She stilled. How had he known? How had she not?

His body shook with suppressed laughter. "Ye've never experienced desire, have ye?" he asked as they left the road they were on, taking them out of the sight of the guards.

She glanced behind her, catching a smug look in Iain's icy blue eyes. She stiffened her spine and glared at him. "I'd rather not talk about it right now," she murmured, hot mortification singeing her cheeks.

He nodded his agreement. "Likely best. We need to make haste." And then, without another word, he clicked his tongue and his destrier took off in a gallop. Up ahead, Rory Mac's horse did the same. She supposed the beast could sense the shift of pace of the other animal.

The wind whipped her hair in her face and sliced through her gown. She shivered but was soon shaking and clenching her teeth in an effort to control it. They approached the end of the path, coming close to her father's castle. She was about to tell Iain when he pulled up on the reins and slowed his horse to a stop. Ahead of them, Rory Mac slowed his horse and turned back to look at them. Without a sound, Iain raised a hand and motioned Rory Mac around. The man immediately obeyed without question. Marion's teeth chattered in the silence as she pondered this. Would Iain expect the same blind obedience from her as he apparently got from his men?

Before she could think on it further, he spoke. "Ye're freezing," he said, shifting behind her. His arm released her, and then both hands encircled her as he drew her so close to him that she could feel the beat of his heart through the thin material of her gown. In the next instant, a heavy fabric was laid over her legs and tucked behind her back and under her chin. She glanced down to see the plaid he'd been wearing, and her eyes flew open wide as she craned her neck to look at him.

She gasped as her gaze locked on his bare legs. He wore nothing but a long léine. "You cannot ride around like that! You're naked."

He grinned. "I assure ye, I'm nae. If ye'd care to see me naked…"

He was trying to provoke her. She shook her head. "No."

He stared at her as if he were trying to read her thoughts. "Ye ken ye desire me."

"I don't know a thing about desire," she snapped, though she suspected he was right and that the odd feeling he'd been causing in her was indeed lust.

"It's nae bad ye desire me. I desire ye, too." He said the last as if that fact bothered him, but he spoke again before she could consider why. "'Tis the truth. It will make being married more pleasant for both of us."

"Do you want a pleasant marriage?" If he did, at least that was something. Many men just wanted a wife to give them babies and do their bidding.

He shrugged. "It matters little what I want. We're to be married by the wishes of our kings, so we will be."

"It matters to me what you want," she said. "*I* don't wish for a husband who will treat me poorly."

"I dunnae treat anyone poorly," he replied, his voice gruff. "Simply do as I tell ye, stay out of my way, and we will live peacefully."

She ground her teeth. "So you want a wife without an opinion who will obey your every command?"

"A wife must listen."

His hard, unbending tone irritated her. "You want a dog not a wife," she grumbled.

"Ye've strange ideas about a woman's place, Marion."

Maybe she did, but her mother used to tell her stories every night about her sisters who had married for love and how wonderful their lives were. Marion wanted that. She had longed for a happy family for as long as she could remember, and she had known deep within that the key to that was love. A husband had to love his wife, or at the very least be capable of love, unlike her father. She stilled, fear rising in her chest. She couldn't even say if Iain was capable of love or not.

"Have you ever been in love?" she blurted.

He started at her question. "Aye." The word throbbed with suppressed pain that made Marion instantly curious about what had happened and completely relieved that he could feel for another with such depth. "What happened to the woman you loved?"

"She died," he replied, the words catching in his throat.

Marion bit her lip at how awful it was to lose someone you loved. She'd never been in love, but she had loved her mother greatly and lost her. "I'm so sorry," she offered lamely. "How did she die?" Sometimes it helped to talk of it. At least it had helped her to talk to Angus about the unfairness of her mother's passing.

"She was sick," he replied, his voice like a blast of cold air. "Dunnae ask me of my wife again. Ken?"

"Your wife?" she gasped, unable to control her reaction. "I didn't know you'd been married before."

"There was no reason ye would," he said, his tone still chilly as if her words had opened a wound and he was now irritated. She struggled to find something to say to put him at ease when he clicked his tongue again and his horse began to move.

In the distance, she could see her father's castle, and her thoughts shifted from Iain to Angus. She clutched Iain's hard thigh before she realized what she was doing. When she felt the muscles tense under her touch, she released him, her cheeks flaming.

"We need a plot to get Angus out of the castle," she said, turning to the subject that most needed to be addressed.

"I already have one," he replied dismissively.

She clenched her teeth and inhaled a long steady breath. "I wish to be part of the plot."

"It's best ye learn now, Marion, that ye'll nae always get what ye wish," Iain said, pulling his horse to a stop next to some large trees where Rory Mac was already helping Neil off the horse. Iain dismounted quickly and assisted Marion down. Once her feet hit the ground, she turned toward him, her temper flaring that he too seemed to think her spoiled and pampered.

"I've learned well enough that I'll not always get what I want, but in this, I must demand."

Iain shook his head, his jaw set in obvious determination. "I've spoken, and that is that."

That was that!? He'd spoken!?

She turned away from him before she said some rather unladylike things. She learned in dealing with her hard-hearted father that sometimes it was better to simply do what you wanted rather than ask and be denied. And she wanted to help rescue Angus. It made perfect sense. She knew her father's castle and Iain did not.

━━◦❦◦━━

Iain may not know Marion de Lacy very well yet, but he knew she was angry. Any clot-heid who could see would recognize it from her narrowed eyes and high color. Plus, she turned swiftly away from him and her back was stiff and her foot tapping. He knew she wanted to help, but the best way she could help him was to ensure he did not worry about keeping her safe.

"Marion, turn around," he commanded. When she

didn't budge, he stifled the annoyance that threatened to overflow and decided to try a gentler approach. She didn't know the way of the Highlands, after all. Maybe she didn't understand that she should obey him without command, yet given his meeting with her father, he suspected de Lacy had demanded obedience without question. Maybe that was the problem. Maybe Marion thought he was going to be as cruel to her as her father must have been.

"Marion," he tried again. When she didn't turn toward him, he decided he could waste no more time. He grasped her by the shoulders and spun her around. She stubbornly kept her gaze down. He suppressed an unexpected desire to smile. He wasn't used to being defied, and he should be angry, but instead, he was impressed at her bravery. He hooked a finger under her chin and tipped her face to his until she had no choice but to look at him. "When I'm talking to ye, I'd like to ken ye're listening. Especially when yer safety is involved. Ken?"

"Just because I'm not looking at you does not mean I don't hear you," she said. "And I already told you I want to help."

"Ye did. And the best way for ye to help is to stay here."

She scowled at him and shook her head. "I know the castle."

"And ye ken the men. If ye had to kill one of them, would ye?" When her eyes widened and her lips parted, he nodded. "Ye see, ye'd be a hindrance and nae a help." Before she could say anything, he turned to Rory Mac, who had been standing nearby, silently watching the exchange.

"Keep her out of the castle," Iain commanded.

Rory Mac nodded. "I'll keep her safe."

Iain could tell by the derisive noises coming from Marion that she intended to argue, so he stopped her before she could start. "Nay," he said, his hard tone warning her. "Ye will do as I say and stay with Rory Mac."

"I said nothing," she muttered.

"Ye were going to."

Marion huffed out a breath.

The little hints of how she felt fascinated him. He had to force himself to concentrate on his task instead of wondering what she might do next. "I'll get Angus and yer priest—"

Her brow furrowed. "Why would you collect Father John?"

There was no polite way to tell her this, so he simply stated the truth without preamble. "We need to be wed and the marriage consummated as soon as possible."

A shocked expression settled on her face, and she took a step away from him. "What?" she demanded in a hoarse whisper.

Rory Mac laughed deeply, and Iain scowled at him. "Tend to Neil."

"But I already—"

"Do it again!" Iain clipped.

"Aye, Iain." Rory Mac turned and went to the tree where Neil lay with his eyes closed.

Iain stared through the darkness at this woman who was to be his wife. She was a stranger, yet he already knew she was brave and loyal, and he did not want to add to the pain he assumed she'd already had to endure.

He stepped toward her and touched her elbow. Her body trembled under his fingertips. Was she going to faint?

She surprised and impressed him by shoving his hand away, notching her chin up, and pushing her shoulders back. "Since I know it's not a great need for my person that's driving you to force me to be wed in wee hours, I suppose on the dirt upon which we stand will do..."

Guilt pricked him for where her innocence would be taken, but there was no choice. The marriage needed to be completed with the joining as quickly as possible. "Nae. We'll find a nice patch of soft grass *somewhere*," he teased in hopes to lighten the grave situation, but her sharp intake of breath told him she was not amused.

"How considerate of you," she retorted. "I suppose you feel the need to seal the marriage before we flee."

The time for teasing was over. "I dunnae like the circumstances anymore than ye do, Marion. We'll flee first, then see to the other."

"You're mistaken if you think joining your body with mine will stop my father if he's made up his mind to defy King Edward."

"I dunnae think our joining will stop yer father, Marion, but it will make ye mine in the eyes of my clan."

"And what about in your eyes, Iain?" she demanded, her voice belying her anxiety. "Will that make me officially yours?"

His gaze slid over her voluptuous body, barely visible now in the dark, but he could remember every detail from her long slender neck to her delicate fingers to her round bottom that had pressed between his thighs on the horse. He heated instantly. "Ye were mine the moment I consented to marry ye. Now tell me, where might I find Angus and the priest?"

Her jaw jutted out, but she huffed out a breath and spoke. "The priest will likely be in the chapel near where the stables were, which is where you will likely find Angus, as well, working to create makeshift shelters for the horses. Unless—" Her words halted, and she gulped. "Unless

Father has tied him to the post where he beats people and left Angus as an example."

Iain's gut twisted in disgust. "Does yer father do that often?"

"Yes," she whispered, her right hand finding her left and her fingers curling around her wrist. She rubbed the skin as if in memory of being tied there herself.

It took all Iain's determination not to tell her he wanted to kill her father. She may hate the man, but he was still her father. "Where is the post?"

"The bailey near the front gate."

He nodded. "What can ye tell me about the castle, in case I need to enter?"

"Let me show you," she countered, her voice a hopeful plea.

Though it made a great deal of sense to have her with him as his guide, he could not bear the thought of taking her deliberately into danger. If he didn't come back, Rory Mac would know to flee and take her to safety. Iain didn't even need to say it, the Scots knew each other that well. They'd grown up together, and Rory Mac was like a brother.

"Nay," he said, making sure his tone brooked no argument. "Stay here." He turned and caught Rory Mac's eyes, understanding passing between them. Iain retrieved his sword from his tethered mount, and then he headed into the black night to rescue Angus and get the priest.

It did not take long, even on foot, to close the distance to the ditch that surrounded the castle's outer court. The bridge was drawn and the towers manned, which meant the only possible way into the castle was through the dark, stale-smelling water that filled the ditch. He'd cross the divide from the side of the wall, scale the wooden stockade, and make his way across the bailey to find Angus and the priest. Hopefully they were not in the keep, instead.

Iain crouched low to the ground, hidden by trees, and eyed the stockade, searching for the best place to climb and contemplating how to draw the guards' attention away from the wall. Perhaps another fire?

Just as he settled on the idea, the pounding of horses' hooves filled the silent night behind him, and out of the darkness rode his future wife, the moon shining bright upon her. Her pale hair glowed in the moonlight, like one of the fairies of Dunvegan Castle. God's truth, he blinked to make sure he was seeing clearly, but it was certainly Marion, calling in a loud voice for the drawbridge to be lowered.

As she rode by him, a look of defiance graced her face as his plaid flew behind her and landed near where he was crouched. As he snatched it up and quickly put it on, two thoughts collided at once: she was brave and beautiful, and the combination was potently enticing and dangerous.

Stay here, he'd told her. She'd nodded her agreement, hadn't she?

He thought back to the moment as he slipped down the side of the ditch into the dark waters of the moat. When he dove into the slimy water, the recollection came to him. She'd not agreed. Nay. He'd not waited for it, either. He'd simply assumed she would listen. That was the last time he'd assume anything about the Sassenach.

Four

The second slap from her father was the one that sent her to her knees. She wasn't there long, though. He yanked her up by her hair and jerked her head back until stars danced in her vision. Truly, they did a jig. She blinked and the stars in the sky settled and stilled.

Thank heaven. She was on the verge of being sick, and she'd almost rather die than show her father such weakness. Her cheek throbbed painfully, and she considered that, perhaps, riding into the castle had not been the best idea. When she'd persuaded Rory Mac to walk a distance away and turn his back to her with the lie that she needed to relieve herself, she'd only thought of providing the distraction Iain needed to retrieve Angus and the priest. Hopefully, Iain would consider that if he decided to rescue her. She wasn't at all certain that he would come to her aid, however; he'd likely conclude that having her as a bride would be too much trouble, and Rory Mac would likely agree.

"Tell me the truth," her father roared as he released her head and gave her a shove forward. She almost fell again, but Andrew caught her by the arm. Her father's fist crashed into Andrew's face, letting the knight know what her father thought about his aiding her. Poor Andrew staggered to the ground beside her. She quickly shook her head at him.

"Do not dare to help her," Father ordered as he stepped in front of her once again. "Marion, on my word, if you don't tell me the truth, I'll beat you until you beg for death. Now, where did you go when you fled from here? From whom did you get that horse?" He pointed a gloved finger toward Rory Mac's destrier. Iain's beast had refused to let her mount him.

Marion slanted her gaze toward the bridge on the other side of the bailey. Her father had left Angus tied to the pole at the entrance, as she'd told Iain he might. Just as she was about to look away from Angus's slumped form to answer her father, a large shadow rose up beside Angus. It had to be Iain, she thought, and within seconds, Iain and Angus were gone. Iain may be a strapping Scot, but his size certainly didn't impede his ability to hide. She should have known he'd be clever. Angus had always said Scots were taught the art of shadow dancing from the day they could toddle on two legs.

Slowly, she faced her father once more. "I already told you the truth. Someone tried to snatch me from the hill in front of the castle. I don't know who it was! I fell into the water in the struggle, and they fished me out and then rode me all the way to Newcastle. I escaped when they thought I was sleeping, and stole this horse to return directly to you."

"If you're lying, Marion—"

"I'm not. I swear it." That lie would cost her a great number of coins to Father John, but it was worth it. Perhaps all was not lost.

An idea occurred to her then, one that would lead her father and some of his men away from the castle to make things easier for Iain. "I can lead you to where they took me. I know what they look like."

"Give me their descriptions and the exact position. I'll ride out with some of my men to find them, and you"—he offered a malicious smile—"will stay here and ready yourself for your wedding. Froste will have to be fetched from Newcastle. He arrived earlier and I told him you drowned, so he went into town to—er—deliberate with his brother."

Marion knew that was a lie. Froste had gone into town to seek a whore to warm his bed for the night. That's how distraught he was by Marion's presumed death. She snorted inwardly as she studied her father from under her lashes. So her father truly meant to defy the king. Or maybe he simply intended to claim she'd been married to Froste before he knew of the king's new orders. That was very likely. But it would mean her father had every intention of hunting down Iain and killing him and Rory Mac so they could not tell King Edward otherwise.

Marion needed to escape quickly, now that Angus was safe with Iain. But how? Before she could consider it further, her father spoke.

"Sir Thomas will escort you." Her father nodded to a knight Marion didn't know.

"There's no need," she replied, striving to sound accommodating though she was feeling desperate.

"There is a need, Marion." Her father's dark eyes bore into hers. "Someone tried to seize you. I will see you defended at all times."

It had been years since she'd allowed herself to hope her father might feel any true affection toward her, but that hope had apparently never died as it now flared in her chest. "Father, I'm touched."

"Don't be," he snapped. "I simply can't have you disappearing again before I marry you to Froste."

"Of course," she replied, her face heating with anger at herself. Why had she been so foolish to allow any hope?

She followed the knight across the bailey, over the bridge that covered the second moat, and up the stairs that led to the keep—and her room—while she plotted her escape. She needed to get Sir Thomas away from her door.

She paused as he opened the door and stepped aside for her to enter. "Could you fetch Father John from the chapel for me?" He would normally be there at this time of night, but she prayed he was already with Iain. However, the errand would occupy the guard for a bit. "I have some sins to confess before I marry."

"Certainly, my lady," the knight readily agreed.

Well, it was certainly easy enough to send Sir Thomas away, Marion thought as she walked past him and into her bedchamber. The door clicked shut, followed by the distinct snap of the lock setting in place.

"What are you doing?" she demanded, pressing her ear to the closed door, her pulse ticking up several beats.

"Your father ordered you to be locked in, my lady. I'll return shortly with Father John."

"Wait!" she shouted, even as she heard his footsteps carrying him away from her. She gripped the door handle and pulled on it for several seconds before she forced herself to let go. Desperation wanted to overcome her, but she refused to succumb.

This was terrible! She'd not foreseen being locked inside her chambers when she'd decided to provide the distraction the stubborn Scot needed so he wouldn't get caught entering the castle. And though she'd certainly delivered the needed diversion, she now not only had to escape the castle but she had to escape her room.

Thinking quickly, she decided that once she was out of the keep, she'd scale the keep wall, make her way down the backside of the hill, and swim the treacherous, snake-filled waters to escape and meet with Iain. That was assuming no guards stopped her.

She gulped at the daunting task. At least she knew Iain had Angus, and if he didn't have Father John—she smiled grimly to herself—well, then she would not have to be wedded and joined with him so soon.

She stalked to her bed and ripped off the coverlet, then dragged the heavy blanket—and two others she collected from her trunk—over to the window, which she threw open. Glancing out the window to the ground far below, her stomach knotted. She inhaled deeply, then let it out and muttered to herself as she began to tie the blankets together. Once they were secured, she fastened one end to the iron of the window and dropped the other out of the small space until it dangled toward the ground.

She swung a leg over the window ledge and wiggled out of the cramped space. She gripped the coverlet, sweat dampening her brow with the effort to hold on, and shimmied all the way to the end of her rope. With a hopeful prayer, she glanced below to see if she was close enough to leap. Her heart sank. The ground was still so far away. Climbing back up was not an option. Not only were her hands beginning to cramp but there was no way for her to escape her room with the door locked.

She squeezed her eyes shut, took a deep breath, and released the material. She dropped with a speed that stole her breath and made her body tighten in expectation of a painful landing. She did hit something hard, but it was warm, too, and the landing, though jarring, wasn't agonizing. Her eyes flew open and met an angry—or was that astonished?—blue gaze.

"You returned for me," she said in surprise.

"Aye," Iain growled, setting her roughly on the ground. "And now I'm questioning why." He gripped her by the shoulders and fairly dragged her against the castle wall. "Ye would have broken yer neck had I nae caught ye."

"Nonsense," she replied, annoyed that instead of one word of praise for her creating the perfect distraction for him, he was angry. "I know what I am doing," she snapped.

He crossed his arms over his chest and glared at her. "Do ye now?"

His voice was hard, and she vowed he'd made the question sound threatening on purpose. She notched her chin up. "I do."

His glower became fiercer as he stepped so close to her that his heat overwhelmed her. "Then ye have the priest with ye?"

"Well, no," she hedged, not willing to admit quite yet that she didn't have everything in hand. "We will simply have to make haste to the chapel and find him. I thought you would have done that with Angus and been away from the castle by now," she snapped.

"Ye thought that, did ye?" He pressed closer to her, his hands coming to either side of her shoulders.

She could feel the anger rolling off him in waves of scorching heat that seemed to create steam from his wet body, hair, and clothes. Fear lodged in her throat, but she refused to show it. She squared her shoulders. "I did. I created the perfect opportunity for you to do what you needed. You should have trusted me to escape and find you outside the castle walls."

"I should have trusted ye?" Incredulity shook every

word as his face came very close to hers. "*Ye* should have trusted *me*," he growled. "I am your laird."

Her heart pounded viciously, but she forced herself to speak, praying she didn't sound scared. "Not yet you're not."

He blew out a long, hot, clearly angry breath that fanned her face. "Ye ken ye have nay choice but to marry me."

Her gut clenched with bitterness at the truth of his words, but she refused to acknowledge out loud that he was right. Instead, she said, "Where is Angus?"

"When we saw yer father's knight leading ye to the keep, Angus said ye were surely being taken to yer room. We decided that he'd get the priest and I'd come for ye."

"Because I'm yours?" she asked, feeling slightly bemused by his nearness, his masculine scent, and the power that he projected by his sheer size.

He laughed. "Nay, but ye *are* mine." The words held a ring of finality she did not dare argue with.

"Then why did you come for me and not Angus when he knows the castle and you don't? Oh no!" she cried suddenly and clutched Iain's arm. "Angus is hurt."

"Just bruised. He'll mend, but he's slower than usual and was uncertain he could properly defend ye if the need arose."

He took her hand in his big, warm, rough one, and a jolt shot from her fingertips straight to her stomach. "Come. We're meeting them outside the castle where I presume Rory Mac is still waiting for me as I bid the *two* of ye to do," he said pointedly.

'Twas true that it was hard to pull her thoughts away from the tingly sensation Iain's fingers were causing, but somehow she managed. "Don't blame Rory Mac. I deceived him."

"I dunnae doubt it," he grumbled, "but the man should ken better than to fall prey to a woman's charms."

"Well, in his defense, he doesn't know me."

Iain made a derisive sound in his throat. "Ye're nae helping his cause," he said and then pulled her into the wall of brick that was his chest. She pressed her hands against the sinewy muscle and froze, enraptured by the fast beat of his heart tapping against her fingertips.

"Sassenach," he said gruffly. "There will be time enough for ye to show me how much ye desire me, but now we need to leave."

"Are you always so arrogant?" she managed, though her throat felt thick and her thoughts spun a little.

"Aye," he replied. "Now let's go meet the others."

She gasped, suddenly realizing the consequences of sending the guard to fetch the priest. What if the guard had come upon Angus retrieving Father John?

"We may have a slight problem," she said.

"What?"

Marion bit her lip. "I sent the guard to get the priest in the chapel," she blurted, thinking telling it quickly may make it less terrible. It didn't.

"Why'd ye do that if ye intended to escape?" he demanded.

"I didn't know that Father's knight was going to lock me in my room," she grumbled. "I thought I'd escape while he was fetching Father John."

"And that's what ye call knowing what ye're doing?" he growled.

"Oh, do be quiet," she snapped. "I've put up with my father being cruel to me for twenty years, I'll not put up with twenty more years of it from you. I'd rather chance a future with the MacDonalds."

His hands came to her shoulders and gripped them. "I highly doubt ye have any chances with the MacDonalds at present, Marion. Yer uncle Gowan surely kens about our marriage. David likely told him because of his position. And I ken yer uncle. He would have agreed to bind me to him through marriage to ye himself. So even if ye went to him begging nae to wed me, I'd nae trust his help. I'm yer only hope, whether it pleases ye to accept the truth or nae."

⟨✦⟩

Iain cursed himself as tears filled Marion's eyes. She blinked rapidly and glanced away, and when she turned her face to him again, no tears trailed down her fine-boned cheeks, but the unmistakable glistening of unshed tears did shine in her lovely eyes. Presently, the only person Marion needed defending from was him. He released his hold on her shoulders and gently cupped her face.

"I'm sorry," he said, uncertain what else to say. It had been a very long time since he'd held a woman so familiarly, and Marion's silken skin under his rough fingertips filled him with a need he'd forgotten.

"Don't worry yourself," she whispered. "I'm aware no one really wants me." She blinked up at him. She was trying so valiantly to be brave, but her lower lip trembled, and all he could think about was that he'd caused her pain. He wanted to take it away. With no other intention but that one, he pressed a kiss to her forehead, hoping to soothe her.

She quivered beneath his fingers, and his chest tightened. He had desired Catriona, to be sure, but it was a cautious need because she had always been sick and frail. But life and strength simmered from Marion, and he realized with a relieved start that he'd not have to be cautious with her. Guilt assaulted him, as if his relief was a betrayal of his love for Catriona.

He took a deep breath, glad that they needed to go and he could store this away to consider later. "We better make our way to the chapel to see if Angus needs help."

Marion nodded, an eager look on her face. "We can go to the side of the keep and scale the wall, but then we'll have to carefully descend the hill, swim the ditch waters, and cross the bailey to get back to the chapel."

Iain studied her. "The water is filled with snakes."

She bit her lip and nodded. "I know. It will be dangerous."

"Aye. So will crossing the bailey in the dark. Yer father's men may shoot arrows at ye, never kenning they are assaulting ye." Iain's blood rushed through his veins as he stared at Marion. He had to protect her. He could not fail to protect a woman that was his again. He grasped her chin gently. "If ye dunnae listen to everything I say, I'm going to flay yer bottom when we're away, ken?"

"I ken," she replied, surprising him by mimicking him.

He chuckled at her cheekiness. "Stay by my side. Dunnae speak. No matter what."

"But you may need my help if we encounter one of my father's knights. I may need to influence them to—"

He shook his head. "I doubt ye'd be able to influence them to do anything now, and I will nae need help defending myself against a weak Englishman."

Her eyes narrowed. "Pride is one of the seven deadly sins."

"I'll keep my pride and chance that it will nae be the

thing to kill me," he replied and started them on the journey.

━━━◦❦◦━━━

"I see living in England all these years has nae lessened the craftiness of a MacLeod," Iain said, surveying the blazing buildings from his crouch near the wooden wall Iain and Marion had just scaled.

"If it is indeed Angus," Marion murmured as she twisted the dripping skirts of her gown.

Even soaking, the woman was so beautiful his body hummed. With her wet hair slicked away from her face, her perfect bone structure was even more striking, but what he truly found enticing was the bravery she continued to display. She'd not batted an eyelash when they'd slid down the steep hill and then swam the freezing waters, only to have to climb the wall.

"I dunnae think any man here would set fire to yer father's home besides Angus, do ye?"

She shook her head, her teeth chattering. "No, I don't. Do you think that means—"

"I think it means Angus needed to redirect the knights' attention to get to the priest in the chapel. What I don't ken is whether he has him or if they are still in there."

"So how will we find out?" she asked as she vigorously rubbed her arms.

The desire to wrap her in his embrace and give her the heat from his body swept over him, but he couldn't allow himself to be distracted. They could both pay for the folly with death. "We'll have to get to the chapel, but in this frenzy"—people filled the bailey, helping to smother the kitchen fire—"we should be able to get there unseen."

"And then if Angus and the priest are not there, or if they are and we need to help Angus, we will triumph, and then we will all simply go back over the wall and swim the moat to freedom." Her voice trembled slightly, showing the tiniest hint of concern at what they were facing.

Iain took her hand for one brief moment and squeezed. "Dunnae worry," he soothed. "Are ye ready?"

"No," she said with a laugh. "But let us go anyway."

"Follow me," he said, staying near the wall to keep to the shadows. They came to the chapel quickly, but battle-ready knights flanked the door. Iain was certain Angus had to be in there. He needed to draw their attention away, so he could cast aside one knight and then the other. He looked at Marion and knew he had to forget his pride and ask for the help he'd boasted he'd not need.

When he leaned close to her and slipped his hand around her neck to pull her near for a whisper, she started but did not make a sound. From inside the chapel came a roar, followed by a bellow.

"Angus," Marion breathed, turning her head toward Iain's so that her lips accidentally brushed across his. Her eyes flew open wide, and a strangled sound escaped her. The burning desire to claim her mouth swept through Iain and almost took his senses, but he fought the primal craving and instead leaned toward her ear.

"I need yer help," he whispered.

"You need *my* help, you say?" she whispered back, suppressed laughter in her hushed tone.

"Aye, I am resigned. Now, will ye help me or nae? If ye dunnae, I'm going to have to kill more knights to get to Angus and the priest."

"You leave me no option," she grumbled.

"Aye," he agreed with a grin. "I'm a Scot, Sassenach.

There's nae need to give ye an option because I ken what's best, but I do speak the truth. Either ye can draw away the knights or I'll have to charge through them with my sword."

"I will do it," she hastily replied. "How do you suppose I should proceed?"

He hated that he had to use her at all, but he knew the knights would not hurt her. A simple plot was often the best one. "Step forward on my say and call out for help. Hopefully, they'll both come to yer aid and I can catch them unawares."

"That's a sound plot. There are no other reasonable choices, as there is only one entry," she replied, to his amusement. Marion's mind seemed to work more like a man's than a woman's, calculating danger and assessing risks. Iain liked it. "I don't know either of those knights. They must be new, so I don't think I can coax them to trust me, so yes, your plot is best." Iain bit back a smile as she continued. "What should I do when they are upon us?"

"Move back and ye duck."

"That's your idea?" she demanded, her voice incredulous.

"Yer lack of faith is noted," he grumbled under his breath. "There are only two of them."

"Indeed," she whispered sarcastically. "I suppose it takes at least ten Englishmen to bring a Scot down."

"Nay. I've seen a Scot brought down by one," he replied. "But I'm nae weak or foolish. Twelve is the likely number it would take to fell me."

"Only twelve?" She cocked her head. "Hmm...I'm not sure I should marry a man who can be felled by a mere twelve knights."

He laughed softly. He liked her sense of humor and the

fact that she was not afraid to tease him. God's truth was he liked almost everything he'd learned about her so far. Except her stubbornness. He was used to protecting and fighting for himself, but a burning awareness that he once again had someone to guard rose in his chest, made his heart pound and his blood course through his veins and rush in his ears. What if she was accidentally injured?

He gripped her chin and turned her face to his. "Dunnae forget to duck the moment I stand."

"Why don't you give me a weapon?"

He was about to argue, but the rightness of it made perfect sense. He'd seen her wield a dagger with skill. He withdrew one of his sheathed blades and handed it to her. "Ye'll nae need to use it," he promised.

She touched her hand to his heart and pressed her fingertips there. "I'm sure I won't."

An ache, poignant and sweet, throbbed. Whatever that feeling was, he didn't have time for it now. Grasping his sword, he nodded. "Go. Now."

As she sprang up and called to the guards, he tensed and readied himself to move. Both knights rushed toward her as Iain had hoped, and when they were upon her, Iain leaped up, wielded his sword, and struck the first knight in the chest. The man fell to the ground, dead, and as Iain pulled his sword out of the man's chest, the other knight was lifting his sword to strike. Just as the sword dislodged and Iain raised it again, Marion sprung forward and stabbed the knight in the leg with her dagger. Iain scowled that she should risk her life but was impressed by her still. He lunged toward the knight as the man howled and felled him with another blow to his legs. When the knight went down, Iain gave him a swift punch, making him swoon, and retrieved the dagger he'd lent Marion. He rose and glared at her.

"Ye could have been killed," he growled and turned away not waiting for her reply. He was certain she'd argue, and he had neither the time nor the patience. He charged into the chapel, which was empty except for one knight, the priest, and Angus—who was tied to a chair.

The knight came at Iain with his sword raised high. Iain didn't hesitate. He swung his sword low, slashed his gut, and when the knight doubled over, Iain hit him in the back. The man fell to his knees, and while he was trying to get back to his feet, Iain withdrew his blade and used the hilt to knock the man in the head hard enough that he swooned. The knight fell forward onto the ground.

"You must be the MacLeod," the priest said, his eyes wide and his hands twisting together.

Angus grinned from the chair to which he was tied. "He is, Father John, but dunnae fear. He'd never harm a godly man."

"Unless the man was trying to kill me," Iain retorted, purposely eyeing the priest while stepping around the felled knight and striding toward Angus.

Before he even reached the Scot, Marion sprinted past him and kneeled in front of the man. "Angus!" she cried out. "I'm so happy to see you!"

She threw her arms around him, and Iain faltered for one moment, struck deep to the core with the love she had for this man. Had Angus been like a father to her when her own had not? It had to be so. Angus was far older than she was for it to be anything else.

"I'm safe and so are ye," Angus said, soothing her.

As Marion and Angus spoke at once, each trying to ask the other what had occurred since they'd been parted, Iain silently untied Angus and then gripped Marion under the arm and raised her to her feet.

She looked up at him. "What are you doing?"

"Getting married," he replied, reaching out and snagging the priest by the elbow when the man looked like he might flee. "Marry us quickly," he commanded the priest.

Marion gasped. "Here?"

"Aye."

Shock made her green eyes sparkle even brighter. "Now?" she squeaked.

He knew at once she'd hoped to delay, and he could not begrudge her. He had hoped to never marry again himself, but fate didn't care what they wanted.

He slung his arm over her shoulder without releasing his hold on the priest. "Aye, Marion," he said gently. "Here and now. It is for yer protection. If I were to be killed, my clan would come for ye as my widow. They would defend ye with their life."

She heaved in a breath, as if to argue, but Angus stood and spoke. "He's right, Marion. I ken ye had other ideas—"

"What ideas?" Iain demanded.

She looked up at him, her cheeks turning scarlet. "It's nothing," she mumbled.

He released the priest with a warning glare and moved her far enough away that they would have privacy. "Tell me," he said. He didn't want to enter into the marriage with secrets between them.

She sighed, her face turning redder than he would have thought possible. "I wished to marry for love," she whispered and cast her eyes downward.

He felt as if he had suddenly been robbed of his ability to breathe. His lungs tightened. *Love.* He had no use for the emotion or the word. It pained him to know what he was about to say would hurt her, but he wanted to be certain she understood. "I want no part of love."

She quickly glanced back up at him, her gaze locking with his, and her lips parted slightly. "You cannot mean that."

The misery that still haunted him from losing Catriona weighed especially heavy in this moment when faced with the stark truth that he was marrying yet again. "I do mean it, Marion, and I'm sorry. I have been married before. I loved my wife, and when she died, so did my desire and my ability to love that way again."

It was as if a light went out in her shining green eyes. She stared at him for a moment before inhaling a ragged breath and forcing a sad smile. "I see." Her voice trembled, and he was afraid she would cry and hated himself for being the cause of it once more.

He grasped her hand. "I will be a good husband. I'll keep ye safe and treat ye kind. I'll give ye everything that is mine."

Her sad smile turned brittle. "Just never your heart." Sorrow encumbered her words.

"Nay," he agreed, feeling more like a clot-heid with every word. But he could not change how he felt. "Nae my heart."

She slipped her hand from his. "Thank you for your honesty. I suppose we better hurry and marry." She shifted her face away, but not before he saw her lower lip tremble.

He cursed his own miserable self, but with nothing left to say, he turned to the priest and Angus, who glared at him but said nothing. "Get on with it, Father," Iain said.

The priest paled. "But Baron de Lacy—"

"Is planning to defy his king's orders that Marion marry me." Iain pulled out the scroll, but since it was so soaked it was no longer legible. He threw the useless thing to the ground. "That was the decree, but it's ruined. Marion has seen it."

Marion nodded. "King Edward commanded it, Father John. You know I'd not lie to you."

"I know, Lady Marion," the priest quickly replied. Beads of sweat appeared on his forehead. "Let me see... Where to start..."

"Isn't the usual place the homily on the sacrament of marriage, Father John?" Marion offered.

Iain glanced at her. She had the most innocent expression on her face yet she had drawn up to her full height, which brought the top of her head to Iain's shoulder. The woman was slight in body, but in spirit she was a giant. She had stored away the hurt he'd just caused her and was gallantly facing her future. Pride swelled dangerously within his chest.

The priest nodded as he withdrew a white cloth from his robes and dabbed at his forehead. "Your full name?" he asked Iain.

"Iain MacLeod," he replied. "And Angus MacLeod will be the witness," he added in an effort to hurry the priest.

Father John frowned at Iain before looking to Angus. "Angus, are you a willing witness, or do you fear the MacLeod will kill you if you decline?"

"Father," Marion chided. "That was not very fair. Iain would never kill a man for such a thing. He has assured me he only kills those who try to kill him first."

Iain laughed at the priest's suddenly pale face and Marion's attempt to defend him. He was pleased she was showing such faith in him and such understanding already. "Go on, priest," Iain commanded. "We must escape this place presently."

Angus came to Marion's other side. "Father, I willingly

witness for Marion." She quickly hugged Angus, who patted her back.

Father John nodded and rushed through the rest of the ceremony, sighing when it was over. Iain glanced at the priest, deciding what should be done. "Ye better come with us," he said. "Baron de Lacy will likely kill ye when he learns that ye married us."

Marion nodded. "Yes, Father John, you must come."

"No," the priest said stubbornly, surprising Iain—and Marion, as well, by the way her jaw dropped open. "I swore long ago to save your father's soul, my dear, and I'll not abandon my sacred vow, even if it means my own death because he's angry that I married you."

Marion threw her arms around the priest, who looked distinctly uncomfortable with the contact. "I'll pray for your safety, Father John, and for my father to stay his hand and his temper."

Father John nodded as he disentangled himself from Marion's hold. "You should go."

"It's daft for ye to stay, vow or nae," Iain said. "The baron will kill ye, I'm sure."

The priest shook his head disapprovingly. "I would think a man such as you would understand a sacred vow."

Iain scowled. "I do, but in this case, I dunnae think getting yerself killed is the best way to keep the vow of reforming the baron. Ye kinnae reform the man if ye're dead."

The priest frowned at Iain. "I'm willing to risk such things."

"There are smart risks," Iain said, "and then there are dim ones."

Marion gasped, and Angus laughed. Marion patted the priest on the arm. "I'm terribly sorry, Father John, for Iain calling you dim."

Iain frowned. "I did nae—"

"In my bedroom," she continued, cutting Iain off with words and a sharp look, "in the gold cup are my coins. Please take five—no, you better make that six—and give the rest to the poor tenants."

The priest mumbled his agreement, and Iain's patience snapped. He grasped Marion's hand and tugged her toward the door. "Why did ye tell the priest to take the coins?"

"I'm buying indulgences," she explained. "One is for your sin of pride. One is for the knights you killed. One is for when I lied to my father. Two are for Angus—" She glanced at Angus with a grin and then eyed him with reproach. "*He* refuses to take up the custom of indulgences and he is almost as proud as you are. And I bought two more for whatever sins you commit during our escape."

Iain shook his head at her strange ideas of forgiveness as he pulled her to his side and stepped through the exit and into the bailey.

Noise and thick smoke from the burning kitchens hit him like dual waves, and his eyes watered. A white cloud seemed to blanket the entire bailey, which was helpful in that it made it harder to see them, but it also made it more difficult to see their enemies.

As they headed toward the wall they needed to scale to gain the moat, he motioned to Angus behind him, gesturing for him to flank Marion's other side. The Scot gave a nod, but as he moved to do so, a man came out of the mist with his sword swinging in a high arc. Instinctively, Iain reached for Marion to shove her behind him, but she hurdled forward with a shriek. Iain felt his jaw drop as his heart tripped over itself. He yanked Marion back with a roar as the knight's sword came within a hairsbreadth of cutting her.

For a moment, Iain could not move. Everything around him seemed to fade away as he stared at the material of her gown. He half expected the material to suddenly gape open and for blood to gush out. When nothing happened, relief flooded him, even as crazed anger consumed him. He wasn't sure if he was more furious at Marion or the fool knight who'd almost killed her.

He snapped his gaze to the man—Marion could be dealt with later—and took one step to close the distance between them. He was young, his face blanched, eyes wide, and hands trembling. At any other time, Iain may have taken pity on him, but if the fool had possessed a truer aim, Marion would have been bleeding to death right now.

He deflected the oncoming sword with his forearm, grabbing the hilt of it as the knight swung low by Iain's hand. The man tried to pull back, but Iain easily took possession, swung the sword swiftly upward, the steel slicing through the air with a hiss, and pointed the tip at the man's throat.

"Ye almost killed my wife," Iain growled.

"Your wife?" The man glanced at Marion, who nodded.

His eyes grew wide with disbelief. "I would never harm Lady Marion," the knight said and smiled at her in a way Iain didn't care for at all. As if there was something special between them. And he wasn't the first knight who seemed lovesick when he spoke of Marion. The knight Andrew had sounded miserable when he'd said he'd failed to protect her when she went missing, as if her loss was very personal.

Iain scrubbed a hand across his face as the man met his gaze once more and sneered at him. "I was trying to kill *you*."

"I ken that," Iain replied with a nod. "'Tis the only

reason I'm going to let ye live. That, and I want ye to deliver a message to Baron de Lacy from the MacLeod." When the knight didn't readily agree, Iain pressed the tip of the sword against his throat.

"Iain, please!" Marion cried. "Peter is a good man!"

Iain narrowed his gaze on the knight as he curled his fist tighter. He didn't like that Marion was pleading for the man's life as if she cared for him, but then again, he didn't want his future wife to be uncouth, either. "Marion is mine," he said, continuing with his message for de Lacy. "If he's bold enough to defy his king and come after her, then tell him he should be ready to die. Ken?"

"I understand," the man snarled.

"Good."

With that, Iain hit the man with the hilt of his sword, causing him to faint. As the man thudded to the ground, Marion moved to Iain's side and patted his arm. "Thank you for not killing him."

He glanced down at Marion, and his chest tightened a bit. He wasn't sure how to feel about it, so he shoved the confusion away. "Quit trying to save me."

"You needed me," she retorted, her expression wounded.

He set his jaw. He didn't know why Marion thought she needed to protect him, but now was not the time to argue. "Come on."

Within moments, Iain, Marion, and Angus had scaled the wall and slid down the ditch, plunging into the freezing water once more. As they swam silently across, Iain could not take his eyes from Marion to ensure she was safe. When they reached the other side and he helped her out of the ditch, he felt her body trembling violently.

"Are ye cold?" he asked, drawing her to him with one hand and reaching down to help Angus with the other.

She nodded. "Yes, but also worried about what will happen now."

He could hear the fear in her voice and feel it in the way her fingers curled tighter around his hand. "Dunnae fash yerself, Marion. Ye're my wife now, and I'll defend ye with my dying breath."

She tugged her hand from his and set both of her hands on her hips. "I'm not worried about that."

Her confidence in him filled him with pleasure, until he realized she'd not actually said she was not worried *at all*, just not about that.

As the three of them moved toward the place where Rory Mac and Neil should have been waiting, Iain watched her hips sway in the moonlight, but when he turned to meet Angus's angry glare, he pulled his gaze away. The man may think of her as a daughter, but Marion was now Iain's wife, and he was getting tired of the Scot glaring at him.

"What are ye worried about?" he questioned to her back as she marched ahead of him.

"If you don't know, then it's not worth my breath to explain," she snapped without breaking her stride.

Iain let her leave, as he suspected her worry lay with his telling her he would never love her, and there was nothing he could say to ease that worry. Angus coughed, none too discreetly, until Iain finally looked at the man. "What?" he barked.

"Let me ken when ye need my advice," the Scot offered with a chuckle.

Iain frowned. "I'll nae need yer advice on how to deal with my wife," Iain bit out and stalked ahead, each step making him wonder why he felt like there was a possibility he could rue that statement.

Five

Several hours later, Marion clenched her teeth as the horses drove relentlessly forward over the rocky terrain of Scotland. To her right, Rory Mac glared at her, still clearly angry over her taking his horse. She understood, but it seemed to her he could forgive her. After all, he *had* gotten his destrier back when two of her father's knights had ridden out of the castle and Rory Mac had apparently overtaken them. He had retrieved not only his horse but one more. She'd said as much to the man after she, Iain, and Angus had escaped her father's castle and met up with Rory Mac and Neil. Rory Mac had only growled at her as she'd spoken. Apparently, Scots were *very* attached to their horses.

She looked away from Rory Mac with a sigh. Every time she was jarred, her bottom and back cried out. Iain MacLeod was the devil himself. She started to turn around on the horse to tell him so, but his big hand came to her shoulder and stayed her movement. "Dunnae move. Ye risk losing yer balance and falling off."

Angry, she blew at a strand of hair dangling in her face. The man may never intend to give his heart to her, but he could at least give her his respect. All he'd done since they'd escaped her father's castle was order her about. "I'm not one of your men you can constantly command."

"True enough," he agreed. His tone was so soft and pleasant that a bit of her anger slipped away. "Ye're my wife." The implication that she was also to be ordered about was clear in his now-flat tone.

Her anger spiked to near eruption. "I'm not your wife fully yet," she snapped.

"By the time the sun sets again ye will be," he replied. His easy banter irritated her even more. It was as if her anger amused him. She ground her teeth against saying another word to the man until he treated her with respect.

As the horse galloped forward, the clopping of his hooves drummed in her ears and her mind returned to Iain telling her that he'd buried his love, and his heart, with his late wife. Even if Marion had wanted to be hurt that he'd so bluntly told her that he'd never love her, she could not be, not really. They barely knew each other. What she did know of him, besides the fact that he was brave—fiercely so—and honorable, was that he was in grave pain from his loss. He'd not said it in words, yet when he'd spoken of his late wife his tone had been raw, as if simply thinking of her pained him. She'd felt it like an enormous wave washing over her.

She clenched her hands and pressed her lips together at the memory. She was married to a man in love with a ghost. In spite of his declaration that he'd never love again, she could not help but wonder if it was truly so. She didn't even know if she would ever want this man's love, but she wanted the possibility of it. Not a lifetime of being forsaken.

When the sun started to rise, she was sure they would pull over to hide and rest, and relief poured through her. Her body ached all over, her head pounded, and her stomach growled. The desire to beg him to stop strummed through her, but she held off until she thought she might fall off the horse. That's when she realized her idea not to talk to him until he showed her respect was foolish. She had to talk to him, but she vowed she would make him see she deserved respect and not to be ordered about.

Her mouth was so dry that she had to swallow several times before speaking. "Will we stop now that the sun is up?"

"Nay."

Marion didn't consider herself a weak, helpless woman, but she was on the verge of collapsing or crying. She couldn't decide which would be worse. Crying, she concluded, would be worse, shameful even. One could help weeping, but collapsing really was quite involuntary. "I'm going to slide off the horse from exhaustion," she protested.

"Ye will nae. I command ye to stay upright."

Her face burned with anger. He'd done it again! She curled her hands into fists with the desire to hit him. "You cannot simply demand a person not collapse," she grumbled.

"I can."

"You cannot! You rude beast," she snapped. She was normally so sweet tempered, but he really was bringing out the worst in her.

"Who's rude?" he replied with a chuckle.

That did it! It was simply the last thing she could handle. "Did you command your first wife around so? Did you demand she ride a horse until she was so exhausted she could hardly keep her eyes open?"

"Nay," he said quietly. "She was a gentle creature. Ye are different."

"Is that praise or condemnation?" she asked, utterly

perplexed and angry with herself for bringing up the subject of his deceased wife when she knew it pained him.

"Praise, Sassenach," he replied, his tone soothing.

All the anger rushed out of her with the air she blew from her lungs. An absurd sense of happiness filled her, and she decided to somehow keep herself on the horse, upright and silent, to prove to him she was worthy of his admiration. Admiration was a stepping-stone to respect, and from there, who knew what the future could hold for them.

Hours later, as night was falling, they crossed into MacLean territory and Iain finally relaxed. He was good friends with the MacLean laird, Alex, and their clans were at peace. Iain slowed his horse to a walk as they climbed a steep path, and he inhaled deeply and appreciatively of the fresh air. He silently signaled to Rory Mac and Angus to stop. Angus glowered in return. Iain didn't know if it was because the older MacLeod had been squashed on his horse with Neil for most the day or if it was because the man had been listening to Iain's exchange with Marion.

It wasn't long before he found out, though. After he carefully gathered a snoring Marion into his arms and dismounted Olaf, he caught Rory Mac's eye and then inclined his head toward Angus and Neil, the latter of whom was awake but had a stark-white face and sweat-dampened brow.

"Gather wood and ready a place to rest. I'll be back to help in a bit," Iain said as he gazed off toward the river in the distance and the thick trees where Marion could have some privacy.

Rory Mac nodded, but Angus dismounted faster than

Iain would have thought the man capable of moving. The surly old Scot stalked toward Iain, and agitation rippled through him. He was too damn tired to exchange words, but it appeared unavoidable.

"Ye dunnae deserve her," the Scot accused.

Iain refused to take offense. Angus clearly thought of Marion as his own kin.

"Maybe I dunnae," Iain said, "but she's mine now."

Angus shook his head. "Ye're a young fool if ye think that. She may be yers by marriage, but ye'll never possess her body and soul until ye open yer heart te her."

Iain clenched his teeth. "I dunnae want a lesson from ye on these matters. Ye forget I'm yer laird."

"I dunnae forget at all," the man whispered fiercely. "I ken ye're the laird and that ye are due my respect because of it, and I ken I risk chastisement talking to ye so."

"I chastise no man for his opinion, Angus. But dunnae lecture me. Now if ye'll excuse me." Iain didn't wait for an answer. He turned away, taking care not to let Marion's head flop back. He leaned her cheek against his chest and walked over to the stream in the distance. He didn't look back to see if Rory Mac and Angus were seeing to the horses and gathering wood.

They knew what to do, and in truth, he could not look away from Marion's face. Her beauty took his breath. Awake, she was a fiery fairy. A force, to be sure. One minute angry and the next smiling. Defiant. Belligerent. Brave. And possessing a kind heart. He lowered them both carefully to the grass, setting her in his lap as he leaned against the tree. She stirred a bit but didn't wake. Her hand came to rest by her cheek, over his heart.

As the cold from the ground seeped into his skin, he worried she might get a chill. As carefully as he could manage, he moved her forward with one hand, and with the other, he took off his plaid, now dry from the day's ride, and laid it over her. Then he tucked it around her legs and under her chin until only her lovely pale face showed. Then slowly, ever so slowly, he lowered his head to hers and listened to her deep, measured breaths.

Her breaths held the ease of good health. Relief made him sag a bit. He was a fool. He'd told himself he'd not care for her at all, but the moment he'd said his vows in the chapel and she'd said hers, he'd felt an undeniable connection to her, as if an invisible rope bound them to each other.

He stared down at her dark lashes, which fanned her pale cheeks, and he traced a finger over the slope of one delicate cheekbone. She shivered in her sleep but did not awaken. He'd not wanted another wife but now he had one. The only way to move forward was with care. He'd seen the distressed look in her eyes when he'd told her that he'd never love her. She was his wife now and he didn't want to hurt her, yet he was afraid he would. His past had left scars on him.

Tiredness made his thoughts unclear, and he closed his eyes to rest.

Dreams haunted his sleep as always, but this time, Marion joined Catriona in his dreams. He was in a thick forest, searching for someone who was calling to him in desperation, as he often did. The woman turned out to be Marion instead of Catriona, though, and he awoke with a jolt.

When he opened his eyes, Marion's face was inches from his and she was studying him. He shifted his weight, and she wiggled her bottom. His reaction to his wife was instant and painful. He wanted her so.

Her eyes grew wide, and she scrambled off his lap and to her knees beside him. She looked beguiling as she pulled his plaid around her and her wild hair tumbled around her face.

A sharp yearning to feel her beneath him grew stronger. He took a deep breath and reminded himself that he needed to be slow and gentle. She would likely be afraid at first, never having been with a man, and he would likely be a bit crazed, as it had been a very long time since he'd touched a woman. The year before Catriona had died, their joining had stopped when she'd become so weak. The idea of taking another woman had repelled him—until Marion.

He cleared his throat, realizing she was still staring at him. "Why are ye studying me?"

She pressed her small hands to her knees. "I am trying to understand you."

"And have ye succeeded?"

She shook her head. "No. You confuse me. You've ordered me about since I met you, and not once did you consider my needs on the road, but when you did stop, you apparently held me in your arms so I could sleep and wrapped me in your plaid to keep me warm. So I know you *are* capable of being mindful of me."

He frowned. "How did I nae consider yer needs?"

"You refused to stop even when I told you how tired I was."

"That was for yer safety, Marion. Had I stopped before we reached MacLean land, it would have been verra dangerous. We had to travel quickly so Froste and yer father would nae have time to overtake us before I arrived in allied clan territory."

She nodded. "I suppose, but now that we are married, and they do not know if you've"—she cast her gaze down—"you've joined with me. I'm not so certain they'll follow, especially Froste. I'm sure my father will strive to keep the man as an ally. He'll likely offer him money, which he was no doubt trying to avoid by using me and the land I'd bring, for his aid instead."

Iain gaped at her. His wife thought her only appeal was the land that had been attached to her. It made him angry that her father had obviously never praised her one bit. "Marion," he started, intent on correcting how she perceived herself, "even if there were no land attached to ye, I imagine Froste would still come for ye."

Her brow wrinkled. "Because he does not like losing, I suppose."

"Well, aye," Iain agreed. "But also because ye're beautiful and bold, and ye're the sort of woman that, well—" He stopped. He could not tell her she was the sort of woman to stir desire with a mere look. And the sort of desire a man could not easily forget. With her moonbeam hair hanging in heavy waves down her back and her large grassy eyes sparkling with laughter—and alternately burning with her ire—she was a woman no man would want to lose, especially a man like Froste who, as she'd said, did not like to lose.

Iain shrugged lamely. "He'll come after ye, I swear it, but I dunnae think he's foolish enough to come before he is certain he can retrieve ye without difficulty. But ye dunnae need to fear. I'll defend ye, as is my duty."

The talk of duties brought to mind one that would be pleasurable. He needed to truly make her his. Just thinking of bedding her made his blood heat.

He reached out and ran a finger across her ankle, which was peeking out from beneath his plaid. "Marion," he said, his throat husky with need.

Her eyes went wide, and she stood abruptly. "I'd like to wash before supper," she said. Her voice wobbled, and she pulled the plaid even tighter around her body.

He'd scared her, or rather, she was scared of the joining. As much as he ached to take her now, he would force himself to give her as much time as he could to reconcile what was to happen. Unfortunately, there was not much time. The marriage had to be consummated.

He stood slowly and looked at her. She was nibbling her lip, clearly ill at ease. He inhaled a deep breath of the chilly night air, hoping it would cool his lust. "Let me search the river first and make sure it's safe."

"Are you worried?" she asked, her voice pitching a bit higher.

"Nay," he assured her. "Just careful. I'm always careful."

After they walked down to the stream, he quickly verified that the area was not dangerous. "Do ye want me to stay near?" he asked. "Will ye be afraid if I go ready a place for us to bed down?"

Her eyes widened more than they had earlier. God's truth, she looked more afraid of the idea of lying down beside him than she had at the idea that someone might want to steal her away.

"I don't frighten easily," she replied boldly, though her voice shook. "Go on back to the men."

"Dunnae wade too deep," he said, surveying the river one last time. It was fairly low right now, but that didn't mean she could not get injured. "In the dark ye could lose yer footing. If ye need me, simply call for me."

"I'll not need you," she replied with a sure tone.

He bit back a grin, wondering what his wife would think if she knew her walking about in his plaid greatly undermined her effort to appear brave and unaffected.

The minute Iain walked out of sight, Marion sagged. There were so many emotions swirling in her that her head ached. She'd felt disappointed and worried earlier with Iain's blunt words about love, but then he'd praised her fortitude and she'd felt a small sliver of hope, which had blossomed when he'd told her he thought her beautiful and bold, and well—

She laughed aloud. It didn't even matter that he'd never finished the sentence. That he thought her bold thrilled her. Beauty was fleeting, but she supposed she wasn't unhappy that he found her pleasing, except she was nervous about consummating their marriage. She had always thought when it was time, she would know the man and love him. Could she love this man someday? Perhaps. He certainly was the sort of honorable, brave man she'd envisioned marrying, except for the part about not ever loving her. What if she fell in love with him and he never returned her love? The thought made her slump to the ground with a groan.

Sitting on the cold, thick grass, she kicked off her shoes. When her feet made contact with the wet ground, she shivered. She had not realized how cold it was, likely because Iain had held her. She blushed at the memory of how sinfully good it had felt to be wrapped in his arms. She wiggled her toes and sighed as she wearily got to her feet to unlace her gown.

A short time later, she was muttering to herself and saying every unladylike curse she'd ever heard Angus and the guards mutter when they'd not known she was listening. Her maid had helped her lace this gown, and she could not get it undone by herself, no matter how she contorted her body. Her head began to pound harder as she stared longingly at the river, which held the promise of removing the grime from her father's moat from her skin.

She peered over her shoulder and saw Iain, Angus, and Rory Mac in the distance. The three of them stood around a small fire. If she called out to Iain, she knew he'd come directly. She bit her lip, remembering the desire in his eyes and his thick voice. He may not ever love her, but he wanted her. And she wanted a bit more time before the joining.

Besides, how was she supposed to earn his respect if she could not remove her own gown?

Marion squeezed her eyes shut. Calling him over to help was not an option. A woman who needed aid disrobing was not a woman a fierce laird like Iain would ever come to rely upon. Her gut clenched with a sudden realization: she wanted him to rely on her and need her because, even if he never loved her, a man who relied upon and needed a woman would never discard her. Not like her father, who had been so callous and eager to give her to another.

Resolved, she struggled for several more minutes until frustrated tears stung her eyes and she collapsed onto the cold grass, drawing her legs up to her chest and pressing her head against her knees to allow herself a good pitiful cry. Just as she was getting started, a hand clamped roughly over her mouth. She was pulled off the ground as another hand slid around her waist and then her back was pressed against the length of a man's armored body.

The man who held her breathed heavily, his stench of sweat and horse making her wrinkle her nose. Fear tingled across her skin leaving gooseflesh. Was there any way to free herself?

Before she could answer her own question, another man appeared from the darkness and stepped in front of her. "Hello, Lady Marion," the man whispered. "Froste sent us to fetch you."

She could barely make out the knight's features in the dark, but she got a glimpse of the burn scars that ravaged his face, and her blood ran cold. Malcolm Basset was Froste's most trusted, most vicious knight, and his loyalty had been sealed when Froste had rescued him from the man's own father, who had set Malcolm on fire.

Malcolm pulled his lips back in a snarl as he slid his calloused hand around her neck. "Froste says we must bring you back alive, but he told me how you fled him, Marion. I'd like to kill you, but he'd not like it."

Marion's heart pounded as she desperately tried to determine how to escape.

"Forget what you'd like, Malcolm," the man holding her and covering her mouth hissed near her ear. "Let's get on with it. I want to kill the MacLeod and be done with Scotland. We must follow orders," the knight added.

"I know," Malcolm snarled. "But she does not deserve to be Froste's wife." Malcolm squeezed her cheeks so hard that tears stung her eyes. "You're likely not even chaste anymore, are you?"

Marion's skin crawled with the question, and the knight holding her chuckled as Malcolm stared through the darkness at her. "On further thought," he said, his voice taking on a husky tone that made bile rise in her throat, "let's enjoy her first. If she's not chaste—"

Malcolm's fist flew by her face so fast that she screamed, but the clammy hand covering her mouth smothered the sound. Malcolm's fist met her captor's nose with a sickening crunch, the hand dropped away, and she was shoved aside. The man lunged at Malcolm, and Marion saw her chance. She dashed past the men who were locked in combat, but just as she filled her lungs to scream for help, she was hit from behind and went crashing to the ground, crushed under the weight of a body and its armor. She was going to die.

Horror filled her until she was pulled up by her hair and came face-to-face with Malcolm, who clamped his hand over her mouth once more. "We want you to scream, but not just yet. We need to have you placed perfectly so we can ambush the MacLeod and his men."

Driven by rage and fear, Marion brought her fist up and started to hit Malcolm in the face. Behind her, she heard the quick clank of armor, and then her hands were grabbed and pulled roughly behind her back.

"I've got her," Malcolm growled. He jerked her toward him and encircled her body with his arm, nearly crushing her ribs with his grip. He lifted her off the ground, and before she knew what was happening, he dragged her into the cold river as the other knight moved to the bank on the other side. She started to shiver, watching helplessly as the man withdrew two daggers that gleamed in the moonlight. Her breath seized in her chest. They thought to make her scream to bring Iain running and then the knight would throw the daggers at Iain. Even if he missed, Malcolm had his sword, and Iain would not be prepared. She could not scream, no matter what they did to her. She could not call Iain to his death.

Her fear must have shown on her face because Malcolm's grin widened as he stared at her. "Don't fret. I won't harm you, though I want to. Now do your duty as Froste's future bride and scream."

Immediately, his hand moved from her mouth to her windpipe and pressed.

"I won't scream," Marion managed to choke out before Malcolm's fingers crushed her throat a bit harder, cutting her words off.

"If you don't scream, you'll die, and I vow to you, the MacLeod will die either way."

She'd have no part in helping them kill Iain, even if it meant her own death, which it likely would. It was becoming harder and harder to draw air and stars were dancing in her vision, yet she was determined not to scream.

⌘

When Iain found a good spot for them to sleep, he spread out a blanket and then quickly caught a rabbit for supper. Angus glared at him as Iain skinned the rabbit beside the fire.

"Say yer grievance with me or stop yer glaring," Iain said.

"Is that the command of a laird?" The old MacLeod faced Iain and braced his legs as if preparing to fight.

Rory Mac shook his head with a laugh. "I dunnae think he likes ye, Iain."

Iain ignored his friend's prodding and stared at Angus. "That's the request of one man to another, Angus. I may be laird, but I strive to treat all my men fairly. If ye think I've done ye some wrongdoing then I'd like it to be confessed so we can solve it. Though as we've only known each other a day, it baffles me what that could be."

Angus's stance immediately relaxed, and he moved

closer to Iain and sat on the tree stump next to him. "Marion is like a daughter te me."

"I thought so," Iain replied, moving over for Rory Mac to sit down, too.

"I want the best for her," Angus continued.

Iain set the rabbit down. "Are ye implying I'm nae best for her?"

The man notched his chin up. "I'm saying she's already had a lifetime of feeling unloved. I heard what ye said te her at the chapel."

"What did ye say?" Rory Mac asked in a deceptively innocent tone.

Iain gave Rory Mac a warning look, but his friend simply grinned in return. A tick started in Iain's jaw as he met Angus's gaze once more. "I will treat her well."

Angus shook his head. "Treating her well will nae be enough. Marion has a tender heart that yearns for affection."

"I yearn for affection, too," Rory Mac said, mimicking a woman's voice with a chuckle.

Both men glared at him. He had the sense to look chagrinned. He stood, unsheathed Marion's dagger, and silently handed it to Iain. "I think I'll go check on Neil and gather some more wood."

"Verra wise," Iain said as he set Marion's dagger on his knee. When Rory Mac walked away, Iain faced Angus. "She will nae yearn as my wife," he stated, then picked up the rabbit and began skinning it once more, wishing the matter to be sorted. When after a minute, Angus did not move from in front of Iain, he looked at the man once more. "What?"

"She will yearn because ye will nae be able te give her what she truly desires. And I'm nae talking about a night with ye."

Iain clenched his teeth. He had always been one to allow his men to speak freely, but at the moment, he considered that a change may do. "I dunnae talk matters of the heart. I'm a Scottish warrior, nae an Englishman who speaks prettily. Ye've been gone from Scotland too long. Ye're soft."

"I'm nae soft. Just smart enough te see what ye dunnae. Ye can be a widower te one woman ye loved yet allow another into yer heart."

"Cease yer talking, Angus," Iain growled. He didn't want to think about Catriona, his heart, *or* allowing anyone else to make him weak, and he refused to continue this conversation.

A determined look crossed Angus's face. "Maybe she should come live with me, since ye dunnae really want her around," the Scot prodded. "Ye can be married in name only, that way she will be safe and ye'll have met Edward's conditions for talks of David's release."

"Nay." The word boomed from Iain deep in his chest, but instead of the fear he'd hoped to raise in Angus, the older man smiled slightly.

"Why nae? If ye're as lacking in emotion as ye claim, then any wench will do te smother yer lust."

"Any wench will nae do," Iain bellowed. "Marion belongs with me."

"Aye, she does," Angus agreed, surprising Iain with his words and his grin. "I feel much better now that we had this talk. I thank ye for obliging me."

Iain gaped at the man. "Ye tricked me," Iain muttered. "Ye said something ye did nae mean in order to see how I would reply. What are ye trying to decide about me, old man?"

Angus picked up the rabbit he'd killed and started to skin it. "I am wondering if she had any hope of melting a wee bit of that thick ice around ye."

"Listen here, ye daft old fool," Iain growled. "She does nae have a hope of melting a thing as there is nothing to thaw." His heart was dead, and that was how he wanted it. Desire could not harm him, but love—love when lost left pain that could kill a man.

"Ye dunnae need te be angry," Angus said good-naturedly. "Ye can protest all ye want, but I dunnae think ye can stop what's already happening. If ye wished for no emotion between ye, ye'd join with her and many others. Ye want only her."

Iain never allowed himself to show anger, but it pulsed through him in fast, hard beats. He did want only her, but that had nothing to do with anything but lust. The thought rang false in his head, but he shoved the doubt away and concentrated on his annoyance. "I can stop whatever I wish. I'm laird. If I dunnae want to feel anything for her, I won't. It's as simple as that."

Angus cocked an eyebrow at him. "Simple, ye say?"

Iain was just about to answer when Marion's scream echoed through the night. The high-pitched piercing sound of her fear ripped across his heart and tore away the scab of indifference that had been covering the gaping wound left by Catriona's death. His reaction was instantaneous, as if he were an arrow shot from a bow. He dropped the rabbit, gripped Marion's dagger, sprang up, and barreled past Angus into the blackness without hesitation, his feet pounding over hard rock, soft dirt, and branches. As he dodged limbs and shoved shrubs out of his way, Marion let out a string of the foulest curses he'd ever heard from a woman's lips. In spite of the edge of concern driving him forward like a crazed man, he grinned. No doubt, sharp on the heels of her curses she'd mentally calculated how many indulgences her perceived sin would cost her. His life certainly would not be dull with Marion.

He burst through the trees, expecting to perhaps find that she'd ignored his advice and waded too far into the river, but what he saw brought him to a stunned halt. Marion stood knee-deep in the water, and behind her stood a tall man dressed in armor. The knight had his hand around her neck, and when he pulled her backward and thrust her under the water, a red haze covered Iain's vision. He was going to kill that man for daring to hurt Marion. He didn't give a damn if it angered King Edward or David. He'd start a hundred bloody wars if that was what he had to do to keep his wife from harm. And her melting him or whatever nonsense Angus had sputtered had nothing to do with it.

Six

She'd screamed.

That fact pounded through Marion's head as she kicked her legs and clawed at the hands holding her underwater. By God, she'd scream again if she got the chance. She dug her nails into soft flesh, but the hand squeezed harder.

The desire to live overrode the shame of failing to keep Iain from harm as her lungs burned with the need to call for help again.

Malcolm wrenched her back to the surface just as she was sure she was going to die. She coughed violently, water spewing from her mouth and racking her body. Over the sound of her hacking, a war cry split the air, as well as her fear and the very chambers of her heart.

He'd heard her!

She blinked her watery eyes and searched the darkness for Iain. He thundered out of the shadows and toward her, white mist rising from the ground as if it were smoldering. The fog parted with each of his strides, and his sword sang in a high arc over his head. In all the nights, she'd stood on the rampart and watched her father and his men return from battle, she'd never seen a man look as fierce and frightening as her husband did. He didn't seem like a mere mortal; he seemed like a god intent on decimation as he charged into the river.

The pressure against her throat disappeared in a flash as Malcolm raised his hand to give the signal for his comrade to throw the daggers.

"Danger on the left bank!" Marion shouted and pointed.

Iain looked to the left at the same time Malcolm shoved her backward and under the water again. For a moment, she thought he would hold her there until she was dead this time, but then his hand disappeared and she came up in a rush, rubbing the water out of her eyes. Malcolm was just ahead of her, his sword poised to kill. Marion scanned for the other knight on the left bank but didn't see him. When something touched her leg, she jerked and then shrieked when she realized it was the other knight floating on his back in the water with a dagger—one that looked suspiciously like the one Angus had given her—sticking out of his neck, the only patch of skin that was not protected by armor.

When the dead man started to sink, Marion reached down and pulled the dagger out of his neck. Her stomach roiled with queasiness, but she stood upright in time to see Malcolm swing his sword to try to hit Iain in his left side. She tried to scream a warning, but her voice came out rough and her throat protested any further use.

Iain didn't need a warning anyway. He moved in a blur she could not follow. It was like trying to capture the moment a storm turned deadly. He opened like a sky filled with torrential rain and poured his fury on the other knight.

Yet Malcolm's fighting prowess had not been exaggerated. He took blow after blow from Iain and did not fall. And then, when Iain raised his sword to strike once more, she heard Malcolm exclaim, "Die!" She gasped when she thought she knew why. Iain's left side was exposed! Marion splashed forward toward Malcolm, raised her dagger, and plunged it into his back—or attempted to. The dagger did not go through the armor. It splashed into the water and disappeared. There was no time to look for it.

Malcolm spun around, eyes wild, and swung his sword toward her neck. She screamed as Iain's sword glimmered in the moonlight above Malcolm, then came down and ended the man's life with a sharp blow to his head. He dropped into the river directly in front of her.

Her legs trembled and threatened to give out, but Iain wrapped her in his embrace. She buried her face against his chest, sagging into him. They stood for a moment, face-to-face, both panting heavily.

"Wife." His voice held a faint tremor, as if some emotion had touched him, and she could almost feel her hope rising in the air.

She lifted her gaze to his. "I'm sorry." With her hands fisted by her side, she waited for Iain to tell her how disappointed he was in her. That was what her father would have done.

In the distance, Angus was calling her name and Rory Mac was shouting for the MacLeod. Iain called out that they were fine, that he'd killed two of Froste's men, and to give them a moment. Then he caught her gaze once more.

"Ye're sorry?" he asked, sounding incredulous. "Ye've nothing to be sorry for, Marion. I'm to keep ye from harm, and I failed."

"But you didn't," she exclaimed. "You just saved me!"

"There'd nae have been a need if I'd nae left ye down here alone." His tormented tone made her breath catch, and when he looked at her, there was anguish in his eyes.

He tugged a hand through his hair in obvious agitation. "Can ye forgive me?"

"Forgive you?" Her heart swelled almost painfully. Iain had asked *her* forgiveness, which meant he thought enough of her to want her forgiveness, if nothing else. She swallowed the large lump in her throat. Not once, in all her years, had her father ever asked her forgiveness for anything; he was always quick to tell her what she'd done wrong to make her feel small and unworthy. Iain was not like that. For all his gruffness, he was also gentle.

"I can forgive you," she said, "if you can do the same for me."

He cupped her face. "Why do ye think ye need my forgiveness?"

"I vowed to myself I'd not scream because that's what they wanted," she said, motioning behind her. "They wanted me to scream for you so you would come to my aid, and then they were going to kill you."

"I suppose I've the answer to the question of if Froste intends on defying Edward," Iain said, his voice hard. "Nae that I really thought otherwise."

Marion shivered at the idea. "Do you think Froste sent more men?"

"Nay," Iain answered. "I think the arrogant clot-heid imagined those two would complete the mission. We'll make our way to Alex MacLean's hold tomorrow morning and warn him that knights may be passing through these parts."

"Marion," came Angus's worried voice.

Marion peered around her husband's enormous frame to see Angus and Rory Mac standing at the bank of the river. Angus held a torch that illuminated both men's faces.

Rory Mac was the one who spoke first as Iain took

Marion's hand and led her to the men. "I told the old man
to do as ye ordered Iain and give ye a minute, but he was
fretting over the chick like a hen."

Marion supposed she was the chick and Angus the hen.

"I'm nae stunned," Iain replied, his tone not indicating
if he was angry that Angus had disobeyed him. That was
another big difference between her father and Iain. Her
father would have punished Angus for daring to defy him,
even though Angus was clearly worried for her. Iain
seemed to understand this, and even if he did not like it, he
was in control enough not to show it and to allow Angus to
see her. Warmth toward Iain filled her heart.

"Are ye hurt, Marion?" Angus asked, his voice shaking.
"I could nae move swiftly enough te help ye," he grumbled, rubbing his leg.

She regarded his leg. "Have *you* been hurt?"

He shook his head. "Just sore from yer father's beating."

"Oh, Angus!" she cried out, angry with her father and
mad at herself for not seeing to his wounds sooner. "Let
me help you," she said, starting toward him.

Angus shook his head. "Nay, lass. I'll tend te my own
wounds. I ken how. Yer place tonight is by yer husband's
side."

She glanced at Iain to protest, and he shrugged. "If ye
wish to tend to him, do so."

"Nay," Angus said, the stubbornness she knew well
clear on his face. "Ye go with the MacLeod."

Rory Mac made a derisive noise from his throat. "I'll
tend the old goat," he said to Marion. "Tell me what to
do."

She quickly explained it to him, and when she was
done, Rory Mac looked to Iain. "I suppose we will head to

Alex's tomorrow."

"Aye," Iain replied. "He should know that he might get English visitors on his land." Iain's tone had turned sour.

Rory Mac nodded and then grinned. "Are ye nae worried Marion will be taken with the MacLean?"

Iain scowled. "I'm nae worried a bit."

"Why would you think I'd be taken with the MacLean laird?" Marion demanded.

Rory Mac's satisfied chuckle told her she'd reacted exactly as he'd hoped. "He's got quite the reputation, and the lassies find him verra pleasing to their eyes. Some visiting ladies have even been known to slip into the MacLean's bed when their own husbands are asleep." Rory Mac wriggled his eyebrows at her.

"I'd never do such a thing," Marion exclaimed, knowing she was only adding to Rory Mac's pleasure at getting a rise out of her, but she could not help herself. "I can't imagine a man more attractive than my husband, and I'm sure he'll please me so much in bed, I'd never dream of another man!"

Angus broke into a coughing fit, Rory Mac roared with laugher and Iain gave her an approving yet amused look. She considered what she'd said, and heat flooded her cheeks. She wasn't sure what to say now. She did think Iain very attractive, and she was sure he was very capable of his husbandly duties. But heavens, she wished she'd not blurted that.

"Go away," Iain demanded of the men, saving Marion from having to say anything at all. Rory Mac immediately departed, but Angus looked as if he might protest. "I wish to be alone with my wife," Iain added before Angus could speak.

Angus still looked as if he wanted to argue, so she gave

him a quick nod to let him know she would be fine, and he nodded back, finally leaving Marion and Iain alone in the dark. She could barely see Iain's face, but she could feel his heat and his power, as if it were vibrating out of him. Suddenly, she wanted him to hold her, touch her, make her feel alive when she had almost died. The need grew fierce in an instant, hampered only by the fear that she may not please him. Yet on that fear came another. What if he thought of his dead wife, and he found Marion lacking in comparison? Before she could consider any more of her fears, he slipped his arm behind her legs and lifted her to his chest.

Her body instantly warmed at his touch. She slid her arms around his neck and locked her hands behind his head. "What are you doing?" she asked in a breathy whisper.

"I need ye, Marion. I need to ken ye're alive and nae harmed. I see ye and ye seem safe now, but I need the knowing that only being with ye as yer husband can provide. Is it too greedy?"

"No," she croaked, a strange tightening occurring in her belly.

Iain walked some distance away, past the trees where they had rested earlier to a more private thicket. A blanket lay on the ground, and he kneeled and deposited her gently upon it. She thought he'd sit beside her, but instead, he stood looking down at her. The moon must have broken through clouds because she could see the outline of his strong body, though not all the details of how he was formed. She had a sudden sharp desire to feel him since she could not see him, but she was too shy to ask.

Silently, he stooped before her, lifted her again as if she weighed no more than a blade of grass, and settled her, straddling him, in his lap as he sat down. They were now face-to-face, and he was hard as steel everywhere, and even though he was wet from the river, he was hotter than a blazing fire. Embarrassment caused her to shift, but his large hands clutched her hips.

"Be still a minute, Marion. I'm intent on being slow and tender with ye, but if ye move at all, I'm afraid I'll take ye like a mindless beast, I want ye that much."

His words made her feel oddly giddy and light-headed. "You want me that much?"

"Aye. It's been a long time since I've been with a woman."

"You *are* a beast," she growled, angry that she'd momentarily thought his need was solely due to her. It seemed any woman would do. She pressed her palms against his thighs to stand, but he caught her around the waist and guided her firmly back onto his lap. She wiggled to free herself, but it was no use. His fingers curled around her waist, unmoving and unrelenting.

She tried to turn her face from his, but he took hold of her chin and made her look at him. Even in the darkness, she could see his burning eyes. "I did nae mean it like that."

"I don't care," she muttered, irritated with how much she actually did care. Why was she letting hope grow inside when she knew he would hurt her?

"Ye do," he said fiercely. "And I like verra much that ye care."

"I don't," she protested weakly, her heart pounding. She didn't want to let herself care for him if he was never going to love her.

He cupped her face. "Listen to me. I ken I just hurt ye, and I'm sorry. I did nae mean I wanted ye simply because I'd nae been with a woman. I've had plenty of opportunity to ease my desire. Ken?"

"I *ken*," she said, pleased that she'd not screamed at him as she wanted to. "Women must offer themselves to you all the time. I suppose because you are an attractive and mighty laird. What is it you're trying to tell me?" She poked him in the chest. "Are you trying to tell me that you could ease your desire whenever you choose? That you do not need me?"

He captured her fingers with his when she poked him again. One of his large hands wrapped around hers, and the other delved into her hair to slip through her tresses and cup her head. He brought her face so close to his that his warm breath fanned her lips when he spoke. "I'm trying to tell ye that I've nae wanted a woman since my wife died. Though opportunity has been plenty, I've nae cared. I figured that part of me died with her. But it has nae. Ye have awakened me."

"I have?" Her body tingled with shock and pleasure. If she personally had awakened that, maybe she could awaken his heart in time.

He nodded and then brushed the pad of his thumb across her mouth. The tingling intensified and her breasts grew heavy, her nipples taut. *This...this* had to be desire. She licked her lips, liking it very much. If simple desire felt this good, desire born of love must feel like Heaven. She wanted Heaven.

He didn't answer her. Instead, he covered her mouth with his. The kiss was consuming, demanding, and showed her that he liked it as much as she did. His lips massaged hers, and then his tongue slipped inside her mouth, swirling, teasing, taunting. She'd never been kissed before him, but she'd imagined quite often what a passionate kiss would be like. Yet her imagination had not captured it. Not really. Kissing Iain was like swimming in the water of the sea. It was like racing on one of her father's horses with the wind whipping through her hair. Like hitting a target in the center on the first try. It was everything exhilarating she'd ever done combined, but it was so much more.

She could not think, except to concentrate on the slide of his hand down her neck, over her back, and to her bottom. Suddenly, her gown was being pulled up over her thighs as his fingers deftly kneaded her skin. His mouth blazed kisses against her shoulder, across her collarbone, and to her lips.

A pulsing need sprang to life between her thighs and shot a sharp ache up into her abdomen. Before she knew what had happened, he'd unlaced her gown and the front of it was draping open. He pulled her chemise down, and his mouth, hot and seeking, found her breast. His hands cupped her bottom and hoisted her up, closer to his mouth while he suckled in long, heady draws. Every sense she possessed sparked to life and screamed for more.

She could not get close enough to him, or maybe it was that she could not get him close enough to her. She wanted to feel all of him against her, bare flesh to bare flesh. She wanted to be consumed, and as that thought occurred, it ceded to another. She needed relief.

"You're torturing me," she whispered hoarsely to the top of his wet head as he flicked his tongue over her bud, then took it into his mouth. A moan wrenched from between her clenched teeth, and he chuckled.

"Aye. I'm torturing ye because ye need to experience the pleasure ye can only find when the pain of the yearning finds release."

"I don't understand," she murmured, running her hands up the rippling muscles of his bare back to grip his corded shoulders.

He lifted his head and grinned. Her breath caught at how happy he looked. She'd made him happy, if only for a moment.

"Ye'll understand soon enough," he replied.

Before she could even order her frenzied thoughts to form a clear reply, he had slipped off the last of his clothing and tugged her gown and chemise off. She shivered when the cold air hit her damp skin, but he settled her onto her back on the blanket and his body came close to warm her. His hands traced over her knees, sliding down toward the inside of her thighs to part them.

She tensed as she stared up at the sky, suddenly afraid once more, but she refused to show it. She didn't want him to be disappointed.

"Marion," he murmured as he applied light pressure to her inner thighs until she allowed them to be opened all the way. "Dunnae be afraid. I vow to ye I will go slow and be gentle."

She curled her fingers into the cool grass. "I'm not afraid of you. I'm only afraid you'll find me lacking."

Suddenly, he was looming over her with his hands on either side of her upper arms, his body hovering above hers, his face directly over hers. He looked down at her. His hair had come out of the twine that tied it back, and it hung down the sides of his face. "I will never compare ye to Catriona. Ye are as different as winter and summer."

"Which am I?"

"Does it matter? Each time has a purpose, aye?"

She nodded.

"I want to do things to ye, Marion. Fierce things. Things I would nae have dared with—" He stopped with a curse. "Will ye trust me?"

She already did. God help her. He had her trust completely in this moment. She hoped he didn't prove her
foolish to have given it so easily. "I trust you."

"I'll nae take that lightly. I vow it." He leaned forward,
brushed his lips to hers, and then feathered kisses down the
center of her chest, over her belly, and to the juncture
between her thighs. When his fingers parted her and his
lips found her sensitive spot, she gasped and drew her
thighs together. She would have squeezed his head
between her legs, but he pressed her thighs back apart as
his tongue tortured her sweetly.

She'd never experienced anything so sinfully wonderful
as the slide of his tongue against her tender flesh. Coherent
thought left her, and soon she was moaning, thrashing, and
begging him to end the pleasurable torture. And he ended
it in a way that left her feeling as if she had been filled with
vigor and then drained. There was nothing left in her. Not
a speck of ability to move. But she knew instinctually they
were not done.

When he came up to hover over her, he lifted her
bottom off the ground, and in the next second she felt his
hard staff pressing against something inside her. She started
to ask him to wait, but her words were lost in another gasp
as he eased into her and broke through whatever barrier
was there. He stilled, filling her completely, and she was
suddenly nervous about his size.

"This hurts," she murmured, tears stinging at her eyes.

"I'll nae move until ye say," he replied, his voice gravel-
ly, as if he too were in pain.

Tears trickled out of her eyes, and she sniffed. He
leaned down and kissed the left and then the right sides of
her temples, taking her tears into his mouth. That gesture,
that simple display of wanting to take away her pain,

restored her faith and destroyed her fear.

"Will it feel better if I let you move?"

"Aye. I think so." The strain of waiting vibrated in his voice. "I think it will feel verra good, but if it does nae and ye want me to stop, I will."

"You vow it?"

"Marion," he growled. "I'd rather die than hurt ye."

Her heart ached with his sweet words. "You may move."

He didn't say a word, but she felt the tension in his still body spring loose as if he'd barely held it in control. He began to move then, and within seconds, his words proved true. It felt very good, indeed. So good that after a few more minutes she was demanding he move faster and harder as the pressure of before, that pulsing ache, blossomed to life again and demanded satisfaction.

He went slowly, though, moving in languid, almost careful strokes, until she growled her dissatisfaction and clawed at his back. "I'm not glass underneath you, Iain. You will not break me. Quit holding back."

"Ye're sure?"

She could hear the strain in his voice again.

"I'm sure."

Seven

*H*olding himself back had been agonizing, but he'd not wanted to hurt or scare Marion. But when she begged him to take her, he could not contain himself any longer. He did not unleash his need; his desire for her *took* him, and he lost control. Each of her moans increased his craving further until he took her first on her back, then above him while he guided her motions, and then from behind. His fingers worked frantically between her thighs as his body hummed with each stroke in and out of her hot slickness.

He could not get enough of her, and while he had a deep fear that he would hurt her, he was unable to control himself as he'd done all those years with Catriona. Marion was warmth and health and bursting with a desire that seemed to match his own. Her body welcomed him and wrapped around him, compelling him forward. His blood rushed through his veins and beat a quick cadence in his ears. He pumped into her, needing to consume her and needing to be consumed. He forgot himself completely as the sweet, sharp ache of pleasure gripped him and he claimed her as his, now and forever.

He shuddered as his seed poured into her, and then he came to rest beside her, panting as he pulled her into the crook of his arm. As he gazed up at the sky, brilliant with its specks of starlight, such contentment filled him that he felt at once uneasy at how simple it would be to forget his past pain and loss. He didn't want to forget Catriona. Loving her and knowing her had, in part, made him the man he was today. Yet, deep in his gut, he feared that he might forget her with the craving he already felt for Marion.

Marion shifted in his arms, and he gazed at her and traced the delicate slope of her cheekbone up to her closed eyes and over her pale hair. She was so different in appearance and personality from Catriona, but God help him, Marion pleased him mightily, and he desired her in a way he'd not known before. It was an insatiable hunger, whereas it had been a comfortable, careful need with Catriona. An easy slow thing, pleasurable but not devouring, because she had been too weak for him ever to allow himself that sort of greedy pleasure.

Marion, however, was not weak. She had begged him to take what she wanted to give him, what she knew she could.

"Marion." There was much he could not say—truthfully, he didn't even begin to know how to—yet he could tell her how she'd pleased him. He also wanted to verify that he'd satisfied her and not hurt her. "Marion," he whispered again.

Her answer was a snore, deep and sated.

He smiled in amazement that his wife could have fallen asleep so easily after napping not long ago, but he supposed with the long ride, having to fight for her life, and his pleasing her so—he grinned with pride into her fragrant hair—she would be exhausted. Personally, he was starving. He gently extracted his arm and set Marion on the blanket, then retrieved his plaid and laid it over her before rummaging in the satchel he'd brought earlier for some bread, cheese, and wine. After partaking in all three but still saving some for Marion, he lay back down on the blanket beside her and listened to her even breaths.

Things would be good and well between them. How could they not be with the desire that burned so bright for each other? With that thought, Iain fell into the first deep sleep he'd experienced since Catriona had died.

Iain awoke before Marion the next morning and he disentangled himself from his wife, who had wrapped her arms and legs around him during the night. He retrieved his plaid and folded the part of the blanket he'd been lying on over Marion instead. He laid the food he'd saved for her on top of his satchel and set it by her head before going down to the river to wash. Once he was clean, he dressed quickly and went to check on Angus, Rory Mac, and Neil. Angus had already packed his horse, as had Rory Mac, except Rory Mac was now reclined against a tree.

He grinned at Iain. "Finally ye're awake. Late night?" he teased.

Iain ignored Rory Mac's question and walked over to Neil. "How do ye feel?" he asked. The man still looked pitiful.

"I've felt better. I'm sorry if I'm slowing ye down."

"Dunnae fash yerself," Iain rebuked.

Iain sensed someone standing behind him, so he turned to find Angus staring at him. "Did ye remember what I said te ye about Marion?" Angus demanded.

Iain could have simply reminded Angus he had no right to demand anything from Iain, but instead, Iain nodded. "I remembered."

Angus peered at him suspiciously. The older man stepped closer. "Did ye go te sleep with Marion in yer thoughts or a ghost?"

Rory Mac sat up from his spot in the grass with a smirk on his face. "By the screams coming from yer direction, I'd say ye went to sleep with yer new wife in yer thoughts. Ye look tired, too," the Scot commented with a chuckle. "I ken I'm tired. I could nae sleep over the noise."

"Shut yer mouth," Iain and Angus ordered as one. With a look of understanding, they silently agreed that his joining with Marion was not a topic to be discussed by anyone.

Rory Mac waved a dismissive hand at Iain. "Hold yer anger. I was only teasing. I'm glad to see ye're finally moving on. And ye, ye old goat, I suppose I'm glad an old man like ye has someone to care about."

Iain's worries concerning Catriona roared to life with Rory Mac's words and stirred his ire. "I will never forget Catriona. No one could ever take her place."

Rory Mac's gaze locked on something or someone behind Iain.

Iain knew it was Marion even before he turned to see her standing close behind him. She'd donned her gown, which was bunched oddly as if she'd had trouble lacing it. She had a pained look on her face, and he instantly knew she'd heard his words.

"Marion—" He started to apologize and faltered. How could he say he was sorry for something that was true? He could not say he didn't mean it. He couldn't say she'd misunderstood. "Did ye see the food and drink I left out for ye?" he asked instead, aware that he was hurting her, though he didn't want to be.

"Yes, thank you," she replied, her tone sounding withdrawn and slightly cold to him. He could be imagining it, he supposed. He tried to catch her gaze to meet her eyes, but she looked around the camp, evidently avoiding him. "I see we're packed and ready to depart. I hope you were not waiting on me."

"Nay," he replied and stepped closer to her. She subtly shifted away from him.

Iain glanced at Angus, who shook his head, and then Rory Mac, who simply shrugged. It seemed the best thing to do was continue on their journey. Even if he could think of the right words to comfort her, he'd not say them with Angus and Rory Mac listening. "We'll depart now, unless ye need a moment."

"No." She shook her head, her voice tired, even slightly sad.

Once he had settled behind her and the horses started toward the MacLean's hold, Iain thought about Marion and why she continually put herself at risk to defend him when he'd told her not to. Did she think she had to prove her worth? He suspected it was a possibility, given that her father likely made her feel insufficient. He wanted to ask her about her life in England, but he'd rather be able to see her face and expressions in case she tried to conceal the worst from him. Yet, he wanted to let her know he was thinking of her and that he would make it clear to his clan that she was important to him.

"When we get to my home, I'll have a bedchamber made for ye next to mine."

She turned around sharply, almost toppling herself. He had to grab hold of her arm to keep her on the horse and turn her back around. "You're giving me my own bedchamber?"

He could hear the shock in her voice. He had to hide his sudden grin because he was that pleased that having a grand bedchamber made her happy, even though she'd sleep in his every night. He knew it was not the custom, but he personally thought a man not sleeping with his wife was foolish. "I am. And ye can make it grand. It will be the grandest room in the castle."

"Oh, Iain, thank you! I, well—"

He thought he heard her sniff.

"Thank you," she said. "Thank you for being so considerate and thinking of me. Will it be acceptable for me to alter Catriona's bedchamber, though? If not, I can leave it or take a different room—one less grand."

Talking of Catriona with Marion was not what he had wished, but he didn't want her to feel uncomfortable, as if she were taking something that had belonged to Catriona. "It will be fine. Catriona did nae have her own bedchamber. She shared mine."

Marion cocked her head to the side. "You never offered her one?" The confusion was evident in her voice.

"Nay. I preferred she sleep with me, and she thought it was silly to have a chamber she'd never use."

Marion hunched her shoulders forward. "I see," she responded in a small voice that made him frown. "Have I upset ye?"

"No," she immediately responded, her reply snappish. "I'm simply tired from last night."

Guilt for letting himself act so freely and take her with such abandon overcame him. "I'll nae bed ye tonight," he proposed reluctantly.

"Please stop talking," she said. Her tone was not an order but more a plea.

Perhaps his wife was shy about bed talk. Well, he'd not

say another word about last night, then. The problem was, with her pressed between his thighs on the saddle, all he could think about was last night and how she had felt in his arms. But instead of saying something else that might embarrass her further, he said nothing.

Several hours later, Marion shivered as she scrutinized the cloudy gray sky, and when Iain pulled her against his chest and wrapped an arm around her waist, she didn't try to move away or protest. Her desire not to freeze to death overrode her hurt and anger at herself for the moment.

She bit her lip as her vision blurred with the threat of tears. She blinked, a few trickled out of her eyes. She prayed they'd not hit Iain's hand. She didn't want him to know she was upset by his earlier words that his first wife, Catriona, could not be supplanted. Of course she couldn't. It wasn't his feeling that way that was upsetting, though. It was that there was never going to be a place in his heart for her. He'd told her it was so, but hope had started to grow with his praises and the way he watched over her. And then last night…

The things he'd done to her and the way he'd made her feel… Well, she'd thought it was the beginning of something special, that a connection had been forged between them. She'd even foolishly gone to sleep with hopes that she may one day have a piece of his heart. But she'd never have his heart. His desire was all he was willing to give of himself.

And it was made worse knowing she could not even say he just wasn't a sharing and loving man. Obviously, he had been—with Catriona. *She* had shared his bed. Soon his whole clan would know that he didn't care for Marion enough to allow her to do the same. It was humiliating and hurtful. She felt too much like the child who had always tried to do everything to please her father to gain his love but had never been enough. She simply refused to exhaust herself trying to gain Iain's love when it was clear he had no intention of ever giving it.

She had to be stronger and colder; she could not hope for something that would never be. When he made her feel warm with a compliment or a touch, she needed to remind herself it was merely lust and would never be more. She could not allow herself to lower her defenses. He was like a handsome conqueror who could storm her heart and take it if she were not very careful, and she knew too well the heartbreak of wanting love from someone who was not capable of giving it.

Iain squeezed her a bit tighter in his arms, and his fingers fanned across her belly, gently rubbing as if he knew her thoughts. It was so typical of a man to want to take from a woman but not give in return. Marion held onto this thought and let it fuel her anger. He wanted to take his pleasure but give nothing back. Her cheeks heated at the memory of the way he'd lavished kisses on the most sensitive part of her body.

She worried her lip as she thought. She had to confess that he'd given her pleasure and had seemed to love doing it.

He was giving her protection. He was quick to keep her safe and care for her. Her heart tugged remembering how he'd come to her rescue with Froste, then at her father's castle, then again at the river. So he'd give his life for her but not his love to her? It was a depressing thought and one that, along with her aching body, exhausted her.

She had no idea what to do besides try not to allow herself to be hurt too much by him. The best way she knew to do that was to keep herself away from him, emotionally and physically, as much as possible.

With that thought in her head, she braced herself for the cold, and shifted slightly forward. But within moments, her teeth were chattering. Within an hour, being cold had so exhausted her that she could no longer keep her eyes open. She closed them and allowed her body to sway with the cantering of the horse.

Eight

Iain hadn't realized Marion had fallen asleep until she suddenly slumped forward. He caught her and gently leaned her against his chest. With her head resting against him, he tightened his hold around her waist, feeling each deep breath she took.

He could not resist pressing his lips to her head and inhaling her fragrant scent. She stirred in her sleep, and wiggled her bottom, immediately making him hard. He clenched his teeth.

His need for her had grown with each hour she rode between his thighs. Why had he made that foolish offer not to bed her tonight? Sometimes the best thing for sore muscles was to use them again. He immediately shoved the greedy thought away. He suspected that idea did not hold true for the soreness of losing one's innocence. As he held her close, her fragrant flowery smell surrounding him, her soft body languid in his arms, and her silky hair blowing against his face, that same fierce need to keep her from any harm rose in him.

If Alex was not such a good friend, Iain would forego the MacLean hold and head directly home. He had an uneasy feeling about stopping at Alex's. While what Rory Mac had said about Alex was true—women did seem to find him irresistible—that wasn't what was making Iain nervous. He trusted Alex, and he wasn't worried that Marion would be untrue. He knew her well enough now to discern she was honorable. It was Alex's men that made Iain tense. They were known for their violent ways, which was helpful in wartime but not when it came to women. They were not going to be able to resist staring at Marion with desire, and *that* was going to make him angry. He needed to show the men immediately that Marion belonged to him, and he'd not abide any man looking at her with lust.

These thoughts were still in Iain's head as he led them up the winding trail to Alex's hold. He expected to encounter guards at the main entrance to the castle grounds, but as Iain and his kin curved around a bend, a large, loud group of men on horseback came out of the woods. All laughter and talking stopped when the men saw them.

Rory Mac brought his horse up to the side of Iain's as the men approached, and Angus, with Neil sitting in front of him, came to flank Iain's other side. The MacLeans smelled of sweat and animal blood, and Iain could see that several of them had dead deer and rabbits strapped to their mounts. One man had great spiky antlers strapped to his horse along with a satchel soaked with blood. The man had the blood of the animal smeared under his eyes and down the bridge of his nose to show he'd made the greatest kill of the day, and it was to this man that Iain looked.

Angus spoke in a low undertone. "That one will have the feeling of power from the kill flowing though him."

"Aye," Iain agreed, following Angus's gaze to the man Iain had already marked as trouble.

The painted man moved ahead on his stallion and approached, the other eight slightly behind him. Iain didn't have time to gently wake Marion. He gave her a hard shake, and when her eyes fluttered open, he whispered in her ear. "We're at the MacLean hold. Dunnae talk until I say ye can."

She stiffened in his arms, but her gaze darted to the side. She must have seen the men, because her eyes widened and she gave a quick nod.

"Well, if it's nae the legendary MacLeod," the painted warrior said with a trace of contempt.

Iain gripped the reins of his destrier. He didn't like being at the disadvantage with the stranger knowing his name. "And who are ye?"

The man grinned. "Do ye nae remember me, then, Iain?"

Iain studied the man for a moment—sparse red hair, blue eyes, and a jagged scar above his upper lip. Iain recognized that scar. He'd stood over Bridgette MacLean as she'd clumsily sewn the gash in her cousin's lip together. Alex had given it to him for disobeying an order and nearly getting ten clansmen killed rescuing him.

"Ye've grown, Archibald," Iain said to the once impulsive and impetuous boy now turned man. He was careful to keep his words void of emotion to disguise his surprise. The last time he'd seen Archibald MacLean, he'd barely come to Iain's shoulder. The man now almost looked Iain eye to eye.

"That happens in four years. Ye'd nae be amazed if ye'd seen me, but since I was banished from battles..." Bitterness tinged Archibald's words.

"Ye should consider yerself fortunate," Iain said, irritated that the man still seemed to be foolish. "If ye were my clansman and ye disobeyed my orders in battle and nearly got my men killed trying to rescue ye, I would have banished ye from the clan. Alex is a much kinder laird than I am."

"I do consider myself fortunate," Archibald said. "And I'm nae angry with Alex, if that's what ye think. I'm angry with myself for the battles I missed and the men that died when I ken I could have saved them."

"I see ye learned humility in your time in the stables," Rory Mac added with a snort.

Archibald smirked at Rory Mac. "I've about as much humility as I remember ye having. And I dunnae speak anything but the truth. I was always one of the best warriors, even when young. Ye ken that. What I lacked was patience and forethought."

Iain spoke before Rory Mac could reply. Rory Mac and Archibald tended toward quick-heated anger, and Iain did not want to break up a fight. "Are ye saying ye have learned those two things?"

Archibald grinned. "If I had nae learned those two virtues, do ye think Alex would have let me join his forces once more?"

"Nay," Iain said. "I dunnae. Welcome back."

Archibald accepted Iain's words with a tilt of his head, but the man had already pointedly shifted his gaze to Marion. "I'm sorry for the loss of Catriona," he said, his tone sincere.

"I thank ye," Iain replied, feeling uncomfortable. It had been quite some time since he'd had to withstand the looks of sorrow and pitying words. It used to be that his chest would tighten, but it did not now, surprising him. Maybe time was finally healing the wound, or maybe he was just learning to control the gut-wrenching reaction that occurred when someone reminded him that Catriona was gone.

Archibald slowly swept his gaze up and down Marion in a manner that made Iain instantly aware that the man liked what he saw. Iain had a sudden, intense dislike for Alex's cousin. Angus must have felt it, too, because he growled low in his throat.

Archibald smiled as he stared at Marion. "So who do ye have here? Is she a gift for Alex?"

"She is nae a gift for Alex," Iain said through clenched teeth.

On either side of him, he saw Rory Mac and Angus each touch their weapons as Marion's hand clutched Iain's thigh. He wanted to press his palm over her hand to reassure her that she was safe, but to show he cared might make her even more appealing to Archibald. Even as a young lad, he had always pursued what he thought he could not attain. Iain did not wish to start his visit with Alex by thrashing his cousin if it could be avoided.

Archibald's grin widened. "Excellent. I'll take her." He started to reach forward as if to grab Marion off Iain's horse, but Iain whipped out his dagger and pointed it at the man. Archibald may have grown into a man, but the heart of who he was had not changed a bit. The only way he'd accept the truth is by having it clarified with a threat.

"She's nae a gift for anyone." Iain glared at the man. "She's my property, and I dunnae share what I own."

Marion grew even tenser in Iain's arms. Didn't the woman know he'd not let any harm come to her?

"What's yer name?" Archibald demanded of her.

Marion inhaled a sharp breath as if to answer, but Iain cut her off. "Her name is the MacLeod's wife," he growled. "That is what ye may call her unless I say otherwise. Do ye ken?"

Archibald eyed Iain for a long moment, then Iain's

dagger. He nodded with a smile. "I did nae ken ye married again. Is she a Scottish lass? Such things usually reach us quickly."

"Nay. She's from England."

"Och, that explains it, then. I'm sorry for ye," Archibald said, shaking his head. "Come. I'll lead ye to Alex."

Iain didn't correct Archibald's assumption that Marion was a cold Englishwoman. It was better to let him think that so that he'd not bother with her.

Iain simply nodded and motioned for Rory Mac, Angus, and Neil to follow.

If it were possible to spit fire, Marion was sure she'd be shooting blazing flames out of her mouth and nostrils right now. She was that mad. She glared ahead as Iain guided his horse toward the towering, foreboding hold in the distance. She was about to tell him exactly what she thought of him instructing people to call her "the Mac-Leod's wife," and just as bad was his obvious distaste for his English wife, but the man with the dark gaze, Archibald, placed himself beside Iain and started asking him questions about their king, David, and his captivity in England.

Through the anger roaring in her ears, she learned that David had been imprisoned in England for eleven years already. She'd not known it had been that long. Father had mentioned the King of Scots before, and what he'd said was that King Edward wanted a Scottish king he could control, and David was not a man to be controlled, which was likely why he was still imprisoned. She knew little else because Father didn't consider her worthy of talking to about—or capable of understanding—politics. Perhaps she'd ask Iain later. She thought he'd likely tell her more of the history, at least.

She sat silently as they rode, but when Marion heard the man Archibald refer to her once more as "the Mac-Leod's wife," she felt as if smoke was coming from her, but no one seemed to notice or care. She cut her gaze to her left and met Angus's eyes. Her stomach clenched at the pity and worry swimming in her friend's green gaze.

I'm sorry, lass, he mouthed.

She nodded and quickly turned away, not wanting to show her anger to him. Even though Iain was Angus's laird, she didn't doubt that Angus's loyalty was with her, and because of that, she didn't want him to see how upset and hurt she was by Iain's treatment. Knowing Angus, he'd lose his temper and say something he should not. Iain may be a reasonable man, but she doubted he'd stand for one of his clansmen telling him how to treat his wife. Besides that, she was married now, and she was Iain's "property," as he'd so rudely told everyone. She squeezed her hands together. If she'd had any doubts that Iain only cared for her for the pleasure she could give him, she had none now.

With Iain referring to her as "the MacLeod's wife," everyone would soon know he had little regard for her. She gritted her teeth at the familiar pain of being the one who didn't belong. Her father had been quick to point out often that she was only half-English, and now she supposed she was only half-Scottish, and worse, an intruder in Iain's life and his clan. Though Rory Mac had been nice enough, as well as Neil, she suspected once his clan saw she was not loved by Iain, they would ignore her, just as most everyone had done at her father's home.

She jerked a hand through her hair, and her fingers

became stuck in the tangled mess. She slowly unthreaded her fingers from her matted locks and brought her hands in front of her. Dirt smudged her skin and had caked itself under her nails. She could only imagine how awful she must look.

Maybe her appearance had embarrassed Iain and that was why he'd treated her so. The thought made her frown. If it was, the man was a shallow goat. She almost wanted to not bathe until they reached his home just to teach him a lesson, but the fact was that her skin itched and so did her scalp, and she really did feel dirty. No, she wasn't going to forego a bath, if she could get one, just to torture him. There were other ways to do that. Well, really only one, which was to deny him her body. She doubted he'd force her to join with him, at least not here at the MacLean hold. The problem was that she had enjoyed his touch, too.

Just the memory of it made her feel warm and tingly. But perhaps if she refused him until he at least gave her the respect she deserved, he'd treat her better. She could feel her brows pulling together. Would those actions make him treat her better or make him so angry he became a brute? Oh, how she wished her mother were still alive and she could ask her what to do. She needed advice, but she had no one with whom she could talk. Certainly not Angus. Just the thought of trying to tell him these particular problems burned her cheeks.

When the horse suddenly stopped, she was surprised to realize they had arrived at the MacLean's hold. She stared at the enormous castle, and her jaw dropped. A mountain rose in the sky behind a mammoth mound of stones, and the castle seemed to stretch into the blue with the mountains. To one side was a great cliff, and on the other a jagged rock covered in green moss seemed to grow toward the sea.

Iain lifted her up and off the horse before she could protest that she could manage on her own.

Archibald dismounted his own horse and stepped toward them. "Alex is down by the sea." The man looked away from Iain and to her. "Do ye want to take her to meet him now, or will it just be us? It will determine the path we take to get to him."

Iain shook his head. "She can await me in my chamber."

Marion wanted to smack her husband—hard. She was going to need to pay another indulgence for that sinful thought, but really, how was she supposed to help it?

"Laird." Angus spoke up. "Perhaps ye should present Marion te—"

"Nay," Iain said, cutting off Angus's words.

Marion silently prayed he'd say nothing else. It was humiliating, and Iain clearly did not consider her worthy of meeting his friend.

Iain took her by the elbow. "I'm sure ye want to clean up before meeting Alex."

She forced herself to nod, and she struggled not to narrow her eyes at him. "Of course. I wouldn't want to shame you, *my lord*."

Iain frowned at her, then addressed Archibald. "Is there a clanswoman about who can show Marion to the bedchambers and bring her fresh water?"

Archibald's answer was a loud, long, shrill whistle.

Within a minute, a young woman came stomping down the castle steps, her flaming-red hair flowing behind her in the wind. No one spoke as she progressed down the steep stairwell, but a few of the men whistled at her. When she got to the last step, she set her hands on her hips and gave the men an icy stare that silenced all of them. Marion was instantly envious. She wanted to learn that look.

The woman tossed her long red hair over her shoulders as she walked toward them. "I've told ye a hundred times nae to whistle at me, Archibald. If ye want me, cart your arse up the stairs and fetch me. I'm nae a dog, but a woman."

Archibald grinned. "I ken well ye're a woman, Bridgette. Shall I show ye?"

She snorted. "Nae unless ye want to make yerself seem a fool."

Laughter erupted from the men, except a scowling Archibald, as Bridgette swept her gaze over Iain's small party. She paused on Marion—who she acknowledged with a raised eyebrow—and then Iain, at whom she batted her eyelashes. "Well, well, if it is nae the MacLeod. Did I nae tell ye the last time I saw ye that one day ye would be begging me to marry ye. Have ye come to beg, then? I'm afraid the line is long."

"Aye," said a man standing directly behind Marion. "I'm in it."

"As am I," another man said.

"Me as well," replied a third man whom Marion couldn't see, nor did she care if she could. The only person whose reaction she cared about was Iain's. He'd told her he'd not been attracted to a woman since his wife had died, but maybe now that his lust had been awakened, he'd desire many other women. Her stomach twisted. The idea made her feel ill. If Iain was untrue to her, she'd leave, even though she had nowhere to go. She'd figure it out somehow.

A smile tugged at Iain's lips, and Marion's heart jerked. Was that a flirtatious smile? He rubbed a hand across his stubble. "I see yer brother has nae made progress taming ye."

She snickered. "Did ye think he would?"

"For his sake, I'd hoped. I ken well what a trouble-seeking sibling is like, as I have three of my own."

"Since ye mentioned yer siblings..." Bridgette batted her eyes. "How is Lachlan?"

"Still nae the man for ye."

"Is that because ye want to be the man for me, Iain?" Bridgette stepped very close to Iain and drew her hand down his chest. Marion stiffened. She really didn't want to act unladylike in front of a bunch of strangers, but her temper was rising, which truly was something that did not happen often. She didn't even really have a temper. Except for when she was near Iain. *He* brought it out in her. And now *Bridgette* did, too. It must be full-blooded Scottish people in general. Marion quirked her mouth. But not Angus. He'd lived in England so long he acted more English than Scottish. And not Neil. And really not Rory Mac, either, though he did like to tease.

Iain moved Bridgette's hand from his chest and finally turned to acknowledge Marion. It was all she could do not to glare at him for ignoring her for so long. "This is my wife."

Marion stepped forward as Archibald said, "She's called 'the MacLeod's wife.'"

That did it!

"My name is Marion," she growled through gritted teeth.

Iain gave her an amused look, but Bridgette's gaze rounded in surprise before she frowned. "Truly I'm stunned ye married again, and a Sassenach at that. I dunnae understand men one bit."

Iain suddenly looked very uncomfortable. "She's half-English, half-Scottish. She's the MacDonald's niece. And I married to gain David's freedom."

His words were like a blow to Marion's gut. It was one thing for her to know he would never love her, but did he really need to announce how he felt to everyone? Her cheeks heated with searing embarrassment.

She straightened her spine, lifted her chin, and caught Bridgette's eye. "And my only choice was to marry him or be forced to marry a malicious knight intent on overthrowing my king."

Out of the corner of her eye, she saw Iain frown at her, and she heard the men murmuring around her, but Bridgette's hearty laughter and the woman linking her arm through Marion's, captured her full attention.

"I like her," Bridgette announced to all the men standing there looking confounded. Bridgette stared at her. "I like ye. And I never like other women. Come, then." Bridgette tugged on Marion's arm. "I'll get ye a bath drawn and a decent gown for supper." The woman eyed Iain with a smirk. "Is she sharing yer chamber, per yer odd custom, or shall I give her one of her own?"

"Give her a chamber next to mine if it's nae too much trouble."

"It's nae any trouble, but the castle is cold and the night will be long," Bridgette said in a teasing voice.

"I ken," Iain said dully. His gaze flicked to Marion. "Stay in the chamber until I come to fetch ye for supper."

She curled her hands into fists. "Stay in the chamber?" she sputtered, disbelieving how he had ordered her so—and in front of others.

"Aye," he replied.

She opened her mouth to tell him no, but Bridgette

gave a sharp shake of her head. Marion frowned. Maybe Bridgette knew something Marion did not. She clamped her jaw shut and forced a nod as Bridgette guided her up the stairs.

Marion had never been so humiliated or felt so unwanted in all her life, and that meant a great deal seeing as how her father had made it perfectly clear that he had only tolerated her because of the match she could one day make. As she picked her way carefully up the steep steps, she thought of all the foul curses she knew her husband deserved to have hurled upon his head, and then she determined how many indulgences she owed.

She gasped when she realized her tally was ten. She needed more coin and she needed to learn more curses. The man was a heartless beast who deserved more than ten sinful thoughts, no matter how poor it made her.

Nine

Iain followed Archibald, Angus, and Rory Mac down a long steep path toward the sea. Neil had gone with the MacLean men to see their healer and then find a place to rest. Iain had purposely slowed his pace as the men talked ahead of him. He listened to the steady sound of his feet against the steps, the hum of the water in the distance, and the underlying whistle of the wind blowing into his face.

If the occasional sound of a man's voice didn't invade his thoughts, he would have forgotten they were there. All he could see in his mind were Marion's hips gently swaying as she departed with Bridgette. She was going to drive him to madness with the seductive way her body moved. Did she mean to entice him? With the pinched look that had come over her when he'd told Bridgette to give Marion her own chamber, he half wondered if she had wanted to sleep with him in his bed.

The very thought of holding her again made him throb with need. If she wanted to be in his bed tonight, and she wasn't too sore, he certainly would oblige. He'd have to find time to get her alone and try to figure out how she felt, as well as to explain that he'd not meant to reveal that he'd only married her to secure David's freedom. Bridgette's comment about him marrying again had filled him with guilt, and he'd blurted it out, which was unforgivable and mindless. Marion had haunted his dreams last night instead of Catriona, and he woke today consumed by thoughts of his new bride. Her bright smile and quick wit. Her bravery in her desire to defend him and the strange way she thought to give coin to the church to reduce the consequences of his sins.

He liked it, and her, very much. So much it bothered him. He'd sworn never to forget Catriona. He couldn't allow Marion to do that, yet she was his wife now. Before he could think on the matter any further, they arrived at the water. Alex stood with his back to them, but he turned at their approach, his hearing sharp as ever.

A broad smile spread over his face when he saw Iain. "MacLeod! Rory Mac!" Alex strode toward them and clasped Rory Mac on the shoulder and then did the same to Iain. "I was nae expecting ye but am glad ye're here. I could use yer counsel."

Iain quickly presented Angus and then asked, "For what do ye need our counsel?"

A distinctly wary look came over Alex, and he slanted his gaze toward Archibald and Angus, who had stepped aside when Alex had approached them. "We can talk about my problem in a minute. What brings ye to my home?"

"I am coming back from England and needed to warn ye of something."

"England?" Alex said, his face pinching. "Why would ye want to go there?"

"I did nae want to but was compelled to do so. David sent word that he needed my help."

Alex nodded. "In being returned to Scotland? I am guessing that's why ye were summoned."

"It was. He asked me to take a wife to aid in the cause

of getting King Edward to speak of David's release."

"A wife? Ye took a wife?" Alex asked with a significant lifting of his brows.

Iain nodded.

"From which clan?"

"She's English. Well, partly. She's the daughter of Baron de Lacy, but she's the niece of the MacDonald."

Astonishment wiped the smile from Alex's lips. "A devil's bargain, then?"

Iain heard Angus shifting behind him, as if readying to lunge for the MacLean. Iain didn't like referring to Marion as part of a devil's bargain, but neither did he want to discuss his wife in front of Archibald. "Something like that," he replied.

Alex turned abruptly toward Archibald. "Why are ye all still standing here? Do ye nae have training with the men that can be started without me? Must I be there to oversee ye, Archibald? If I must, then ye nay longer shall be on the council."

Iain had not expected the news of Archibald's status, given the younger man's troubles with taking orders in the past, but considering that Archibald was Alex's only male relative, Iain understood that Alex wanted to ready Archibald to become laird if Alex died. Iain surveyed Archibald for his reaction. Typical of a reckless man, he was openly scowling rather than controlling his reaction.

"Ye ken ye dunnae, Alex," Archibald snapped. "I thought ye may have need of me here."

"I dunnae—"

"Ye may," Iain interrupted. "Who's yer best tracker?"

"Of man or beast?" Alex asked.

"Man," Iain replied, not bothering to hide the worry he felt.

Alex tilted his head toward Archibald. "He is."

"Then send him out now with some men to verify that the area around yer castle is safe."

Alex cocked up an eyebrow. "And who would dare enter my lands who's nae welcome?"

"Froste," Iain replied, knowing he need not explain who Froste was because Alex knew of the knight from tournaments, as well.

"Froste? Why?" Alex inquired, his voice tight now.

"I'll explain it all to ye, but I'd feel better if ye sent out a scouting party presently." Iain eyed Archibald, knowing he needed to at least explain exactly who might be coming and what they would want. "Froste and his men's surcoats are adorned with snakes, and there may be other knights with them—Baron de Lacy's. His men wear a fire-breathing dragon. They'll be coming for my wife."

Archibald's eyes widened. "I thought ye said ye married her to foster David's freedom?"

"I did. I married her by decree of King Edward."

Archibald scowled. "Then why—"

"That's enough questions," Alex thundered. "It's nae for ye to ken. Report to me about the scouting when ye're finished."

"Aye, *laird*," Archibald growled and stomped off.

Iain caught Rory Mac's eye. "Ye ken what to do?"

"Mind Marion and keep her safe," the Scot replied with a wink.

"I'll be doing that, as well," Angus added, his voice daring Iain to argue.

A smile tugged at Iain's lips. In truth, he was pleased to have both men watching his wife. "I see ye've nae forgot the way of highland life, Angus."

Angus snorted. "That's the way of life everywhere,

laird. More so in England than here. There's nae many men a body can trust in an English household. I barely slept some nights once my lady grew te be such a comely lass. I worried some foolish knight would nae control himself when faced with her beauty and take liberties."

The very idea of another man touching Marion made Iain's blood heat. "Does the baron nae have control of his men?"

Angus stared at Iain for a long moment and then gave him a look as if the answer was simple. "Can ye say for certain that no man in yer entire clan would dare te take liberties with Marion once they behold her?"

Iain felt himself stiffen. "I would kill any man, including all three of my brothers, who dared to touch my wife in any way other than to defend her, greet her, or guide her," Iain stated.

"That did nae answer my question, but yer words make me happy," Angus said with a small smile.

"I trust all my men," Iain added. "They are honorable and faithful to me."

"Aye." Angus nodded. "I imagine ye earned their dedication by treating them fairly. Baron de Lacy kinnae claim the same." Angus spit toward the ground. "Service through fear and greed is different from service through respect and a sense of family from a clan, ye ken?"

"I do," Iain replied, even more aware now of how lonely Marion's life must have been in such a home. She'd been fortunate to have Angus. "Set yerself outside her door and go where she goes." Iain looked between Angus and Rory Mac. "Ken?"

Rory Mac gave Iain a smug look. "I ken ye so well that ye did nae even have to give the order."

"I ken, as well," Angus interrupted. "I've been shadowing Marion long afore ye took her te wife, laird. No rudeness intended."

"Am I to take it," Alex said from beside Iain, "that ye are nae displeased with having to marry the Sassenach?"

"I was," Iain responded.

Alex chuckled as Iain faced him. "And now?"

"And now I'm nae," he growled.

Alex raised his eyebrows. "I can see ye dunnae wish to discuss it. All I shall say is that I'm glad ye are finally burying yer dead wife."

The words, similar to Rory Mac's earlier ones, had Iain clenching his teeth against his sudden ire. He motioned for Rory Mac and Angus to leave, and the men exchanged a knowing look that Iain did not miss. They understood he was angry, which irritated him even more. He didn't like people guessing his emotions.

Once Iain and Alex were alone, Iain said, "I've nae forgotten Catriona. Marion kinnae take her place."

"No one said ye should forget her. Nor do I think yer new wife could take the place of yer old one. Now, enough on the subject. Tell me the whole tale of de Lacy, yer wife, Froste, King Edward, and David."

Iain quickly relayed how Edward thought Froste and de Lacy were plotting to overthrow him, and how Edward refused to even speak of releasing David until he acquired a Scottish laird with a powerful army to marry Marion. Iain relayed that he was certain King Edward also suspected nothing would stop the men from trying for the throne, but he had bought himself a distraction, time, and had effectively forced Iain to become his ally in the hope of finally getting David returned to Scotland where the King of Scots belonged.

Alex nodded. "And so the distraction Edward created is

working thus far."

"Aye," Iain said grimly. "It appears so. Now that ye ken all, tell me of yer woes."

Alex blew out a frustrated breath. "Bridgette refused an offer of marriage from the Campbell's son. I wanted her to accept as it would have helped bring peace, but she did nae feel compelled."

"And ye did nae make her accept?" Iain asked, confounded. He was glad he had brothers. Though they stirred plenty of mischief, they'd never endanger a peace treaty simply because they didn't wish to marry a woman.

"I did nae," Alex responded, his words stiff. "I vowed to my mother on her deathbed that I would nae force Bridgette to marry any man she did nae love." Alex stared hard at Iain. "I kinnae tell ye how many times I've wished I never consented to that, but when ye look at yer dying mother, it's verra hard to deny her anything. So I consented, thinking it would likely never be a problem. But Bridgette wishes to marry for love," Alex groused. "She dunnae seem to care what her foolish desire did to the possibility of peace. I explained to her that marriage is about duty, nae foolish fantasies."

Iain nodded to show his agreement, but his marriage to Catriona had been more than duty. In the beginning, he'd married her because he felt obligated to watch over her. She'd come to him after her father had announced that he was going to marry her to Gowan MacDonald, Marion's uncle, and Iain had not been able to let the fragile girl he had known for years be chained to a man known for his temper and deceitfulness. Catriona had confessed her love to Iain, and he knew his time to marry was coming, so he'd married her. Yet love had grown from duty. And now he'd wed Marion out of duty. Passion was there for certain, but the other emotion? He could not allow it again. It was a foolish fantasy, as Alex had claimed.

He sensed Alex staring at him. "Sorry. What did Bridgette say when ye told her that?"

"Only men who have never been in love spout such drivel." He offered Iain a disgruntled look. "And she said I was a cold Scot." Iain was surprised when Alex's scowl turned to a grin. "I don't mind that part so much."

"Aye," Iain replied without hesitation as he scratched at his stubble and thought about how nice it would be to wash off in the sea. That idea spawned another, one of Marion naked and soaking in a tub. He'd never bathed that way himself. His father had always said such a thing was for women and weak men, and it had stuck with him, but the idea of climbing into a pool of warm water where Marion reclined with rivulets sluicing over her skin and him rubbing soap over her soft breasts and tight stomach made his blood hum. He'd never last a night without touching his wife. And once he touched her, he'd have to take her, he wanted her that much. It was a gnawing, growing hunger.

Alex coughed loudly. Iain snapped his gaze to his long-time friend. "I was—"

"Thinking about yer new wife by the lusty look on yer face."

Iain grinned. He couldn't help it, but a grin was not an omission, and he'd rather cut off a finger than admit he'd been lost in a fantasy about bathing with his wife. Alex would annoy him about it until death took the man and silenced him. He needed to draw his friend's attention away from him and Marion, especially when he was so confused about his new wife.

"Bridgette is sweet tempered as ever, I see," Iain jested.

Alex rubbed the bridge of his nose. "She's more trouble than ever. And her obstinacy has increased with each year she ages. When I told her I considered being cold a necessity in any husband I'd allow her to marry, she threw a pot at me. I've never known a woman to have the temper of a man. She needs lessons in being obedient. Maybe yer new wife could give her some? In fact"—Alex gave him a pleading look—"maybe Bridgette could travel with ye to Dunvegan for a short visit."

Iain held up his hand to halt his friend. "I'd nae look to the Sassenach for help on making Bridgette obedient."

"Nay?"

Iain shook his head. "She's rather like a man herself."

"Why are ye grinning?"

"Am I?" He struggled to straighten his mouth. But God's truth, he liked Marion's spirit. Though, she *would* have to learn to obey him. He would never want to extinguish the fire that burned in her.

"Ye are," Alex said, his voice displaying his bewilderment.

Iain shrugged. "Can a man nae grin when talking of his new wife?"

Alex shook his head and chuckled. "Go on. I'll nae give your secret away."

Iain frowned. "What secret?"

"Ye're happy, my friend. Whether ye want to be or nae, ye are. And I want to meet the woman who has done that. But first, yer counsel on my problems if ye can keep yer thoughts on me."

"Of course I can," Iain said, contemplating what he had learned of Alex's difficulties so far. "Why do ye want to send Bridgette away?"

"Because the Campbell laird wants retribution for the

wrong to his son. If she goes with ye—"

"Ye think things may cool."

Alex rubbed the back of his neck. "Aye. What say ye?"

"I'll take her." Maybe she and Marion would become friends, and Bridgette could be Marion's ally when they all returned to his home. Knowing Catriona's sisters, Marion would need a friend, and Bridgette, with her liveliness, could be the perfect supporter.

"Thank ye," Alex said, obviously relieved. "Can ye stay tomorrow or must ye depart?"

He wanted to get home, but then he thought of Marion and the long journey still remaining before they reached Dunvegan Castle. If they lingered one more day, some of Marion's aches from traveling would ease and she could rest up for the second half of the journey. "We can stay for another day."

Alex nodded. "Good. We'll hunt tomorrow to salute our being together again."

Iain smiled. Alex prided himself in being the best hunter, but the last time they'd hunted together, Iain had killed more animals. Iain chuckled. "Does it take yer sleep at night that I shot more deer than ye last time?"

Alex grinned. "Aye, it does, and tomorrow I'll take my rightful place back as the best hunter. Yer men are welcome to come. I can leave Archibald to guard Marion, if ye're worried. He'll be annoyed, but it does good to remind him he's nae laird."

Iain frowned. "Does he try to act like the laird?"

"Nae overtly but he does subtle things, such as alter orders I've given."

"Why do ye allow that?"

"I dunnae. Which is why he's so often in trouble. Do ye want me to tell him to stay with Marion tomorrow?"

"Nay. She's like a daughter to Angus. I'll leave him to guard her."

Alex nodded and added, "I think I'll leave Archibald anyway. He was insolent earlier."

"That might be best," Iain agreed, thinking of Marion. "Trouble does seem to find my wife."

Alex chuckled. "Bridgette has a knack for finding trouble, too, so the two of them together likely need minding."

"I'm nae worried about today," Iain replied. "I told Marion to stay in her bedchamber until I came for her, so I'm certain she will."

"Well, since ye're nae worried, come to the training fields with me. Some of my men need a good lesson in humility, and ye're just the man to give it to them."

What Iain really wanted to do was go see if Marion was bathing and possibly join her, but when Alex smiled devilishly and said, "Unless ye kinnae bear to be without yer new bride for a few hours."

Iain shook his head. A strong pull to Marion already burned within him. Relinquishing the chance to see her now was the perfect opportunity to prove he was master over how he felt about her. "Seeing her at supper will be soon enough," he said, willing himself to feel it deep into his bones.

Ten

"Are you sure this is a good idea?" Marion asked Bridgette as the woman strode ahead of her and led them deeper and deeper into the woods, and farther and farther away from the castle and bedchamber—which she'd yet to see—where Iain had ordered she await him.

Bridgette suddenly stopped and whipped around to face Marion. "Do ye prefer I take ye to yer chamber to wait like an obedient dog for Iain to come fetch ye, or do ye want to come with me to see the traveling seer? Since ye followed when I gave ye yer choices, I guessed ye had a bit of courage and liked adventure. Perchance I was wrong."

Nervous, Marion caught the inside of her cheek between her teeth. She didn't think she believed anyone had the ability to tell the future, yet since she'd never met a seer, she couldn't say for sure whether she believed or not. She wasn't feeling very curious about it at the moment, though, as the shadows grew long and the sunlight faded. And she desperately wanted to remove her grimy gown and bathe.

But she'd allowed her anger at being ordered about to cause her to make a reckless decision. At least her anger seemed to be cooling, but unfortunately so did the temperature. It still would have been wiser to stay in her bedchamber until Iain returned and then talk to him. If Iain discovered she had deliberately disobeyed him, she was certain he'd be angry. The man seemed to be awfully concerned with her safety, and she doubted he'd consider it safe for two women to go traipsing alone through the woods. And he'd be right. They should go back.

She swallowed. "It's just that—"

"Ye're afeared?" Bridgette interrupted.

Marion hated to be called a coward. "No, but I am considering how angry this will make Iain if he comes to get me and we've not yet returned."

Bridgette plunked her hands on her hips. "Do ye care if he's angry? Do ye like being ordered about, then? Ye did nae seem to care for it when he did it. Yer eyes narrowed and yer face got all red."

"That is insensible," Marion snapped, irritated that this woman who barely knew her was making judgments about her character. "I don't like being ordered about, but well, my marriage has not started well," she blurted, feeling suddenly overwhelmed.

Bridgette's face, which had been set in hard lines, suddenly softened, and her eyes widened. She rushed to Marion and threw an arm around her shoulder. "I could see that! That's why I'm trying to help ye! I ken Iain. He and my brother have been friends since before I was born. I could see that ye like him but that he's still clinging to Catriona's ghost."

Marion cringed that Bridgette had discerned so much from their short encounter. "What makes you think I like him?" She didn't bother to ask what made Bridgette think Iain was still in love with his dead wife. That was obvious enough by the things he'd said, but she'd thought she'd concealed that she wished her husband cared for her.

Bridgette rolled her eyes. "Ye stare at him with the

longing of one who desires to be seen, for one thing."

Marion's cheeks burned. "Oh," was all she managed to say. She was so embarrassed.

Bridgette patted Marion on the shoulder again. "For another, I saw the way yer face fell when the clot-heid told me to get ye yer own chamber. Is he refusing to complete the marriage?"

Marion's mouth parted with shock. Is this what having a friend was like? One discussed private matters with the other? She'd never really had a friend, but she desperately wanted some counsel, and Bridgette seemed to know a thing or two about men. "Actually," she started. She cleared her throat, which made her voice come out as a cracked whisper. "We completed the marriage last night. And he made it clear then that he, er, um, desires me."

Bridgette nodded. "Go on."

Marion caught her lip between her teeth. "Maybe it's more correct to say he *desired* me? I'm so confused! And I wish I knew why I even care!" She pressed her fingertips to her temples, which now pounded thanks to her husband the clot-heid, as Bridgette had so aptly called him.

"Ye should thank God that he put me in yer path," Bridgette announced, her tone slightly smug but also excited.

Marion lowered her hand from in front of her face and looked at the other woman. "I should?"

Bridgette nodded. "I can clear the confusion for ye and help ye get Iain's attention, and then his love."

"You can?"

Bridgette nodded again. "Did ye nae see the way all the men hung on my every word?" she asked, as if it explained everything.

"I did, but do you care for any of those men or their

attention?"

Bridgette frowned. "Well, nay, but I could charm the man I do love, if only I were near him long enough."

"Who do you love?"

"Can ye keep a confidence?" Bridgette asked, a secretive smile coming to her face.

"Of course." When Bridgette looked at her doubtfully, Marion added, "My mother was a Scot. She was the daughter of the MacDonald laird."

"Well now," Bridgette crowed. "That's good to ken!" Then she pitched her voice lower. "I have loved Lachlan MacLeod for as long as I can remember."

"But you've never been around him long enough to compel him to love you back?"

"That's exactly right. Neither my brother nor yer husband will let me be alone with him because they dunnae trust I could bring him to heel, but I vow I could if given the time."

By the fiercely determined look in Bridgette's eyes, Marion was inclined to believe the woman. "I'm not saying I want my husband's love, but if I did, how do you think I could win it?"

"Well, first, ye want it and ye ken it. Ye're just afraid to admit it because ye dunnae want to be hurt. That's natural."

"Perchance," Marion agreed reluctantly.

Bridgette frowned at her. "The first thing ye must do is embrace what ye want. No one ever gets what she desires without pains. My mum taught me that. Ye must say what ye want aloud and be ready to accept the hurt and happiness that it will bring ye, nae only when ye're trying to get it but even after ye've attained it. Great love calls for great risk, but it reaps great reward." Bridgette nudged her in the side. "Go on. Declare yer desire."

Marion's chest tightened painfully. She had vowed never to try to make someone love her again as she had tried with her father, but she knew she wanted Iain to care for her and she agreed that a great love would demand great sacrifice.

She gulped in a breath. "I want my husband to love me." Not that she loved him yet, but she thought she could eventually. If he acted like less of a clot-heid and more like the man that had held her in his arms last night.

Bridgette clapped. "Dunnae ye feel better having said it aloud?"

Marion paused and considered how she felt. Her stomach was turning and her mouth was very dry. She shook her head. "I feel ill."

Bridgette snickered. "That's the beginning of the sacrifice for the love that will come."

"What do you think I should do to gain Iain's love, or even to get his desire to return?"

"What makes ye think ye lost his desire?"

"He told me he would not bed me tonight," she confessed, her face scorching. "I must have done something wrong last night." Though he had seemed to like their joining a great deal at the time.

Bridgette tapped her chin as she walked, and her gaze traveled over Marion. "I'll nae ask for details."

"Thank God!" Marion blurted, which caused Bridgette to laugh.

Once Bridgette composed herself, she said, "We must first work on yer appearance. Ye look affright."

Marion grimaced and raised her hand to her hair, but Bridgette caught her hand and squeezed it reassuringly. "We all look affright after travel. We'll clean ye up afore supper when we return to the castle. That should make him remember why he wanted to bed ye from the start. I have a gown ye can borrow that is sure to reawaken his desire, though I dunnae think a man who cares nae for a woman stares at her the way he stared at ye. His eyes were full of fire."

"Truly?" Marion asked in awe.

Bridgette nodded, but Marion thought perhaps her new friend was just being nice.

"What else besides the bath and the gown? What do you recommend?" Having a friend was wonderful. Not that Angus had not been a friend, she thought guiltily, because he had, but he was more like a father than a friend, and she could never talk to him of the things she and Bridgette were talking about.

Bridgette motioned Marion forward. "Let's talk as we walk. If we dunnae move quickly we'll nae have time to visit the seer and make it back afore anyone finds us missing."

Marion nodded and strode beside Bridgette down the dense trail that was growing deeper in shadows. As they walked, Bridgette cleared their path with a dagger she removed from her boot, and Marion thought of the dagger she'd lost in the river, the one Angus had given her. She was sad to have lost the gift, but she needed to acquire a new dagger. A bow and arrows would be lovely, as well. She'd never owned a set, though she was an excellent shot. Father had refused to allow her to own weapons. Both daggers she ever had, Angus had secretly given her.

Her musings were interrupted when Bridgette spoke. "I think ye must have done something right last night because I swear it was desire burning in Iain's eyes today, so what I think must have happened or is happening is that

Iain feels guilty about wanting ye. He's a good man, and this may be hard to hear, but he loved Catriona fiercely."

It wasn't hard to hear. That he'd loved Catriona was not the problem. In truth, it was a good thing because it proved he had the capacity to love fiercely. The problem was, his ability and desire to love that way again seemed to be gone. Where did that leave her? She hated to think that she was bound to a man for life who would never love her. And in spite of her earlier foolish thoughts about leaving him—she *knew* they were foolish—she had nowhere to go. And besides that important fact, she'd much rather stay and have a good, strong marriage.

She wrung her hands together while ducking under a swinging branch as she finally answered. "I know he loved her. And I know he thinks no one can take her place, but I have no wish to do that. He told me right before we were married that he would never love me, that he had no desire to love the way he had again."

"Oh," Bridgette said. The one word was low and accompanied by a wince. "That is bad."

Marion's shoulders sagged. "I know. There is not much hope for a future that begins that way."

Bridgette stopped on the trail, patted Marion on the shoulder, and then pointed toward a hill. "The seer is over that hill in a cave." Bridgette looked back to Marion. "I think what ye must do is first make Iain mad with desire and then show him that he kinnae live without ye and how ye make his life better. He will nae be able to help falling in love with ye, no matter what he may think currently."

Marion nodded. That seemed like good advice, except she had spent so many years trying to show her father that he could not live without her and he had never grown to love her. The idea of torturing herself in that same way made her stomach knot, but she could not deny the longing she felt. She'd always dreamed of having love and a family, and Iain was her husband now. If they never loved each other, her dream would be dead.

"I'll try," she said.

Bridgette grinned. "When I fell in love with Lachlan it was as if lightning struck me. One day, he rescued me from a man trying to seize me, and I knew then that I loved him. How did ye and Iain come to be together?"

Marion quickly told Bridgette of King Edward's decree, her attempt to escape marriage to Froste, and Iain rescuing her.

Bridgette sighed, a wistful smile tugging at her lips. "Did ye fall in love with him after he rescued ye, then, as I fell in love with Lachlan?"

"I don't love him," Marion asserted, her chest tightening. "I don't plan on being that vulnerable and allowing him into my heart until I know he is willing to offer love in return."

Bridgette snorted. "If ye ask me, ye already love the man."

"I didn't ask you," Marion snapped.

Bridgette smirked at her. "Defensive people are usually trying to deny something."

"I cannot possibly love him! I have only known the man for a few days!"

Bridgette moved around Marion and started climbing the hill toward the cave as she spoke. "I only knew Lachlan for two days afore I understood he was the one for me." Bridgette swung around and looked down at Marion from the top of the hill. "My mum knew my da only four days afore she loved him. So dunnae try to tell me ye kinnae love him yet. Love is nae only for those who have known each other for a long while. If it is, then ye may as well give up hope because Iain knew Catriona all his life."

Marion's breath caught in her chest. That was exactly what she feared, that she was the biggest sort of fool to hope Iain could ever love her with the same depth he loved his first wife. That was the real problem, she realized. She didn't simply want his love as she'd told Bridgette. She was greedy, and she'd waited all her life to be loved. She wanted him to love her fiercely and completely and with an intensity that rivaled, but was not the same as, what he had felt for Catriona. And then she could love him the same way in return.

Eleven

Marion stood at the opening of the cave, where Bridgette had instructed her to stay. A raspy, crackly voice that sounded as if it had been well used floated on the wind from within. She could hear that the seer was speaking, but she could not determine what she was saying. As Marion waited, she stared at the orange sun and watched it lower in the sky. Soon they'd be returning to the MacLean hold in the dark, and it would be much too late for someone to not have discovered they had left the castle.

"Bridgette," she hissed into the cave. "Bridgette, we must go!"

When Bridgette suddenly appeared without a sound, Marion yelped. "You Scots must be taught at birth how to move without making a sound," she grumbled.

Bridgette laughed. "Nay. They wait till we can walk," she said with a wink. Then she looked up at the sky and frowned. "I'd nae known I was in there so long."

"Well, you were," Marion said, wrapping her arms around herself for warmth. "We need to depart. We'll have to run back to the castle to get there before it's black as pitch. I just pray that Iain doesn't come for me before then. I don't think trying to tempt a man who is angry with me will be very effective," she finished, thinking of Bridgette's earlier advice.

"Ye're likely right," Bridgette said with a giggle. "Let's away, then."

Just as they started to leave, the old seer called out from within the cave. "Wait! I've something to say to the MacLeod's wife."

Marion glared at Bridgette. "You told her my name was the MacLeod's wife?"

Bridgette's eyes were wide as she shook her head. "Nay. I did nae tell her who ye were. Just that I had a friend with me."

The hairs on the back of Marion's neck prickled, and her skin tingled with fear as the seer emerged from the cave. Weathered lines and crevices marked the woman's face. Her hair was stark white, her eyes bright blue. She had high, sharp cheekbones and thin, cracked lips. She was very small and hunched, and appeared almost frail. The cape draped over her shoulders didn't look as if it would keep her warm, either, and Marion was filled with the sudden desire to bring her back a warmer one.

The woman smiled, showing teeth darkened with age. "Come closer, Sassenach."

Marion exchanged a nervous look with Bridgette. If her friend had not told the seer who Marion was, then the only explanation for the woman knowing these things was that she truly *was* a seer. But that was impossible! Yet, if it wasn't...

Marion found herself moving toward the woman as she considered the possibilities of what she would want to ask if the woman really could see her future. When she was standing directly in front of the seer, she clutched Marion's hand in her cold, bony one. And no wonder her hands were freezing!

As the seer's fingers squeezed Marion's harder, she wanted to tug her hand away, but she forced herself to stand still. The woman's penetrating blue gaze held Marion's.

"Ye're nae sure ye believe in me," the seer stated as a fact.

Marion wet her lips. "It does not seem possible that someone could tell the future."

The woman tapped one of her long fingers against the back of Marion's hand. "Ask me what ye wish. I could sense that ye did nae believe from inside my cave. Ye'll see ye're wrong."

Marion's mind raced with all she would love to know, but what if the woman told her something she didn't want to hear? And how would Marion even know if it were going to truly happen or not? Still, she blurted out the thing she wanted to know the most. "Will my husband ever love me?"

Suddenly, the seer grasped Marion's fingers so tightly that it felt as if her bones were being crushed. Marion gasped and tried to pull away, but the woman jerked her close with a surprising show of strength. Her blue eyes grew cloudy, and she stared through Marion rather than at her. "Thrice he'll stare how he feels for ye in the face, and thrice he'll deny it. But if the Fairy Flag flies again, then the love that is now but a seed in his gut will have found a way to his heart and will grow into a vine that stretches to the heavens. It will be a new love. Nae the same as any that grew afore it, but strong, true, and a blessing."

"Old lady," Bridgette hissed, "why must ye always speak in riddles that dunnae make sense? Will the man love her or nae? Will Lachlan love me or nae?"

The seer cackled. "Maybe, maybe nae. I ken the possibilities from what I read of yer actions up to the moment I hold yer hand. But after ye part with me, if ye change the course I saw, I kinnae say for certain that yer future will remain the same."

Bridgette growled in response, grabbed Marion's elbow, and pulled her away from the seer. "Waste of time coming here," Bridgette snapped. "We must go."

The seer reached out lightning-quick and clasped Bridgette by the hand. "The Sassenach will save yer life. For it, she'll demand a favor, and ye must give it to her or ye'll nae get the man ye desire."

Marion was in a daze as she turned to follow Bridgette, but the seer grabbed her arm once more, stopping her departure. Marion looked over her shoulder to find the woman very close and staring up at her. "Find a warm cloak and bring it to me tomorrow."

Marion sucked in a sharp, stunned breath but nodded. "I'll try."

"Nay. Ye must. It will bring about the first denial of his feelings for ye. There must be three denials afore he will accept how he feels."

Bridgette tugged Marion away before she could reply. Once they were a few steps from the cave, Bridgette paused. "I'm sorry I brought ye there. The woman has gone mad, I think. As if ye'd ever save my life! I'm much stronger than ye."

Marion ignored Bridgette's accidental affront. "She knew my thoughts," Marion replied, her voice wobbly.

"What?" Bridgette gasped.

Marion could hardly see Bridgette's face it had gotten so dark, but she could see the whites of Bridgette's eyes, and she knew by how big they were that the woman was stunned by her words.

"The seer knew my thoughts," Marion said again. "I thought about how thin her cloak looked and how I wished I could bring her another, and then she told me to bring her a warmer cloak tomorrow."

"I dunnae ken," Bridgette said. "Perchance she saw pity in your eyes when ye looked at her, or yer gaze lingered on the garment and she seized the opportunity to get a warmer one."

"Yes, perchance," Marion replied, not really believing that was what had happened. She wasn't sure she believed what the seer had said, either, but she wasn't sure she didn't. But she knew without a doubt that she'd find a way to bring the woman a cloak tomorrow.

"We need to run," Bridgette said, interrupting Marion's thoughts. "We're starting back much later than I intended. Do ye think ye can match pace with me?"

"Of course I can," Marion boasted. "If I knew the way back, you'd be the one having to try to stay with me, and I daresay you'd fail."

"Oh, a challenge!" Bridgette said with a laugh, and then, without warning, she turned sharply and took off down the hill. Marion burst into action after her.

It didn't take long to realize what a hazard the dark was. Marion nearly lost her footing several times when she tripped on rocks and fallen branches, and more than once, a tree limb scraped her cheek when she failed to see it in her path and bat it away. After a few minutes of racing across the craggy terrain, her breaths were coming in gasps and there was a sharp stabbing pain in her right side. But she refused to slow down and let Bridgette pull too far ahead.

Marion could tell her new friend was still close because she could hear the pounding of her shoes against the ground, though she could not see her. Darkness had so swallowed the light of day that she would not have been able to see in front of her face at all if not for the bright moon. She wasn't sure how long they'd been running, but sweat was dampening her brow and the back of her neck, rivulets running down her back. She knew the temperature was dropping from the cool wind against her face, though she was not cold. Around her, the night came alive with sounds of animals venturing out. Deep-throated croaking and shrill shrieking filled the air. Something buzzed very near her ear, and she swatted at it as she ran.

The path they were on narrowed and began to curve sharply. They must have been going along the mountain ledge they'd traversed on the way here. She'd not been afraid when she'd followed Bridgette around the ledge previously, not even when she'd looked down and realized how high up they were, but now, in the dark, unable to see where to place her feet, her heart raced and her body tensed. She held her left hand out as she ran, taking comfort from the branches against her skin and the fact that she had something to grab onto if she should take a wrong step.

"Be careful," Bridgette called back to Marion. "There's a log blocking the path, and—"

Bridgette's high-pitched scream resounded in the night, and Marion halted, her heart slamming painfully against her ribs. "Bridgette?!"

When no answer came, awful dread filled Marion and made her shake. "Bridgette!" she yelled, a terrible feeling that Bridgette had fallen over the edge filling her. She stumbled forward in the dark, clinging now to the branches on her left as she called for Bridgette. She paused every second to stop and listen and peer into the blackness below.

"Bridgette!" she cried out again, kneeling on shaking legs. She dug her fingers into the dirt as if it could save her were she to lean too far over. "Bridgette!"

"Aye?"

The weak voice came from below, and Marion's chest squeezed with relief as she tried to locate her friend. The moon shifted just enough that its light shone down to reveal Bridgette.

"Oh my God!" Marion gasped, as she stared in astonishment at Bridgette, who had one leg flung over a tree branch that was sticking out of the side of the cliff and was clinging to it. "Don't move, Bridgette!"

"I did nae intend to," Bridgette said, her words fearful, yet slightly amused.

"I'll run back to the castle and fetch help." She could see the castle ahead. It wasn't far now.

"Nay!" Bridgette screeched. "Dunnae leave me! I fear this branch will nae hold me much longer. If ye can get on yer belly and stretch out yer arm"—Bridgette looked up at Marion—"maybe I can grasp yer hand and ye can pull me up?"

Marion's gut clenched. The idea of Bridgette dangling in midair and Marion being the one with the woman's life in her hands terrified Marion, but what choice was there?

"Don't worry!" Marion dropped to her belly and slid as far as she could toward Bridgette, careful to keep most of her weight on solid ground. She stretched her hands as far as she could. "Can you reach me?"

Bridgette raised her head and one hand, but Marion could see that it was not going to be possible. Bridgette could not let go of the branch without falling, and the only way she would be able to grasp Marion's hands was if she sat up. Dread curled in Marion's belly, but when Bridgette started to softly cry, the dread turned to determination.

"Collect yourself, Bridgette!" Marion commanded, her tone stern. "I'll get you off that branch!"

"How?" Bridgette wailed. "I kinnae reach ye, and we've nothing else for me to grab."

Marion bit down on her lip, hard. If only they had rope, or cloth, or—She fisted the material of her skirts in her hands and stilled, her heart tripling its beat. "Bridgette! I've got it!" she shouted as she began to tug off her gown. "I'll hang my gown down to you, and when ye see it, grab it!"

"Ye're removing yer gown?! I dunnae think Iain will like that!"

Distraught laughter bubbled up from Marion. "I think he'll understand in such circumstances." Though she doubted he'd be too understanding about the fact that she'd disobeyed his order to stay in her chamber. She shook her head and kept her attention on her task. The rest was not important now.

Once her gown was off and she stood in her chemise, she sat on her bottom at the edge of the cliff, her legs bent to her chest and her heels digging into the dirt. This position would allow her to use the strength from her legs and back combined. The cold, wet grass made her shiver as she slid across it, or maybe it was her nerves. Whichever it was, she had to take a few deep breaths to still her shaking hands.

She carefully wrapped the material of the skirt around her hand, and then she clasped her hands together and called down. "Here it comes. Be ready."

"I'm ready. I dunnae enjoy hanging on this branch."

"Do you see it?" Marion asked.

"Aye," Bridgette called, and Marion felt a sudden pull on the gown.

"I'm afeared to let go," Bridgette wailed.

"Don't be," Marion replied in the most soothing voice she could muster. "I will not drop you." They may both go over the ledge, but she'd not break her vow, even if it meant her own death.

With a low moan, Bridgette grabbed both sleeves of the gown very slowly, and Marion instantly felt the tug on the material. "Knot your hands in the gown and try to slide toward the edge. Perchance there is rock you can put your foot on to aid you." She hoped there was.

The minute Bridgette started moving on the branch, Marion's whole body was jerked forward. She bit down on her lip, and the taste of blood filled her mouth. Spitting it out, she leaned backward and pulled the material tight, praying to God that it would not rip.

"I see some rocks I can use!" Bridgette cried from below. "I'm going to let go with one hand and grip one of the rocks, and then I'll pull as ye pull."

"I'm ready," Marion answered, her words a pant from the exertion. Sweat dripped down her brow and into her eyes, and suddenly the pull on the material increased, making Marion's body physically move. She dug in her heels harder and pulled back. Her arms and legs burned, her lip stung where she had bitten it, and her head throbbed. She heard Bridgette's grunts, and she knew every time the woman latched onto another stone because she could move a little farther away from the ledge. Finally, she saw Bridgette's head crest over the edge of the cliff.

Marion gave a great tug, and suddenly Bridgette was lying on top of her and they were laughing, crying, and panting. After a few minutes, Bridgette pushed herself off Marion and rolled onto her back.

Marion turned her head to look at her friend. She

frowned when she realized Bridgette's forehead was cut. "You're bleeding."

"So are ye," Bridgette said.

Marion raised a shaking hand to her sore lip and pressed a finger to it. "I suppose we better return to the castle."

Bridgette snorted. "I suppose ye better put yer clothes back on, unless ye want to see what yer husband is like in a temper."

"I've seen his temper," Marion said, thinking of how he'd looked when he'd come toward the men who had held her captive at the river, "and I'd rather not see it again." She shivered as she forced herself to stand and put on her gown. It had been filthy before but now the garment was a ripped, ragged mess. When she put her arm in the sleeve, she noticed only a few threads kept it attached to the dress.

"Dear God above," she murmured, thinking about what could have happened and what Iain would say if he saw her before she managed to get to her appointed bedchamber and change into one of Bridgette's gowns. "Iain cannot see me like this!"

"Dunnae fash yerself," Bridgette replied as she held out a hand to help Marion. "I dunnae want to get caught any more than ye do. My brother is already angry with me for refusing an offer of marriage. Come"—Bridgette grabbed Marion's hand—"Let us make haste. But more carefully this time."

Twelve

*I*ain strode ahead of Alex into the torchlit courtyard, anxious to see Marion. He'd not intended to train with Alex's men for so long, but every time he had tried to leave, another man challenged him, and Iain could not let a challenge go unanswered. He knew very well his pride was a sin, and the sin had cost him precious private time with Marion. She'd likely been fretting waiting in her bedchamber as he'd commanded her to do.

A vision of her asleep on the bed, perhaps not dressed anymore, filled his head and made him ache for her, so when he suddenly caught a glimpse of her coming out of the woods with Bridgette, Iain squeezed his eyes shut, certain he was imagining it. Yet, when he opened them again, she was still there.

Iain thought immediately of his conversation with Alex earlier when they had agreed that Bridgette and Marion likely needed minding when together. Iain stopped walking, and Alex came up beside him.

"What is it?" Alex asked, confusion furrowing his brow.

Iain did not remove his gaze from his wife, who had just passed by a torch and looked directly at him. Her eyes went wide, and she had tried to duck back into the shadows, her hand darting out to grasp Bridgette's.

"I believe Bridgette and Marion found trouble," Iain

said dryly as he pointed toward the two women. Anger started to simmer as he watched his wife try to crouch behind a tree.

"Bridgette MacLean," Alex roared. "If ye dunnae come out from behind that tree and bring the MacLeod's wife with ye, I'll break my vow to our mother and marry ye to the Campbell tomorrow."

Bridgette immediately popped up, yanking Marion up with her. He'd give it to the lass, he thought grimly, at least she knew when she'd been caught, which was more than he could say for his wife, who was trying to wrench free of Bridgette's hold. But though he didn't doubt Marion was strong, apparently Bridgette's fear of marrying the Campbell gave her superior strength at the moment. She dragged Marion forward and then paused after a few steps, the women whispering fiercely to one another.

"It appears yer wife may be afraid to come to ye," Alex said, amusement in his voice.

"Aye," Iain agreed, irritated that Marion was apparently fearful of him. True, he was angry, and there would be consequences for disobeying his orders, but any sort of punishment would never include hurting her. He was a reasonable man, after all, and not quick to anger the way her father had been.

When Marion tried to tug her arm away from Bridgette again and the right shoulder of her gown suddenly slid down her arm to expose her skin, all reason fled Iain and anger flared bright orange. Beside him, Alex cursed under his breath.

Iain stalked toward Marion, his gut clenching as he stopped in front of her and took in her appearance. Blood stained her lips and her exposed right arm was streaked with crimson. Bridgette didn't look much better.

Iain gripped Marion by the arm, intending to pull her to him, but when she winced, he immediately loosened his hold. "What happened to ye?"

She shot a worried glance at Bridgette, and Iain's mind leaped to a dozen vile possibilities, all of which ended with him killing whatever man had hurt his wife. A haze descended on him, his vision almost blurring.

He raised his sword. "Point me in the direction of the man who defiled ye. I'll bring ye his heart, I vow it." He cupped the back of her neck and drew her toward him, pressing his lips to her ear. "I'm sorry, Marion. I've failed ye. I'll nae ask forgiveness."

Her eyes grew wide, and her hand came to his cheek. "Iain, no. You do not understand." She bit down on her lip and winced again. "I need to ask *your* forgiveness. I disobeyed your order, and well, the truth is I do hate to be ordered about," she said quickly. "But I should have restrained myself and—"

"I compelled her to come with me," Bridgette blurted, glancing beseechingly from Iain to Alex, who had come to stand by them.

"What do ye mean?" Alex thundered.

Bridgette notched her chin up. "I needed to visit the seer and I did nae want to go alone. On the way back, I fell and she risked her life to save me."

"That's not true!" Marion said.

Iain shifted his gaze between the women, his rage receding and amusement rising to the surface. They'd obviously formed a fast and loyal friendship in the few hours they'd known each other. He was glad for Marion that she'd made a friend and gladder still that her appearance was due to trying to save Bridgette and not from harm done to her by another. Yet she put herself in danger by not listening to him, and he'd have to speak with her about that. And think of some sort of punishment. Yet the truth was, he could not imagine punishing Marion. He'd had the same problem with Catriona, and he sometimes feared it was why she'd done as he'd told her not to and swam in that freezing water, in spite of her poor health.

"Of course it's true!" Bridgette replied, bringing Iain's attention back to where it should be. Bridgette scooted away from Alex, who looked as if he wanted to throttle her with his pinched mouth and flaring nostrils. "Ye did save me!"

"No, no. I helped you save yourself," Marion said, her embarrassment obvious in her trying to belittle her courageous act.

Iain smiled behind his hand. Only his wife would be so selfless as to refuse to take credit for rescuing another.

Bridgette looked thoughtful for a moment. "I suppose that's true enough. I did do much of the work hanging over the edge as I was, and I had to find the footholds."

Iain and Alex let out a collective groan that caused both women to look at them. Iain wanted to grab Marion and kiss her soundly, but he could not let her think it was acceptable for her to disobey him.

"I require an explanation," he said in a hard, stern tone.

She sucked her lower lip between her teeth, then promptly released it with a hiss. "I know."

Bridgette cleared her throat. "Iain MacLeod, if ye're going to be angry at someone ye can direct yer temper at me. I talked yer Sassenach wife into going with me, and I ordered my maid to sit in her bedchamber and claim to be Marion should anyone knock."

That explained why Rory Mac and Angus had not come to tell Iain that Marion was gone. The men didn't know. He could hardly fault them, though. Nor could Iain lay complete blame at Bridgette's feet. Marion should have obeyed him, in spite of her new friend's compelling words.

His wife let out a small sigh. "Bridgette, that's really so kind of you to try to—"

Marion gasped as Iain whisked her off her feet. He needed to be alone with her now. Not just to chide her but to make sure she was not hurt.

With one hand under her legs and the other around her back, he met Alex's gaze. "My wife and I will be upstairs until supper. It seems we have some things to discuss." Iain could see the smile Alex was fighting, but his friend managed to keep his face blank.

"I ken. I'll see ye at supper and hopefully yer lovely wife, as well, as I've yet to formally meet her."

Iain nodded but did not bother to present her. There'd be time enough for that, and the need to touch her was making him shake. He turned to stride away just as Alex started talking in a rush of angry words at Bridgette.

Marion gazed up at him with a frown. "That was very rude not to—"

He glared at her, caught between anger for her disobeying him and relief that she really did seem to be safe now. Marion fell silent and dropped her gaze to his chest.

"Where is your bedchamber?" he demanded.

"Bridgette mentioned that it was up the stairs and to the right," she mumbled. Her small, pitiful voice made him wince with guilt that she was worried, but God's truth, the woman needed to worry a bit so she'd not repeat what she'd done.

He took the stairs two at a time, and when he came to the top and rounded the corner to where her bedchamber was, Angus and Rory Mac scrambled to a standing position from the spot by her door where they'd been sitting. Both men gaped at Iain.

"How did she get out of the bedchamber?" Rory Mac asked, his brow furrowed. The man looked at the closed door and then back at Iain.

"My crafty wife never went in the bedchamber," he growled as he set Marion on her feet. "Knock," he demanded.

Marion's eyes widened. "But—"

"Knock," he said more harshly, though he did feel bad about it. She had to understand there were consequences to her actions, and he'd just realized how to best make her see it.

Her shoulders drooped as she stepped to the door and knocked.

"I've a stomach malady," a woman called from within. "Please leave me."

Beside Iain, Angus hissed, and Marion turned back toward them, her cheeks stained with her embarrassment.

"Ye ken better than te lie," Angus chided. "And te force a servant te lie, as well." Angus caught Iain's eye quickly as if to say, *Allow me.* Iain nodded, relieved that someone else would prove the point. He was loath to cause Marion any further embarrassment.

Angus placed his hands on her shoulders. "Ye could cost the woman in there her position in this household if the MacLean decides she's nay longer worthy."

"Surely, he'd not do that!"

"He could," Angus replied.

A look of horror crossed Marion's face, and she slipped from Angus's hold and started past Iain. He snagged her by the elbow. "Where are ye going?"

"To talk to your friend and beg him not to do such a

thing."

Iain met Angus's gaze. "Leave us."

"Likely wise." Angus chuckled as he walked past them toward the stairs.

Iain expected Rory Mac to follow, but his friend just stood there with a look of amusement on his face.

"Why are ye still here?" Iain growled, his patience slipping away.

Rory Mac's smile grew to a grin. "I thought ye may need my counsel in speaking to yer wife since ye've nae had to do such things in so long."

"Rory Mac," Iain warned.

The Scot threw up his hands in a gesture of surrender. "I can see ye nae want my help," he said. "I'll just go see how Neil is faring."

"Where is Neil?" Marion asked.

Rory Mac chuckled. "The healer has told him he must stay abed, which has made him verra angry."

Marion nodded. "The healer is wise."

"Aye, but that does nae make it easier for Neil," Rory Mac replied, then turned and departed.

When the corridor fell silent, Iain faced Marion. "Alex is a reasonable laird and would nae punish a servant for following the command of his sister. But ye did nae ken that. Ye simply consented to what Bridgette proposed." When Marion opened her mouth to speak, Iain held up a staying hand. Truly, he didn't want to admonish his wife. He wanted to take her in his arms and bring her pleasure. Yet certain things had to be said for her own good. "Ye disobeyed me."

Her chin jutted out. "I'm not a dog."

He frowned. That was the second time she'd mentioned this. Something needed to change, and he was willing to admit it might be the way he was treating her. He was used to giving orders and simply being obeyed. And the truth was, Catriona had done as he'd said, until the very end, and had never questioned him. It had not occurred to him until just now that he was interacting with Marion, who was headstrong and certainly not meek, as he'd always interacted with Catriona. He'd told Marion that a wife must listen, but he would try to listen, too.

He took Marion's hand in his. "I dunnae think ye are a dog, but I see that I've been ordering ye about. I want to explain and see if we can come to an understanding."

Her eyes widened in clear shock. "You want to come to an understanding with me?"

"Aye," he said simply.

Marion threw her arms around him and hugged him hard. "Thank you, Iain."

He ran his hands up the length of his wife's small back and pressed her close until her body molded to his. Had he known that simply telling his wife he wanted to understand her would please her so—and get her in his arms—he would have told her the day they'd met.

"Why do ye thank me for wanting to understand you?" Really, he thought he knew, but he didn't want to make assumptions.

Marion pulled back and traced her finger along his chest. His muscles jumped to awareness under her tender ministrations. "My father never tried to understand me. He did not think me worthy enough of understanding, so it means a great deal to me that you are making an effort." She offered him a sweet smile that made his breath hitch.

He cleared his throat and forced himself to concentrate on what he wanted to say and not how nice she felt pressed against him all womanly and soft. "Ye must understand that as leader of a clan of six hundred men, I kinnae have my wife openly defying me. Why would they think they need to follow my orders if my own wife does nae?"

She quirked her mouth. "I can understand what you mean, but do you never take the counsel of your men if they challenge your orders?"

"They dunnae challenge me."

She arched her eyebrows at him. "None of them? Ever?"

He started to say no but stopped himself. "My brothers and Rory Mac," he admitted. "But they never challenge my orders in public. Only in private."

She grinned. "Then if I ever challenge one of your orders, may I do so in private, as well?"

He liked very much how sweetly she'd asked and had not demanded it. "Aye," he agreed easily. "But," he continued, wanting to make sure she understood, "I may nae concur with yer argument, and if that's the case, ye'll simply have to accept my choice, as do all my brothers and Rory Mac. I dunnae give orders without great thought, Marion, and today's order to tell ye to stay in yer bedchamber was for yer safety."

She inhaled a shaky breath. "I know, and I'm sorry."

He kissed her on her forehead. "I'm sorry, too."

"Thank you," she burst out and circled his waist once more to hug him.

He grinned down at the top of her head. His wife was very affectionate, and he liked it very much, and he'd like it even more when they were alone. With that thought in mind, he unwound her arms, took her hand, and opened the bedchamber door. The maid, who had been sitting doing embroidery, hurried to her feet, her eyes wide. "My lord, I—"

He held up his hand. "I ken ye were commanded to feign being in here. The matter has been settled to my satisfaction, and I dunnae blame ye. Ye may go."

The woman did not hesitate. She rushed past them, nearly tripping in her haste to get out the door. When the door shut, Marion giggled. "I feel awful for causing her worry," she said, contradicting her laughter.

"Ye dunnae seem to feel awful."

"I do," she said, smothering another laugh. "But when she looked like a fearful child, I could not help but think of how silly I must have looked trying to hide from you in the courtyard."

Iain chuckled. "Aye, ye did look silly when ye knew I'd seen ye."

"I was afraid," she admitted.

"Why?" he asked, turning her toward him and threading his hands into her hair. "Would yer father's consequences have been great?"

"Yes," she whispered, her eyes taking on a faraway look.

"Marion, I will never hurt ye."

She nodded quickly, but her eyes still appeared haunted. He wanted to wipe away those bad memories and replace them with new, happy ones. Hopefully, they could start now. "I want ye in my bed and my arms tonight, but if ye're too sore from last night or today—"

"I want to be in your bedchamber tonight, Iain," Marion said in a shy whisper. Iain's heart jolted as desire overcame him.

He gazed at his beautiful, battered wife. "I suppose I should keep ye near me to keep ye out of trouble."

She grinned at his words. "I suppose you should." Her voice was full of contentment, which pleased him mightily.

They quickly left her bedchamber, and as he opened the door to his own, she said, "I always knew following my own mind would have benefits someday."

He started to reply when a throat was cleared behind him. He turned to find a young maid. She curtsied. "My lord, the MacLean bid me see if ye needed anything. He thought ye might be alone and need help bathing yer back," she said, batting her eyelashes at Iain.

Marion stiffened beside him. He fought the desire to grin. He liked that his wife was jealous. He liked it very much, indeed. It showed she cared for him, though he didn't care for the thought that she would believe he'd ever be untrue to her. "My wife will bathe my back," he said gently, so as not to embarrass the girl for simply following Alex's orders.

Marion plunked her hands on her hips. "You can let all the maids know that I'll be the only one to ever bathe the MacLeod's back again." She glared at him, as if he'd implied otherwise. Then she whipped her gaze back to the stunned maid. "And make sure to tell your laird, as well," Marion snapped.

The woman's face went pale. "Yes, my lady."

Marion offered her a sweet smile. "I'm not angry with you, so please do not be worried. Truly, I'm a nice person. I really don't even have a temper."

"Yes, my lady," the maid said again, giving Marion a dubious look.

Iain's side ached with the desire to laugh. He cleared his throat. "It seems I cause it in her. She's verra jealous of me," he said to the young woman as she backed out the door. He shut it behind her, and when he turned around, Marion was frowning at him.

"Why did you have to tell her that I'm jealous of you?"

He did laugh then as he reached out and pulled Marion against the length of his body. He brushed a bit of her loose hair out of her eyes. "Because ye are. And she'll forgive jealousy but nae meanness."

He ran his thumb very lightly across Marion's bruised lips. She tensed but then relaxed against him. Her curves pressed against him reminded him of the night before and made him go hard with longing. He traced his fingertips down her scratched arm to her breasts and cupped one of them as he circled his thumb over her taut bud. Need pounded through him as she pushed even closer to him.

"I like that ye're jealous over me," he admitted, his voice almost hoarse with desire.

She pursed her lips as she brought her hand to his chest and laid her palm flat against his beating heart. "What about you?" she asked. "Are you jealous over me?"

"Nay."

She frowned and tried to move away from him, but he caught her at the elbow and brought her hard against him once more, so that her breath whooshed out when her body collided with his. "I dunnae get jealous ever." He just didn't want anyone to touch her or stare at her overly long, but that was different.

She quirked her mouth. "Why is that?"

"Because I am the master of my emotions, Marion. I dunnae allow myself to feel what I dunnae wish to feel."

Her brows dipped together. "How nice for you," she grumbled. "We simple humans are often ruled by emotions. Some people even think that when great emotion strikes, such as deep love, or anger," she quickly added, "one cannot control oneself."

"I always control myself," he managed to get out, in spite of the fact he could feel his control slipping away. He wanted to throw her on the bed, rip off her gown, and worship her body.

"I suppose you are not jealous because you do not wish to feel anything for me," she said, glancing down.

The hurt in her voice sliced through him. His guilt, his own tortured mind, was hurting her. He was a clot-heid. Shame poured over him as he hooked a finger under her chin and lifted her face until he found her glorious green gaze on him once more, and this time his heart jolted with feelings for her. Shock vibrated through him. For a long moment, he said nothing as he realized that the connection he felt to her had already strengthened.

"I feel things for ye," he admitted finally, "in spite of the fact that I dunnae want to."

"You do?" she asked in a shaky whisper.

He nodded. "Aye."

A loud knock came at the door.

"Who is it?" Iain demanded, irritated by the interruption.

"We've bathing water for ye."

Iain released Marion, strode to the door, and let the two boys enter with big barrels of steaming water. As they filled the wooden tub, he studied his wife, standing there nibbling on her hurt lip with her flushed cheeks, yet her head was still held high. She was a fine woman, and he was struck with how very fortunate he had been. He could have been wedded to a cold woman, indeed, but Marion was hot as a burning log, and he was glad for it, in spite of the unwanted emotions she stirred.

When the boys finished, Iain closed the door and turned slowly toward his wife. He didn't want to talk anymore, and he prayed to God she'd let it be. He didn't understand what she stirred in him, nor what he was going to do about it, but he comprehended completely how much he wanted her.

He walked slowly over to her and stopped a hairsbreadth from her. "Shall we bathe?"

Her gaze widened, and he was afraid she was going to say no, but she nodded. "That would be nice."

Nice was not what he had in mind, but he kept that thought to himself. When she started to raise her hands, as if trying to disrobe herself, he caught them in his and shook his head. "Let me," he said, moving around to her back. "Tell me what happened to you and Bridgette."

As he slowly started to undo her gown, her soft melodic voice filled the silence as she explained very matter-of-factly how she and Bridgette were racing back to the castle in the dark, of Bridgette's fall off the mountainside, and how Marion had risked her own life to save Bridgette's.

"Ye're courageous and foolish," he said, meaning it. The idea that she could have died helping Bridgette made his insides twist into a tight coil. Yet, had she not helped, he'd have thought her a coward and the behavior shameful. So he couldn't fault her.

She glanced back at him as he lowered her gown over one silky shoulder and then the next. Her green eyes flashed with anger. His wife, in spite of her protest to the contrary, had quite a temper. He liked her show of spirit. He liked everything about her thus far, except her disobeying the orders meant to keep her safe.

"What would you have had me do?" she demanded. "Let Bridgette fall?"

He turned her around to face him as he caught the soft material next to her skin and dragged it downward over her high, firm breasts, lower still over her tiny waist, and down farther past her rounded hips and lush bottom. His blood sang through his veins as he moved his gaze inch by pleasurable inch over her long legs and flat stomach back up to her eyes.

"If ye'd obeyed my order to stay in the bedchamber, then ye would have never been in such a dangerous position. But I'd never have ye leave someone in need."

He could see her jaw visibly clenching. He expected her to argue so was surprised when she said, "Perchance could we call your commands to me 'requests'?"

He chuckled. "Fine, *requests*," he answered as he motioned for her to step out of her chemise. "But dunnae ever tell my brothers or Rory Mac I consented to this."

A wistful look swept across her face. "You have a big family."

"*We* have a big family," he replied and helped her remove the chemise, out of which she had yet stepped out. She blushed and tried to cross her arms over her chest, but he lowered her hands to her sides and drank in the sight of her. "Ye're so beautiful."

She sucked in a sharp breath, which made her chest rise higher, taking his lust along with it. "You're blind, then," she said flippantly.

"Nay." He tentatively flattened a palm against her stomach and eyed her.

"I'm not in pain," she encouraged.

"I see ye clearly, Marion. It's ye who does nae see yerself. But I find I like that." He traced a sensual path to her breast with his other hand. "What did ye learn today?" he asked as he circled her taut bud with his fingers. The pink nub strained tighter and his own body felt as if he were being stretched to near breaking.

"I learned," she murmured, "that following Bridgette will likely get me into trouble." Her voice was so husky and alluring.

He'd meant to ask if she had learned anything from the seer, but he let her misinterpretation of his question pass. He wanted no more talking, just touching. He cupped her entire breast and lowered his head to trace his tongue in a slow circle around the bud.

She moaned and pressed herself into his hand. Desire gripped him in an unrelenting iron hold. All he could think about was how he wanted to suckle her and enter her. His lips found her flesh again, and he drew the bud into his mouth, aching ecstasy filling him. He pulled and released her flesh until ragged moans came from her and she arched fully toward him, making him doubt that he could control himself any longer.

He removed his clothes deftly as he continued to torture her with pleasure, and when he was naked, he released her breast only to grasp her under the bottom and heave her to his waist. He half expected her to protest, but a violent need to be inside her claimed him. When her legs circled his waist, her hands gripped his back, and her mouth pressed to his ear to beg him to take her, he lost all reason. He closed the distance between them and the door, and he took her there, suspended in air, soft perfect flesh against hard battle-scarred flesh. He entered her again and again, until sweat dripped from his skin and every nerve in his body burned with pleasure.

He did not stop until he felt he'd explode, and his seed poured into her. His body shook with the release as she cried out, and he slumped against her. Her breath fanned his ear, cool air caressed his damp back, and the realization of how he'd taken her like a rutting pig hit him.

"God," he murmured as he pulled back and caught her bright-green gaze. "I'm sorry."

Her forehead immediately wrinkled. "You're sorry? What for? That was...that was..."

He slid her body slowly off his staff and then lowered her gently to her feet, bringing his hands to either side of her waist and pinning her against the door. He'd not be surprised if she tried to run away from him, beast that he was. "I dunnae ken what came over me."

She blushed. "I'd like to think it was desire."

He felt his eyes widen. "Oh, to be sure. But I did nae mean to take ye like a wild beast. I intended to be gentle."

She cast her eyes down and he followed her gaze, watching as she curled her toes under her feet. "I like the way you took me," she said, barely above a whisper.

He was instantly hard again and so pleased with himself that he knew it to be a sin of pride, but one that would likely be forgiven since he was only so pleased because he could bring her pleasure. He wanted very much to pleasure her again. All night long, if he thought she could bear it. Perhaps, he'd ease her into the idea. He forced back the grin he could feel stretching his cheeks and cleared his throat as he stared at the top of her pale head. His wife was lustful and had an appetite for bedding to match his own. It was a new situation for him. He sent a silent prayer of thanks to God for this unexpected gift.

"Perhaps we could take a bath? I believe there's still time before supper," he said, eyeing the tub and Marion's voluptuous body. She'd tempt the devil to sainthood if that were what it took to bed her. The thought made him grin again, just as Marion looked at him.

She cocked her head. "Why are you grinning?"

"I'm grinning at ye, wife. Ye please me." He grabbed her hand, pulled her to him, and kissed her soundly on the mouth, as he'd failed to do in his desire-fueled haze moments ago. She tasted wonderfully sweet, and she smelled of wet grass mingled with heather and earth. He liked it immensely. "Come. Let me bathe ye." There was much more he wanted to do to her, but he'd bring that idea into her head one kiss at a time.

They walked hand in hand to the steaming tub. He held her steady as he helped her in, and then he simply stood for a moment and stared in wonder at the little water nymph that was his wife. She'd promptly leaned back into the water, her blond hair floating around her. Slowly, she sat up, her hair dripping and slicked back from her face. She drew her legs up to her chest and wrapped her arms around her knees as she stared at him. The water made her creamy skin glisten. She looked utterly beautiful and utterly vulnerable.

A trickle of fear ran down his spine as he thought about what tonight would have been like if she'd fallen to her death while trying to save Bridgette. His breath froze in his lungs at the idea. The realization that he cared for her too much already hit him hard, but he didn't think there was a thing to be done about what had already happened. He simply needed to be more guarded in the days to come, but tonight, he wanted to enjoy her.

He gripped the side of the wooden tub and stepped in behind her, the water sloshing against the dark wood boards and sluicing over both of them as he sat down and pulled her between his thighs and into the safety of his arms.

A small sigh escaped her as she settled against his chest and laid her head back. Her dark eyelashes fanned downward to veil her eyes. He held perfectly still, wanting the moment to suspend in time. He knew from losing Catriona that savoring such moments when he was in them was wise. He closed his eyes and memorized the way Marion's bottom curved against him, the silky feel of her skin brushing his own, and the weight and warmth of her body pressing so trustingly against his chest. Slowly, he opened his eyes and devoured the sight of her lovely legs and the delicate appearance of her arms, which belied the strength she had shown when saving Bridgette.

Marion had courage, it seemed, for everything she faced. But did he?

He squeezed his eyes shut again, a single thought drilling into his brain. He had the nerve for battle, the mettle to lead his clan, the willingness to sacrifice himself to protect anyone in his care—or anyone who simply needed him—but did he have the courage to give himself to a woman fully, heart and soul, again? He didn't know, but he suspected he'd never have all of Marion unless he offered all of himself.

Suddenly, she stirred and leaned her head all the way back until her eyes locked with his. Her pink tongue darted out to lick her lips, and then she spoke. "Iain, could I—" Her cheeks reddened considerably. "Would you let me—" She bit her lower lip and started to turn her face away, but he caught her chin and held her steady.

"Never be afraid to ask me anything, Marion."

She nodded, blinking rapidly. "Would you let me touch you?"

For a moment, confusion filled his mind. She was already touching him. Then she moved away from his chest and twisted around until she faced him. Her hand dipped under the water and came between his thighs. Her gaze drew downward to his staff, and understanding made him hard as stone.

"Ye can touch me anytime ye wish," he fairly growled,

his voice rough with barely restrained desire. "Ye never need ask."

She nodded again and slowly ran the tip of her fingertips lightly over his rod. He'd kept his silence through a thrashing during which he was tied to a post, and he'd kept his silence while having many a terrible battle wound cleansed with fire, but he could not keep his silence at her touch. A deep, guttural groan escaped him as his muscles flexed and his blood rushed through his veins. By all the saints, he swore that every drop of blood in his body went to his staff; the thing fairly throbbed with the need to be within her.

He saw the delight that brightened her green eyes. She brought her gaze to his once again. "Do you think it's a sin for me to kiss you there?"

"Nay, Marion." His voice vibrated in his ears. "I think it'd be a sin for ye to deny yerself, and me, such pleasure."

She laughed. "Well, even if it was a sin, I have to confess I'd chance it and beg forgiveness later."

"I like a bold lass."

She cocked her eyebrows. "Any lass?"

He remembered their conversation from earlier and her jealous nature. "Nay," he assured her. "Only ye."

"Stand up," she said, her voice throaty and her green eyes half-closed.

"Is that a command?" he teased.

"Aye, laird," she murmured. He stood immediately, water dripping off him, and without another word, she kneeled and clutched his thighs. Her fingers curled around his muscles as her mouth found the tip of his shaft. Searing lust exploded in him as her tongue circled him. When she took the tip into her mouth and sucked, he pressed toward her, and as he did, a pounding came at the door. She jerked back, her eyes wide with fear.

"Go away!" he roared.

"My lord, the MacLean sent me to fetch ye."

"I dunnae give a care if God himself sent ye to fetch me. Get away from my door."

Marion clamped a hand over her mouth, her eyes crinkling with mirth as merry laughter trickled from her. Iain's heart expanded within his chest, a deep happiness spreading through him. It was so foreign, so forgotten, and so surprisingly welcome in this moment.

"Laird," came the frustrated Scot's voice from the other side of the door. "Alex begs yer attendance. Archibald has returned with his report, and Alex believes ye may want to hear it. What say ye?"

A hundred foul curses filled Iain's head as he held his wife's gaze. "I must go."

"Must you?" she asked and gave him a lustful look that made him want to stay, but if Alex thought Iain would want to hear the report now, there must be news. Until he knew what it was, he'd keep what Archibald was out doing to himself. There was no sense in worrying Marion needlessly.

"Aye," he grumbled.

She looked crestfallen but didn't pout.

As he got out of the water, he called to Alex's man that he'd be down shortly, and then he quickly dressed. When he turned back to Marion, she was humming gaily and washing herself with a bar of soap that the servant had brought. He strode over to the tub, his need for her a hunger gnawing in his belly. Bending down, he settled his forearms over the edge and crooked a finger at her.

She leaned forward, but he motioned her closer until every breath she exhaled was one he inhaled. "If I'm verra fortunate, I'll be back before we must go down for supper and we can continue with yer sinful ways, if ye're willing?"

"So I was doing it right, then? I wasn't sure." Her face, neck, and even the tips of her ears flamed red.

He couldn't resist teasing her. "I think," he said, making his tone serious, "ye may need a good deal of practice before ye get it just right."

"Really?" she said, her small shoulders drooping slightly.

He chuckled as he claimed her mouth with his and gave her a long kiss. When he pulled back, he cupped her neck and rubbed his thumb over the long, delicate column. All he could think was how this woman was now in his care, and he never wanted anything bad to happen to her again.

"Nay," he said gently. "I near went mad with what ye did. I imagine I'd now be a simple fool if we'd nae been disturbed."

A smirk came to her lips. "I thought I might be doing it right by your response."

He scoffed at that and stood, not wishing to part with her but knowing he must. "I'll return soon."

She nodded and started humming to herself again as he departed.

When he entered the great hall and saw Alex looking grave and surrounded by a group of his men, plus Rory Mac and Angus, Iain knew the news was not good. He strode to the table and sat next to Rory Mac at the bench, which put Iain face-to-face with Archibald. "What did ye find?"

Archibald rubbed his knuckles for a moment before he spoke. "I thought I saw a man with a surcoat with a snake on it, but I kinnae be sure and I lost the trail. I'm sorry."

Iain nodded and caught Alex's gaze. "I'll be riding out to search."

"What?" Archibald said, sounding incensed. "I'm the best tracker here. It's insensible for ye to go. Isn't that the truth of it, Alex?"

Iain kept his calm, as Alex looked angry enough for both of them. Alex slammed both his fists against the table, his eyes narrowing into slits. "Ye overstep as usual, Archibald. And ye boast too much. Ye're a verra good tracker, but that dunnae make ye unfailing, nor does it mean another man will nae be able to find a trail ye lost." Alex turned his gaze back to Iain. "I'll go with ye, as will ten of my men. Will that suffice?"

Iain nodded. "That should be plenty."

"I'll go, too," Archibald added, his eyes darting from Alex to Iain.

"Nay," Alex said in a now dangerously calm tone. "For failing to obey, ye'll stay here."

The man's nostrils flared and his hands curled into fists, but he kept his silence.

The men all stood, and Iain, Rory Mac, and Angus faced one another. "Rory Mac will come, and Angus, ye'll stay."

Rory Mac nodded but Angus crossed his arms over his chest and glared. "Is it because I'm older?"

"Nay," Iain assured the man. "It's because I need ye to go upstairs and tell Marion that I'll nae be back as soon as I thought, and then see her to supper in my stead."

"Why dunnae ye go tell her ye're leaving yerself?" the man demanded.

"Because Marion will want to come, and I dunnae have time to argue. If I send ye, there is no time wasted when an Englishman could be getting away."

"Seems sound," Angus agreed. "I'll simply tell her ye had something to attend to with the MacLean. That way she'll nae be worried about ye while ye're gone. She tends to fret over those she cares for." Angus gave him a pointed look.

"Seems sound," Iain repeated dryly, purposely over-looking Angus's efforts to get any more information from him.

Within moments, Alex's men were ready to depart, and as Iain and Rory Mac started for the courtyard, Iain turned back to Angus. "Keep my wife safe from harm." He knew she'd be protected here, but there was a tension in his chest that he didn't like.

Once they found the trail, which was not where Archibald had told Alex it was, they followed it for hours to no avail. By the time they rode back into the courtyard of the MacLean hold, the hour was very late and Iain was sure Marion would be sleeping. After they saw to their horses, several of the men, including Rory Mac, Iain, and Alex, headed to the great hall for some drink to warm their bones. But after only being in the hall with the raucous men for a short time, Iain stood, knowing he only desired his bed and his sleeping wife in his arms.

Alex and Rory Mac both grinned at him.

"Up to see yer wife?" Alex asked.

Iain nodded. "She'll be asleep."

Rory Mac snorted. "That never stops me with Alanna."

"Which must be why Alanna is always so testy," Iain retorted.

Alex snickered, took a sip of his wine, and then stood.

"I'm to bed, as well. The hunt will start at dawn, if ye still intend to ride with us," he said with a challenge.

"Of course," Iain said. "Sleep is for the weak."

"I sleep every other night," Alex boasted. Then he bid the remaining men good night and motioned Iain to the door.

"Every other night?" Rory Mac commented, falling in step with Alex and Iain as they departed the great hall and headed toward the bedchambers. "I only sleep every four nights," he said, grinning. "Ye can be certain I'll be hunting."

As they turned the corner, they ran into Archibald, who was oddly—or so it seemed to Iain—lurking about the hall still fully dressed.

"Did ye find the knight?" Archibald demanded, and Iain concluded the man had been awaiting their return only to make sure he had not failed where they'd succeeded. Had he been stalking the corridors since the moment they'd left? Archibald was as proud as he had ever been.

"Nay," Alex said and brushed past Archibald. Tipping his hand in the air, the MacLean laird disappeared down the hall.

Iain lingered for a moment and faced Archibald, and when it appeared the man was going to go around him, he stepped in Archibald's path. Rory Mac moved to Iain's side.

"The trail was nae at the stones as ye said," Iain said to Archibald.

"The trail was there," the man retorted. "Ye must have missed it, which is why *I'm* the best tracker. Now if ye dunnae mind, MacLeod? It's late and I'm tired."

It was pointless to argue with the man. Clearly, he'd not relent that he'd been wrong or confused, though either possibility seemed odd to Iain given what Alex had said of his cousin's tracking abilities. Maybe they had missed the trail. The one they'd found hadn't been that far away from where Archibald had said it'd be. Iain moved aside and motioned for Rory Mac to do the same.

Once Archibald disappeared down the corridor, Rory Mac spoke. "He needs a lesson in humility."

"Aye," Iain agreed and started toward his bedchamber. "A man who kinnae admit he's wrong has a lifetime of problems to come."

Rory Mac grinned. "If he were in our clan, I'd be happy to teach him with my fists."

"I'm sure ye would." Iain chuckled, then paused. "I'll see ye in the courtyard in the morning."

Rory Mac mumbled his farewell, and Iain opened his door and entered his bedchamber as quietly as possible. The moonlight trickled into the space, bathing the form of his sleeping wife on the bed, and he moved toward her. Unclothing quickly, he carefully slipped in beside her, but she immediately stirred and turned toward him.

"Where have you been?" she asked drowsily.

Iain quickly told her what had happened, and he could see Marion worrying her lip in the moonlight.

"If Archibald really did see a knight, it had to be one of Froste's men," she said.

"It is likely," he said, pulling her into the crook of his arm. "But ye're safe here. Alex has increased his guards threefold, both at the stronghold and throughout his lands. By dawn, no Englishman will be able to make a move on MacLean land without encountering a MacLean. So if Froste sent more men, they'll nae have a hope of escaping."

Marion pressed up on her elbows, her long hair falling over the front of his shoulder and onto his chest. "Iain, will you tell me about David? My father never spoke to me except to order me about, and I'd like to know how David came to be captive in England."

Iain bit back a tired sigh. He didn't have the heart to deny her, though he didn't have much time to sleep. Sleep could wait. Making his wife feel valued could not.

"For years, David has been fighting to stop yer king from crowning another, a man of King Edward's choosing, as King of Scots. Do ye ken about King Edward putting his apprentice, Edward Balliol, on the throne?"

She nodded.

"Balliol was a fraud, ye ken?"

"Do you mean he made a false claim to rightfully be King of Scots?"

"Aye," Iain replied, running his hand up and down the length of her back and then lower over her delectable bottom. She sighed and snuggled back against his chest. Desire for his wife flared once more, in spite of how bone-weary he was feeling. He wondered groggily, and with a great deal of amusement, if he'd always hunger for her as he did now.

She tapped her fingers on his chest. "Are you not going to continue?"

He chuckled. "Aye. I'm sorry. Yer pretty bottom stole my attention."

She gave him a coquettish smile. "I'm pleased to hear I can distract you, and I'll be happy to distract you further...after you tell me a bit more."

Iain purposely rested his palm on her backside and then spoke. "David was sent to France for his safety for the brief time Balliol was in power. But while he was gone, his representative fought to restore David to power and succeeded. David returned in 1341 and took control of Scotland. But he was captured by King Edward when

David invaded England on behalf of the French, who were fighting the English in Normandy." He glanced at Marion, who was listening intently, and kissed the top of her head before continuing. "David is a worthy king. He loves Scotland and he wants peace with England, but he will nae lie down and let King Edward trample on him to get it."

She nodded. "Do your people love David?"

"*Our* people," he corrected her gently.

A grin spread across her beautiful face. "Yes, our people."

"Aye, they do," he replied and trailed his fingers from her bottom up toward her breasts. He traced the curve of her left breast, and she wiggled against him.

"Are you trying to tell me something, my lord?" Her voice was teasing, and he answered her question with a long, drugging kiss. The intensity of desire that sprang forth surprised him, but what surprised him more was that Marion's desire seemed to match his own, even at this late hour. Soon they were locked together in passion, which ended in them tangled in each other's arms and Iain totally sated and exhausted.

He closed his eyes, thinking only to rest them for a brief moment, but he found he did not have the strength or the desire to open them again.

A pounding at the door woke Iain. His eyes flew open and he started to sit up when he remembered Marion was lying on him. He eased out of bed, cursing the fool who dared to bang so loudly on his door. Wrapping his plaid around him, he stalked to the door and threw it open.

Alex stood there grinning at him. "I see ye're nae

ready. Are ye nae coming with us, then? Too tired, perchance?" Alex teased, while trying to peer around Iain.

Iain shoved his friend back into the hall. "I'll be there presently." With that, he shut the door, quickly dressed, then went over to Marion and gently shook her. He was about to give up on rousing her to say farewell when she opened one eye.

"Must we wake already?" she groaned sweetly.

"Nay," he said and pressed a gentle kiss to her lips. "I'm meant to hunt with Alex this morning. Ye may sleep as long as ye wish."

"Mm-hmm," she responded, her eye shutting.

He smiled and opened the door, glancing back over his shoulder at his wife, already asleep once more.

Thirteen

"How did you do this?" Marion asked later that morning as she kneeled in front of Angus and tended to his foot.

Angus's face flushed red, and his gaze flickered from Marion to Bridgette, who was leaning forward to see over Marion's shoulder.

"I told ye," Angus grumbled. "I was trying te help that clot-heid Archibald after he fell into an animal trap, and he pulled me in with him. When I hit the ground, I hurt my foot."

Archibald stood facing them, and he glared at Angus. "I told ye three times already, I did nae intend to pull ye in, ye stubborn fool. I outweigh ye! I told ye to keep yer footing. I should nae even be here," he growled. "I should be on the hunt, but the *laird* once again sees fit to punish me, though I've nae done a thing wrong."

Marion tried not to take offense that Archibald considered guarding her and Bridgette with Angus a punishment. She understood he was angry about being forced to stay behind. The two men continued to argue as Marion wrapped a cloth around Angus's swollen, rather bluish foot.

She paused for a moment, blew a strand of hair dangling in her eyes out of her face, and exchanged a long look with Bridgette and motioned for her to follow. "I'll be back in a moment," Marion told Angus and Archibald, but they were bickering and neither man acknowledged her.

Once Marion and Bridgette were far enough away, Marion spoke. "Angus cannot join me to visit the seer as intended. And I don't think going alone is wise, even with the guards about."

Bridgette nodded and nibbled on her lip. Marion had told her earlier that morning when she borrowed a fresh gown that she intended to go to the seer. Bridgette had understood and found Marion a thick cloak to take the woman. "I could go with ye again."

Marion frowned. "I thought Alex told you not to leave the courtyard today."

Bridgette shrugged. "He did, but—"

"Then you should not," Marion interrupted, thinking on her talk with Iain last night about why he gave the orders he did. Alex likely wanted her to remain in the hold because of the possibility of one of Froste's men lurking about, which was why Marion thought taking Archibald with her to the seer was now the best solution since Angus was hurt. She simply had to go to the seer. She could not explain the pull, but it was there. And as for being safe... Well, guards were now everywhere and Archibald was a fierce warrior. Besides that, she'd borrowed a dagger from Bridgette, which she was wearing in a sheath around her waist. "Would you stay with Angus so he'll rest his foot and then Archibald can come with me? Otherwise—"

"Aye!" Bridgette exclaimed. "Ye dunnae need to say more. I'd do near anything to be rid of Archibald for the day." The two women giggled as they strolled back to Archibald and Angus, who were still bickering.

Marion quickly finished dressing Angus's foot, and then

she stood and stretched, her body a bit sore from yesterday with Iain. The mere thought of the intimacy they had shared heated her cheeks and made her belly flutter. She'd woken this morning shocked at her boldness. She could not say what had come over her. Well, she could—*lust*. Her husband made her lustful. And Iain's kindness and thoughtfulness in taking the time to tell her about David made her heart throb with pure happiness. He thought her important enough to have a meaningful conversation with him. The thought made her cheeks ache to grin, but she managed to refrain. She didn't want to explain a silly smile to anyone. She sighed with contentment, then gave herself a shake. Standing around sighing would not do. There was something important that must be done.

She set her hands on her hips and hoped her expression looked stern as she stared down at Angus, who sat on a log looking very disgruntled. "You must stay off that foot today," she commanded.

"Bah!" he grumbled. He promptly stood up and then winced in pain as he stumbled backward and gripped his injured foot. He'd have fallen on his bottom if Archibald had not moved quickly and caught him.

Archibald deposited him, none too gently, back on the log. "Sit there, ye stubborn fool. When ye're ready to go inside, I'll help ye."

Marion scowled at Angus. "If you don't stay off that foot, you'll make it worse."

He didn't look as if he cared, so she decided to lie a bit. "I've seen a man lose a foot because it became so swollen that the blood stopped flowing to it."

Angus went pale as he stared at his foot. "Who?"

She waved a hand dismissively. "You didn't know him. Just a man from the village."

Angus nodded. "If I stay off it today…?"

"I'm quite sure it will be much better by tomorrow," she supplied.

"It will have te be," he grumbled as he glared at Archibald. "Help me into the great hall. Marion, ye can sit with me there until Iain returns."

"I'll sit with ye," Bridgette quickly offered, sliding Marion a knowing look.

"Ye can sit with us, as well," Angus said, not realizing that Marion intended to leave.

Marion gave Angus what she hoped was a convincing smile so he'd not argue too much. "I mean to visit the seer."

"Ye kinnae—"

"I can," she said firmly. "Archibald can come with me, and you can watch Bridgette." Marion smiled sweetly at Archibald. "Would you mind coming with me?"

"If that's what Bridgette wishes and if she vows to stay with Angus."

"It is, and I do," Bridgette instantly replied as she handed Marion the cloak she'd been holding while Marion tended to Angus. As Marion took the cloak, Bridgette grasped her hand and drew her near. "Will ye ask the seer something for me?" she whispered.

Marion nodded.

"Will ye ask her if my brother will be safe should I leave here?"

"I will," Marion replied, "but where are you intending to go?"

"With ye," Bridgette said in a hushed tone. "Ye must coax yer husband into agreeing that ye need a friend when ye go to the den of women who will be waiting to torment ye."

Marion frowned. "Who's waiting to torment me?"

"Catriona's sisters, of course. She has two, and they're going to hate ye."

"Why would they hate me? I've done nothing to them."

"Ye are a naive lass," Bridgette said, matter-of-fact. "They're going to hate ye cause Catriona is dead and ye're alive. Nae that they need any more reason, but if ye need one it's known by many that Catriona's eldest sister, Fiona, has been hoping Iain would take her for his wife."

The news that she had more to contend with than her husband not wishing to ever love again bothered her, but there was nothing she could do about it currently, so she moved to Angus and patted him on the shoulder. "Stay off that foot!"

"I'll ensure he does," Bridgette promised.

Archibald and Marion helped Angus into the hall and got him situated in a chair while Bridgette fetched him some food. Once Marion was satisfied that Angus would do as she had said, she and Archibald set out for the seer's cave.

They walked in silence for a good while, and Marion decided Archibald would likely not speak at all unless she spoke first. He seemed a man of few words. She glanced at him from under her lashes as they climbed the mountain, and he held branches back for her to pass with ease. For being cousin to Alex and Bridgette, Archibald looked nothing like either of them. Bridgette and Alex were both tall, lean people. Though Archibald was tall, he was certainly not lean. Everything about him was thick from his chest, to his neck, and even to his fingers. And whereas Alex and Bridgette both had heads of unruly hair, Archibald had almost no hair left on his head, which was surprising considering how young he looked.

"Were you reared near Alex and Bridgette?" Marion asked.

He didn't look at her as he answered. "Aye."

Marion scowled. It was going to be a long walk there and back if they didn't speak at all. "Do your parents live here, as well?"

"Nay. My mother died in labor and my father, Alex's father's brother, was killed in battle when I was but a wee bairn."

"I'm so sorry," she replied. "Was it a battle with another clan?"

"Aye, the Campbells. But my father was nae killed by a Campbell."

Marion frowned. "What happened to him?"

"Alex's father cut him open with his sword," he said, his tone cold and unforgiving.

Marion gasped. "He murdered him?"

Archibald did not answer for a minute, and Marion could see his jaw clenching and releasing. Finally, he said, "Nay. It was accidental."

She blew out a relieved breath. "That must have been awful for him to be accountable for his own brother's death."

Archibald shrugged and kicked a branch out of the way. "I dunnae ken. He never talked about it. And when I was old enough to ask what had happened to my father, Alistair refused to speak of it. And he'd ordered everyone else to nae speak of it, either." He motioned her to continue walking.

"Then how did you learn of it?" she asked, glancing to her right and over the same ledge Bridgette had fallen off the day before. Her stomach clenched with the thought of what could have been.

Archibald held his hand out to her to help her up a rocky embankment. For a moment, she hesitated, and he laughed. "I vow nae to tell yer husband ye took my hand if ye dunnae want."

She scowled at Archibald as she set her hand firmly in his. "Iain is not the jealous sort."

The Scot howled with laughter, and he continued to chuckle until they were off the embankment and headed up the steep incline. He released her hand and then spoke. "Iain MacLeod may have nae been one to be jealous afore, but I can assure ye, he is now. One but has to see his face when he's lookin' at ye to know that."

"What is it you think you see, Archibald?" Marion didn't particularly care to discuss Iain with this man, though she wasn't quite sure why. Perchance it was his claim to know so much about Iain.

Archibald didn't look back at her as he walked. "Possession burns in his eyes and wavers in his voice. I never saw or heard that from him afore. I dunnae think he even knows about it himself yet."

If Iain was jealous, it meant he cared a bit. Yet, why would he be jealous over her but had not been over Catriona? Marion bit her lip. Did that mean Iain didn't trust her to be true?

"I'm sure," she said slowly, not wanting to appear as if she were searching for answers about her husband, though that's exactly what she was doing, "Iain showed jealousy over his first wife."

"Nae that I ever seen," Archibald said. "But then, he and Catriona knew each other all their lives. Ye ken?"

No, she didn't *ken*. What did that have to do with jealousy?

She clamped her mouth shut, not wishing to talk anymore. Her mind swirled as they walked in silence, thoughts of how she'd never compare to Catriona rising up to torment her. Heavens, she could not be jealous of a dead woman! It was pathetic, and she knew better than to compare herself to Catriona. They were different, as Iain had said, but nevertheless, by the time they reached the seer's cave, Marion's stomach was a big bundle of tight knots.

The old woman came out from the cave before they could even call for her. The woman's gaze narrowed on Archibald, and her nostrils flared. Marion turned toward him and was surprised by the guarded look on his face, as if he had secrets he thought the seer might discern.

The seer motioned Marion to come closer, and when she was within arm's length, the woman grabbed her hand and pulled her even nearer. "Did ye have any more questions for me today, my lady?"

Marion was about to say no when a question popped into her head. She leaned even closer to the woman so Archibald would not overhear. "You said yesterday that Iain would fly the Fairy Flag, did you not?"

"Aye," the seer responded in a low tone, releasing Marion's hand.

"Can you tell me what the Fairy Flag is and why it's flown?" She had been too embarrassed to ask yesterday when Bridgette was present; Marion hadn't wanted to appear as if she knew nothing of her Scottish heritage, even though she didn't.

The seer motioned for Marion to move even farther away from Archibald, and when they stood inside the cave, she spoke. "The Fairy Flag is the most prized possession of the MacLeod clan. Their honor and the very existence of their clan depend on the preservation of the flag."

"Where did it come from?" Marion asked.

The seer smiled knowingly. "It was a gift to a MacLeod chief from his fairy wife. She was allowed to marry the man on the condition that she had to return to the land of the fairies after twenty years with him. When twenty years came and she had to go, the fairy gave the flag to her husband. She told him that if a grave time of need came and he were to wave it, help would come—but only on three occasions. She warned him that on the third waving, either the clan would have total victory over their enemies or would be destroyed."

Marion's stomach pitched to the ground at the implications. "How many times has the flag been waved?"

"Twice," the seer answered in a low whispery voice.

A chill raced down Marion's spine. *Twice!* "The flag must never be waved again!" she said, eyes wide with panic. She could not let him risk his clan for her.

"If the danger is great, then the laird may decide the risk is worth taking."

Marion's heart stuttered. "If you see Iain waving the flag in the future, does that mean there will be danger to the clan?"

"The need will be of the one afore the many."

Bridgette was right. It was utterly annoying the way the woman spoke in riddles. "Will the clan be in danger or not?" Marion demanded, her breath coming out in a puff of white fog.

The seer slowly cocked her silver eyebrows. "Aye," she cackled. "And ye will be the cause of the danger that comes to MacLeod land."

Icy fear twisted inside of her, and her heart was beating so fast she pressed a hand to her chest. "Me?" She immediately thought of Froste and her father.

The seer nodded. "Do ye want to ken anything else?"

Even with the cool temperature of the air, sweat moistened her palms. She trembled as images of Iain in the midst of a great battle with her father and Froste's men flooded her mind. The seer had said she only knew the future up to the point she'd touched you, and that the future could change if you changed your actions. Marion swallowed. She was too afraid to ask anything more about herself, but she had promised Bridgette she would convey her question.

"Bridgette would like to know if her brother will be safe if she journeys to the MacLeod lands with me."

"Aye. For a time."

Marion started to breathe out a sigh of relief, but the seer squeezed her arm and Marion's hair on the back of her neck suddenly prickled. The woman's deep eyes pierced her. "She'll take the danger with her, and the danger will become yers."

Suddenly, the seer pulled her gaze away from Marion and looked past her to Archibald. "Come," she commanded loudly. "Let me take yer hand."

Marion turned to see what he'd say.

He shook his head. "Nay, old woman. I dunnae wish to learn my future. Only God should ken that."

In this moment, Marion rather wished she hadn't let the seer touch her, either. She found she suddenly, desperately wanted to leave. She thrust the cloak at the woman. "I must return to castle," she said.

"Oh, aye," the seer replied. "Ye can leave, but that will nae change what I've told ye."

"Hush yer trap," Archibald snapped. "Come, Marion."

This time, Marion gladly followed Archibald, and as they started back, she didn't try to make conversation, lost as she was in worry about what trouble she might cause Iain's clan.

When Archibald cleared his throat, Marion met his hooded gaze. "Ye asked me afore how I ken what Alex's father did to mine…"

Marion nodded.

"Alex told me. It took him until I was fifteen to do so, but on my fifteenth birthday, his father died and Alex told me the story. Do ye ken, up until then, I'd imagined my father must have done something terrible since no one would speak of it? I thought perchance he was a traitor or a coward, but Alex told me he was verra courageous and his father had been tormented with guilt over what had happened."

"You must have been very glad to learn the truth," Marion said quietly, seeing the pain etched on Archibald's face and hearing the catch in his voice.

He stopped and gave her an incredulous stare. "Glad?" His hands were fisted at his sides, his knuckles white. "I was nae glad. I was angry that no one had been courageous enough to disobey the mighty laird's command to nae speak of what happened. They all let me believe my father was a bad man, that I should be ashamed."

Marion reached toward him to give him a reassuring pat on the arm, but he jerked away. She licked her lips, a nervous feeling sprouting in her belly. "I'm sure they didn't know that you felt ashamed of your father. They were simply following the orders of their laird."

He said nothing for a long moment, but he continued to walk. Finally, when she thought he was not going to speak on the subject again, he said, "I'm sure ye're right."

To her, his words sounded false and forced, but she didn't comment. She simply quickened her pace toward the castle and, hopefully, Iain.

Fourteen

*I*ain muttered to himself as he strode up the path toward where he'd been told the seer lived. When he'd returned to Alex's hold not long before, Iain had been exhausted, but his anger at learning where Marion had gone had woken him right up. He couldn't believe Marion was as foolish as to go back to the seer's when she knew Froste's men could be about. It didn't lessen his fury that she had taken Archibald to watch over her. It increased it because Archibald should have known better. The man was too sure of himself to think he was so invincible that he could take Marion from the safety of the castle.

Iain stalked up the steep embankment, aware that he needed to get control of himself before he saw Marion and Archibald. He took a few deep breaths and regarded the rocky cliff. As he was considering the best way to make his way up it, Marion and Archibald crested the hill. Iain watched, his eyes narrowing, as they descended hand in hand. Once they were on flat ground again, Archibald didn't let go of Marion. He faced her and said something that Iain couldn't hear. But even if he'd been standing right next to them, he doubted he'd have heard Archibald's words over the roar of his blood in his ears.

He would keep his calm. He repeated the thought in his head as Marion and Archibald looked his way as one.

Archibald released Marion's hand.

"Iain!" Marion cried out, scrambling toward him so quickly she slid, arms flailing, the last few paces to him. He caught her around the waist to stop her forward motion. She laughed as she peered up at him, her cheeks pink from the cold and her eyes glistening. "How was the hunt?" she asked, touching his cheek. Her hand was warm, and Iain suspected it was because Archibald had been holding it. Iain moved her hand away from his face, and unmistakable hurt filled her eyes. It normally would have given him pause, but he was livid.

"Ye kinnae be so foolish as to think it's safe to visit the seer when there is a verra real danger of Froste's men lurking around here."

Her eyes widened, then narrowed. "You said I was safe, and that Alex had increased his guard. And you also said that by dawn a knight would not have a hope on MacLean land, so don't look at me as if you're angry."

He stared at his wife, disbelieving. He had said all that, but he'd not meant she was so safe that she could go running off, and especially not without him. She was safe with him, not Archibald. "Ye misunderstood me."

"So I'm not safe?" she demanded, her eyes blazing.

Iain moved his gaze to Archibald. "Ye are safe with me, Marion. Only me. And Archibald should ken that I'd feel that way."

"Why are ye so churlish?" Archibald asked in a goading voice.

"Ye think me churlish?" Iain challenged, his temples pulsing with ire. "This is mildly annoyed, but if ye take my wife's hand again, I'll show ye just how churlish I can be. Ye ken?"

"Oh, I ken," Archibald said with a smile directed at

Marion, not Iain, which only served to make Iain angrier. "I'll take my leave and let ye walk yer wife back in the *safety* of only yer company."

Iain nodded. "That seems a wise choice."

Archibald laughed and looked at Marion again. "I'd say ye have the answer to yer question," the man said before turning and departing.

"What question?" Iain demanded.

Raw hurt glittered in her eyes as she stared at him. "You're jealous," she said, her voice coming out as a choked whisper.

For a moment, he was too surprised by her accusation to offer a response. *Jealous? Him?* The woman was daft. "I dunnae get jealous."

"I know," she groaned.

Confusion pricked him, and he ran a hand across his stubble. "You seem distraught by that."

She pressed her lips together and glared at him. "Your keen understanding fills me with wonder," she muttered.

He narrowed his eyes. "If anyone should be angry, Marion, it's me."

A flush colored her cheeks and her eyes flamed brighter. "You wouldn't be angry that I went to the seer with Archibald if you trusted me!" she snapped.

He was about to deny it when it struck him like a hard blow. She was partially correct. He would still be angry because she put herself in danger, and Archibald assumed too much by thinking he could protect Marion on his own, but her accusation was true in that he *was* jealous. He became jealous every time another man looked at her or dared to touch her. It was irrational and unlike him, but it wasn't her. It was him.

"It's nae because I dunnae trust ye," he said.

Her eyes grew wide. "Then why? Archibald told me you were never like this with Catriona."

He stilled at the mention of Catriona. Marion was right, he'd never gotten angry when a man looked at Catriona overly long or touched her to aid her, and he would not have minded Catriona asking any of his men to accompany her somewhere for her safety. But he had known Catriona all his life and had trusted her fully. He did not yet really know Marion. His gut tightened as he looked at her. He wanted to know her. God help him, he did.

He sighed. "I dunnae trust myself; therefore, I dunnae trust ye. So I suppose ye're right. I'm sorry."

He expected her to become angrier at his words, but she stepped close to him and put her small hand on his arm. "What do you mean you don't trust yourself?"

"I dunnae want to get close to ye," he admitted.

Her jaw went slack even as her body grew rigid. She removed her hand and started to step away from him, but he grabbed her arm and held her still.

"Let me go," she demanded, hurt underlying her tone.

"I kinnae." He swallowed hard. "I dunnae want to let ye go. Even as I fight against getting close to ye, ye're pulling me toward ye. Don't ye see?"

"I am?"

Her voice held a depth of hope that he feared he would destroy with his own demons. But he'd not lie. "Ye are," he replied. "I need to think on some things."

"How long do you need to think?" she asked, making him laugh.

He circled his arm around her waist and tugged her close until her soft breasts pressed up against his chest. When he inhaled, her freesia scent filled his lungs. "I kinnae say for certain." He didn't know if he could ever give her what he knew she wanted, but he wasn't going to say so and cause her undue pain. He was struck with a thought, though, that he could not keep from her. "Do ye trust me fully?"

"I do," she answered without hesitation.

"But ye were jealous, so it must mean ye dunnae trust me."

She quirked her mouth. "Not at all. I trust you. It's those women who stare at you worshipfully that I don't trust."

His chest expanded with happiness at her honesty. "That's good. A wife should trust her husband."

She frowned at him. "What else is the duty of a highland wife?"

"To love her husband," he replied, regretting the words the minute they flew from his mouth. Marion made him lose his control in more ways than one, it seemed.

A wary shimmer came into her eyes, and she shifted away from him as far as she could until he stopped her. "I'm not about to love you until you show me you can love me," she said, her voice breaking.

"That's understandable," he replied, "but I think ye'll nae be able to stop yerself from loving me." He grinned at her.

He watched as she struggled not to smile, and when her body defeated her will and a lovely smile settled on her lips, his body stirred at the sight. She tossed her hair back as she stared up at him. "You think you're that enticing?" she asked playfully.

"Oh, I do," he said, his voice husky with the sudden burning need for her. "I'd hazard I'm so enticing that ye'll let me take ye now."

A scandalous look crossed her face. "In broad daylight?

With *danger* lurking?" Her eyes twinkled as she toyed with him. "I would not be so bold."

He grinned as he slid his hand around her waist but paused when he felt a dagger sheath. He was about to ask her where she had gotten it but decided the question could wait. He brought his hand to her breast and cupped the delectable flesh. "But I would, Marion. I've been thinking of taking ye in broad daylight since the ride here. It was all I could do nae to pull ye off my horse yesterday and bury myself in ye."

"Oh my," she murmured, her chest rising with her inhalation. "You want me that much?"

"I do," he readily admitted. "Do ye ken what the motto of the MacLeod clan is?"

She shook her head. "I'm sorry to say I don't."

He traced his hand from her breast to her lips. "It's *hold fast*, and I've held fast since yesterday to the idea of being inside ye with the woods around us. I dunnae think I can wait any longer."

"Well, then, I suppose it's my duty to please you," she said huskily. "I've held fast to something, as well, Iain."

"Have ye now?" he managed to choke out, though his heart pounded so viciously that talking seemed almost impossible.

She nodded as she slid her hand between their pressed bodies and found his hard staff. He groaned as she squeezed him. "I made a vow to myself to see if I could make you a simple fool." She stared boldly at him.

"Well, I'd nae be one to cause ye to break a vow ye've made yerself," he said, deftly unlacing her gown and tugging at her bodice until her breasts spilled out.

She gasped as he took her in his mouth and tortured her until she screamed her pleasure so loudly that he covered her mouth in a kiss so the MacLeans wouldn't come to investigate. But not long after, when she took the length of him in her mouth and stroked him until he was sure he'd never have a rational thought again, it was his guttural cry that filled the woods without a care for anything beyond making the wildly tempting woman in his arms as happy and sated as she was making him.

When they were spent and they lay wrapped in his plaid, he caught sight of the dagger in its sheath, which lay beside her gown. "Where did ye get the dagger?"

"Bridgette loaned it to me so I could defend myself. As you know, I lost my other one. And I need it for my safety," she said with obvious defiance. But what did she think she was rebelling against?

He cupped her cheek. "Do ye think I'll take it from ye?"

Her gaze shifted about before settling on him once more. "You took mine from me before and told Rory Mac to not return it."

He scowled. "Only until ye did nae want to use it on me."

"Well, since it was never returned to me, how was I to know if you would truly allow me to have my own weapons? Angus had the dagger I lost in the water made for me."

He frowned. "Why did Angus have a dagger made for ye?"

"Because he's the one who taught me to use a dagger. My father would not have done such a thing with me. He would not have done anything with me, really. Besides scold me and punish me." The last words had been whispered and she glanced down.

His chest tightened, and he hooked a finger under her chin and brought her sad gaze to his once more. "What did

Angus teach ye of the dagger?"

"He taught me to aim straight and throw true. I could show you," she said shyly, "if you'd like."

"I'd like it verra much," he assured her as he leaned forward and pressed a gentle kiss to her lips. "And we can go hunting together when we're back at Dunvegan."

"You'd take me hunting with you?" Her eyes widened with surprise.

"Aye, it would be pleasing to take ye. Though, I've never hunted with a woman."

"Never? Not even—"

"Nay," he interrupted, realizing it was time to return to the castle. "Nae even Catriona. Let's dress. We can talk as we walk back to the hold."

They dressed quickly, and as Iain took Marion's hand in his when they started walking, she peered at him. "I like that there is something we will do together that you've never done with anyone. It seems as though it's just ours."

He thought about it and couldn't see how it could be a betrayal of his vow not to forget Catriona. He smiled at Marion. "I like it, too," he replied with a squeeze of her hand. "And when we get to Dunvegan, I'll have a dagger and a bow and arrows made for ye."

She sucked in a delighted breath. "I always dreamed that my father would one day come upon me and see how talented I was with a dagger and the bow, and then perchance he would be filled with such pride that he'd not even be angry that Angus had taught me. And then," she gushed, her words quick as she was caught up in her memories, "he would finally find me worthy of loving."

Her admission of her dreams was like a dagger plunging into his gut. He stopped walking and looked at her. "Ye are worthy of loving." He knew damn well his words would sound false to her, given what he'd told her before, given his own struggles. "It is nae ye but yer father who is nae worthy."

He gave her a long kiss, trying to imprint that knowledge in her head. "Nae ye," he said once more and started them walking again.

For a long moment, she said nothing, and then, very quietly, she said, "Then it seems being worthy of love does not assure anyone wants to give it to you."

He could not respond because she was right, yet every part of him rebelled against agreeing.

After a lovely feast that night, they arose early the next morning to depart for Dunvegan. They had a road journey, as well as a sea journey, ahead of them, yet Marion was already anxious about going to Iain's home, given what Bridgette had told her of Catriona's sisters. But Marion also had a sense of newfound hope. At dinner the night before, Bridgette had asked her brother if she could go to Dunvegan with Marion to help her adjust to life in the Isle of Skye, and he'd thought it an excellent idea. Marion had been surprised by his easy agreement, until Iain told her later that night about how Alex had spoken to him the day they'd arrived, requesting that he take Bridgette for a time to allow a cooling period for the Campbell she'd snubbed.

Marion was thrilled that Bridgette was coming but not so thrilled that Alex had appointed Archibald to accompany Bridgette to Dunvegan. He was to keep her out of trouble. Astonishingly, Archibald didn't oppose the duty. The man had actually seemed unconcerned, though he may have hidden his annoyance well, since he did leave dinner early.

As they were packing the horses to depart, Marion realized Archibald had not come down from his bedchamber, so when he rode into the courtyard from the direction of the woods, she was stunned to see him.

"Where have ye been?" Alex demanded.

Archibald scowled. "Can a man nae even say farewell to a lass without being challenged?"

Alex blinked in clear surprise. "I did nae ken ye had a lass. Who is it?"

"Ye dunnae ken her," Archibald said, rather evasively.

Alex waved a dismissive hand at Archibald. "Fine. Keep yer secrets. Ye may take them with ye."

"I will," Archibald grumbled.

Iain and Rory Mac exchanged a wary look. They didn't seem to want Archibald to come any more than Marion did, and suddenly she felt bad for the Scot. He seemed to be an outlander in his own home, just as she'd been.

With that in mind, she walked toward his horse and looked up at him. "Archibald, I'm glad you are coming with us." She searched her mind for a nice compliment to give him. "You increase our group's strength and defenses, and that is always a good thing."

Archibald gave her a surprised look, but then he offered a small smile. "Thank ye, Marion."

Iain came up behind her and set his hand on her shoulder. "She's right. Ye do aid us, and we welcome that. My wife is wise."

Marion turned and beamed at him. He'd complimented her in front of everyone. Things were going so well between them now that Marion's hope swelled a little further.

It only took a few more minutes for everyone to say their farewells, and then they were bound for her new home, where she would hopefully feel as if she belonged.

As the rough sea made the birlinn dip continuously, Marion's weary body felt as if she had abused it with a month of travel, though in reality, the trip from the MacLean hold to the farthest reaches of Scotland had been two and a half weeks. But the breakneck pace at which Iain had ordered the crew to row, in spite of the turbulent waters, had left her battered, bruised, and seasick. She'd tried to appear brave so that Iain would not know just how uncomfortable she was as she sat huddled in his plaid, but the God's truth was that she was afraid she'd never be warm again. Yet, she had to stay in the fresh air, rather than seek shelter, or she would most assuredly become sick again. Even now, her stomach roiled.

The Isle of Skye and Dunvegan Castle could not come into view soon enough for her. The chill from bathing in the icy rivers and sleeping outside in the winter-kissed highland air, followed by the chill from the constant breeze blowing off the water and being sprayed when the boat dipped had settled a cold deep into Marion's body.

She seemed to be the only one bothered by the weather or freezing water, however. Iain had slept with his chest bare every night of their journey, and she was certain the only reason she'd not perished from the freezing temperatures was because she fairly burrowed into him until he wrapped his arms tight around her. His body gave off heat like a fire, and she did her best to drink that heat up.

Yet, it wasn't just Iain who had appeared unaffected by the weather; it seemed all Scots were oblivious to it, from Angus, Neil, and Rory Mac to Archibald and Bridgette.

Bridgette had even hummed when they'd bathed in the frosty river, and at this moment, she stood at the front of the birlinn without a cloak, her red hair whipping in the wind. Marion's teeth chattered so strongly that even if she'd wanted to join in on the humming, her frozen lips would likely fail her.

She frowned as she tried to curl into a tighter ball under Iain's plaid. The birlinn dipped sharply, reminding her it wasn't just the way the cold had affected her that seemed to separate her from the others. They didn't seem a bit queasy. None of them. She couldn't understand it. No one had retched over the side of the birlinn except her, and when they'd been on horses before taking to the water, the others had not asked Iain to stop so they could relieve themselves. Again, only her.

When she finally requested he stop, she'd seen the amusement in all eyes but Iain's. He'd looked exasperated. And when she'd heaved over the side of the boat, they'd all made comments that it was to be expected, as if her being half-English made her inherently weak. Even Bridgette and Angus, who should have been squarely on her side, made the comments. Only Iain had said nary a word. He'd watched her with wary eyes, though, as if he expected her to fall over and die at any moment.

The birlinn dipped yet again, and this time a spray of water came over the edge and drenched her. She had to clench her jaw until pain shot through it to stop the violent chattering of her teeth, which she was sure everyone could hear even above the hum of the rowing men. She was not weak; the Scots simply were not normal.

The birlinn entered the loch with the ship that was transporting the men's horses directly behind it. Soon someone called out the sighting of land. Marion peered out from the plaid and then parted it, her eyes going wide at what she was sure must've been Dunvegan Castle.

"Iain," she called loudly over the noise of the water, oars, and sudden chatter of everyone on board.

Iain glanced over his shoulder from where he stood a few feet away, frowned, and then made his way to her, concern etched on his face. "Are ye going to be sick again?"

"No," she said, willing it to be so, even as her stomach roiled. "Are we home?"

"Aye, Marion," he said, his voice catching. "We're home."

She parted the plaid more and an icy wind caressed her cheeks, but she left the garment open, entranced at the sight of Iain's home. Dunvegan Castle sat like a crown high atop the steep rocky cliffs of the seashore. Its stone walls seemed to reach Heaven itself. It sat very near the edge of the bluff, and as she stared at the square keep and the turreted tower, she inhaled a sharp breath. The high land the castle stood on was completely surrounded by a curtain wall, and it appeared the only entrance was through the seagate.

"What is it?" Iain asked her, taking her hand in his.

Instinctively, she curled her fingers around her husband's hand. "I thought my father's castle was surely the most impenetrable, but Dunvegan would be impossible to breach. You'd see your enemies coming long before they reached you."

He squeezed her hand. "It is as close to invincible as a home can be, but there is nae a place anywhere that is invincible."

She looked at him. "How would anyone get inside?"

"By drawing us out," he said simply.

As the birlinn glided closer to shore, Marion thought

she heard pipers playing. "Is that—"

"Aye," Iain interrupted. "They're welcoming us home."

"Us?"

"Me and Rory Mac," he replied. "But when they learn of ye and our marriage, they will welcome ye, as well."

She did not miss the steely determination beneath his words. "Iain," she said hesitantly, trying to determine the best way to ask him to let her try on her own to befriend his people.

"Aye?"

"I am a bit concerned about your clan liking me."

"Dunnae worry," he replied. "I'll command them to do so."

She bit her lip. It was just as she thought. She loved that he wanted to keep her safe, but his actions would actually make the task harder for her. She was sure of it. "Iain, you cannot command them to like me. They will resent you—and me—if you try to make them accept me directly. I beg you to let me win their friendship on my own."

She watched his eyes narrow. "There are some that may nae be nice to ye if I dunnae command it."

"Are you referring to Catriona's sisters?"

"Aye," Iain replied. "Her mother has passed. How do ye ken of her sisters?"

"Bridgette told me, but I can defend myself," Marion stated firmly, feeling more sure of herself than she ever had before. Being away from her father and with Iain, who truly offered her respect, had helped her to see that it was not her duty to constantly try to prove she was worthy of admiration, but for others to see her worth and recognize it. And if she'd not broken under years of her father's harsh treatment, two women would not defeat her. She also had Bridgette as an ally.

Iain studied her for a long moment and finally nodded. "I'll let ye try," he said.

She exhaled with relief.

"But," he added, causing her to tense once more, "if anyone gives ye any trouble at all, ye will come to me, tell me, and let me attend to them. Ken?"

She understood, but she'd never utter a word if someone was unkind. She would simply get them to like her by meeting their dislike with care. She wanted Iain to see that she could manage without help. What she did not want, above all, was him thinking he needed to worry about her or protect her every moment. He'd never relax around her enough to let her close if he was anxious about her.

"Marion, did ye hear me?"

"I did. I understand," she replied, without actually agreeing.

Iain squeezed her hand. "Verra well. Ready yerself."

She laughed. "You act as if we're about to be descended upon."

He stood and brought her to her feet with him. "It will nae be long," he said looking up toward the castle.

Marion followed his gaze through the growing darkness and up, very high, beyond the battlements. On the barmkin, blazing torches suddenly appeared, and the sound of the pipers floated down the seawall stairs in clear notes. By the time the birlinn reached the shore, was secured, and they left the ship, hundreds of torches made a long, curving line down the stairs.

The mist seemed to part as the first torches came near. Three tall men led the line, their heights and steps matching, making them seem almost as one person. Their plaids flapped with the force of their strides as they walked.

The man in the center moved ahead of the others and reached Iain first.

"Brother," his voice, though deep, was crisp and clear. "It's good to have ye back. And Rory Mac, as well. And Neil," the man said in surprise, then looked quizzical. "And is that Bridgette MacLean?"

Bridgette moved to Marion's side, dropped into a curtsy, and gave the man a coquettish smile. "Yer eyes dunnae deceive ye, Lachlan MacLeod. 'Tis me."

"It's good to see ye, Bridgette," he said politely and turned his attention to Archibald, who stood behind Marion. "And who are ye?"

Iain stepped forward and clasped Lachlan on the forearm. "Ye remember Archibald, Alex's cousin?"

"Aye. Welcome, Archibald."

Archibald offered his greetings, and then Iain quickly presented Angus without much explanation, which Lachlan accepted without protest, but Marion could hear murmurs from the men behind him.

"It's good to be back," Iain exclaimed. "I missed home."

A look of mischief swept across Lachlan's ruggedly handsome face. "Did ye now? Are ye getting soft, then?"

Iain chuckled. "Nay, but the food in England is awful—"

"Worse than here?" Lachlan asked with a chuckle.

Iain scowled, but it gave way to a smile. "Aye, I ken it seems hard to believe."

"And the women, were they too ugly for ye to bed?" asked the man on Lachlan's right, the only one with light hair.

As Angus growled behind her, Marion stiffened at the comment and at the laughter that erupted from the group of men that she suspected were Iain's brothers. These men—the blond-haired one, Lachlan, with his deep russet locks, and the dark-headed man—matched Iain in height and had eyes of the same shape.

"Cease talking, Cameron," Iain snapped at his fair-haired brother, even as he reached out and clasped him affectionately by the forearm.

"Why? Is it nae the truth?" the Scot demanded, laughter in his voice. "Are yer bollocks now aching for a highland lass's touch?"

"If they are," the man with the shoulder-length brown hair said, as he stepped forward and gripped Iain by the arm Cameron had just released, "then I say *finally*."

Iain's three brothers nodded as one, and the dark-haired man grinned. "Fiona has done naught but annoy me constantly about when ye may be returning. She's fairly itching to take her sister's place as yer bride."

"Then she will be disappointed to hear what I have to say, Graham," Iain said, his voice cold.

"What?" Graham asked, clearly startled.

"What do ye mean?" Lachlan demanded, appearing more irritated that he didn't know of the news already than he did surprised.

"What do ye have to tell us?" Cameron asked and grinned as his gaze came to rest on Marion.

She drew herself up to her full height and squared her shoulders, just as the first wave of MacLeods bearing torches reached them. A woman with bland brown hair and small beady eyes smiled before casting her gaze down. Another woman, beautiful and dark-haired with golden eyes, stared straight at Iain with a more-than-welcoming look.

Marion narrowed her gaze as Bridgette briefly squeezed her hand. The golden-eyed woman had to be Fiona.

Iain looked behind him and held his hand out to Marion. Holding her head high, she stepped forward and slipped her hand into his. He drew her to his side in a way that seemed to be proud. She could not stop her smile. "This is my wife, Marion, of the house de Lacy," he announced in a loud voice that instantly silenced all talk around them.

Marion heard several sharp inhalations of breath, and then the beautiful woman spoke.

"Were ye forced to marry the Englishwoman?" she demanded, her gaze settling on Marion and filling with disdain.

Iain slid his arm around Marion's shoulders and hauled her to his side as she held the woman's gaze. Iain gave Marion a squeeze. "Fiona, ye ken better than to ask such a foolish thing. No man could ever force me to do anything I did nae wish. I wed Marion of my own free will."

Marion would have kissed him for his proclamation if it would not have shocked everyone.

The woman tossed her long dark hair over her shoulder. "I dunnae believe it," she mumbled under her breath, but loud enough that Marion heard her. She was sure others had, as well, because she saw several men stiffen. The woman shook her head as she glared at Marion. "Catriona must surely be wailing in her grave."

Iain's body went rigid against Marion, and he inhaled a long, deep breath before he spoke. "Yer sister is nae wailing in her grave because she's dead."

The barely controlled anger in his voice made Marion bite her lip. She wanted to do something to diffuse the building discord, so she stepped forward and dipped a quick curtsy. "I'm pleased to meet you."

Fiona raked her gaze over Marion. "Ye will nae take the place of my beautiful, sweet sister." Fiona took a deep breath, preparing to say more, Marion suspected, but then

Iain spoke.

"Hold yer tongue, woman," he growled. "I've nae the patience for such nonsense tonight."

She grimaced and turned as if to leave, but the homely woman beside her gripped Fiona's arm. "Ye should make yer greetings to the laird's wife," she said, finally looking up once again. Her brown eyes rested momentarily on Marion, but then settled on Iain, who smiled at her.

"Elspeth is right, Fiona," Iain agreed.

"Welcome," Fiona said bitterly.

Marion smiled and prayed it appeared gracious. "I hope we can become friends."

Fiona stared at her in stony silence, flicked her gaze to Iain, and then turned and shoved her way through the silent crowd. The whispers started immediately afterward, and would have likely grown to a dull roar, but Elspeth moved toward Marion and said in a loud voice, "I'm glad ye're here, my lady. I can see by yer beauty why the MacLeod wed ye."

From somewhere in the thick crowd a woman called out, "I guess ye won't last through yer first highland winter."

Iain made a disgusted noise from his throat, and Marion caught his gaze, beseeching him with her eyes not to punish whoever had spoken. He inclined his head in understanding, and she spoke in a loud clear tone. "I'm half-Scottish. My mother was a MacDonald, I'm not weak, and I *love* the cold."

Bridgette poked her in the side at the bold-faced lie about the cold, and behind her, she was fairly certain Angus was coughing to cover up his laughter.

Iain leaned close to Marion and whispered in her ear, "Ye did well. That was Alanna who spoke out from the crowd. She is Fiona and Elspeth's cousin and Rory Mac's wife. She was also Catriona's closest friend. The rest of them should be more pleasant."

"The rest of them?" she asked, suddenly afraid he meant she was to greet the whole gathered crowd. Pray God, not each one of them. She was exhausted.

"Aye." He waved a hand toward the crowd. "They'll be expecting to meet ye now that they ken of ye."

"Now?" she whispered. "I likely look horrible."

"Nay." He brought her hand up between them and kissed her fingertips. Sparks shot from the point of contact through her entire body. His hot breath caressed her skin as he spoke again. "Ye look like ye could make a man a fool."

Before she could respond, he abruptly dropped her hand and stepped forward. "It's good to be home!"

A deafening cry arose from the crowd, and by their happy faces, she knew Iain was beloved. When the noise faded, he spoke once more. "As I'm sure ye heard moments ago, I've married. This"—he swept his hand toward her—"is my bonny bride, Marion."

More cheers, but these sounded less enthusiastic. She lifted her chin a notch and kept her gaze on Iain, who raised his hands to quiet the crowd. As he was waiting for them to quiet, Bridgette surprised Marion by stepping around her and whispering in Iain's ear.

Iain grinned and nodded his agreement, then said, "In honor of Marion, we will have a feast tonight!"

Cheers and thundering applause exploded, and as Bridgette came back to Marion's other side, Marion gave her a look of thanks, to which Bridgette winked. Marion did not have time to catch Iain's gaze to thank him, however, as his brothers came forward and greeted her one by one with welcoming, crushing embraces. If they were not happy about Iain's marrying her, she could not tell. She could not say the same for the rest of Iain's clan. The men were generally friendly, except for a few of them, but the women were cool at best.

Marion dragged herself up the seagate stairs a good deal later and followed a stone-faced servant to Iain's bedchamber. Hers would need time to be prepared, for which she was actually quite glad. She eyed the enormous bed sitting on a dais in the center of his room, and a physical ache to lie down and sleep came over her.

Marion's eyes burned, but as the servant woman promised to bring up water for her to bathe, she surveyed the room and dazedly took in her husband's bedchamber. A beautiful tapestry hung over his bed, and there were two matching chairs in the right corner with a table between them. Marion stared at the table where something lay, and her gut twisted with the realization that she was looking at an unfinished tapestry of embroidery.

"That was my lady Catriona's," the servant quickly supplied. Marion had been concentrating so hard on trying to determine what she'd been looking at that she jerked at the woman's words.

The woman hurried past Marion and stopped at the tapestry. "I'm sorry, my lady. If I'd known the MacLeod was going to bring home a new wife, I'd have cleaned the room. I did try afore, but he forbade me clearing any of her possessions." The servant snatched up the tapestry. "I'm sure he'll want me to gather them now, though."

"I'm not so sure," Marion replied, a mixture of hope and insecurity flowing through her. She certainly did not expect Iain to remove Catriona from his room and heart, but if he could make space for Marion she could bear it. Still, the clearing of Catriona's things would be his to do—and only when he was ready. "You should leave them."

The woman's eyes rounded, but she dropped the tapestry and hurried from the room, mumbling that she'd be back shortly with water. Marion eyed her surroundings. She knew Catriona had been dead two years now because she had asked Angus, but it was painfully obvious standing among her things just how greatly Iain still mourned his dead wife. What else of Catriona's remained? Suddenly, Marion had a burning desire to know. She strode over to a trunk and, with some effort, opened it. Gowns, dainty slippers, and a hairbrush and hair combs filled the trunk. A short inspection of the rest of the room revealed that the tapestry had been the only thing left out. Everything else of Catriona's appeared to be in the trunk.

Marion walked slowly to the table and picked up the embroidery. Two intertwined hearts had been stitched on the fabric, along with the Gaelic word *daonnan*, which meant *always*. She knew the word because Angus had taught her a bit of the language.

Marion swallowed the large lump in her throat. Had Catriona known she was dying and wanted to leave something behind for Iain to look upon and think of her? It seemed likely so, but the woman must have known she didn't need to leave anything. Iain would never forget his first wife, and Marion would not wish it to be any other way.

Before she could contemplate it more, a knock came at the door, and Marion opened it to find two young servants. She quickly directed the boys to bring in the wooden tub and buckets of water they carried. Once everything was set up, they informed Marion supper would be served shortly and told her where the great hall could be found.

Marion hastily bathed, washed her hair, and combed it out, and then she sat on the bed to rest her eyes for a moment. A few minutes later, she was lying on her back and snoring soundly.

Fifteen

Marion woke with a start and a yelp. Bridgette loomed over her in the darkness that filled the room, except for the candelabra Bridgette held, which lit her face in an orange glow. "Well," Bridgette said, eyeing Marion with a smile, "this certainly explains why ye've not come for supper."

Marion glanced down and gasped as she realized the linen she'd wrapped around her body when she'd gotten out of the tub had slipped down to her stomach. She snatched it up. "You could have said something," she grumbled, heat making her cool skin instantly burn.

"I just did," Bridgette replied with amusement. "I've the same parts as ye. Now, be quick. Supper has been on for some time now, and your absence has been noted."

Marion leaped to her feet. "Did Iain send you to get me?"

"Nay. Angus did."

Marion frowned. "Surely Iain sees I'm not there."

"Well, Lachlan does nae seem to see I'm there at all, so maybe it's a problem with all MacLeod men. He's nae even given me a proper greeting, and I dressed in one of my finest gowns for him. I had some created in a fashion I saw at a fair, more like the one ye were wearing when I met ye but nae so loose. It does nae seem to matter, though. I could prance through the hall naked and Lachlan MacLeod would nae see me," Bridgette grumbled.

"You look lovely," Marion offered, eyeing the rumpled, travel-worn gown that lay out on the bed, the one that Bridgette had loaned her at the MacLean hold. Her skin itched with the thought of putting on the gown so stiff with dirt.

Bridgette snickered, and Marion looked at her friend, who was motioning to the chair in the corner. "I brought ye a clean gown. I thought ye might nae wish to come down in the other one."

Marion hugged her. "You are so kind."

"Come." Bridgette waved her to the chair. "It's one of my new gowns, I like ye that much."

Happy tears pricked Marion's eyes. She had a friend. She had a husband that was kind, brave, respectful, and seemed to be softening—she hoped—and now she had a home where she would, with good fortune, never feel like an outlander again.

Bridgette held up the gown, and Marion slipped into it. With Bridgette's help, she was laced quickly, and then Bridgette stepped back.

"Ye look stunning!" she exclaimed.

Marion was about to thank her, but Bridgette's sudden fierce frown stopped her.

"What is it?" Marion asked, reaching for her friend.

"Ye look so bonny that Lachlan will likely stare at ye the rest of the night and still nae see me."

Marion could feel the blush on her cheeks. She waved a hand at Bridgette. "That's silly. You are a vision."

Bridgette quirked her mouth. "I ken!" she said with a giggle. "Which is why I kinnae understand why the one man I want to see me dunnae. All these other men fall over themselves to be near me, except Lachlan. It's as if he does nae even ken I'm there."

"You poor, poor thing," Marion cooed sarcastically. "It must be difficult to be wanted by many."

Bridgette scowled. "I ken how I must sound, but having a pretty face has nae been to my benefit, as much as ye may think. No one pays me any heed when I speak, and what benefit is a pretty face if the only man ye want does nae seem affected by it?"

"I understand," Marion replied. She linked her arm through Bridgette's. "We will simply have to come up with a plot to get Lachlan to see you. But right now, I'm starving and I don't want to miss my opportunity to eat supper."

Bridgette's eyes grew wide. "We must make haste! Once they put the food out, Scots—men and women both—tend to fall on the trenchers as if they've nae eaten in a year. If we're fortunate, they've nae brought out the rest of the food yet."

"And if we're not fortunate?" Marion inquired.

"Then there will likely be nothing left and we'll have to either ask the kitchen women for more, or if it's like my home, we'll go to the kitchen later and slip our own food out of the stocks."

"If there's none left, I'd rather procure my own food than put anyone to any more trouble," Marion said.

"I feel the same way. Come." Bridgette tugged her out the door and toward the stairs. "Let us hope that tonight we are fortunate."

Marion nodded and hurried down the stairs with Bridgette to the great hall below.

With the general merriment in the great hall, combined with Iain's growing concern that Marion had not yet shown for supper and the fact that he could see Fiona and Alanna whispering at the long table to the right of the dais, he missed what Lachlan had said to him. He only knew Lachlan had addressed him at all when his brother gave Iain a half-exasperated, half-amused look.

Iain took a long drink of his wine, trying to force himself to attend to his surroundings as he usually did. "What did ye say?"

"I asked if we should be expecting trouble from the knight yer wife was supposed to marry."

Iain didn't need to ponder his answer. "Aye. And from her father, as well."

"Her father?" Lachlan asked, incredulity saturating his words. "Should we nae call her father an ally now that ye married his daughter?"

Iain shook his head. "Baron de Lacy wanted her to wed Froste and would have defied the orders of his king to make it so."

"But why?"

Iain sat back as a serving wench appeared before him. "Laird, it's good to have ye home," she said.

"Thank ye." He nodded as she set the trencher of meat before him. She leaned forward, licked her lips, and batted her eyes in invitation. Iain turned away only to find Lachlan eyeing the wench. Iain gave his brother a hard kick under the table.

"What was that for?" Lachlan demanded, his face flushing red.

"Do ye nae think it's time to commit yerself to one lass?" he hissed.

Lachlan's jaw tensed. "I would if the right lass were

willing."

"I'm willing," the serving girl said with a giggle.

"Return to the kitchen, Lillias," Iain said evenly.

"Why'd ye do that?" Lachlan demanded, as Lillias walked off, swaying her hips. "Are ye jealous because she turned her sights to me so quickly?"

"Nay. I dunnae wish for anyone but my wife. And ye ken as well as I do that Lillias is nae the right lass for ye, so dunnae trifle with her emotions."

Lachlan drummed his fingers on the table and smiled devilishly. "If I trifle, I'll make sure she knows I dunnae wish to marry her. Will that suffice, *laird?*"

Iain grunted. "I suppose. Why do ye nae find a lass who ye could care for?"

Lachlan scowled. "Who says I have nae but that she's nae willing?"

"What do ye mean?" Iain asked.

Lachlan scrubbed a hand over his face and glanced to his side, where Graham sat in conversation with Cameron. When Lachlan turned back to Iain, he wore a guarded expression. "Nothing. I mean nothing."

Iain was about to question his brother further when a frenzy at the entrance to the great hall captured his attention. Whistles came from a table near the front, and one of the benches scraped the floor as several of the younger, rowdier of Iain's men seemed to be good-naturedly fighting among themselves to get to whomever was coming into supper. Within seconds, Broch, one of the larger of his fighting men, walked through the crowd, Bridgette on one arm and Marion on the other.

Iain's breath caught deep in his chest as he stared at his wife. Her pale blond hair framed her creamy face, and her eyes shone blindingly green like two luminous stones. Her red lips beckoned to be kissed, and her gown... He clutched the edge of the table as desire raged through him. Her rich blue gown clung to her curves and pushed her breasts upward, invitingly and teasingly. He'd never seen a gown cut as low and tight as hers. Lust and jealousy seized him in an iron grip. He shoved his chair back and ignored Lachlan's gaping stare.

Iain circled the table in one stride and stood before Marion in three more long steps. Holding out his hand to her, he said, "Ye're late." Jealousy, which he rationally knew to be misplaced, was there and getting the better of him.

Marion's brows dipped together. She released Broch's arm while thanking him and slipped her arm into the crook of Iain's elbow. "So you did see I was not here."

"Of course," he replied. "If ye'd nae appeared in a minute, I was going to go ensure ye were fine."

Marion grinned.

"Come sit by me," he said. "I'm sure ye must be hungry."

***

Marion eyed the seats at Iain's table. All of them were taken by his brothers. Broch was seating Bridgette at a table. There was one seat empty beside her. The seats around Bridgette were occupied by Catriona's sisters, Rory Mac, and a woman Marion assumed was Rory Mac's wife, Alanna.

Marion took a deep breath. This could be the perfect time to get to know Catriona's sisters and extend an olive branch. "I'll sit by Bridgette."

Iain frowned. "It's traditional for the laird's wife to sit

at the head table." Iain's jaw set with obvious determination, making Marion smile. She was pleased he wanted her near him. If it were not for the fact that she believed earning the friendship of Catriona's sisters and cousin would ease her entry into Iain's clan, she would have gladly taken the seat beside him.

"All the seats are full," she replied.

"Cameron knows to move now that ye've arrived. They were simply telling me about what happened in the clan while I was away."

"Iain, I'd like to sit with you, but I think it will help me with the other women if I can win the favor of Catriona's sisters and cousin."

"Ye'll never do that with Fiona and Alanna," he replied grimly, but then quickly added, "nae by fault of yer own, though, ken?"

"Well," she hedged, nibbling on her lip, "perchance I can prompt at least Elspeth to like me."

He looked doubtful, but he nodded. "Possibly. Since Catriona died, Elspeth has been the most sensible."

"Was Catriona very sensible?" Marion asked, pleased he felt momentarily comfortable enough to talk about his first wife.

"Aye. Until the end when she decided she was ready to die."

He'd said it with no emotion, yet his eyes held a depth of pain and regret he'd not shown her thus far. It twisted her heart. She squeezed his hand, wanting to ease the hurt she knew still throbbed within him. "Perchance she was weary of being ill?"

His eyes widened a fraction, and he stood in silence for a long moment. "Do ye ken, I never thought of that? Only of how she seemed to simply decide she was finished with life."

Tears welled in Marion's eyes at the idea of how desperately weary Catriona must have been to welcome death.

Marion took in the powerful man before her, so battle-hardened yet with such a tender heart. Having been Iain's wife the short time she had, she knew with every beat of her heart, with every breath that she took, that she'd fight death with all her might not to leave his side. The revelation stunned her. It blossomed and moved like fire through her veins, making her skin prickly and the hairs on the back of her neck stand up. Everything around her disappeared. The noise faded, except for the faint sound of the inhalation and exhalation of the man facing her. The smells of the mutton and freshly baked bread vanished, and all she could smell was Iain. His scent of pine, the sweat of his labors, and a faint trace of wood smoke and sweet wine surrounded her. She inhaled deeply.

She *loved* Iain.

She stared at his strong jaw, chiseled face, and soulful eyes. She loved her husband. He'd captured her heart, though she'd intended not to give it to him unless he offered his own to her. He'd taken hers so quickly, she wondered if she'd ever had hope of keeping her heart as her own. She blinked and raised her hand to swipe at the tears at the same time he touched his fingers to her face.

"What's this?" he asked.

She swallowed. "I cannot help but think of Catriona and how exhausted she must have been to desire the end of her life. It makes my heart ache for her and for you."

"Ah, Marion," he said, his voice ragged and catching on her name. "The things ye say stun and please me."

"I want to please you," she whispered, aching with just

how much, but not because she still worried she was unworthy. She wanted to please him simply because she loved him.

He brushed a finger quickly across her lips, a devilish twinkle coming to his eyes. "Ye do."

She heated from her belly to the juncture between her thighs at his obvious reference to what they had done together.

"Come," he said, taking her hand. "If I keep standing here staring at ye and thinking on what we could be doing, I'll throw ye over my shoulder and leave the hall, and that certainly will win ye little favor with the women."

Marion giggled as Iain led her to Bridgette's table and then solicitously waited for her to take her seat before excusing himself and striding back up to the dais. She watched as he strode the few steps, the muscles of his powerful legs flexing. He settled himself, and though Lachlan immediately started talking to him, Iain's heated stare stayed on her. All she could think about was that she loved him. It pounded through her, at once thrilling and frightening.

"The MacLeod did nae want ye to sit by him, I see," said someone directly across from Marion. She drew her gaze away from Iain and met the derisive flashing eyes of Fiona.

"I wanted to sit with all of you to get to know you," Marion replied.

"There was nae a need for that," Fiona snapped. "Bridgette here has talked about ye since she sat down." Fiona scowled at Bridgette, who met the woman's dark look with one of her own. Marion wanted to hug her friend for trying to help her. She offered Bridgette a smile and then took a piece of meat off the almost-empty trencher and one of the last two hunks of bread left on the platter before her.

Marion understood that Fiona was angry at her because the woman had wanted to be Iain's wife, but she also suspected the woman was afraid of what would become of her now that Marion was here. She had to find a way to assure Fiona that she was still an important part of this clan.

"Tell me, Fiona, who took on the position of mistress of the castle when your sister passed away?" Marion asked as she took a bite of the bread, or attempted to. God's truth, it was like biting into a stone. Marion frowned and set the bread back on her plate. Someone needed to teach the women in the kitchen how to properly bake bread.

"I did," Fiona answered, her tone defensive. "I suppose ye want to do it now?"

Marion stabbed at the meat with her knife. Her stomach growled, but the blood leaking from the obviously undercooked meat deterred her from trying it. She glanced swiftly around and saw that most of the women at the table had left a good portion of their food untouched, and Bridgette appeared to have eaten nothing. Tomorrow, Marion would talk to Iain about what could be done. But tonight, she had to face a larger problem.

She held Fiona's gaze as the women at the table shifted their eyes between the two of them. "I think Dunvegan is possibly so large that it needs a mistress of the castle and an assistant. What do you think?"

"I think," Fiona said, her words wrapped in scorn, "I dunnae need an assistant to run this castle."

The woman was making it hard to like her, but then again, Marion had known it would be difficult, though she'd hoped she was wrong. "*I* need an assistant," she said pointedly.

"Ye think ye're strong enough to be mistress of the castle?" Fiona demanded, her brows rising in disbelief.

Marion opened her mouth to respond, but her words were cut off by Bridgette's. "Marion is stronger than she looks," Bridgette said and gave Marion a sympathetic smile.

"I certainly hope so," the curly redheaded woman sitting by Fiona crowed. "Ye look as if a strong highland wind would blow ye away," the woman said, her hand coming to rest on her rounded belly.

"Alanna." Rory Mac growled at his wife and gave Marion an apologetic look. "She's with child," he offered as his way, Marion supposed, of explaining his wife's sour mood.

Alanna glared at Rory Mac. "What does being with child matter?"

In answer, Rory Mac dragged his bread through the sauce in the trencher and stuffed the entire piece in his mouth.

Marion stifled her nervous laughter at Rory Mac's actions and the dissension of the table in general.

"It's good to finally meet you, Alanna," Marion offered.

The woman drew her russet eyebrows upward. "Is it now?"

Marion clenched her teeth at Alanna's mocking tone, as most of the women at the table snickered and laughed, save Bridgette and Elspeth. Rory Mac, with a dark look, stood abruptly and left the table to take a seat at one occupied by only men, including Angus, who Marion noticed was turned around watching her. Marion didn't blame Rory Mac for leaving. She would rather sit elsewhere, as well, but this was a battle, and if she fled, she'd be defeated. "Yes, it is good to meet you. Iain tells me you are cousin to Fiona and Elspeth." When Alanna's mouth twisted cynically, Marion realized her error. "And of course, Catriona, when she was alive."

"Aye," Alanna clipped, "*and* Catriona, who was the best of *all* of us."

Marion was more angry than hurt at the hostility of Catriona's sister and cousin, but being hostile in return would solve nothing.

Beside her, Bridgette took a deep breath, drawing Marion's attention to her. Bridgette looked as if she could spit fire, and Marion felt her eyes go wide. *Oh dear!*

"Marion is nae weak," Bridgette bit out, "and she is just as good as Catriona was, ye bunch of wee petty women!"

Marion touched her friend's arm. "Bridgette, I can defend myself."

Bridgette didn't even flick her gaze to Marion. She simply narrowed her eyes, her cheeks turning an alarming shade of red. Belatedly, Marion recalled the men teasing Bridgette about her temper. This must be to what they had been referring. Bridgette slapped her palms on the table, the noise so loud and unexpected that all conversation quieted at their table and those surrounding them. Bridgette started to rise, but Marion grasped her arm, desperately pulling her back into her seat.

"Bridgette, please," Marion hissed.

Bridgette waved a hand at Marion. "Allow me to handle these witches."

"Witches!" Fiona screeched. Marion cringed. "Are ye calling me a witch?" the woman demanded, staring at Marion.

"No!" Marion exclaimed.

"Aye!" Bridgette fairly shouted. "Ye act like an old ill-tempered witch! And if ye're nae careful, yer sour disposition will get ye banished from the clan."

"And just who's going to banish me? Nae Iain. Her?" Fiona speared Marion with a dark look. "She could nae banish an ant from its bed."

"She's pulled me up from the cliff of a mountain and saved my life, and she did nae blanch when she heard the seer's prophecy," Bridgette exclaimed. "She's strong and courageous."

"Ye met a seer?" Elspeth asked, her brown eyes wide with curiosity.

"It was nothing," Marion rushed out, praying Bridgette would say no more.

"Nothing?" Bridgette exclaimed. "The seer told Marion that Iain would fly the Fairy Flag to save her."

Marion hastily looked over her shoulder, praying that Iain was not listening. His eyes were trained on their table, though conversation around him clearly continued. Thank goodness, she didn't think he could hear what was being said.

"If the MacLeod did nae fly the flag to save my sister, he'll nae fly it to save the *Sassenach*."

Marion gritted her teeth. This was not going well at all. "I never thought—"

"I tell ye, he's going to fly it," Bridgette interrupted.

Fiona shoved back the bench that she, Alanna, and Elspeth were sitting on, and she stood. "Iain!" she called across the hall, her voice ringing out like a shrill whistle above the hum.

Marion froze. Aside from tackling the woman, Marion could think of no other way to stop her from speaking.

Iain's gaze sharpened on Fiona. "Aye?" he answered, not even having to raise his voice as the room had fallen into silence.

"It seems yer new wife thinks ye're going to fly the

Fairy Flag to save her."

Whatever Iain felt about Fiona's statement didn't show on his face. His face showed nothing but mild interest. Lachlan's jaw, however, was hanging open.

Marion felt as if the heat of her embarrassment would set her body to instant flames. "No," she said, hurrying to explain. "I didn't. I don't. It wasn't me."

"Oh, forgive me," Fiona said dramatically. "A seer told yer wife that ye would fly the Fairy Flag to save her. Tell her, MacLeod. Tell her how it will never be so. Tell her that the flag may only be flown one more time and ye would nae fly it to save her! Tell her ye'd only risk flying it to save the clan. Tell her! Tell her how the clan comes first, how the clan will always come first!"

Marion wanted to shrink away and disappear. She felt two hundred pairs of eyes on her, and it was worse than anything she'd ever felt. It was worse than years of being invisible to her father, and then only being seen for how he could use her. And Iain, she knew, could not let the questions go unanswered with his clansmen looking on, and she feared his words would be like tiny cuts to her heart.

Sixteen

*I*ain cursed under his breath. He'd known something was stirring at Marion's table by her worried look and the angry ones around her. As he swept his gaze across the waiting crowd, he realized he had no choice but to answer. Something inside him tightened painfully as he settled his gaze on Marion. If he only had himself to consider, he'd fly the flag to save her life without hesitation. Yet he was chief of the clan, and he always had to consider the entire clan, and Fiona knew that. He'd married Catriona because she'd needed him, but also because the clan had wanted it. He didn't regret it, and he grew to love her greatly, but he always considered the clan's needs and desires above his own.

"Iain," Lachlan hissed beside him. "Ye must answer."

Iain nodded and spoke without taking his eyes off Marion. "Ye all ken that the flag can only be flown three times, and on the third, it will either destroy our enemies or destroy us. And ye all ken it's already been flown twice."

"Aye," came answers from nameless faces in the crowd.

"It was flown first when the MacDonalds battled us," said a woman.

"And again during the plague," said Lachlan.

"Aye." Iain had to choose his next words carefully to

preserve Marion's feelings. As he considered how to say what he must, his heart thudded in his chest and his ears. "When the flag is flown again, it will be for the good of the clan, as is my duty."

He hoped Marion understood. As he stared at her, she did not seem upset. Her face did not fall, nor her shoulders slump, but then Marion was used to trying to appear brave. Wanting to draw all attention away from the Fairy Flag and what he would and would not do, he motioned for the bard to come forth and begin the entertainment.

"Ye answered well," Lachlan said.

"I dunnae ken that I did," he admitted. "I answered as my duty demands."

"Aye, brother, I ken ye did. I hope yer wife will understand."

Iain hoped so, as well. He glanced toward Marion through the crowd. Fiona was saying something to her, and whatever it was, the color had drained from Marion's face. Iain's gut tightened as she stood, waved Bridgette off, and moved toward the door.

Iain stood, but Lachlan caught his arm. "Brother—"

"What?" Iain demanded. "There is nothing wrong with me speaking to my wife."

"Of course nae," Lachlan said. "It's just a surprise to see ye show emotion. It's been so long."

"My wife does strange things to me," Iain admitted, baffled by his own reactions to Marion.

Iain caught Marion by the waist just as she stepped outside the great hall. The corridor was empty, so he turned her into his arms and slid his hands around her back. When she did not look up but stared at his chest, he sighed. "Look at me, Marion."

Slowly, she lifted her gaze to his.

"Why are ye leaving supper?"

"I'm tired," she immediately replied, her gaze skittering away.

He hooked a finger under her chin and turned her face back to his. "Dunnae lie to me."

"I am tired," she said stubbornly, tilting her chin upward.

He brought a hand to the curve of her back and pressed her closer. "Are ye distraught over what I said regarding the Fairy Flag?"

"No! It's not that. I knew how you would answer. You don't love me."

Something in the way she said the words, as if there were more to say but she feared doing so, made him go completely still. "Do ye love me?"

Her eyes went wide. "Of course not!" A rosy flush covered her cheeks, her neck, the top of her chest. "That would be foolish, not to mention too soon." She bent her head and shuffled her feet. "It's not as if I really know you." Fascinated, he watched as she brought her hand to her hair and began to spin the golden strands around her finger. "I *do* know you are kind and honorable."

He grinned at the top of her head.

"And you are fiercely faithful and true, and I think you may be the most courageous man I know."

"Ye only think?" he teased, his chest tightening with every word she spoke.

Her head came sharply up, and she smirked at him. "I have known many courageous men."

He frowned at her. "Ye have *known* nary a man but me."

Her blush deepened. "There is knowing, and then there is *knowing*. And aye," she said in the loveliest attempt at a Scottish burr, "ye're the only man I've ever *known*, and I'm glad of it."

"Ye did nae answer my question," he said in a low tone. The need to hear her answer roared like a tempest inside of him.

"I've forgotten it," she replied, looking utterly innocent except for the blush still on her cheeks.

"Do ye love me?"

She scrunched her nose in the most adorable way. "I've no coin left," she grumbled.

"Coin? I dunnae ken…"

"I've no coin to buy an indulgence, so I cannot sin."

He frowned. "How would ye be sinning?"

"It would be sin to lie to you!" she burst out.

Iain stared at the beautiful, confusing woman before him, and he felt his caution slip. "So ye do love me?"

"Yes," she groaned.

Something deep within him shifted. She was his. In body. In heart. Now what of her soul?

She was his completely. He took her by the face and covered her mouth with his, sweeping his tongue around her sweet, welcoming caverns. He was greedy for wanting her love when he knew he had none to give in return, but he wanted it anyway. He'd give her other things.

A throat cleared behind him. Iain broke the kiss and turned to see Lachlan standing there grinning and staring. Iain glared at his brother until he finally looked away.

"Yer absence is being noted. I hate to take ye away from yer wife"—Lachlan gave Marion an overly appreciative glance that made Iain grit his teeth—"but ye really should stay for the rest of the feast, as it's in honor of yer safe return to us with yer bride."

Iain pressed Marion's hand to his chest. "Join me?"

She shook her head, refusing to meet his gaze. "I truly am tired. I'll just retire to my chamber if it's been readied."

Iain frowned. He'd hoped Marion would have decided she wanted to sleep with him and not in different chambers. He knew he'd offered her the chamber, but it had only been to try to please her. He wanted her with him. "It's nae ready," he said, glad for it. "Ye'll have to sleep with me."

Whatever she was feeling, his wife, who usually wore her emotions on her face like clothing, simply nodded, expressionless. "If you wish."

"I'll nae be long," he promised.

She nodded and turned to leave, disappearing around the corner as he stared after her.

"Ye watch her like a hungry man watches a deer he intends to consume."

Iain faced Lachlan. "She makes me feel like there's an insatiable hunger in me."

"Why does that make ye frown? It seems a good thing to me."

Iain scrubbed a hand over the back of his neck. "I'm nae sure I can keep my control with her." She'd already made him forget himself in the bedchamber, but he wasn't going to share that.

Astonishment crossed Lachlan's face. "Ye've never lost control afore her, have ye?"

Iain turned away, not wanting Lachlan to see the truth. He'd loved Catriona, but she'd not stirred a storm in him as Marion did. He felt at once guilty and disturbed. What was it that Marion did to him? He abruptly turned back to his brother. Whatever it was, he'd not discover the answer in the great hall while his wife was upstairs. The sooner supper was over, the sooner he could go to her and try to sort out the knots she'd tied in him. "Come. We must get back to the feast."

Lachlan looked as if he might argue, so Iain brushed past him, strode into the great hall, and resumed his seat with his other brothers. It seemed an hour had passed as he listened to the bard, and then he sat as several of his clansmen came to speak to him. Finally, his people started to disperse, and he stood.

"Iain," Cameron said, "I need a moment."

Iain barely held in the desire to refuse his brother's request. Cameron had been sitting at the table with him all evening and there had been much time to talk, but obviously he wanted a private moment.

Iain nodded. "What is it?"

Cameron glanced around the great hall, as if to verify they were alone. "I've been speaking with Raghnall and he is certain he can build us the faster ships we discussed. He's demanding half the payment for them now."

"What do ye think?" Iain inquired. He knew what he thought they should do, but he wanted his brother to decide. It was time that Cameron asserted himself and felt the pressures and rewards of making decisions. As the youngest MacLeod brother, Cameron had yet to truly find his place.

Cameron tugged on his beard. He was the only one of them who wore one. "I think we should pay him as he requests, but I should personally oversee the building and make sure he completes it quickly."

Iain nodded. He was pleased with Cameron's decision. Faster ships were worth the money for the speed they could bring in battle. "Very well, then. Proceed."

Iain started to rise again, keen to get to Marion, but Cameron went on. "Do ye want to see the drawings

Raghnall and I did?"

Cameron wore an unmistakably eager expression that
Iain could not deny, no matter how much he wanted to
rush upstairs to Marion. "Of course," he replied, hoping
Marion would stay awake for him.

Marion awoke the next morning, when Bridgette thoughtfully came to lend her another gown until she could have
another made. Once Bridgette had departed, Marion stared
first at the indentation in the fine feather mattress on Iain's
side of the bed and then at the pile of clothes he'd discarded
in front of the bed, the ones he'd worn yesterday. So he
had slept here but had apparently awoken and left. She
sighed as she started to dress for the day in the gown
Bridgette had brought her, questions and concerns swirling
in her head. She still could not believe that she loved Iain
and that she'd foolishly told him. But she had not wanted
to lie to his face, and she'd seen no other option but to offer
the truth.

She worried that her confession was the thing that kept
Iain only by her side while she was asleep, and it was
making her feel slightly queasy. Coupled with the awful
things Fiona had said to her last night, Marion wanted to
climb back into bed and hide from the world. But she'd
never been a coward before, and she was not going to
become one now. After a servant came and helped Marion
tie her gown, Marion went to Catriona's trunk, drawn once
again by her curiosity.

Catriona had died so young and so unfairly, so the
niggle of jealousy Marion felt toward the woman made her
feel awful. Fiona had told her at the feast that Catriona had

confessed on her deathbed that Iain had wanted to fly the Fairy Flag to save her, but Catriona had vowed that if he did, she'd fling herself from a cliff. The woman was selfless. For the good of her clan, Catriona had made her husband stay his hand.

Marion swallowed the large lump in her throat. Iain had loved Catriona with all his heart. He'd loved her so much he'd been willing to put the needs of the clan after his need to save his wife. Marion's heart twisted. He'd never love her that way. He'd said himself that he'd never fly the flag for her, and even knowing that, she'd confessed her feelings.

What did she do now? She glanced around the bed-chamber, feeling like an intruder and out of sorts. One of the few places she felt truly comfortable was in a kitchen, and the kitchen here certainly could use her help. She wondered if Iain would frown upon it as her father had, until he realized how much better the food tasted with her directing the staff.

She heaved a sigh as she started for the door. She was going to have to go search out Iain and gain his permission to make some changes in the kitchen. The prospect of locating the husband who seemed to be avoiding her was daunting, but if she was going to get the MacLeod women to like her, she had to start somewhere besides Fiona and Alanna, both of whom clearly despised her.

A while later, after searching for Iain and not finding him, she ran into Bridgette, who insisted on helping her locate him. Marion knew Bridgette had only agreed because she wanted to see Lachlan. Still, she was glad for the company. The first two servants they stopped to ask thought the men were at the stables, but they only found Angus there. He spent some time demanding to know what had happened last night, and after Marion had told him, she had to soothe him to ensure he'd not confront Fiona. Once he was calm, he told her that Iain and Lachlan were training by the water. Before Marion and Bridgette made their escape from the stables, however, Archibald appeared, red-faced because Bridgette had apparently been evading him, and insisted on seeing the women safely to Iain.

Archibald spoke of the sea as they descended the seagate stairs, and Marion stared out at the water of the loch and recalled the breathtaking cerulean water of the sea that lay directly beyond it. Today, birds blanketed the sky, calling in loud squawks from above. And still higher than the birds could even hope to reach were scores of dark storm clouds.

Marion imagined Iain was readying his men for a possible attack from her father and Froste. At least Marion hoped that was the reason behind the early training rather then the alternative of Iain avoiding her.

Before she saw Iain, she heard steel crashing against steel. The sounds of battle led them across the land and around the corner of the cliff wall like a torch in the darkness. She gasped at the sight of her husband standing in the center of a circle of Scots. He was shirtless with his sword raised above his head, his brother Lachlan facing him.

They circled each other, obviously very nearly matched in expertise from what she watched. Iain would serve a blow, his thick, bulging forearms the only sign that the sword weighed more than a feather. As he brought his sword down for the third time and Lachlan met him in the air, the corded muscles in Iain's stomach tightened like bands sewn together perfectly. He backed Lachlan so close to the edge of the large circle that the crowd of men had to shuffle back to keep from being overtaken by the fight.

"Yer husband is the most skilled fighter I've ever seen," Archibald commented.

"Me as well," Marion murmured, awed by the unbridled power that flowed from him.

"Lachlan is fiercer," Bridgette inserted, ever loyal to a man who did not seem to appreciate her.

Marion glanced at Bridgette to give her a sympathetic smile, but her breath caught at the jealousy she saw flashing in Archibald's eyes. He truly cared for Bridgette, yet Bridgette pined for Lachlan. For a heartbeat, Marion's problems seemed less complicated. Until she saw that the fight had ended and Fiona had appeared from around the corner with a bucket of mead and a cup for Iain.

Fiona dipped the cup in the bucket and handed it to Iain, who took it with a grin. Marion's temper snapped. She stormed across the rocky terrain, or she tried to storm, as the uneven land made her progress wobbly and slow. She barged through the men who appeared rather stunned to see her, but she did not stop for a single nicety, as she normally would, until she stood face-to-face with Iain, who was so bold as to bestow a smile on her after the one he'd just given Fiona.

She plunked her hands on her hips and glared up at her husband. "I need to speak to you now!" She'd meant to ask him and not demand. And she'd certainly not meant to yell a command at her husband in front of his men, but Fiona had put her hand on Iain's arm, and well, Marion simply felt as if she were going to explode.

Iain tried to shrug Fiona's hand off his arm as he stared down at Marion, who by her glittering eyes, high color, and flared nostrils was in a fierce temper about something. Iain's gut told him that *something* was Fiona and her hand on his arm. His wife loved him *and* she was jealous. *Of Fiona.* He grinned, even as he contemplated how to address the problem of Fiona and assuage Marion's delicate feelings. Whether his wife ever realized it or not, he'd already ascertained she was delicate. Oh, she was tough on the outside, but beneath that outer shell of iron, her core consisted of pure soft love and a giving heart.

When Fiona refused to move her hand, he removed it for her and took Marion by the arm. As he guided her away to a cave, he barked an order over his shoulder for Lachlan to keep training the men.

Once Iain and Marion were hidden by the cave walls, he turned to face her. He meant to chide her for ordering him about in front of his men, but her teeth were chattering as the wind whipped her pale hair against her face. She reached up, twined her hair quickly, and then crossed her arms over her chest.

He frowned. "Why are ye nae wearing a cloak?"

"I left my mother's behind to make it appear as if I'd drowned."

"I did nae ken it was yer mother's cloak yer father spoke of. I'm sorry for that and that I've nae appointed one of the women to sew ye another. That was rude of me."

She shrugged. "Bridgette loaned me a gown, but she only has one cloak. Usually, the mistress of the castle would attend my needs, but as Fiona hates me and is so busy attending to *your* needs, I doubt a cloak for me—or any clothing, for that matter—is on her mind at all."

"Now, Marion," he started, but her scowl silenced him.

He sensed she needed to speak.

"I do not like the way Fiona looks at you and touches you."

"Neither do I," he immediately agreed. "What do ye want me to do about it? Do ye want me to marry her to someone from another clan?" He easily could. He had briefly considered the idea, but he was reluctant to send her away without giving her time to adjust to his new bride.

Marion shook her head. "No. That would only make all the other women hate me. And I'm still not certain I cannot gain her favor. I just need time."

"One month," he decided. "That's enough time for the woman to stop acting like ye're the devil and I'm a prize to be won."

"You're no prize," Marion grumbled.

He caught his wife around the waist and pulled her to him, crushing her softness to his bare skin. The contact instantly aroused him. "Ye did nae think that the night before last when ye screamed and moaned in my arms," he whispered huskily in her ear, contemplating and reluctantly dismissing the idea of taking her here in the cave. His men were too near.

Marion shoved back against his chest, but he refused to loosen his hold. She looked up at him, her annoyance apparent on her face. "Well, I certainly thought so last night when you failed to join me in bed as you said you would."

"Did ye want me to join ye?" he asked, nipping her ear and then brushing kisses down her neck to her collarbone. She shivered in his arms.

"I wish I'd wanted it a little less than I did," she admitted, her voice full of misery.

He lifted his head from where he had been kissing her

collarbone and caught her eye. "I like verra much that ye long for me to join ye in bed."

"Do you?" The suddenly doubtful look on her face made him ache to reassure her.

"I do. I wanted to come directly to ye last night and bury myself between yer welcoming thighs, but Cameron would nae quit talking."

"And you could not refuse your brother's request," she said in a soft voice.

"I could nae. Are ye angry?"

"Angry? No. I'm happy. I wish, well... 'Tis nothing."

"What do ye wish? Tell me what ye desire and I'll give it to ye." At this moment, he wasn't sure he could refuse her anything.

"I wish I had family that loved me the way you clearly love your brothers. The only person who loves me is Angus, and while I do think of him as family, it would have been nice if my father loved me, or if..." Her words trailed off into awkward silence, but she didn't need to finish her sentence. He knew what she'd been about to say. She wanted his love. She already had more of him than she understood, and the amount she'd managed to claim already worried him. If he were to lose her...or to forget Catriona because of the wild emotions Marion sparked in him...

"It's a foolish girl's dream," she blurted.

"Marion," he started, not even sure what to say. "I—Ye mean a great deal to me."

She looked as if he'd hit her. He cursed himself. He wanted to give her something she wanted, something that in her mind meant she was important to him. "I'm going to make certain yer bedchambers are readied today."

"Thank you," she whispered, looking even more dejected than she had seconds ago.

He frowned. "Do ye nae want that?"

"I didn't," she said, surprising him, "but I'm thinking now that it is possibly best."

"Why are ye thinking it's best now?" he demanded, losing his temper. The woman was making him crazy.

"You took my love from me like a thief in the night!" Accusation barbed her words. "From this point on, I refuse to give you any more."

"Love kinnae be stolen, woman."

Her eyes popped open wide, and her jaw clenched. "It can! You took mine without my knowing it, but my eyes are wide now," she said, motioning wildly in the air. "From now on, I'm going to guard my heart from you. You won't give me yours, so I refuse to give you more of mine."

"Laird," came a deep voice from outside of the cave. "Yer brother is wondering if ye'll be returning or if we can cease the training now."

"I'm coming," Iain roared, without taking his gaze from his wife. "I must go."

"Go, then!" She waved a hand at him.

He'd never been dismissed by anyone other than his father. He crossed his arms and stared, unblinking, at her. "Ye leave," he ordered, regretting the words as he said them. A wounded look flickered in her eyes. "Marion," he reached for her as she scuttled away from him.

"I'll be happy to leave!" she growled and stomped out of the cave.

In one stride, he caught her by the elbow and swung her around. "Marion," he whispered hoarsely while wrapping his arms around her. "I'm sorry. I'm sorry that I'm hurting ye. I dunnae want to."

"I know you don't mean to hurt me," she replied as she

pushed against him for space he refused to give her. Finally, she stopped trying when he simply tightened his hold. Her stormy gaze locked with his. "I'm sorry for my temper."

He noted she did not take back the words about guarding her heart from him, yet he released her. When she did not take a step back, he laced his fingers with hers. Now that he had her love, he wanted more, not less. He was in no position to ask it, though.

"Was there a reason ye sought me out down here?" he asked.

"Yes. I wanted your consent to change some things in the kitchen. I, er, saw that the bread was quite stale at supper. I think I can be of help to the women who do the cooking."

"Ye dunnae need my consent to oversee the kitchen. Ye are the mistress of Dunvegan now, nae Fiona. I will speak to her, and ye should do as ye wish."

Marion looked imploringly at him. "Please don't speak with her. You'll make things worse. I'll handle Fiona myself, as I've said."

"Fine," he agreed, glad Marion seemed less upset now. "Then I'll be training for the rest of the afternoon if ye need me."

Her eyes widened. "Do you always train for so long?"

"Nae. Unless I'm expecting trouble."

"Froste and my father," she said, nibbling her lip.

"Aye, but ye dunnae have to worry. I'll defend ye with my life, and so will my clan." He thought his words would remove the concern from her face, but all the color leeched from her skin, leaving it looking nearly translucent.

"That's exactly what I fear," she said. "I'd never want you to give your life for me."

"That is what a husband does, Marion—keeps his wife from harm."

She slowly pulled her hand out of his. "You sound like my father, cold and uncaring. What of love? What of a happy life shared between a man and a wife?"

He hesitated, warring with himself. It was as if his thoughts were cleaved in two. Part of him liked her idea of how they should be and part of him feared it.

She waved a hand in his face. "Pay my question no mind!"

"Marion—"

"Please dismiss it from your thoughts," she replied evenly.

"If that is what ye wish," he said, feeling as if he had taken the cowardly way out.

She sighed, then spoke again. "If Froste and my father come here, could they defeat you?"

"Nay," he said with force to assuage her fears. He had confidence in his men.

"But they'd have more fighting men." Her voice shook with her worry.

"My clan is fierce, Marion, and Dunvegan would be difficult to breach. And I have allies I could call upon."

"Oh yes!" Relief washed over her face. "King Edward."

His mouth dropped open at her words. "Nay. He's using me to draw your father and Froste's attention, but I'm sure *yer king* will call on me if and when they turn their sights on the throne."

She scowled. "I suppose he's no longer *my king*."

Iain smiled even as creases appeared on her forehead. "Why would King Edward expect you to help him if he will not help you?" she asked.

"Because he has David."

"But I thought part of the reason you married me was to get King Edward to discuss David's release. I was a condition."

He didn't like how she referred to herself, though it was true. "I think of it like this," Iain said. "Getting King Edward to talk of David's release has several parts to it, like gates that must be opened. I married and opened the first gate, which brings me closer to the next gate. Now Edward must tell me what more he requires, moving me closer to talks with him."

She quirked her mouth in obvious thought. "What do you think will open the next gate?"

"Well, if yer father and Froste attempt to take the throne, I'll refuse to go to King Edward's aid until he draws up terms for David's release, but if they do nae attempt the throne and all settles, I imagine Edward will want money. Either way, I expect to be summoned back to England or invaded by yer father and Froste in the near future."

Her hand fluttered to her neck. "What do we do until then?"

He drew his wife against him once more, wanting to feel her and wanting her to feel safe. "We account for all possibilities, and then we ready for each so we are always victorious."

Seventeen

Marion thought about what Iain had told her all the way to the kitchen. If her father and Froste came here to wage war against Iain and his clan, she would simply have to dissuade them from fighting. She could not allow Iain or any of his people to be killed because of her. Beyond that, she was haunted by the memory of the seer's words. If the seer had seen a need for Iain to fly the Fairy Flag, that had to mean her father and Froste would be coming. And if Iain flew the flag, the seer had said it would mean he had accepted his love for her.

Marion gritted her teeth to keep from crying out. The seer had said the third waving could save the clan or destroy it, and while Marion wanted Iain's love, she did not want it if it destroyed his clan.

As they neared the kitchen, Marion turned to Bridgette, who'd been walking quietly beside her, and whispered so Archibald would not overhear her. "I cannot let Iain ever wave the flag because of my father and Froste."

"Ye dunnae want Iain to love ye so much that he'd fly the flag for ye?" Bridgette asked in a hushed voice.

"I don't want him to go to war for me," Marion said, twisting her hands. "If it ever seems that he might, you must vow to me that you will help me stop it."

"So ye believe the prophecy?"

"I don't know for certain," Marion whispered. "But I'm not willing to risk it."

Bridgette nodded. "I feel the same. I'll do as ye ask. I dunnae want to go against the seer, if she may be correct."

"What are ye two ladies whispering about?" Graham, Iain's younger brother, asked as he came out of the kitchen and nearly collided with them. Graham was the smallest of the MacLeod brothers—not that he was small. The other men were simply like enormous oak trees while Graham was a slender pine. Marion had only spoken to him for a few minutes since arriving at Dunvegan. Of the four brothers, he seemed the quietest.

"I'm stunned to see a man in the kitchen," Bridgette teased.

Graham's neck flushed red. His friendly dark-brown gaze flicked over Marion briefly and then turned to Bridgette, where it lingered. Marion inhaled slowly as she watched him staring at Bridgette. He liked her! She'd bet her last coin on it, if she had a coin.

"Graham!" Bridgette, grinning mischievously, snapped her fingers in his face. "Are ye woolgathering?"

Marion felt instantly sorry for him. It was clear that Bridgette did not see him as a possible husband.

"Sorry." Graham cleared his throat. "I was in the kitchen asking Cook to make baked pears for the last course tonight."

"But that's my favorite!" Bridgette exclaimed.

"Is it?" Graham said, as if he was surprised, but Marion didn't believe the surprise was genuine. He'd known baked pears were Bridgette's favorite. He shrugged. "I had a strong hunger for it. It's my favorite, as well."

"I kinnae believe that in spite of all the meals we've all eaten over the years, Graham MacLeod, I never kenned that about ye."

His dark eyes grew even darker, almost black. "There is much ye dunnae ken about me, Bridgette MacLean."

Marion blinked. Graham was trifling with Bridgette! Marion held her breath and prayed Bridgette would sense his adoration and be gentle with him.

Bridgette laughed. "Such as?"

"Why do ye nae take a walk with me in the garden and I'll tell ye?"

Bridgette frowned, as if she could not think of a single excuse to give him. "I dunnae think—"

"If Bridgette walks with ye, so do I," growled Archibald.

"I dunnae need a minder!" Bridgette snapped.

Graham immediately stepped to Bridgette's side. "Ye heard the lady."

"I heard," Archibald snapped. "But I've orders from the MacLean to nae leave her alone."

"She'll nae be alone," Graham said with a smirk.

"She needs a man by her side who can defend her," Archibald barked.

Oh good Lord! Marion saw a fight brewing. She moved closer to the men, who were now standing so close they almost touched. "You are both strong, bold men capable of defending Bridgette. However, I need someone to come with me to move some things in the kitchen," Marion lied and stared pointedly at Archibald. She knew Bridgette likely didn't truly want to stroll with Graham, given she desired his older brother, but Marion pitied him. Being the youngest and the smallest could not be easy among this lot.

Archibald sighed but nodded. "I'll be happy to aid ye any way ye wish, my lady. I'm sure ye picked me because—"

"Yes, yes, come with me," Marion interrupted and hurried off, leaving Bridgette and Graham standing alone in front of the kitchen doors.

The chaos of the kitchen was shocking. She stood in the entrance with Archibald beside her and gaped at the scene. A score of cooks ran around shouting at one another, and women who surely had to be the bakers—if the dough covering their arms was any indication—traded nasty and very loud barbs. Meanwhile, the poulterers—ten of them that Marion could see—all seemed to be waving their knives and cursing instead of actually preparing the birds for supper.

She glanced quickly at the shelves and saw that many were almost bare and not properly stocked, either. Fiona may have been mistress of the castle, but she clearly did not care about it, or at least not the kitchen, which was odd since she would benefit from a well-run kitchen.

Marion cleared her throat. When no one even glanced her way, she turned to Archibald. "Can you whistle?"

He narrowed his eyes at her, confused. "Aye."

She'd tried for years to master whistling, but the only way she could manage it was by inhaling air, and that never produced the loud, shrill whistle she longed to make.

"Would you mind?" she asked him.

His brow stayed wrinkled for a moment, and then it slowly smoothed and he grinned. "I'd love to." He put his fingers up to his mouth and let out the loudest, shrillest whistle Marion had ever heard. She was awed, jealous, and immensely pleased.

The occupants of the kitchen came to a complete standstill, and silence permeated the room.

Marion cleared her throat, suddenly very nervous. "Good day. I wanted to present myself to each of you."

"We ken who ye are, my lady," said a woman with salt-and-pepper hair and kind eyes. "Many of us were gathered by the sea when the laird returned and presented ye." The woman glanced around her. "And those of us who were nae there have certainly been told of ye." The woman wiped her hands on her dark apron, leaving a trail of flour across its front. She stepped forward and offered an awkward curtsy. "I'm Kyla, Neil's wife."

"Neil!" Marion smiled, inadvertently touching her ear as she thought of the man who Froste had mutilated twice now. "I did not know he was married. It's a pleasure to meet you."

The woman grinned broadly. "Likewise. Neil told me how ye risked yer life to help him, and then how ye dressed his ear. I was hoping for the opportunity to thank ye, and tell ye simply to ask if I can ever do anything for ye."

Marion was aware that the entire kitchen staff was listening to their conversation. This would be the perfect time to tell them of her intention of being involved in the running of the kitchen, but she needed to make certain she didn't sound obtrusive. She wanted them to see her as a peer, not a Sassenach that suddenly appeared and told them what to do.

"Actually, Kyla, I would very much like to learn about how things are done in the kitchen here, and in other areas of the castle, as well. You see," Marion said sincerely, "I was mistress of my father's castle in England, but I fear that is very different from overseeing a grand Scottish castle. Would you help me learn?" Marion purposely met the curious gazes of the women surrounding her, and she was very surprised and pleased to see Elspeth standing among them. Marion settled her attention on Elspeth. "Would you all help me?"

"Of course, my lady," Kyla immediately replied, and others, Elspeth included, quickly echoed their agreement. "What would ye like to ken?"

Marion smiled. "Well, the first thing I'd like to know is if you would all please call me Marion."

"As ye wish it, my lady—er, Marion."

"Excellent!" Marion looped her arm through Kyla's. The woman's eyes widened, but she did not pull away. "Are you head of the kitchen?"

"I was," Kyla murmured, bitterness tingeing her voice. "But when Lady Catriona passed away, her sister Fiona took her duties upon herself and declared that we were nae to do anything without asking her first." Kyla glanced pointedly at Elspeth. "But Fiona never comes to the kitchen and kinnae be bothered with the needs of the kitchen."

"Truly, she does nae want to be bothered with much that does nae pertain to her own needs," Elspeth added, glancing shyly at Marion.

"I see," Marion replied softly. It sounded as though Fiona simply liked to lord over people. Marion took a deep breath. "Well, I'm mistress now, and I firmly believe it's good to have different people running different things. You all know this kitchen and the castle's needs better than anyone. I'd like to appoint someone to head the kitchen, who will then deliberate with me." Murmurs of agreement filled the room. She had been careful to use the word *deliberate* because she wanted the women to understand that they had a voice and a say in what was to happen.

"Would everyone be in agreement with my appointing Kyla as head of the kitchen?" Hearty agreement swiftly came. "Wonderful!" Marion glanced sideways at Kyla. "Would you please counsel me as to who you think should head the bakers, and the poulterers, and the other areas of the kitchen?"

For the next hour, Marion followed Kyla around the kitchen as the woman personally presented Marion to each person whom she felt should run a part of the kitchen. At the end of the hour, Marion was parched from all the talking and she noticed Archibald had found a chair in a corner and looked as if he was about to fall asleep. She excused herself from Kyla and went over to Archibald and assured him that he did not need to stay with her. He offered a weak protest but then left at her behest. Once it was just Marion with the kitchen ladies, who seemed willing and ready to accept her, she felt a sense of real hope.

The women gathered around a large rectangular table in the middle of the kitchen and partook in a light morning meal. As they ate, Marion entreated them to tell her what they thought needed improvement in the kitchen. The cooks themselves readily admitted the food was not as good as it could be, but they were adamant that it was because things were so disorganized and the food stores were not properly stocked. Marion told them that she would oversee the stocking of the kitchen herself and that together they would strive to please Iain. While he never complained of the lackluster meals, he never complimented the food, either. Marion could tell it had hurt the women's pride, and having known just how it felt to want to be noticed for your efforts, Marion was determined to see that Iain and the other men were so impressed by the meals that they'd rave about them.

As she departed, she promised to speak to Iain about gathering the proper spices and supplies the kitchen needed. True to her word, Marion spoke with Iain that night as they lay in his bed.

"Iain, have you noticed the food at Dunvegan tends to be bland?"

He frowned. "Aye. It used to be much better."

Marion wanted to lay the blame at Fiona's feet where it belonged, but she restrained herself. "The kitchen is not being properly stocked. The cooks tell me they don't have the herbs they need, nor enough barley and rye to make the bread and mead. And they don't have any honey from the beekeepers to sweeten the food."

"Well, then they should simply procure some," he said and pulled her toward him to kiss her on the lips. As his hand slid lower to cup her breast, she gently pushed him away. She wanted him very much, but she wanted to discuss this first.

"They are afraid to do so because Fiona told them that she was head of the kitchen and she'd gather all the supplies or appoint someone to do it, but she has not done so."

Iain grunted. "Did ye tell them ye're mistress of the castle now and to follow yer command?"

"In my own way. I think it's best to show them they have nothing to fear by gathering what the kitchen needs myself this first time, but I'll need help."

"Ye need me to help ye?" he murmured as he nuzzled her neck.

She blinked at him in surprise. "Heavens, no! I'd not ask you to waste your time on such matters, but I will need someone to carry the heavier things. I wanted to make sure it would be acceptable if I asked Archibald to help me."

Iain stopped kissing her neck and met her eyes. "Nay. I'll help ye."

"You're sure?" she asked skeptically, aware the offer

was only made out of jealousy.

"Aye," he replied, slipping his hand back under her clothing and cupping her breast. His fingers moved deftly and quickly over the hardened nub. "We'll go at dawn, and afterward, ye can show me what ye ken of shooting a bow."

Marion's eyes widened. "Really? Do you have that much time to give me with all your training?"

"I will always have time for ye, Marion," he responded, his voice low and husky. And before she could tell him how pleased she was, his mouth claimed her breast and all her thoughts fled, save one: her husband certainly knew how to pleasure her.

The next morning, after several hours of gathering what the cooks needed and then taking the stores to kitchen—to the delight of the cooks—Iain and Marion set out into the woods adjacent to the castle. When they arrived at a lovely spot dotted with trees, Iain pulled two bows from his sack. One of them was the perfect size for Marion, and she could not help but wonder if it had been Catriona's.

It must have shown on her face, because as Iain was passing her the bow, he said, "I had Graham make it for ye."

"What?" she gasped. "When? There hasn't been enough time for such a task."

Iain chuckled. "Aye. Graham is lightning-quick and excels at making all weapons. I asked him to make these the night we arrived." Then Iain produced a dagger that Marion had not even noticed before. "I also had him make this for ye to replace the one Angus gave ye."

Tears filled Marion's eyes as she took the dagger in her free hand. "Iain, I'm so touched."

He smiled. "Good. I'd hoped ye would be. Look at the dagger's hilt."

She handed the bow back to him, so she could do so.

"*Teaghlach,*" he said when she looked at the inscription. "It means *family,* and ye are a part of mine. An important part."

Marion's heart tugged and she sniffled, even as he lowered his head and brushed his lips to hers. "Vow to me ye'll never forget it," he said.

She looked deep into his eyes, wondering if this was his way of offering her something in place of his love, but she pushed the thought away and concentrated on the goodness of his gifts. "I'll not forget. Now, shall I show you how I can shoot?"

"Aye. And then we can practice using the dagger. Yer skill needs a bit of work."

"Don't let Angus hear you say that," she grumbled.

Iain laughed. "He taught ye fine, but now ye'll learn from the best."

"You arrogant man," she said with a chuckle.

Much later, Marion realized Iain's words had not been arrogant at all, but simply truthful. His skill with the dagger and the bow amazed her, and as the sun set, they gathered their things and walked hand in hand through the woods.

"That was the best day I've ever had," Marion said shyly.

Iain stopped and pulled her into his arms. "It was a perfect day, aye?"

She nodded.

"I never did anything like this with Catriona," he said, surprising her with his openness. Marion didn't comment, hoping he'd reveal more, and he did.

"I allowed being laird to consume almost every waking moment, and I never took time like this with her. I regret that."

Marion's throat tightened at the pain in his voice. Was he wishing Catriona were here instead of her? Or was he trying to tell her that he did not want to repeat the past? She wanted to ask him, but she was afraid of the answer, so she kept silent all the way back to the castle.

Several days later, as Marion worked in the kitchen learning how to cook some of Iain's favorite dishes, Kyla came to stand by her. "My lady," Kyla started, her voice tentative.

"Marion," she corrected.

"Aye. Marion." The cook grinned. "I dunnae mean to cause offense, but I see that ye seem to wear the same gown each day."

Marion felt her cheeks heat. "Yes, I had to leave my home rather hastily, and there was no time to pack gowns. Bridgette loaned me one, but it became filthy and tore on the trip here. Bridgette did lend me another that I wore to supper the first night, but—"

"Ye need nae explain it," Kyla said, a mischievous twinkle in her eyes. "Yer gown was the talk of the kitchen, and I ken well that ye could nae wear it about in the day to do work. So the gown ye have on is yer only one?"

"It's not even mine," Marion said. "It's Bridgette's. I've been meaning to ask about getting someone to sew gowns and a cloak for me."

"I'm a fair hand at sewing, if I say so myself," Kyla said.

"I'd be honored if ye would allow me to sew ye some gowns. I've never sewn anything as fancy as ye wear, but I'd like to try."

"That would be lovely," Marion agreed. "Thank you."

"If ye'll come to my cottage later today, I'll fit ye. I sewed a few gowns for Catriona, and she requested a more fitted style, so I do have some experience. I have some material at home, as well, and I'm sure some of the girls in the kitchen will be happy to lend ye a gown or two until yers are ready so ye dunnae take all Bridgette's gowns," Kyla said with a wink.

"I'll lend you one," Elspeth offered.

"You're certain?" Marion asked. "I don't want to cause any trouble for you."

"It won't be any trouble at all," Elspeth said with a smile.

Once Marion got directions to Kyla and Neil's home, she and Elspeth left for Elspeth's cottage so she could fetch a gown for Marion to borrow. Marion's stomach turned as they neared the home and she saw Fiona going inside.

By the time she and Elspeth reached the front door, it swung open and Fiona came charging out carrying a basket full of embroidery. She stopped, and her eyes narrowed. "What are you doing here?" She glanced between Marion and Elspeth and then speared Elspeth with a stare. "And why are you with *her?*"

Elspeth jutted her chin out at her sister. "She needs to borrow some gowns until she has new ones made, and I've one stashed in a trunk that none of us wear."

Fiona's lips parted, and she gasped. "She can't wear that gown!"

"Of course she can," Elspeth replied. "Don't be so petty. Think how pleased the MacLeod will be when he sees that ye're striving to be civil."

Though Marion didn't love that Fiona needed coaxing to be nice to her, especially in the hopes of gaining Iain's favor, it did immediately work.

Fiona fairly grinned. "How clever ye are, little sister."

Elspeth bit her lip. "I just remembered that I forgot to add a spice to my soup! I must make haste to the kitchen. Fiona, please retrieve the gown for Marion."

Fiona scowled. "I don't see why I have to be the one to—"

"Fiona, please!" Elspeth begged. "I must go tend to the soup!"

"I'll come back another time," Marion offered.

"I'll do it," Fiona grumbled.

Elspeth called a thank-you as she disappeared back in the direction from which they had come not moments ago.

Marion felt Fiona's glare on her. She took a deep breath and met the woman's gaze. "I don't want to be enemies."

"Nay?" Fiona snarled. "Then leave."

Marion's anger stirred. "Why do you hate me so? It's not my fault your sister died. I don't want to make anyone forget her, and I'm sorry I took the place you thought was to be yours."

"Ye're nae the first," Fiona snapped. "I'm the eldest, and by all rights, I should have married Iain but Catriona stole him by gaining his pity."

"I thought Catriona was the eldest," Marion said.

Fiona's eyes flashed. "Nay! I am. Always have been. Catriona stole what should have rightfully been mine. Everyone thought she was so sweet and kind, but I knew better. She wanted to be mistress of Dunvegan Castle, so she used the only thing she had, her frailness, and she gained Iain's favor with it. When she died, I bided my time and waited patiently for him to heal."

Marion's stomach turned. Fiona would never forgive her and they would never be friends. Fiona now saw Marion as the newest person to take a position that she believed belonged to her.

Marion straightened her shoulders. "Fiona, I have taken charge as mistress of the castle." She did not want to shun the woman; that would only make things worse. So Marion would keep Fiona busy and distracted. She tried to think of some of the more innocuous tasks where Fiona could not cause too much trouble. "I'd like it very much if you would remain in charge of teaching embroidery and dance to the ladies."

Fiona's mouth dropped open, and her nostrils flared. "Ye think to do everything else yerself, do ye?"

Marion shook her head. "Not at all. I intend to make someone head of each area of the castle, and we'll all work together. Will you help?"

Fiona's eyes darkened, and her mouth pinched. "I'd nae help ye even if remaining part of the clan depended on it."

"Well, then," Marion said, her temper brewing, "It's a good thing it does not."

Fiona flinched, and Marion saw the woman curl her hands into fists. She surprised Marion by swiveling on her heel and storming into the cottage. The door slammed behind her, and Marion stood alone, gaping at the slab of wood. She sighed. She supposed that was her signal to depart.

She hesitated for a moment, wondering if there was something she was missing. It felt as if there was, but what it was she was not certain. Taking a long, deep breath, she concluded that even if she was missing something, it didn't change the fact that Fiona wanted Iain and she could not have him. Marion turned to leave but stopped when the door behind her banged open. She turned around to see Fiona stomping out carrying a gown and a hair comb. Marion's eyes widened when she saw the luxurious green silk gown. It looked like a gown she'd once seen the queen wearing when she'd passed through with the king, not here at Dunvegan, where the women wore loose, practical gowns of drab wool.

Fiona thrust the gown and hair comb at Marion. "The hair comb matches the gown. The gown needs a good airing, but I imagine it should fit ye well enough until yer gowns are made. Ye should wear it tonight to please Iain."

Was this the woman's very awkward attempt at trying to be civil? If it was, Marion would do her best to reciprocate. "Thank you, Fiona, for retrieving Elspeth's gown for me."

Fiona gave her a tight smile. "Ye're welcome. I'll see ye at supper."

With that, Fiona left Marion standing alone once again. This time, though, Marion didn't hesitate to turn and make haste back to the castle, rather excited at the prospect of putting on the lovely gown.

She took care washing for dinner, brushing her hair until it shone and then pulling one side up to secure it with the comb. She would have pinned all her hair up, but it was thick and she would have needed several combs. The gown was snug in the chest when she put it on, which made sense as Elspeth was not as shapely as Marion. It was not cut overly low, but because it was tight on her, it pushed her breasts up higher than she would normally dare. She didn't think it was indecent, however.

When she was readied, she sat on the bed, awaiting the supper horn and half hoping Iain might return to the room before supper to lead her down. But when the horn blew and he didn't appear, she supposed he must have been occupied and made her way toward the great hall.

The roar of the hall quickly faded into silence as she walked into the room. She furrowed her brow as everyone stared at her, but then she realized it must have been the gown that was enchanting them so.

To her right, Angus stood, came to her side, and offered her his arm. "Ye look lovely, lass."

Uncomfortable with being the center of the clan's attention, she gratefully slipped her arm through Angus's. "Thank you," she replied, her voice as shaky as her legs. "Angus, is it my imagination or do people seem to be staring as if my appearance stuns them?"

He glanced to the left and right as they walked. "Aye. They do look a bit stunned, but I'm sure it's because they've never seen a lass as pretty as ye are in a dress quite like this one. Are things going smoothly for ye?"

She bit the inside of her cheek against her desire to confide in him and take the comfort he would offer. Angus would fret and interfere if he knew how much Fiona hated her. She patted his hand. "It is improving."

As they neared the dais, Iain, who'd been in seemingly deep conversation with his brother, turned and looked at her. He started to smile and then, suddenly, it slid off his face. His lips parted, and then he pressed them together in a hard flat line. Her stomach plummeted to the floor. Did he think the gown too immodest? If he did, there was nothing that could be done about it now.

Angus led her directly to her husband, who for a long moment said nothing but simply stared at her, his eyes darkening with what appeared to be fury.

"What game are ye playing, Marion?" he snapped.

The sharpness of his words pricked her like a bush of thorns.

"I don't know what you mean," she said stiffly, aware that he'd spoken loud enough that his voice had carried over the hush that had fallen in the hall.

"Yer gown," he growled.

Anger surged through her. So he *was* displeased with the gown. She curled her hands into fists, feeling as if she could turn herself inside out and it would never be enough for him.

"I had to wear something," she retorted. "I've no gowns of my own, and I cannot borrow Bridgette's every night for supper. I am getting more gowns made."

"Wear the one ye had on earlier. Go change." It was a command, and a hard one. His face had closed, and coldness radiated from him.

She could not believe how insensible he was being, simply because he thought her gown immodest, but she was not going to be ordered about. It was as if she was standing in front of her father again, desperate to please him and failing, and then being treated cruelly for no reason. She tilted her chin up. "I'll not change. This gown is much like I saw the Queen of England wear, and she is a modest woman, if indecency is your worry."

He'd already looked down at the trencher in front of him. His head whipped up, and he speared her with a dark look that made her shiver. "Marion," he said, his voice lower but no less forceful, "if ye dunnae go willingly to change out of that gown, I'll throw ye over my shoulder and carry ye up to our bedchamber and change ye myself. And if I have to do that, ye'll nae like the consequences."

She inhaled a sharp breath at the anger rolling off him. What had happened since she'd seen him earlier today?

This was not the kind man she had come to know, the man who had given her the special dagger and the bow. "You'd haul me away and shame me over a gown?"

"Ye shame yerself by wearing Catriona's wedding gown."

A wave of shock slammed into Marion, making her dizzy. She gripped Angus's arm tight so that she'd not fall. He looked at her swiftly, worry filling his eyes, but she shook her head at him and prayed he'd not remark on her sudden swaying.

Iain placed his palms flat on the table as he stared up at her. "How did ye think I'd respond when ye took the gown out of her trunk? I am sorry if ye think I'm being harsh, but ye kinnae—" Pain streaked across his face before a mask of stone descended and she could no longer read his emotions. "Ye kinnae just wear her gowns," he finished quietly.

"I didn't know," she whispered, her voice cracking as she struggled to hold back the tears clogging her throat and filling her eyes. Angry with herself for her weakness, she dashed a hand across her eyes. "I did not take this gown out of her trunk in *your* bedchamber. It was loaned to me." Each word trembled as she fought against herself to be strong, to be cold, not to care. "I would never try to take her place in your heart," she choked out, removing her arm from Angus's grasp. She turned stiffly and walked through the hall, even as Iain demanded she stop, and proceeded back out the way she'd come with her head held high.

She met the gaze of each person staring at her, and fierce determination not to be cowed burned in her veins. The last gaze she met was Fiona's, who almost appeared regretful. Marion didn't believe that for a moment.

By the time she reached Iain's bedchamber, she was shaking. All she knew was that she had to get out of this castle. She yanked off Catriona's gown and hastily put on Bridgette's. There would never be a place in Iain's heart for her. She'd been foolish to hope for it. If he wanted only memories of Catriona, then that's what she'd leave for him. With her heart racing and her hands trembling, she carefully took Catriona's gowns out of the trunk and laid them on the bed. She swiped at the tears filling her eyes and then quickly made her way out of the castle and to the water. She needed fresh air and wanted to be alone.

It was much easier to slip out than she had presumed. No guards stood at the doors, for they were all in the great hall with their laird. Moonlight filled the night while white mist swirled in the damp, cold air. Marion shivered as she climbed down the seagate stairs, her arms wrapped tightly around her waist. The wind blew hard against her tingling cheeks, making her eyes burn and her lips sting.

When she reached the shoreline, she took in short tiny gasps of air from the long descent. In the watchtower on the ramparts, she could see light flickering, so she stayed in the shadows as much as possible. She moved toward the water, feeling almost beckoned by the distant hiss of the waves in the air. She wanted to be numb, to think of nothing. She kicked off her shoes and stood where the water just caressed her toes. Closing her eyes, she breathed deeply and searched for a peace she wondered if she would ever find.

"Did you discover a way into the castle where we'll not be seen?" a deep voice demanded.

Marion's eyes flew open as her pulse increased. She twisted around to see two men coming from the left, where Iain had been training with his men that morning. Ignoring her racing heart, she dropped to the ground and began crawling over the rough land toward the cave where she and Iain had spoken. As she crawled, the hair comb that Fiona had given her slipped from her hair, her long blond tresses falling over the right side of her face. She could hear the men approaching from behind her as she reached the tall grass and dove behind it.

"Froste said it needs to be a route by which at least twenty men could enter before the MacLeods know they are inside," the man added.

"Why can't we simply strike from the outside?" asked another man. "Why must we try to enter the castle?"

Marion crouched in the tall grass, the roar of her blood filling her ears.

The deep voice spoke again. "Froste says the MacLeod must die, and we must seize Lady Marion."

Bile filled Marion's throat. Froste had sent men to find a way into the castle so he could kill Iain! It would clearly pave the way to marrying her and getting the land and title he so coveted, especially if her father became king.

The men paused very near her. "Do you not think it's strange that Froste thinks he needs twenty men to kill one?"

The other man chuckled low. "No. Have you seen the MacLeod?"

"No."

"Well, I have. I saw him in a tournament in England. He's not human. He fights with the power of a god and the heart of the devil."

"Well, then I'll enjoy killing him," the other man replied as they started to move away.

She waited until she felt they were far enough away that they'd not see her, and then she stood and started to run for the stairs. But when her slipper caught on a rock, she went down hard, slamming her head against a large stone as she fell.

Eighteen

Iain sat, ignoring the frenzy that had erupted the moment Marion had departed. His anger quickly gave way to guilt. He'd overreacted. There was no way Marion could have known she'd put on Catriona's wedding gown, yet his reason had been subdued by his emotions. Emotions he'd been able to keep tightly locked down until now.

"Are ye nae going te go after her?" Angus demanded in harsh, angry undertones.

Iain stared at the archway through which Marion had fled. He was going after her without a doubt, but he'd drawn enough attention to their argument, fool that he was. He'd let the attention of his clan turn back to their meals, and then he'd slip out.

He clenched his fists. He never lost his temper—before Marion came into his life, that was. She made him feel everything, every damned thing a thousandfold. She was the spark that brought him to life, but she was also the very thing that threatened to wipe away his memories of Catriona.

"Did ye hear me?" Angus growled, coming much too close to defiance, which Iain could not allow from any of his clansmen, even though he understood Angus's ire and fully agreed that he deserved it.

"I heard ye. Now find a seat. I ken how I acted is un-forgivable."

"Aye," Angus grumbled. "Ye dunnae deserve her."

"I ken," Iain replied. "But she's my wife now, whether I deserve her or nae."

"Aye, she is yer wife," Angus snapped. "Ye'd be well served te remember that. She's nae accountable for yer pain, but she could heal it."

"Ye overstep, Angus. Go sit down with the others."

The old stubborn Scot looked as if he might continue to argue, and Iain admired and appreciated how much Angus cared for Marion and how he was willing to bring trouble on himself in her name. But Iain could not tolerate it. His position as laird was finite; his order must be followed.

Angus's mouth drew into a thin line, but he jerked his head in a nod and turned away. Before Iain could take a deep breath and get his emotions under control, Lachlan gripped his shoulder. "What's the matter with ye?" he demanded in a low voice.

Iain stared at Lachlan, who would never be able to understand what was wrong with him. Iain had been so happy to see Marion when she'd first entered the hall that his blood had leaped at the sight of her. And then when he'd realized she was wearing Catriona's wedding gown and his first thought had been how stunning she looked in it, he'd quickly tried to conjure an image of Catriona on their wedding day. But he could not. All he could see was Marion, her hair flowing and shining like the moon. He could not see beyond her luminous emerald eyes or the way their color perfectly matched the silk gown to even recall how Catriona's eyes had looked in it. His dead wife's wedding dress hugged his new wife's gentle curving hips, tiny waist, and voluptuous breasts, and he heated with desire like he'd never known before her. His body hummed with the memory of how Marion tasted, felt, and smelled, and in that moment, his heart ached with feelings he'd not wanted but could not deny. She was inside of him and he was happy.

But what he was doing was unforgivable. He'd sworn never to forget Catriona, and now it seemed he was failing in another vow. He didn't think he could stop what was happening, though.

"Iain," Lachlan snapped, his tone annoyed. "Did ye hear my question?"

Iain looked at his brother, leaning toward him so no one would overhear. "Aye. I'm my own problem. I must find a way to reconcile what I vowed to Catriona with what I want."

"What do ye want?" Lachlan asked.

"I want Marion."

"Ye already have her."

Iain rubbed his knuckles across his chin. "I want to take all she wants to give me."

"Then take it, brother, but ye must return it, as well— and quickly, afore ye hurt her so greatly she nae wishes to offer it to ye anymore."

Iain glanced sharply at Lachlan. "Ye almost sound as if ye speak from experience, but I ken that kinnae be."

"Nay, it kinnae." A dark look swept over Lachlan's face, but he said no more.

Frowning, Iain followed the direction of Lachlan's stare to the table where Bridgette sat with Graham and Elspeth. Graham put his arm around Bridgette's shoulders and whispered in her ear, and Iain felt Lachlan stiffen beside him. He studied the subtle flare of Lachlan's nostrils and the tick in his jaw.

"Do ye care for Bridgette?"

"Nay." Lachlan had replied so quickly that Iain knew it was a lie.

But Iain also understood his brother did not want to discuss it. And he thought he knew why. "That's good," he hedged, "because I think Graham cares for her."

Lachlan nodded. "Aye, he does verra much. I'm glad it appears she is finally seeing him as a man."

Lachlan sounded anything but glad, but Iain didn't comment further.

He turned his attention to Fiona and Elspeth, who appeared to be arguing. He thought about Marion and what she'd said about borrowing the gown. He watched Fiona as she violently shook her head at something Elspeth had said, and then suddenly both women looked at him. Elspeth stood up, but Fiona grabbed at her sister, and he understood his error, then. Fiona must have tricked Marion to humiliate her, and Iain had inadvertently helped her.

Ferocious anger overcame him as he slid out of his seat, descended the dais, and strode to the table where Fiona and Elspeth sat warily watching his approach. He stopped in front of the two sisters, a familiar pain moving through him for Catriona, but something now burned more fiercely in him: longing. He wanted desperately not to be miserable anymore.

He looked from one sister to the other. "Who gave Catriona's wedding gown to Marion?"

"She did," Elspeth blurted, pointing at her sister.

The blood drained from Fiona's face, so Iain knew it to be true. "I want ye ready to leave my land tomorrow. Pack a trunk."

Fiona scrambled out of her chair and grabbed his arm.

"Iain, it's nae as it seems!"

He scoffed. "Is it nae?"

A look of horror swept over Fiona's face. "Nay, ye dunnae understand!"

Iain clenched his teeth to stifle the desire to shake the woman. "Did ye or did ye nae give Catriona's gown to Marion, knowing it would make me angry?"

"I did, but—"

He took a firm hold of Fiona's elbow and led her out of the great hall so the rest of their conversation would not be overheard. "Ye let Marion wear that gown in here nae knowing what she wore. I'll nae have someone treat my wife that way."

Fiona scowled. "And why nae? Ye dunnae love her."

"Ye dunnae ken a thing about how I feel for her," he ground out. "Listen carefully to me, Fiona. Even if I had never married Marion, I would nae have married ye. I did nae wish to marry again at all, *until her.* Now, go fetch yer sister and get her to help ye pack. John MacDonald has asked to marry ye, and I'm going to let him."

Iain departed without a backward glance and raced to his bedchamber. All he wanted was to see Marion and beg her to forgive him, but when he burst through the bedroom door, he realized the chamber was empty—of Marion. The room itself was most assuredly full—of Catriona's things. Her wedding gown lay on the bed along with the more serviceable gowns she had worn. They covered the bed fully, and Iain's pulse ticked rapidly in his temples as understanding filled him. Marion thought there was no space for her in his life or his heart. He hastily stuffed the gowns into Catriona's trunk and then dragged the trunk to Marion's bedchamber, which was still unfinished. It didn't matter because she was never going to sleep in there.

With the task he should have done the day they arrived at Dunvegan finally completed, he pondered where Marion might have gone. She was likely wandering about somewhere, possibly down below or even out on the rampart. Iain would start in the kitchen, where he knew she felt comfortable.

Kyla greeted him with wide eyes and a quick curtsy when he appeared in the kitchen entry. "Laird?"

"I'm looking for Marion," he explained.

Neil's wife furrowed her brow. "She's nae here. I would think she'd be in the great hall with ye."

Iain nodded. "She was, but I'm a fool."

Kyla's gaze widened further. "Maybe check the tower, if she thought to be alone."

He nodded and strode out the door to the tower. He took the stairs three at a time, sure he'd find her there, but when he didn't, he cursed, his anger at himself growing stronger. Next he checked the stables, where he found Angus, who must have slipped out of supper.

"Have ye seen Marion?" Iain called, breathless.

Angus shook his head, his brow wrinkling. "She is nae with ye?"

"Nay. I dunnae where she went."

"I'll help ye search," the older Scot said, rushing Iain out of the stables.

Together they checked the herb garden and vegetable garden where there were places to sit in seclusion, but they still did not find her. Worry obliterated his guilt for the moment. "Where could she be? Surely, she would nae go down to the water alone?"

Angus scowled at Iain. "Ye do nae ken her very well if ye dunnae understand she'd do such a thing. Her emotions triumph over her good senses sometimes, ye ken."

"I ken," Iain responded, his concern growing. What if she was so angry that she'd left the castle grounds for the woods? The idea of her wandering alone out there at night where wild animals were, or worse... His heart stuttered. His lands were well guarded, but what if Froste or de Lacy had sent someone to fetch her again?

Without a word of explanation, Iain stormed toward the great hall and burst through the door. The chatter in the room died instantly. "I want every man outside now to help me search for Marion."

Before anyone could respond, the warning horn from the watchtower blew in five short bursts, signaling an enemy ship was near. Iain's chest felt as if it were about to explode as men charged toward him.

"Arm yerselves for war," he roared as he headed toward the wall where he always kept his sword. The clank of weapons being readied joined the hum of men talking, and soon Iain strode into the courtyard. His men poured out behind him, armed with swords, bows, and arrows. Iain, flanked by his brothers, Rory Mac, and Angus, led the charge down the seagate stairs, expecting to see the enemy rushing off a ship ready to attack. But when they reached the shore, a ship with a large banner depicting a swirling snake was sailing away under the bright moonlight.

Iain stuttered to a halt, momentarily confused. It was certainly Froste's ship, so why was it leaving before seeing battle?

"Did they decide nae to strike?" Rory Mac asked, sounding just as bewildered as Iain.

At that moment, the man who ran the watchtower, Roland, stumbled across the ground. He fell at Iain's knees. "Laird," he rasped. "I'm sorry. I-I fell asleep. When I awoke, I saw the ship and sounded the horn."

Iain's heart tightened, each beat excruciatingly painful as he stared, frozen in shock, out beyond the loch to the distant sea. *Why would they leave?* he wondered. The possibility that they'd come for Marion and had found her out here, alone, angry, and hurt made fear and anger pulse within him.

"But why?" Lachlan asked, continuing Rory Mac's line of questioning. "Why come here at all?"

Iain's gaze locked on Angus. The old man had bent down to pick something up, and when he rose, he clutched a hair comb in his large hand. Iain stared at it as the image of Marion entering the great hall flashed in mind. Her hair had been pulled up at one side, and this comb... This comb had been Catriona's.

"Marion!" Iain roared, reason fleeing him as he charged into the icy black water. Before he could dive under, hands grabbed onto him and tugged him back.

Lachlan clasped his shoulders. "Ye'll nae rescue her that way."

Coldness seeped through Iain, but it had nothing to do with the freezing temperature of the water. Fear ebbed in the back of his mind, but he shoved it away. There was no time for fear. No time for hesitation. No time for anything but to rescue Marion. He could not lose her. And when he reached Froste, or whoever of Froste's or de Lacy's knights had dared to take his wife, he was going to kill every last one of the men.

⸺⸢⸣⸤⸥⸺

Marion awoke with the left side of her face pressed against the cold wet sand and rough grass. She attempted to sit up, but a strong wave of nausea overcame her. Somewhere in the distance, she thought she heard voices, but she was afraid it might be Froste's men still, so she dared not call for help. With a grunt, she rolled onto her back and breathed in long, measured breaths to calm her roiling stomach.

Her head pounded viciously, and when she raised a shaking hand to her temple, she touched something crusty, likely dried blood, on her forehead. She slowly pushed herself up to her elbows, the nausea still there but not quite as strong. From there, she managed to crouch, her stomach dipping with her movements. She parted the grass just enough so that she could see but hopefully not be seen. Her vision was slightly blurry, but shadows of men with torches swept along the shoreline.

Her breath seized in her chest as she remembered what Froste's men had said they were going to do to Iain. If it wasn't already too late, she had to get back to the castle and warn him of Froste's plan. If she could stay low to the ground, she felt confident she could make it to the seagate stairs and up to the courtyard without being seen by Froste's men.

Infused with determination to help Iain, she began crawling through the grass and over the rocks. The boulders were like a hundred small knives making precise slices across her hands and knees, but she bit back the pain that threatened to defeat her. When she came to the edge of the grassy area, she drew slowly to her feet, teetering where she stood as nausea washed over her wave after wave. She took a step, and her world tilted to the right.

Behind her, she thought she heard yelling, and panic caught in her chest. They'd seen her! Forcing her shaking legs to move was torturous. She tried to run, but her body was heavy and slow. The shouting behind her grew louder, and she pushed herself harder, her legs finally understanding her silent, desperate command. Dirt flew out to the sides as she ran, and when she reached the stairs, she scrambled up them frantically.

Two stairs. Four. Six. Twelve. Twenty. How many more? Thirty. Forty. Fifty.

She lifted her head to check, and everything around her dipped and spun. She tried to gain the next step, but her foot slipped. As she fell backward, a gut-wrenching scream ripped from her lungs.

⌇⌇⌇

At first Iain thought he was imagining Marion when he glanced toward the seagate stairs and saw her racing up them, her pale hair glowing in the moonlight and blowing behind her in the wind. But when Angus started shouting her name, Iain knew a moment of such sweet relief that a shudder ran through his body. He blinked and the respite ended as she swayed precariously. His heart lurched with the knowledge of what was to come, what he could not stop. She flailed her arms wildly about her, and he darted his gaze downward, counting the steep steps to the unforgiving ground. *Fifty steps.*

The world around him abruptly fell away. All sound faded. His vision tunneled onto her, only her. Tumbling. Falling. Hitting the bottom step and lying still. His guttural cry pierced the hum in his ears as he charged toward her, the rough terrain slowing his progress in a torment worse than any he'd experienced in his life. He fell hard to his knees, the stone steps cutting into his skin, but it did not matter. Nothing mattered but her. He'd trade his life to make certain she kept hers.

He gathered her limp, wind-chilled body in his arms. "Marion," he cried out.

She did not move. Did not respond.

"Marion, open yer eyes," he demanded, his throat aching with each syllable he choked out. "Ye will nae die!" he ordered, even as his mind shouted that she might.

Dried blood had caked on her forehead while fresh blood seeped from her blue-tinged upper lip. His hand shook violently as he lifted his finger to her lips and wiped away the blood, so warm against her icy skin. "Please, Marion," he whispered, burying his head in the curve of her neck and holding her tightly. "I need ye," he admitted brokenly in her ear.

"I need you, too," she whispered.

He jerked upward and gaped at her. "Ye're nae dead!"

She offered a faint smile. "Not yet, but if you keep holding me so tightly, I may still succumb."

He pulled her closer and held her against his chest with care, relishing in the faint beat of her heart against his. After his trembling subsided, he held her far enough away that he could see her eyes. A crowd had gathered around them, but he didn't care. He caught her glorious gaze. "I'm sorry. For how I responded in the great hall and for making ye feel there was no place for ye in my life."

The smile she gave him lifted him all the way out of the darkness he'd dwelled in for far too long. She pressed her cold hand to his cheek. "I forgive you."

Nineteen

When Marion awoke, the first thing she saw was Iain slumped in a chair beside the bed. She moved her hand to his and brushed her fingertips over his skin.

His eyes popped opened, and he jerked upright. "Ye're awake."

She swallowed, her throat dry. "How long have I been asleep?"

"A full day. How do ye feel?"

"Stiff," she said as she looked to where the trunk had been. She wanted to know what he had done with it, but she preferred he offer the information. She did not wish to ask. When she pulled her gaze back to his, he was staring at her.

He took her hand in his, brought it to his lips, and brushed a kiss across her knuckles. "I'm verra sorry for my part in yer injuries."

Marion's brows dipped together. "You had no part in my injuries. I slipped."

"Ye would have never been alone outside in the first place had I nae yelled at ye for wearing Catriona's gown." His face was set in hard lines. "I'll nae make excuses for my response. I—"

"You love her," Marion supplied, wishing to spare him the worry of hurting her by saying the words. "You love her, and it pained you to see me in her gown. I understand."

His blue eyes glittered with the hurt he was feeling. "Ye dunnae understand," he replied. "It pained me because when I saw ye in it, I could nae remember what she looked like when she'd worn it. All I could see was ye. All I could feel was my desire for ye. I swore to her that I'd nae forget her."

She took a quick breath of utter astonishment. "You're afraid you'll forget her if you let yourself love me?"

"Aye." The word was a single one, a small one, but drenched with misery deeper than the sea.

Her throat ached with the need to argue, but what words were there to convince him he'd not forget Catriona? She could not imagine loving someone as Iain had loved Catriona and then ever forgetting him. Yes, Iain's memories would likely fade a bit, and he'd make new ones with her, but loving someone new would not erase the love he'd felt for Catriona.

Marion took a long, shaky breath. Deep within, she knew her words would not convince him. He had to realize it himself. "I know not to expect your love," she said, hoping to ease the lines of worry on his forehead. He already knew she wanted it; there was no point in saying it.

He gave her a dark, layered look before pulling her roughly to him. "Marion, ye should expect it. Ye're my wife." He shook his head. "I'm nae good with talk of the heart. Let me try again. What I want to say is that I want to look toward the future, nae dwell in the past anymore."

"What of your fears?" she whispered into his chest.

"They are mine to conquer."

She peered sideways at his strong profile. Did that mean he thought he could defeat them? Did that mean he thought he might be able to make space in his heart to love her?

"What now?" she asked.

He set her away and motioned to the foot of the bed. "I moved Catriona's trunk out of the bedchamber, as I should have done when ye came. This is *our* bedchamber now. I want ye to be comfortable here and feel it is as much yers as mine."

Tears stung her eyes as warmness enveloped her.

He frowned and wiped the pad of his thumb across her cheek to catch her tears. "What's this?"

"Happiness," she said. "You've made me very happy. And I'm terribly sorry about Catriona's gown. I truly did not know. You see—"

He pressed a finger to her lips. "I ken all about it. Fiona admitted what she did."

Marion moved Iain's finger. "I'd like to talk to her." Part of her wanted to throttle the woman, but part of her wanted to try to help ease the pain she must be feeling.

"Ye kinnae."

"Why not?" she demanded.

"She's gone."

"Iain!" she gasped. "What have you done?"

He grimaced at her. "What I should have done months ago when she started hinting that I should marry her. I sent her away to marry another."

"Oh, Iain! How could you?"

"Verra easily," he said, crossing his arms. "I simply sent for the man, and he came to get her. Dunnae fret. He's a good man."

Marion shook her head at his words. "But she surely doesn't love him."

"They've shaken hands and agreed to be bound in

marriage for one year, and if after that she kinnae bring herself to stay married to him, I'll allow her back on the condition that she'll leave for good if she causes trouble again. Either way, she has a year to change her ways."

Iain's explanation made Marion feel a bit better, but still. "The other women will hate me."

"I ordered them nae to," he replied.

Marion choked out a laugh. "We spoke of this before, Iain. It does not work that way."

"It does in the clan, Marion. Ye'll learn."

She refused to argue. She knew he'd done it out of concern for her, and that part made her happy.

He leaned in and kissed her full on the mouth. "Now we need to discuss Froste. Did ye see anyone or hear anything when ye were by the water?"

She nodded, anxiety twisting in her stomach. "I saw two of his men, and I heard them talking. I was attempting to escape their attention when I fell and hit my head, and when I awoke, I saw the torches and presumed more of them had arrived. I didn't know it was you and your men, so I tried to run back to the castle to warn you."

"I thought as much," he said, his mouth setting in a hard, angry line.

A sudden chill took her at the memory, and she rubbed her hands up and down her arms. "They were sent to find a way into the castle."

"Oh, aye? So as to kill me first when they attack," he said, matter-of-fact.

She took a quick, sharp breath. "How did you know that?"

"I'm laird, Marion. 'Tis my duty to ken my enemies. Beyond that, it makes sense. Even if they take ye against my will, they need me dead so Froste can marry ye. I think their aim on Alex's land was to get ye back before the marriage was consummated, and now"—he grinned— "they rightly suppose it has been. Now they must get ye back and kill me."

She studied him, trying to determine what he was thinking, but he'd lowered the mask he so often wore. "Are you not worried?"

"Nay. Froste should be, though. When he comes for me, I'll be waiting. And ready."

Menace wrapped around his words and made her shudder. "What will you do?"

"Kill him," he replied, as if it would be so simple and not dangerous for him at all.

Iain stood, stretched, and started toward the door. Marion clamped her jaw shut as she watched him until he turned the door handle and her mind registered that he was actually leaving the room. "Where are you going?"

He faced her. "To ready my men," he said, as if it were obvious. He studied her long and hard. "Go back to sleep."

"I'm not tired," she protested.

"Ye are. There are dark smudges under yer eyes."

"They are under yours, as well. Perchance you should come to bed with me?"

A smile tugged at his lips. "A verra tempting sugges-tion, but I've yet to deal with the watchman who fell asleep and failed to sight Froste's ship."

Worry quickened her breath. "What will you do to him?"

"His error almost cost ye yer life. He'll go."

She frowned. "Go where?"

"Out of the clan, Marion."

"What?" She scrambled out of the bed and nearly tripped into Iain's arms. "Do you always banish men from your clan when they do something wrong?"

"Nay, but no one has ever done anything that almost cost me ye. I kinnae forgive it."

Her heart swelled that she meant so much to him, but he was being unreasonable. She had to make him see it. "Please, Iain." She ran her hand lightly down his chest. "Be kind and patient with him. For me?"

"What would ye have me do?" he asked, his voice pitching low with what she now knew was desire.

That was a good question. Her mind raced to come up with an answer he'd accept. "Remove him from his post and put him in a lesser position."

"Such as?" He quirked his eyebrows at her. "I kinnae trust him."

"You can make him earn your trust again," she offered. When he didn't look convinced, she seized on the one thing she hoped would work. "If you send him away from the clan, your men will surely blame me." It was true, but she felt guilty for using the fact that Iain would never want to do anything to cause her problems with his clan against him.

He frowned. "I dunnae think so. They ken what an error it was."

"Thinking is not knowing," she chided. "What if you're wrong? Please, Iain."

He sighed. "I'll put him in the stables to feed and water the horses. Will that please ye?"

"Yes!" she said, grinning at him.

Iain chuckled and patted her on the bottom. "To bed with ye. I'll be back later to see if ye are well."

She resisted the urge to scowl at his order. She knew it had been given out of concern for her. "I'm not going to stay abed all day. I feel much better. And lying here would make me feel trapped and worse."

He looked as if he wanted to protest, but he finally nodded. "If ye go outside, take Archibald with ye, but dunnae leave castle grounds with anyone but me."

She clenched her teeth. She knew he was worried. She was, too. But she didn't like feeling trapped. "It's as if I'm being kept prisoner in our home."

His jaw ticked at the side, showing his mounting frustration. "Dunnae think of it that way. I'm simply keeping ye safe until I've dealt with Froste."

"Surely, you do not mean to make poor Archibald attend me every time I want to go outside?" she prodded, trying to make him see reason. "He's supposed to be watching Bridgette."

Iain's expression hardened. "Now he'll watch over both of ye."

"I feel so much better now," she retorted with a roll of her eyes.

He smiled at her, as if a mere smile would make it all better. Her heart betrayed her and tugged as he'd likely intended. His gaze softened. "I'll attend ye when I can. If I kinnae and Archibald kinnae, then Angus can. Or I'll appoint someone else."

She glared at him, to which he responded with a broader grin. He kissed her lightly on the forehead and left before she could say more.

Certainly no longer tired now, she marched to the wardrobe to retrieve the gown she'd borrowed from Bridgette. But when she opened the door, her jaw fell open. A lovely gown of wool, fashioned with wide sleeves and a more fitting cut than the traditional highland woman's garb, hung there. She didn't hesitate to put it on. It fit perfectly. As she struggled with the laces, a knock came at the door.

"Yes," she called out, hearing the frustration in her own short tone.

"May I come in?" Bridgette replied.

"Oh yes!" Marion called back.

Bridgette chuckled when she saw Marion twisting about, trying to tie her own laces.

"Help, please!" Marion begged.

"Turn round," Bridgette demanded.

Marion immediately complied. "Bridgette, have you any idea who put this gown in here?"

"Nay."

Marion frowned, wondering if perchance Kyla had made the gown. Had Iain demanded it or did Kyla still like her? She turned to Bridgette. "Were you there when Iain sent Fiona away and ordered the women to like me?"

Bridgette pressed her lips together, but Marion could see she was fighting a smile.

"Oh no...," Marion whispered. "Do the women hate me?"

"Most dunnae for Fiona being disciplined. Though a few of her friends did grumble, especially Alanna."

"You said *for Fiona being disciplined*."

"Aye," Bridgette said, still struggling not to smile and finally losing the battle. Two large dimples appeared and her eyes twinkled.

Marion knitted her brow. "I hardly think the MacLeod women disliking me should make you smile," she grumbled.

Bridgette had the nerve to laugh in her face. "Ask me why they are griping, Marion."

Marion hesitated, sensing mischief in Bridgette's tone, but then her curiosity prevailed. "Why do they not care for me?"

"It's nae that they dunnae care for ye. Many are envious of ye."

Marion felt her jaw drop open. "Envious of *me?*"

Bridgette nodded.

"Whatever for? There's no reason to be jealous of— Oh!" Her shoulders sagged. "They wish to be married to Iain."

"Well," Bridgette said slowly, her laughter making her voice shake, "I'm sure afore he married Catriona, then after her death and afore ye came along, they wished it, but now they are envious because they long to be married to a man who loves them with as much passion as the MacLeod loves ye."

Marion burst out laughing now, too. "You must be teasing!"

Bridgette frowned. "I dunnae tease about love, and I may even be one of those women who is a wee bit envious. I would love to have Lachlan look at me the way Iain looks at ye."

Marion arched her eyebrows at her friend. "You wish for Lachlan to look at you as if he's tormented by how he should feel for you?"

"Aye!" Bridgette said. "I'd gladly take confusion on his face instead of the blank expression with which he stares at me. Then at least I'd ken he feels *something.* However, Iain does nae look at ye like a man tormented." Bridgette quirked her mouth. "Och. Well, sometimes, but mostly, especially the night ye appeared in the hall wearing Catriona's wedding gown—afore he realized what ye were wearing—he looked like a man verra much in love. His eyes go all soft when he looks at ye and a smile always plays at his lips. Oh! And yesterday, even when ye were nowhere in sight and he sent Fiona away and demanded all the MacLeod women like ye, he looked like a man who would fight the devil himself to defend ye. No man who is nae in love looks like that."

"I assure you, he's not in love with me." No matter how deeply she longed for it, she refused to fool herself.

"I assure ye, he is. Now he may nae have told ye yet..." Bridgette gave her a questioning look, and Marion shook her head. "Och, well, he is still denying it, then. Do ye nae remember what the seer said?"

Before Marion could answer, Bridgette spoke again. *"Thrice he'll stare how he feels for ye in the face, and thrice he'll deny it."* Her accent so mimicked the seer's that gooseflesh appeared on Marion's arms. Bridgette cackled—for effect, Marion knew—but it still made Marion shiver. *"But if the Fairy Flag flies again, then the love that is now but a seed in his gut will have found a way to his heart and will grow into a vine that stretches to the heavens. It will be a new love. Nae the same as any that grew afore it, but strong, true, and a blessing,"* Bridgette finished.

Marion trembled where she stood, exhilarated by the possibility that Iain was starting to truly love her. Yet she also shook with the very real fear that if it was true, and if the seer's prophecy was correct, Iain would eventually fly the Fairy Flag to save the clan, which could only mean the clan was in danger because of her. Her thoughts turned in circles and each loop led to Froste, which led to her father. Before she could think more on it, a wave of nausea overcame her. She barely made it to the bucket before she was sick.

Bridgette hovered behind her as she retched, and when she was done, her friend handed her a linen. "Are ye sure ye feel well enough to be out of bed?"

Marion nodded. "Yes, I feel fine, except I have been rather nauseated in the mornings and haven't had much of an appetite." She gave Bridgette a stern look. "Don't mention it to Iain. I don't want him to worry."

Bridgette stared at her oddly for a long moment. "Marion, may I ask ye something delicate?"

Marion nodded.

Bridgette furrowed her brow. "When was the last time ye had yer flux?"

Marion felt a blush rise to her cheeks, but she cast her mind back and then gasped. "Well before I left England." She could not stop the grin that came to her face. "Bring me the cup over by the bucket."

"Why?" Bridgette asked with a frown.

Marion strode past Bridgette and picked up the cup before scurrying behind the dressing curtain. As she pulled her clothes down to relieve her bladder, she said, "The midwife in the village near my father's home told me that if a woman is with child, her urine will be clear."

Bridgette snorted. "And ye believe that? My mother told me a sure sign was morning nausea. Ye're going to have a bairn!"

A child.

Marion's hand fluttered to her belly as she pulled up her clothing and looked into the cup. She needed proper light to see the color. She dashed to the window, and her breath caught. It looked clear! She and Iain had made a child. Heaven above! Her fingers curled against the skin of her belly as she thought of falling down the stairs and that she could have lost the babe. She exhaled a shaky breath of relief that she had not.

Would Iain be as happy as she was at the news?

Her grin faltered a bit as Bridgette came to peer over

her shoulder. "That looks clear to me. Ye must tell Iain at once!"

Marion nodded. "I will. I just wish…" She let the words trail off. She was embarrassed to say that she wished he loved her. What if he felt he must say the words now because she carried his child, but he didn't truly mean them?

"Ye wish what?"

"Nothing," Marion said, forcing her grin wide once more. "I'll tell him tonight when we are alone. You must keep this a secret until I've done so."

"I vow I will."

"Come." Marion grabbed Bridgette's hand. "I've a feeling he'll limit my leaving the castle even more once he knows this, so let's go. I want to do a great deal today."

⚜

As Marion and Bridgette made their way to the kitchen, Graham appeared and Marion had to suppress the desire to poke Bridgette with her elbow when an irritated look crossed her face.

Graham faced Bridgette with such a look of tenderness that Marion ached for him. "Bridgette, would ye care to go riding with me and Lachlan?" he asked.

Her entire face lit up at the mention of Lachlan. "Yes!" she gushed. "Let me go get my bow."

Graham grinned. "I'll come with ye and we will go to the stables from there."

Bridgette started to dash off and then turned back to Marion. "If ye dunnae need me to stay?"

Marion waved a hand at her friend. "Go."

Bridgette nodded, and she and Graham departed, leaving Marion alone in the hall. She stood for a moment looking down at her flat stomach and grinning, anticipating the quickening. When Marion entered the kitchen, the heat from the ovens and the smells of freshly baking bread and venison assaulted her. Normally, she loved both, but right now they mattered not. She pressed a hand to her stomach and smiled secretly to herself.

Before she could linger on the thought any longer, she caught sight of Elspeth, who paused her stirring in mid-motion. A smile came to Elspeth's face, and Marion released her held breath.

"Marion, it's good to see ye recovered!" she said and laid her spoon on the counter.

Several of the women stopped what they were doing, including Kyla, who rushed over to Marion and embraced her. The woman arched her dark eyebrows as she surveyed Marion. "I see I judged correctly with the gown."

"Oh, Kyla!" Marion exclaimed. "Thank you! It's love-ly."

Kyla nodded and patted Marion's hand. "We all ken what a rotten thing Fiona did to ye. I went directly home after he ordered ye out of the great hall and started on a gown for ye. I decided if it did nae fit quite right, it would do until we could make ye more."

"That was very kind of you," Marion said, running her hand down her skirts and thinking happily that she would need looser-fitting gowns soon. She glanced around the room at the women who were hovering but feigning interest. She felt as if she needed to say something about what had happened with Fiona. "I want you all to know how sorry I am that Fiona was sent away."

She locked eyes with Elspeth, who simply waved a hand as if to say, *Please don't fret.* Marion took a deep breath in the suddenly very quiet room and continued. "I asked Iain to think about letting her stay, but he refused."

Suddenly, comments were coming from every direction, so fast she could hardly tell who was saying what.

"Fiona always acts wanton toward my husband."

"Mine as well!"

"She thought herself too good to work in the kitchen."

"She didn't even cry at Catriona's funeral!"

Marion's cheeks burned with gratitude for what the ladies were trying to do to show her that they didn't care for Fiona overly much, but she also felt a twinge of pity for Elspeth. "I'm sure Fiona has positive qualities, as well," Marion said loudly, purposely looking at Elspeth.

Elspeth shrugged. "I'll nae speak unkindly of my sister, but I'll say she is nae a happy soul and what she did to ye was cruel. I dunnae think what has happened will be harmful to her. She would never have been happy here as anything less than the MacLeod's wife. She thought it her right as the eldest sister, and she always felt Catriona snatched the chance away from her."

"I thought ye were nae going to speak poorly of yer sister," came a sharp voice from behind Marion.

Marion saw several of the women's eyes grow big as they stared at whoever was standing there. She slowly turned and met Alanna's hostile dark eyes. The woman's full lips were pressed into a thin, angry line.

Elspeth brushed past Marion and moved toward Alanna, who flinched away from her. Marion frowned at the odd reaction.

"Alanna, why are ye here in the kitchen?" Elspeth asked. "Ye should be home getting ready for the bairn."

Alanna's hand fluttered to her belly. "I'd feel better about my bairn coming if yer sister were still here." Her eyes cut to Marion. "Fiona acted as clan midwife, though I see many of the women here have forgotten that she helped deliver their bairns."

A hush fell over the group, and some women cast their gazes down. But one woman stared boldly at Alanna. "Ye ken verra well that Fiona killed my bairn."

Marion held perfectly still, realizing there were many secrets that weaved through these women's lives that she did not know.

"Fiona did nae kill yer bairn," Alanna said in a hard voice as she raked a hand through her long, curly red hair. "Yer boy came out with the cord wrapped around his neck and there was nae that could be done! I've told ye this repeatedly, but ye refuse to listen."

"Ye were nae there," the woman spat.

"I was nae, but Fiona came to me distraught and told me what had happened." Alanna turned toward Elspeth. "Tell her, Elspeth! Ye were there! Ye ken. Dunnae let her bitterness destroy yer sister's life any longer."

The woman shook her fist at Alanna. "Elspeth has already spoken to me, and I dunnae need to hear more."

Alanna's shoulders sagged, and she shook her head as her gaze moved from woman to woman and stopped on Marion. "I never thought I'd see the day that MacLeods turned against MacLeods. Then again, I never thought I'd see the day that Iain forsook his love of Catriona, either. My poor cousin!"

With that pronouncement, Alanna stomped out the way she had come, leaving them all standing in hushed silence. Elspeth moved toward Marion, took her hand, and squeezed it. "She's just distraught. She'll quiet once her anger lessens. Catriona and Fiona were her dearest friends."

"But not yours?" Marion asked, surprised by Elspeth's curious lack of emotion over her sister's departure.

Elspeth shook her head and gave a surreptitious glance around. Most of the women had moved away and returned to their work. Kyla was the only one who still stood there with them, and when Elspeth fairly stared the woman down, she wiped her hands on her aprons and gave Marion a smile. "I should go stir the pottage."

"As the youngest, they thought me an annoyance more than anything." Elspeth shrugged and smiled. "I tried to belong, but the three of them did nae wish for me to."

Marion cocked her head. "Do you mean until Fiona thought Catriona stole Iain from her?"

"Oh, aye. I mean until then. Then Alanna and Catriona grew closer, and Fiona decided she would finally be kind to me." Elspeth pressed her lips together, and Marion got the distinct feeling that Fiona's efforts had been too late for Elspeth.

"I am sorry, Elspeth. I didn't have many friends as a child, either." The truth was, Angus had been her only friend until Bridgette, but she didn't feel comfortable enough to share that yet.

"Ye've me now," Elspeth said, linking her arm with Marion's.

Marion smiled. "I'm glad. Can you think of anything I could do to make Alanna a little more accepting of me?"

"Hmm." Elspeth tilted her head in thought. "Ye could take her some of my black pudding. She's nae been feeling well, and she loves it."

Marion rubbed her aching temples with her fingers. Exhaustion was creeping in, but she did want to try to make things right with Alanna.

"That seems to be a good idea," Marion said, nodding.

Elspeth beamed at her. "I'll just get ye the black pudding."

She scurried over to her worktable and came back in short time with a dish of the pudding and a spoon with a heaping serving of the pudding on it. She held the spoon out to Marion. "I brought a bit for ye, too. Do ye like black pudding?"

Marion grinned. "I love it. My father's cook made excellent black pudding."

"Mine will be better," Elspeth boasted.

Marion couldn't resist. She took the pudding Elspeth offered and ate a bite. It was delicious. "Elspeth," she said, "that is the best pudding I've ever had."

Elspeth nodded. "Why don't ye have some more?"

"I couldn't," Marion replied, not wanting to reveal that she was queasy, but Elspeth looked so downcast. "Just one more."

Elspeth laughed, went back to her worktable, and returned with an even bigger bite for Marion. She quickly ate it.

"Another?" Elspeth asked.

Marion held up the spoon. "I'll take this with me and have some with Alanna, if she offers. I really need to go, though. Where does Alanna live?"

"Nae far from here."

Marion bit her lip, thinking on what to do.

"What's wrong?" Elspeth asked, her eyes wide.

Marion sighed. "I just remembered that I told Iain I'd not leave the castle without taking Archibald. I'll have to go find him first."

Elspeth shook her head. "Dunnae fash yerself. Iain will nae ken, and ye'll be back shortly."

Marion shook her head. "He may not know, but I

would. I vowed to him."

"I'll go with ye, then," Elspeth offered.

"That's sweet of you, but I think Iain's intent was for me to have one of his men with me at all times." The look of annoyance that flitted across Elspeth's face made Marion laugh. "I feel the same way about it."

Elspeth forced a smile, and Marion gave her a small wave as she left the kitchen.

She located Archibald in the great hall, and they set off to Alanna's.

They walked in silence for a while as they strolled through the woods. Alanna and Rory Mac's home seemed to be a bit farther than Elspeth had indicated. A sharp pain stabbed Marion in the side as they climbed uphill, and though the air was cold, she suddenly felt warm.

"Archibald," she said, glancing at him on a wave of dizziness. She reached for him as the earth beneath her seemed to shift and another, more intense, pain cramped her belly.

Archibald's eyes widened, and he grasped her when she swayed again. "Marion, what's wrong?"

"I don't feel—"

She doubled over as pain sliced through her stomach, and she broke out into a sweat. "I don't feel well," she said, her voice trembling as the pain pulsed through her belly. Her throat felt as if it was closing, and she gasped a breath of air, then another while grasping her stomach, which was twisting into knots.

"Archibald," she whispered. Her mouth was suddenly very dry and her head pounded so hard that her vision blurred.

"What is it?" he asked, his eyes widening as he hovered over her. He patted her back and then hooked his hands under her arms to help her stand, but when she tried, the agony was so intense she screamed. And then, mercifully, everything went black.

Twenty

Iain sat in the great hall surrounded by his brothers, Angus, and Rory Mac to discuss once again the various ways Froste and de Lacy might try to kill him and seize Marion. He contemplated every possible scenario, thinking they had thought of them all, when a vile one occurred to him. "They could plant a traitor amongst us to lure Marion or myself out, or even to help them get inside."

"Impossible," Lachlan replied. "None of our men are traitors."

Iain didn't want to think so, either, but he had to consider everything. "I hope nae, but I must consider everything. Who amongst us has any reason to be angry or feel as if they have been wronged? Let us think on each of our men and make sure we feel they are faithful."

Before anyone could speak, a loud commotion had them turning in the direction of the castle door. Suddenly, Archibald's voice filled the hall. "Help! Get Iain! Marion needs help!"

Iain shoved to his feet as black fear covered his vision. He raced out of the great hall, his brothers, Rory Mac, and Angus close behind, and came to terrified stop at the sight of Marion in Archibald's arms, her head thrashing wildly back and forth as she moaned.

"Marion!" he roared as he rushed to Archibald and took his wife from him. Iain looked down at her, and his stomach clenched. She was mumbling and her speech was slurred, and he could not understand her. Then she began to twitch and convulse in his arms, white foam coming from her mouth.

All around him shouting reigned, and then Bridgette was beside him with Kyla, screaming at him to lay her on the ground. He kneeled, feeling dazed, almost not in his body, as they pushed him aside to tend her. Bridgette thrust a long piece of her gown that she tore off in Marion's mouth, between her teeth, and Kyla attempted to hold Marion's arms still. But Marion was delirious and fighting Kyla. She clawed at the woman, and Iain moved closer as Lachlan kneeled down. They each held an arm as Bridgette pulled Marion's lids up and looked into her unusually wide pupils.

Bridgette rocked back on her haunches, her face white as a sheet. "I've seen a thing such as this afore," she choked out, tears filling her eyes. "I think she's been poisoned."

Panic rioted through him as he pushed back against her bucking body. "What can we do?"

"Turn her on her side," Bridgette said, swiping at her tears. "We must make her empty her stomach."

Together, Iain and Lachlan did as Bridgette had said, while everyone stood around them murmuring their fear and concern. As soon as the convulsions stopped, Bridgette took the material from between Marion's teeth and stuck her finger down Marion's throat. Immediately, Marion let loose the contents of her stomach. And then Bridgette repeated the process, until there was simply nothing left and Marion fell into unconsciousness.

Sobbing, Bridgette murmured, "I dunnae ken what else

to do. What happens next depends on how much poison she swallowed and when, and whether the dose was fatal."

Fatal. The word hit him like a fist forged of steel. She could not die. She had become like his air. Like water. Like a bright ray of sun that warmed his soul. He loved her. He did. It was simple. It was complicated, too, but it was a fact he would not want to change. He wanted to wrap Marion in his embrace and never let her out of his arms again. He wanted to worship her body and sit for hours learning the secrets of her heart. He wanted to tell her he loved her and that he was the biggest clot-heid of all to have taken so long to realize it. He closed his eyes, and prayed to God that He grant Marion continued life.

When Bridgette gasped, Iain's eyes flew open. He looked at Marion, who was still on her side, and seeping onto the floor around her was blood.

"What's happening?" he shouted at Bridgette as he turned Marion over to see the front of her gown soaked with crimson. He gathered Marion in his arms, careful to cradle her head. His heart beat painfully as he held her.

When Bridgette did not answer but gave him an anguished look, he thundered, "Tell me."

Bridgette, her face pinched, set her hand on Iain's arm. "I vowed to her I would nae tell ye. She wanted to."

"Bridgette," Iain growled, perilously close to losing his control. Angus kneeled beside Iain and looked worriedly at Marion.

Bridgette heaved a breath. "She's losing yer bairn," Bridgette blurted, sobbing anew.

The news tore at his insides, and around him, he could see the shock on his family's and clansmen's faces.

"Come," Bridgette and Kyla both said. "We must get her upstairs to a bed."

"Someone needs to fetch Fiona," Alanna said from her place beside Rory Mac in the circle. Iain blinked at her, realizing he'd not even known she'd arrived. And when he glanced around the room, he realized most of the women from the kitchen were there, all looking terribly upset. Marion had made friends. Happiness and anguish collided at once. Would she live to realize it?

"Fiona?" Iain repeated, angered that Alanna would even suggest that he should bring Fiona back to tend to Marion.

Alanna walked toward him and gave him a determined look. "Aye. If Marion lives, she'll need a healer, and Fiona is a strong one. Set yer anger aside for yer wife."

He glanced at Bridgette, who nodded. "Marion would want that."

Iain curled his fingers tighter around Marion's body, knowing he didn't have much time to decide. He needed to get her to the bedchamber. "What of the bairn?" he asked, his voice cracking.

Bridgette shook her head as tears rolled down her cheeks. "I dunnae ken of a way to save a new bairn nae yet out of the stomach, especially nae this new."

"Iain," Alanna said softly, putting her hand on his arm. "Let Rory Mac go for Fiona. Maybe she can save Marion. It's too late for the bairn."

"Ye dunnae ken that," he argued, tormented.

"I think I do," she whispered, her eyes glassy with unshed tears. "I've lost two bairns myself."

Iain met Rory Mac's sympathetic gaze. "Go," Iain choked out. Pulling Marion close to his chest, he moved toward the stairs flanked by Bridgette and Alanna. He climbed up to their bedchamber and laid Marion on the bed, then stepped back to allow Bridgette and Alanna to clean her. As they worked, his mind turned with what had happened, and a thought occurred that so enraged him that he clenched his teeth until his jaw throbbed painfully. When Bridgette and Alanna were done cleaning Marion, he went to her side, dropped to his knees, and buried his head against her chest.

He listened and caught the sound of her faint heartbeat. "I love ye," he choked out, struggling to control his emotions. "I love ye, do ye hear?" But she didn't. He ran a hand over her flat stomach that had held their bairn. His gut twisted and his throat tightened as he settled his palm there and said a prayer for their child's soul. He was not a crying man. He'd not cried when Catriona had died, though his grief had been all-consuming, yet now tears stung his eyes with grief for the bairn he'd never know, for the possibility that he might lose Marion, for the pain she would feel when she learned she'd lost their bairn. It gripped him in a clutch that made each breath painful.

He forced himself to sit up and turn to Bridgette. She stood in a corner with Alanna, and when she saw him looking at her, they came toward him. He stood to speak to the women. "Ye said Marion had been poisoned?"

"Aye. Her symptoms were all the same as a man in our clan whose wife poisoned him with belladonna."

He scrubbed a hand over his face, fighting back the tiredness threatening to consume him. "Who would do this?" he asked, more to himself than Bridgette, but Bridgette's eyes grew wide.

"I dunnae mean someone here poisoned her. She could have accidentally eaten the berries. They look like fruit."

"Nay." His one word cut through the air and made Bridgette jerk. "Marion knows herbs and medicine. I'm sure she knows the poisonous berries. The only person I would have even imagined might do this would have been Fiona, but she was nae here."

Alanna made an angry sound and then glared at him. "Ye are wrong when it comes to Fiona. Elspeth is the one ye should have sent away."

Iain narrowed his gaze, his heart thumping an angry beat. "What do ye mean?"

Alanna sighed. "I tried to tell ye afore, but ye would nae listen. It was nae Fiona's idea to give Marion Catriona's gown. It was Elspeth's. Fiona refused to do it but, well, she got angry with yer wife and then went ahead and did it against her better judgment."

"Elspeth is a deceiver," he bit out, curling his hands into fists.

"Aye!" Alanna cried. "It's time someone saw the truth in Elspeth. She appears meek, but I ken she brought trouble on Fiona when Rhona's bairn died. Though she knew Fiona was nae to blame, I vow she told the other women she was! And if ye think she loved Catriona, ye're wrong. Elspeth used to laugh at Catriona's weakness, which is why Catriona, Fiona, and I never had time for her."

Iain frowned at the news. Catriona had never spoken ill of Elspeth. Then again, Catriona had never spoke ill of anyone. The thunderous anger growing inside him was threatening to whisk away his reason. "If Elspeth is to blame, she must have more in her possession. Would either of ye ken belladonna if ye saw it?"

"I would," Bridgette replied, looking as enraged as Iain felt.

"Will ye stay here and watch over Marion?" he asked Alanna. She nodded immediately.

When Iain and Bridgette opened the bedchamber door,

Angus was waiting, as well as Kyla, Neil, Archibald, and Iain's brothers. Angus was the first to speak, and Iain had to swallow hard when he saw tears in the man's eyes.

"How is she?" Angus croaked.

"Nae good," Iain managed to say in a steady voice.

"Laird," Kyla said, "may I be of service?"

He forced a smile. "I thank ye. If ye'd stay with Alanna and Marion, Bridgette and I are going to see Elspeth."

"Certainly," Kyla replied and quickly moved past him into the bedchamber.

When the door shut behind her, the questions came at him from every direction. "I'll explain as we go," he said, and as the group worked its way to Elspeth's house—only to find it empty—and then to the kitchen, he told them all he knew.

When he opened the door to the kitchen to find it empty of all the women except Elspeth, Iain knew he had missed something he should have seen long ago. Elspeth was the only one who had not come to attend Marion when word had spread so rapidly of her illness.

"Laird," Elspeth cried out. "Who killed Marion?"

"Who killed Marion?" Angus bellowed. "She's nae dead yet." The older Scot snarled and stepped toward Elspeth, who scrambled away.

Iain reached out and pulled Angus back, though it was hard to see with the anger clouding his vision. He handed Angus to Lachlan and motioned to Graham and Archibald. "Seize her."

The men had Elspeth by the arms just as she let loose a shriek. Iain ignored her screams and went with Bridgette to Elspeth's workstation. Bridgette began to poke around, shaking her head and mumbling. "I don't see anything," she said, slamming her hand against the counter. A tankard fell from the edge, landing between Bridgette and Iain's feet, and dark blue berries poured out. Bridgette gasped and knelt to the ground, carefully picking up a berry with the edge of her skirt. She rose and nodded as her face twisted into a mask of fury. "This is belladonna."

All the blood rushed from Elspeth's face, and she suddenly went limp in Graham and Archibald's hold. Iain stared down at the woman. He wanted answers, but now that Elspeth would be safely locked away, she could wait. Marion needed him.

"Put her in the dungeon," he told Graham and Archibald and then stepped around her without a backward glance and headed back to Marion.

He spent the night watching his wife, who lay still as death until she was suddenly screaming and delirious. She thrashed on the bed and tried to claw at her skin, which had broken into a red, angry rash. He held her until the fit had passed, and then he took the sponge that Bridgette silently handed him and dabbed her until his eyes were so blurry he had to close them.

⚜

Iain woke with a start at the hand on his shoulder, and when he glanced up, Fiona looked down at him. He stood and inhaled a deep breath, stilling as a familiar scent filled his nose. Swiveling back toward Marion, he leaned over and started to lower his head to her chest when Bridgette spoke. "She lives. Barely. Fiona just arrived."

He swallowed. Suddenly, he was back at Catriona's deathbed, and he recalled clearly the sticky-sweet smell of death, hanging heavy in the air like an overly ripe fruit. He shut his eyes tight and then opened them once more to find

Fiona brushing past him.

For several long silent moments, she examined Marion, and then she started talking to—or rather barking orders at—Bridgette, telling her what she needed and to make haste. Bridgette scurried from the room, and Iain moved to Marion's side and took her hand with one of his. He brushed the other over her forehead.

Fiona stood still beside him as he looked down at Marion. "Yer sister did this. She tried to kill Marion," Iain said. He turned to look at Fiona. "Have ye any idea why she would do such a thing?"

Fiona gaped at him, but after a spell, she managed to speak. "I imagine she wanted to have ye for her own. I've thought on why she did what she has done to me, and that is what I concluded. I think it's why she stirred the other clanswomen's hatred of me and why she tricked me into being the one to actually give Marion Catriona's gown. I vow I didn't plot it, but I did do the deed, and my envy is unforgivable."

Iain nodded, not ready to offer any sort of forgiveness, in spite of her apparent regret.

Fiona took in a long rattling breath. "I think Elspeth was intending to rid herself of me from the very start because she knew I hoped to marry ye," she said bluntly, casting her gaze down as her cheeks pinked. "When ye returned with a new bride, I suppose Elspeth simply altered her plot to include ridding ye of Marion, as well. Have ye spoken to Elspeth yet?"

"Nay. I'm afraid my hands would find their way around her neck."

Fiona sighed. "I understand. I kinnae imagine what she was thinking to poison Marion. Bridgette told me of it," Fiona offered before he even thought to ask how she knew.

"I hope ye can forgive me one day."

Iain stared down at Marion, whose breathing was still irregular. "Ye save Marion and I'll forgive ye."

The vigil lasted three days. And though it was the second time he'd stood such a vigil, it was not any easier than the first. Perchance it was harder because he knew the pain that might come.

Fiona had stayed by Marion's side relentlessly, and Iain knew that even if Marion did not live, he had to forgive Fiona. She was as haggard as he was from lack of sleep.

On the third night, moments after his brothers had left the room to report clan news and try to entreat him to let one of them watch over Marion so he could sleep, Marion's eyes flickered open. The moment they did, her hand fluttered to her belly. The bright joy he felt to see her green eyes fixed on him dulled at the thought that he had to tell her of the bairn. He shoved out of his chair, and Fiona stirred beside him. She blinked her eyes, looked at Marion, and smiled brightly, then hastily got up and scurried from the room, softly shutting the door behind her.

Marion watched as Iain, who looked unkempt and tired with heavy beard growth and dark smudges under his eyes, moved beside her bed. He smiled down at her. "Ye're awake."

Her thoughts were not as clear as she would have liked, but she was sure her head would be less muddled once she had a bit of food. She must have eaten something before that had made her ill, but now she was ravenous, which she knew was a good sign for her and the babe.

She glanced at Iain from under her eyelashes, excitement and apprehension stirring in her belly. "Iain, I've something to tell ye."

"So do I," he replied.

The trembling of his voice made her throat tighten with worry. "What is it?"

His large hand cupped her cheek and held it gently. "I love ye."

Tears sprung to her eyes at the words she'd thought never to hear from his lips. "What?"

He leaned close to her, his chest brushing hers, and kissed her with a sweet tenderness that made her feel as if warmth flowed through her.

"I love ye, Marion. I hope ye still want my love because I'm overflowing with it for ye, and if ye dunnae want it, I'll drown."

Her heart hammered at his words and her hand shook as she raised it and pressed it to his cheek. "I want it. It's the only thing I've ever wanted from you." She could not imagine anything better than this moment, except possibly seeing his face when she told him of the babe. "Iain, I'm—" Unmistakable pain flashed in his eyes and stole her breath, and her words along with it. "What's wrong?"

Wordlessly, he gathered her in his arms and shifted her so she was sitting on his lap. He put one arm around her back and one hand on her stomach. "Marion." Her name came from his lips raw and aching, and his fingers curled gently into the flesh of her belly. His eyes held hers, the sadness in them bringing tears to her own, and she knew. She knew what he was going to tell her before he uttered a word.

"I lost the babe." It was not a question, but a statement of gut-wrenching pain.

"Aye." The word trembled from his lips. "Ye lost the bairn."

Her stomach turned violently with the loss as his arms encircled her completely and his hands locked against her spine. Sobs started low and, within moments, were racking her body. She felt robbed. Hollow. To blame. And fearful that his admission of love had been one of pity.

"Let me go," she said through her tears. Yet he held her tighter and began to rock her while whispering of his sadness for their loss in her ear.

She turned her head from his, but his strong fingers came to her chin and forced her to look at him. "Dunnae deny me my grief, Marion. I love ye."

"No." She shook her head, hiccupped with a fresh sob, and blinked at him. "You don't have to say that. You don't have to try to make me feel better."

He stared incredulously at her for a suspended moment, and then he brushed his lips to hers. "I love ye. I would never tell ye so if it was nae true, no matter the pain ye're in. I'm a clot-heid. I tried to deny it, but I'll nae deny it any longer." He kissed her hard on the lips. "*A ghràidh.* My love."

Iain's words were wonderful, yet her happiness was dulled by the agony of losing their child. She nodded at him, wanting to believe him, desperately needing him in this moment. His strength. His arms. His love.

He rocked her as she cried and ran a gentle hand over her head, all the while promising his undying love. It seemed a long while later when she could cry no more. Her eyes were swollen, her head aching, her limbs heavy with fatigue. Iain laid her on the bed and settled beside her, putting his hand once again on her belly.

"One day we'll make another bairn, and I swear to ye, Marion, I'll nae let harm come to ye again as long as there is breath in my body."

Marion settled her hand over Iain's. "You cannot keep all harm from me."

"I can try," he responded.

She nodded, thinking of her lost child and then the seer, of Froste, and her father. She felt sure they would still come, and it would be her responsibility to stop the war her father and Froste wished to start so she could watch over Iain, just as he wished to do for her, until she had no breath left in her body.

Twenty-One

The healing process was slow, both mentally and physically. In the first week of Marion's recovery, Fiona—much to Marion's surprise—was a kind and excellent caretaker. The first thing she said to Marion when she saw her awake was that she was sorry. She then begged Marion's forgiveness for her actions, and Marion forgave her without hesitation, for she could see the truth of Fiona's regret. Perchance her new marriage would make her happy.

Elspeth was another matter. Marion had not seen her since the woman had tried to kill her, but she intended to see her today, as Iain was about to go downstairs where Elspeth awaited him to decide her fate. Marion wanted to go, but Iain had stubbornly refused thus far, saying he would not chance her relapsing.

Marion took a long breath, determined to make him agree. Iain was beside her on the bed where she was reclined—by his orders. "It is my right to go," she said with quiet resolution.

Iain shook his head. "Ye could relapse."

Marion squeezed his hand in hers. "You can carry me down. I'll not even walk."

"Nay."

The man was stubborn, to be sure. Marion would

simply be more so. "I will hear from her mouth why she poisoned me, Iain." When he took a breath to argue, she hurried to speak again. "She made me lose our child, and almost my life. It is my right to hear why face-to-face. It is my right to show her she has not broken me," Marion finished, her voice shaking.

Iain's eyes widened, and then he leaned over and brushed his lips against hers. "No one would ever break ye, Marion. Yer spirit is strong and bold, which is why ye were the only one that could ever release me from my pain. And ye're right, I see that now. Ye should be there."

Marion let out a relieved breath as Iain gathered the blankets around her and then picked her up and wrapped her in one of them. She felt rather silly, but she knew protesting would be futile with her husband.

He carried her downstairs to the great hall and paused outside the door before entering. "Ye're sure?" he asked her, concern lacing his tone.

She nodded as she peered into the large space. Sitting on the dais by the far wall were all Iain's brothers, Rory Mac, Angus, Neil, and two older MacLeods. Together they made up the clan council. The council would give Iain their opinions regarding Elspeth's fate, but the final decision would be Iain's.

In front of the raised dais, Elspeth stood with two clansmen flanking her.

"I'm ready," Marion said, sensing Iain was waiting on her.

When he walked in, the men talking on the dais ceased. They all stood and Elspeth twisted around. Marion's breath caught in her throat. The woman's brown hair was a mess, and she had dirt all over her face. Her gown was torn and her eyes were glazed, but they seemed to clear and flare with hatred upon seeing Marion. Iain's fingers curled tighter around Marion's legs as he strode past Elspeth and to the dais, where Angus offered his spot to Marion.

She shook her head. "You're part of the council."

"I'm nae so old that I kinnae stand behind ye," Angus growled. "Ye'll sit here or I'll carry ye back upstairs myself."

Marion's heart swelled with love for Angus, for everyone up on the dais, as they nodded their agreement and each rose, offering their chairs one by one.

"Sit here, my lady," Graham said. "Ye are one of us."

"Nae, take my seat," Lachlan offered. "Ye are as a sister."

"Take mine," Rory Mac demanded with a smile. "Ye are part of our family."

On it went, with Elspeth watching and scowling. Marion could not help but smile as Iain settled her beside him and she looked to her left and right at her new family. She was a MacLeod in more than name alone.

Iain called the meeting to start, which began with him narrowing his eyes at Elspeth for several long moments. He then read out her crimes. "Elspeth MacLeod, ye're charged with the crime of attempting to murder Marion MacLeod by poisoning. Ye're also charged with the murder of my and Marion's unborn bairn." Iain's voice did not give the slightest hint of his torment, but his hand found Marion's under the table, and he squeezed her fingers hard before continuing. "What say ye? Guilty or nae?"

"I should have been yer wife," Elspeth crowed rather than answering to the charges. When she tried to take a step toward the dais, Marion tensed, but the men flanking Elspeth quickly restrained her. She spat on the ground and twisted her arms to no avail, finally stopping when she must have realized she'd not get loose. "I should have been yer wife!" she screeched louder. "All my life no one ever paid me heed. No one ever even looked me in the face except ye. Ye always looked at me as if I mattered," she cried out to Iain. "And on yer wedding day, ye told me that ye were blessed because ye got two beautiful sisters to defend and honor. I kenned then that ye wanted me."

Marion stole a sideways glance at Iain. His jaw ticked furiously. "I was being nice to ye, Elspeth. It did nae mean I wanted ye. I remember ye looking fearful standing there alone."

"Nay!" Elspeth shrieked. "Ye wanted me. I kenned it. And when Catriona died, I knew ye would want to marry me, but Fiona..." Elspeth twisted around, and Marion only then realized that Fiona stood in the back of the room with the man that surely had to be her new husband since they were holding hands. "Fiona started plotting to steal ye. She thought it her right! But I fooled her! I won. Or I would have!"

Marion's heart ached for Fiona as the woman lowered her head in shame, but Fiona's husband raised her hand to his and kissed it. She lifted her head and smiled at him. He swiped away the tears sliding down her face, and Marion knew Fiona would be fine. She had found happiness. She had never really wanted Iain, and she would have never harmed Marion. She just wanted to be loved, which Marion could understand fully, and Iain—with his kindness and honor—had a habit of making women love him, or think they loved him, without intending it.

"Elspeth MacLeod," Iain boomed, "have ye anything else to say?"

"Ye're mine!" Elspeth shouted over and over.

Behind Marion, Angus's hand came to rest on her shoulder and gave her a gentle squeeze.

Iain shook his head at Elspeth's protestations, and then looked to the council. "What say ye, council members? Banishment or death?"

Death?

Marion's gut clenched. In spite of what Elspeth had done, Marion did not wish her dead. The woman's mind was warped. She held her breath as each member spoke. They were split down the middle with four wanting death and four wanting banishment. Marion stared at Iain, who had the final word.

He scrubbed a hand over his face and then locked his gaze on Marion. "What say ye? What do ye wish?"

He was asking her opinion? It was the greatest honor he could give her, and she loved him all the more for it. "Banishment," she said, her voice clear and loud.

He nodded and turned to look at Elspeth. "Ye are hereby banished for life from the Isle of Skye and Dunvegan Castle to the farthest point in Scotland from this spot. If ye ever stand on MacLeod land again, ye will be killed on sight. Ye will await departure in the dungeon. Take her," Iain commanded and motioned to the guards. And then Elspeth was dragged out of the room screaming and flailing her arms. Fiona followed, Marion supposed, to say her farewells.

"Cameron," Iain said, as he stood and gathered Marion into his arms and pulled her close to his chest. "Ye will go with the guards to see Elspeth settled."

"As ye wish, brother."

Without another word, Iain strode from the dais and up to their bedchamber. He set Marion on the bed, and to her surprise, he joined her.

"What are you doing?" she said, laughing. "Do you not need to attend to clan business?"

"Aye. But it can wait. I've been creating something just for ye in my head." Iain stretched out his long legs as he reclined beside her and took her hand in his. Then, to her astonishment, he began to sing a ballad, and as he started to tell the story, she realized it was about them. He sung of a laird who'd lost his ability to love and the proud, half-English beauty who awoke first his lust and then his heart, and patiently taught him how to love again.

Marion's throat ached with unshed tears of happiness as he finished the ballad. When he was done, he smiled shyly at her and pressed his lips to hers.

"I did not know you could sing."

"Oh, aye, but dunnae tell anyone. Lairds do nae sing," he said most seriously. "My father always told me so."

Marion frowned. "What else do lairds not do?"

Iain rubbed his knuckles over his chin as he looked thoughtful. "Lairds dunnae cry, and lairds always put the clan first, above all else."

"Was your father a hard man?" she asked, thinking of her own.

Iain nodded. "He was hard, but he was good and honorable, and showed us he cared for us."

She quirked an eyebrow. "But never told you so?"

"Nay. Lairds dunnae talk of emotions, either."

She snorted at that, but the conversation went far in explaining why Iain had not spoken to her of how he felt sooner. If the rules about lairds were firmly established early in life, and he'd lived them for so long, it was no wonder it had been so hard for him. "I'm glad you are a different sort of laird from your father."

"Different but the same," he replied. "Speaking of how

I feel is difficult, but I'll do it for ye. But only ye."

She grinned. "Will you continue to sing for me?"

He chuckled. "Aye. But only for ye."

Before she could respond a knock came at the door. "It's Lachlan. May I enter?"

"Aye," Iain called.

Lachlan strolled into the room with a casual grace that made Marion see why Bridgette was infatuated with the man. Though Marion did not find him as handsome as Iain, he was certainly an attractive man with his thick russet hair and his bright-green eyes, which always looked as if he had a secret.

He paused at the foot of the bed and shook his head. "I never thought I'd see the time come that ye would spend all day abed."

Iain laughed. "Now ye have. Have ye come simply to annoy me or do ye want something?"

"Well, *neo-bhriste laird*," Lachlan drawled with a mischievous smile and a mocking tone. "Ye'll nae hold that title much longer if ye dunnae train. Or have ye forgotten ye're wanted dead by the English, and yer wife—" he winked at Marion "—is simply wanted."

"I've nae forgotten," Iain replied with a scowl. "We'll train tomorrow."

Lachlan nodded and turned to go, but when he reached the door, he faced them. "Marion, thank ye."

"What for?" she asked in confusion.

Lachlan grinned. "For nae fleeing from Iain after ye first met him. Ye've made him happy."

"It dunnae show, does it?" Iain asked with an indignation that made Marion laugh.

"Nay." Lachlan rolled his eyes and left.

As Iain wrapped Marion in his arms, she looked up at

him. "What does *neo-bhriste laird* mean?"

She stared at him until he finally answered. "Unbroken laird. The men call me that because I've never been defeated in battle."

He sounded as if he didn't like it, which confused her. "You don't care for it?"

"Nay. I think it's bad fortune to give yerself such a title, as though I'm asking for God to strike me down for being too proud."

Marion nodded. "If I had a coin, I'd give it to you for an indulgence."

Iain roared with laughter until he complained that his stomach hurt.

Later that night, after a quiet game of chess, Marion studied the candlelit bedchamber and a thought came to her. "Dance with me, Iain," she said, wanting to forget her heartache from the loss of their babe in his arms.

"I dunnae ken how."

"You don't know how to dance?" she repeated, stunned.

He smirked at her. "Dancing is nae on the list of things to teach a young Scottish lad who is to be laird."

She nodded, understanding, but... "Surely you danced with Catriona?"

"Nay," he responded, his usual haunted look no longer in his eyes, to her relief. "Catriona did nae care to dance."

"I'll teach you!" Marion exclaimed.

He looked as if he'd rather eat dirt, which made her burst into laughter. "Please," she begged. "It will be lovely and will make me so happy."

"It will make ye happy?"

She nodded, eager to start.

"If ye feel tired, ye must tell me," he ordered.

"I vow it, but I truly do feel quite well."

He helped her up, and they moved to the middle of the bedchamber where she taught him the steps of a country-dance. The fire crackled and roared in the grate, giving the room a toasty warmth. By the time she arranged them in their positions and showed him some steps involved, they were both perspiring.

After they attempted to do the dance a few times, Iain pulled her into his arms. "I think we'd nae be boiling if we took off our clothes."

His blue eyes caught her green ones, and the desire smoldering in his depths sent a shiver of awareness through her of the powerful man that was her husband. He'd not tried to touch her in a physical way once since she'd lost the babe, and she'd been grateful, as her body had been sore and her heart raw. Her heart still ached, but suddenly, with his warm hands pressed against her back and his hard body molded to her, she longed for him to touch her as he had before. She wanted him to fill the emptiness inside of her with his love, with his body.

"I've a confession," he said, his voice husky.

"What is it?" she whispered.

"I only agreed to dance with ye so I could hold ye close like this. I've nay desire to learn to dance, but I've a deep ache to hold ye again."

"I've the same ache," she admitted.

His eyes widened a fraction. "Ye do?"

She nodded shyly. "I do, but I'm afraid."

His gaze caressed her as his hand came to her face and did the same. "What are ye afraid of? That it will hurt?"

She shook her head. Fiona had told her in a matter-of-fact way that because Marion had been so early in the pregnancy, there was no damage of *that* area, so she could resume her marital relations with Iain whenever she felt ready. "I'm afraid of becoming with child again and losing it."

Iain nodded. "I'm afraid of that, too."

Her mouth parted in shock. "You are?"

"Aye, *a ghràidh*." He brought both hands to her face, cupping it, and then brushed a gentle kiss to her lips. "But when we are as one, everything in my world is right and perfect. Ye have given me a gift I did nae even ken I was awaiting."

He could not have said anything more perfect. She cupped his face as he did hers. "I love you."

"And I, ye."

She rose to her tiptoes and pressed her lips to his. When she drew back, his hands slipped around her waist and she found herself lifted off her feet and to his chest.

"Is yer kiss an invitation, *a ghràidh*?"

She shook her head, and though neither his body nor his eyes showed disappointment, his jaw tensed. She barely controlled her giggle. "It was nae a simple invitation, *laird*," she purred in her best Scottish accent. "It was a plea for ye to take me and make me yers once again."

"Ye are mine always," he growled, sweeping her legs up over his arms. "But I'll be happy to answer yer plea one touch at a time."

He strode with her to the bed, set her on her feet, and commanded her to stand still.

She nodded and his hands were suddenly on her, roaming over her body and igniting it in flames. He grasped the edge of her léine and pulled it up over her thighs, hips, and breasts, capturing her wrists with his hand as he drew the garment over her head. He tossed it to the floor and released her hands down by her sides. She stood there utterly naked, his gaze burning and devouring her body. He made her feel beautiful, wanted, and wanton, and as she raised her hands to his chest, pressed her palms there, and felt the thundering of his heart beneath her fingertips, she knew the thrill of the power her touch had over him.

Shaking with desire, she raised up his plaid, and as the material slid over his powerful torso, she marveled at the effect simply glimpsing the perfection of his body had on her. Her heart raced and her stomach fluttered while her core tightened in expectation of what was to come. His gaze held hers prisoner as she moved the plaid to his broad shoulders. She could raise it no more.

"Unclothe," she commanded.

He shot her a wicked grin. "As ye wish, *a ghràidh.*"

Every time he called her *his love*, she felt as if her heart would burst with joy. As he lifted his arms to rid himself of his plaid, she could not restrain herself any longer. She pressed kisses across the hot planes of stomach muscle, and he jerked, groaned, and grasped her by the arms in response.

Before she knew what was happening, she was on their bed with Iain hovering over her. He devoured her mouth in a kiss of possession, then slid his tongue down a path from her ribs to her stomach and lower to the juncture between her thighs. He brought her to quick surrender, her cries of pleasure echoing in her own ears.

Still, she ached for him, and she held her arms out to him when she saw him hesitate above her, unfulfilled in his own need, yet willing to wait for her. His concern and selflessness touched her greatly.

"Come to me," she whispered huskily.

"Are ye sure? I did nae think we'd go so far tonight. Just test the waters, aye?"

"The waters have been tested," she growled. "They are warm and ready."

Oh God. Marion was so beautiful. She smelled of heather and freesia, and the warmth he knew awaited him inside her beckoned to him. His good intentions to bring his wife to pleasure tonight and not take his, to ease her back into their joining, disappeared in a passion so strong it made him shudder.

He grasped her hips and put his shaft at her hot, moist entrance. "I can go slow and gentle," he panted, offering her one last moment to reconsider or command him how to proceed.

"Don't even think of it," she said, her gaze heated as it met his.

His thoughts all fled but one—possession. And with that single driving need, he plunged into her. She immediately clenched around him, fitting him like a silken glove. Need sent him out of his mind, and his body took over. He lifted her buttocks farther, thrusting deeper, harder, faster, his body pulsing and tensing so very close to release.

She arched her back, and he knew she was close, as well. His fingers found one of her breasts and circled her hard bud gently as he stroked in and out of her until his entire body tensed, she screamed out her pleasure, and his own release came. The force of it shocked him, and he stilled, his breaths coming in short pants, his heart beating fast, and his seed flowing into Marion, leaving them both spent.

They collapsed as one onto the bed and lay still, their heavy breathing filling the silence. When his heart slowed, he rolled to his side and traced a finger over her flat stomach. She turned her head toward him, her green eyes wistful. He understood and pressed a kiss to her stomach.

"We will make another bairn."

"And if we can't?" she whispered.

"Then we will be a family, the two of us. And it will be more than enough."

She nodded and clasped his hand with her tiny one. If he could keep pain from ever touching her heart again, he'd give his life to do so.

Iain would have liked to keep Marion in their bedchamber until things were settled with Froste just to keep her safe, but at the beginning of the third week of her recovery, Marion demanded to rejoin castle life. He was about to deny her request when a pounding came at their bedchamber door. Marion burst past Iain, raced to the door, and threw it open.

A frantic-looking Bridgette stood in the doorway with Graham directly behind her. "I'm sorry to disturb ye, but Alanna's been in labor for a day, and there's something wrong. Ye can deliver a bairn, can't ye?"

Marion nodded and was out the door and down the stairs before Iain could protest. Left with little choice, he made haste to keep close to her, pushing Graham to move out of his way.

"How come every time I look ye're trailing Bridgette?" Iain demanded when the women turned the corner ahead of them, going out of sight for a moment.

Graham flushed. "I love her."

"Ye're too young to ken what it means to love a woman."

"I'm nae too young," Graham growled. "I'm as old as ye were when ye married Catriona."

The comment hit Iain like an arrow. He stumbled to a halt. *Catriona.* He'd not thought of her in weeks. Not once. Yet somehow he knew that if she could speak with him, she'd tell him it was as it should be. It was time for him to truly rejoin life. The guilt he felt over breaking his promise to Catriona lifted like a mist. She would always have a place in his heart, but now Marion did, too.

They ran the entire way to Rory Mac's home. Marion and Bridgette made haste to Alanna's bedside, where Rory Mac paced. Iain entreated his friend to let the women work and wait with him outside, but he refused to leave the room. Iain nodded and stood just outside the cracked door, through which he could see Marion and was ready to intervene should she request his help.

Rory Mac barked orders at Alanna to simply push the baby out, and Alanna, in turn, screamed at him to get out of the room. Bridgette started fussing at them to stop but it did no good.

Iain's eyes widened as Marion picked up a plate and threw it to the floor.

The shouting abruptly stopped, and everyone looked at her. She marched up to Rory Mac and poked him in the chest. "If you don't want your wife to die while trying to birth your baby, I think you should leave."

Rory Mac gaped at Marion. "Alanna could die?"

Marion nodded. "Look at her. She's been in labor far too long. Fatigue is setting in, and soon she will be too tired to help the baby come out at all. Your yelling at her is not making it any easier. You must leave and let us help her."

Rory Mac looked as if he was about to argue, but he finally nodded and came out the door. Once it was shut, Iain threw an arm around his friend. "Come. We'll practice combat." It was the perfect task to draw his friend's attention away from what was happening inside, and thankfully, Iain was never without his dagger.

They practiced with their daggers and then took turns shooting Rory Mac's bow while Alanna's yells occasionally punctuated the relative silence.

"I'm going back in," Rory Mac finally demanded after several hours had passed. "Alanna needs me."

"Aye, she needs ye to stay out here and be strong. Ye will be in the way in there, and ye ken as well as I do that she'd nae want ye to see her giving birth."

Rory Mac nodded. "Ye're right, but I feel as if I'll die if I lose her or the bairn."

Iain nodded. "I ken how ye feel, but ye will nae lose them." As the words left Iain's mouth, the sound of a door creaking open caused Iain to turn.

Bridgette strolled out, a large smile on her face, sweat covering her brow, and a baby bundled in her arms. She walked up to Rory Mac and looked up at him as she pulled the plaid the baby was wrapped in down just a bit. "Meet your son," she whispered as she handed the boy over to him. "He was pointing the wrong way to come out, which was why it took so long, but Marion knew how to turn him."

"Thank God for Marion," Rory Mac exclaimed.

Iain nodded, feeling exactly the same way.

By the time Marion and Iain reached the great hall for

supper that night, the news of her saving Alanna and her baby had reached every corner of the castle, in large part due to Rory Mac telling the tale to everyone he saw as he went out to spread word of his son.

Just as they sat down at the dais to eat, Robbie, one of the clan's fiercest warriors, rushed into the hall and directly to the dais. His wife also had been in labor for far too long, and he begged Marion to attend the birth. Marion quickly agreed, and off they set once again.

When they returned to their bedchamber later that night, after Marion had successfully helped deliver another bairn into the world, Iain held her in his arms as they lay in bed.

"What if," she said in a small voice, "I cannot have another child? Seeing the new bairns today made me see that even though I fear losing a babe, I'm more afraid I'll never have one. And then we won't have a family, and you'll be disappointed, and—"

He kissed her to silence her. When he pulled away, he looked into her eyes. "We are already a family, *a ghràidh*. Dunnae fash yerself. We will simply enjoy the process of trying to make a bairn, and if it happens, so be it. If nae, we have each other."

Before more could be said on the subject, a knock came at the door. "Iain," Lachlan called. "A note just arrived for ye from King Edward."

Iain took in his wife's wide eyes. "Dunnae worry," he whispered and kissed her forehead before he went to the door and opened it. He took the scroll from Lachlan, broke the seal, and read.

"What does it say?" Lachlan asked.

Iain suddenly felt Marion pressed at his back. He turned and drew her to his side and then spoke. "King

Edward wishes for me to return to England presently to set the official terms of David's release."

"Why do ye look troubled?" Lachlan asked. "It's a good thing, aye?"

Iain gripped Marion tighter before he answered. "Aye, the release, when it actually happens, will be good. But he also says he's received word that de Lacy and Froste are gathering troops against him, and he feels more certain than ever that he'll need me, er, us"—he locked gazes with Lachlan—"to fight with him."

Marion stiffened in his arms. "So you are going to war?"

"Nae yet," he soothed. "King Edward is cunning, however. He has now promised, in writing, to set the terms to make me believe he will keep his vow. Thus, when called for help, I will aid him."

Marion pressed her hand against his heart. "So you will go to save David."

"Aye. I must."

"I know," she replied her voice stoic, even as her lips trembled. "I wish to go with you."

"Nay. I'm sorry, but the journey is long and yer health is still too fragile."

"But—"

"Nay, Marion. I will nae risk yer life just for the comfort of having ye with me, however much I yearn for it."

~⟊⟊⟊~

Two days later, Iain called for Marion, Bridgette, Angus, Archibald, Rory Mac, and his brothers—except Cameron, who had gone to take Elspeth to her banishment—to come to the great hall. When he had everyone's attention, he spoke. "I dunnae want Marion to leave the castle unaccompanied."

"That's insensible!" Marion blurted, showing the temper she claimed not to have.

When he gave her a long look for breaching their agreement that she'd not challenge his wishes in public, she colored. "I'm sorry," she whispered. Before he could tell her he forgave her, a serving girl from the kitchen entered the room.

"Laird, I'm sorry to disturb."

Iain flicked his gaze to her. "Aye?"

"Torcadal MacLeod is outside and he brings a request from a neighboring clan he was passing through. They wish for my lady"—the girl inclined her head toward Marion—"to come to help in a birth. They heard she has some skills."

When Marion started to rise, Iain caught her hand but rose to stand beside her. He looked at the assembled group. He knew what he was about to say would garner protest from Marion, but it had to be said. "I dunnae want Marion going to any neighboring clans to aid anyone while I'm gone."

"Iain!" Marion gasped.

He glanced at his wife and held her gaze. "Understood?" he asked the group in general, never taking his eyes from Marion. Her gaze had grown stormy, which was not a surprise.

A chorus of agreement met his question. He nodded and faced the serving girl. "Tell Torcadal that Marion kinnae come."

"But, Iain," Marion protested.

He took her hand and squeezed. "I must depart, and I kinnae have ye gone. The worry…"

Her gaze turned soft. "I understand," she whispered.

Once the serving girl left, Iain quickly finished his instructions to the group and then dismissed them. When he and Marion were alone, she spoke before he could.

"I'm sorry. I do forget my tongue sometimes in my anger."

He grinned. "Aye, I ken. I'm surprised ye dunnae still try to pay for all yer sins."

She gave him a dark look. "That's because Bridgette finally told me that Scots don't practice that, and then Father Murdock laughed at me when I told him you all should."

"Dunnae fash, *a ghràidh*. Father Murdock laughs at everyone but me. The man is a drunkard."

"But he's your priest."

"Aye. And drunk as a sow is the way the men like him, as he is likely to turn his eye from sin that way."

Marion slapped Iain on the arm. "You tease me."

"Aye." He kissed her on the forehead, the nose, and then the lips. "I do."

Marion set her hands on her hips. "You cannot truly mean to leave everyone with the orders that I cannot leave MacLeod land if someone from another clan is in desperate need of my services."

Iain nodded. "I mean it. Other clans have healers and midwives of their own. They have gotten by without ye for a verra long time and they can do so until I return. I will have ye safe, Marion. But dunnae fash too much, I should return within a month."

"I wish I could go with you."

"Ye ken why ye kinnae," he replied.

She nodded. "But it doesn't make the parting any less difficult."

"For me, either, *a ghràidh*. That's why I got ye a gift so ye'd think of me while I'm away."

Marion grinned. "I don't need anything to do that. You are here." She touched her temple. "And here." She brushed her fingers to her heart.

He grasped her roughly to him and kissed her again, but this time the kiss was one meant to last her the month. He swept his tongue inside her sweetness and filled her breath with his own. When he withdrew, her bemused look made him smile. "And ye are here, as well." He placed her hand on his heart.

She laid her head against his chest, and for a long moment he savored the soft feel of her skin and the heathery smell that surrounded her. Everything about her—from the way her mouth tilted upward when she smiled to the way she cocked her head when listening to him—was burned into his memory. He forced himself to draw away and then he retrieved her gift from the dais, where he had put it.

When he handed her the cloak he'd had made for her, her eyes lit up. She grinned as she ran her hand over the blue-and-green material. "I love it," she whispered.

He trailed his hand down the slope of her cheek. "It will keep ye warm when I kinnae." He helped her set the cloak on her shoulders and then led her outside to the seagate stairs where his brothers were waiting to bid him farewell. He said his farewells, and then he and Marion walked hand and hand down the stairs to the birlinn. Iain kissed Marion once more, and then he and Neil, who was accompanying him, boarded the readied birlinn.

As they sailed away, he kept his gaze fixed on Marion, until Neil cleared his throat and then nudged Iain. "What?" Iain growled, his mood already sour at having to leave

Marion.

Neil chuckled. "She'll be here when we return, ye ken."

"I ken," he grumbled. "But it does nae make departing any easier."

"Ye've been felled by the lass."

"Aye," Iain agreed. "That I have, and I'm glad of it. Having a lass fell ye is the best way to crumble."

Twenty-Two

Marion threw herself into helping in the kitchen and tending to ailing clansmen and women even more than she had before, but though she was constantly busy, Iain was always on her mind. She marked the days he was gone, and when a month came and went and he did not return, she thought she would go mad.

One day, when she was sitting in the solar, a servant appeared and handed her a note. "My lady, this just came for you."

Hope filled her that it was perchance from Iain, and she had to force herself not to snatch the paper out of the woman's hands.

She quickly read the note, which was a plea from one of the MacLeod families who lived on the outer edge of MacLeod land for Marion to tend their gravely ill newborn babe. She didn't think twice, especially since the family was on MacLeod land. She'd rather risk her life than allow someone to lose a child. She knew all too well the pain of such a loss.

She sheathed the dagger she'd been cleaning, then rushed out of the solar and to the stables to ask Angus to accompany her. But when she arrived he was not there.

"Where is Angus?" she asked a groom.

"Gone hunting with Lachlan and Rory Mac, my lady.

They'll be back late tonight. Angus said the meat stock was running low."

Marion nodded and nibbled on her lip. That left Graham to find and ask. She didn't think Iain would like the idea of her going alone with Archibald on such a journey, even though he had come to like Bridgette's cousin more as time had past. Her husband, she thought with a grin, was jealous, and she actually no longer minded it one bit. He was jealous because he loved her.

Marion left the stables and found Graham in the courtyard with Bridgette. "Graham," she said, racing over to him, "will you accompany me to the Beacons' cottage?"

"Now?" He did not look at all happy about her request. "I just coaxed Bridgette into shooting bows and arrows. I'll go with ye in a bit."

"It must be now," Marion demanded. "Their babe is dying."

"I'll fetch horses for the two of us," he quickly agreed, putting his bow and arrow on his back and picking up his sword.

"I'll come," Bridgette added. "Please fetch me a horse as well."

Graham grinned and departed. Bridgette looked at Marion. "I'd like to learn more of the healing arts. Do ye mind, Marion?"

Marion shook her head then studied Bridgette. "Are you coming for the knowledge or for Graham?"

Bridgette pressed her lips together. "The knowledge, Marion. I dunnae think of Graham that way. He is sweet, but I dunnae have a spark for him. My heart belongs to Lachlan."

"What of Lachlan's heart?" Marion could not help but ask.

Bridgette sighed. "I kinnae tell if he likes me or nae. He seems to avoid me, but then I do catch him looking at me."

Before more could be said, Graham returned with the horses and they readied to depart.

"Where are ye three going?" Archibald called as he exited the castle.

"To the Beacons' cottage for Marion to tend to their ill bairn," Graham explained.

Marion half expected Archibald to offer to come, but his brows drew together in an oddly agonized expression. "I hope the bairn will be well. I'm sure in yer hands, Marion, it will."

"Thank you," she replied, catching the quizzical look that Bridgette and Graham were exchanging, but they simply bid Archibald farewell and departed.

Bridgette looked from Graham to Marion as the three of them rode away from the castle. "That was strange."

"Yes," Marion agreed. "I pity him. I think he does not feel he belongs anywhere."

"He makes himself feel that way," Graham replied in an unyielding voice that reminded Marion of Iain, causing an ache of missing him to throb in her heart. Marion settled into her saddle and listened to Bridgette and Graham tell stories of childhood exploits in the highlands while she thought about Iain.

❧⟡❧

By the time they arrived at the Beacons' cottage, a swirling mist filled the air, which she knew by now was not uncommon for the Isle of Skye. Marion, with Bridgette behind her, knocked on the door, and the husband, Lormac, showed them in, and then he stepped outside so the women would have privacy.

Glynnis, the ill bairn's mother, sat in a chair looking utterly distraught as she held her swaddled child. Marion approached her and kneeled, taking a quick peek at the sweet baby boy's face.

"I'm Marion MacLeod," she offered, though she knew Glynnis likely supposed this already. "This is Bridgette. What seems to be the matter?"

"He will nae take my milk anymore," the woman cried. "And when he was taking my milk, he kept spitting it up. There is something the matter with me! I'm killing my bairn!" Tears coursed down the woman's face, and Marion gently wiped them away.

"Shh," she cooed. "I think your babe is one that cannot stomach human milk. I've seen it before."

The woman gasped. "Ye have?"

"Yes. Do you have any animals?"

Glynnis nodded. "Three goats. One is just born."

Marion bit her lip. She'd only ever seen cow's milk used to feed a babe, but with the choice of leaving the babe to die or trying goat's milk, she would choose goat's milk. She nodded, hurried outside, and told Lormac to fetch some of the goat's milk.

When she went back into the cottage, she looked to Glynnis. "I need some linen."

"On the table," she said in a clearly skeptical voice.

Marion got the linen and ran back to the door, her excitement at possibly saving the bairn growing. It did not take long for Lormac to return. He handed her a bowl of milk and was about to step outside when she motioned him back. "You should watch, too, in case it works."

She dipped the linen into the milk and let it soak. Once it was dripping, she handed it to Glynnis. "Put it up to your bairn's mouth."

The woman frowned at her.

"Go on," Bridgette encouraged.

With obvious hesitation, Glynnis placed the cloth at the babe's mouth, and the babe immediately began to suckle.

"He's drinking!" Glynnis said, stunned, as her husband grinned and kneeled beside her.

For a long while, they all stood around the babe and watched him drink and then waited tensely to see if he'd be sick. When a period had passed and he let out a large belch after Glynnis put him over her shoulder, they all began to laugh.

"Thank ye," Glynnis cried, standing to hug Marion.

"You're very welcome," Marion replied, as the door to the cottage opened and Graham poked his head in.

"It's getting late," he said. "We must return before dark."

Marion and Bridgette nodded, and after providing the Beacons with some further instruction and a vow from Marion to send them a cow for the bairn, they departed.

The sun was starting to set as they rode, and surrounded by trees as they were in the woods, deep shadows rose up around them. Marion didn't feel nervous, though, with Graham beside them and her dagger sheathed at her side. Besides that, they were on MacLeod land. She happily listened as Bridgette and Graham chatted. But when Graham suddenly stopped talking mid-sentence and his hand went to his sword, the hairs on the back of Marion's neck prickled.

"What is it?" she whispered, glancing around them and seeing nothing but trees and descending darkness.

"I thought I saw—Get down!" Graham yelled as he

jerked his stallion in front of them. Marion barely had time to register the command before an arrow flew out of the woods and hit Graham directly in the chest. He slumped over immediately, and Marion heard her scream mingle with Bridgette's. Both women dove off their horses and scrambled to help Graham, who was gallantly trying to push himself up and grasp his sword, but it was futile.

Knights started pouring out of the forest dressed in the all-too-familiar surcoats of Froste and her father. Shock rushed the blood to her head and left her momentarily dizzy.

She forced a deep breath to calm herself when beside her, Bridgette screeched. "Traitor!"

For one brief moment, Marion thought Bridgette was talking to her, but then she caught sight of Archibald coming out of the woods beside Froste. Marion's jaw dropped open as her hand went to her dagger. What was Archibald doing with Froste? Was he a traitor, as Bridgette clearly thought?

Marion raised her dagger at the same time Graham finally managed to bring his sword up and Bridgette lifted her bow.

Froste nudged his horse toward them, and Archibald did the same with his. Marion's heart thumped in her ears as she stared at the two men, Froste offering a cruel smile and Archibald staring almost through them.

Froste motioned to Graham. "Sheath your weapon, boy. You have no hope of winning against so many knights, and if you insist on fighting us, I'll kill the redheaded wench in front of you before I kill you, too. But if you throw down your sword, I vow to let the highland lass live and kill you quickly."

Marion saw Archibald flinch, but she cut her gaze away

from him and toward Bridgette.

"Dunnae do it, Graham." Bridgette's voice was pleading and fearful.

Graham, pale faced and with blood rapidly staining his plaid, held his sword steady. "How do I ken ye'll keep yer word?"

"You don't," Froste said with glee. "But I can vow to you that this woman"—he motioned to Bridgette—"will pleasure all my men here while you're made to watch, and then I shall personally carve her up before killing you if you make me waste time fighting you."

Bridgette gasped, and bile rose in Marion's throat.

"I'd rather die than watch Graham submit to ye," Bridgette yelled and pulled back her bow.

"No!" Graham shouted, and Marion, thinking to save Bridgette and Graham and knowing they were far too outnumbered, grasped Bridgette's bow from her hands.

Bridgette turned to Marion with stunned eyes. "Are ye a traitor, too, then?"

"Of course not!" Marion said. "I'm trying to save your life. Look around you. You'll perchance fell one man, but what of the other twenty?"

"Ah, Marion, my sweet, I would have said it was impossible, but you are more beautiful than I remembered, and your time away has made you wise, as well." Froste's dark gaze penetrated her, making her skin crawl. "I look forward to enjoying your body."

Marion spit at his horse's hooves. "Never."

"We shall see," he replied before turning his attention to Graham. "Well?"

Graham shook his head. "I dunnae trust ye."

Froste raised his hand, motioned toward Bridgette, and barked, "Take her!"

"Graham!" Archibald thundered. "Bridgette will be safe. I swear it. I've come to an agreement with Froste. She will go to England to marry one of his men."

Marion could hardly believe her ears. Why would Archibald do this? Why was he betraying them to Froste?

Bridgette was grabbed by one of the knights then, but she turned toward him and punched him in the nose. The man retaliated with a backhand that sent Bridgette to her knees by Graham's horse.

Graham's eyes blazed with hatred, which he turned on Archibald. "Why do ye betray yer own kind?"

"Because my own kind betrayed me. Alex's father killed my own, and what did they do for me? Keep it secret. Lie to me for years. Leave me to feel shamed by my father. Have me do their bidding and never feel as if I truly belonged. Well, I'll belong when I'm laird. Alex sent me out when MacLeod was at our hold to make sure none of Froste's men were still around, and fortunately for me, one was. I simply sent him back to England with a proposition for Froste." Archibald gazed at the sky for a moment. "And the day Iain left for England I received word that it had been accepted. It was fate, aye, because that very day, I sent Froste's messenger back to tell him to come for Marion, and I'd deliver her to him. The only thing I must still do is kill Iain, which will nae be hard."

Graham spit at Archibald, and Marion's temper flared, prevailing over her fear. "Traitor! Treacherous, filthy traitor!"

When Marion took a breath to say more, Bridgette hissed at Archibald, and he flinched.

"What do you get from Froste in return for killing my husband?" Marion demanded.

Archibald opened his mouth as if to answer when

Froste roared, "Enough! You Scots try my patience. Put down your sword and save the woman or you both die." He grinned maliciously. "Well, I suppose you die either way so it's no matter to me."

Graham looked down at Bridgette, and Marion's mind raced. She had no doubt that Graham would give his life to save Bridgette, but Marion had to try to save them both. If she could provide a distraction, perchance she could give Graham time to sweep down and grab Bridgette. Then they could go for help. It was the only chance they had, and she prayed Graham realized this.

When his gaze met hers, she tried to tell him what to do by looking from him, to Bridgette, to the road. She thought she saw him nod but could not be sure.

The moment Graham's weapon hit the ground, Marion bolted for Froste and plunged her dagger into his leg. Howling, he kicked out at her, his foot connecting with her gut and sending her flying to the ground. All around her, shouting broke out, and she saw Graham's horse take off with only Bridgette on it.

"Graham, no!" Marion yelled, knowing he'd done what Iain would have done. He'd sent Bridgette for help while staying to defend Marion.

Froste strode toward her, but she could not scramble backward fast enough. He clutched her in an iron grip and jerked her about while barking at his men to kill Graham.

Archibald took off after Bridgette as Froste's and her father's men circled Graham. Marion watched in horror as they closed the circle. For one brief moment, he fought them off, and then one of her father's knights plunged his sword downward into Graham's chest and he fell to his knees and then onto his back.

Marion was too shocked to scream, but even if she

could have, Froste yanked her up onto his horse and started to ride away. Marion kicked and screamed then and tried to claw his eyes, and just as she was attempting to grasp the dagger sheathed to his side, something hard hit her square in the back of the head and she disappeared into darkness.

She knew instantly by the rocking beneath her and the smell of salt in the air that she was on a ship. What she didn't know was how long she had been unconscious. Surely, it had not been long enough for Froste to have taken Dunvegan Castle. She also didn't know if Bridgette had escaped. Her head pounded as she struggled to sit up, and as she blinked her eyes to adjust them to the brightness of day, a hand clasped her around the arm and jerked her all the way up.

Bile rose in her throat, and she hastily bent over and retched at her feet. When she sat up, a linen was thrust in her face. She wiped her mouth and met Froste's gaze. "Where are we going?" she demanded.

"Where else but home?" He took a long drink from a cup, then handed it to her.

Her first instinct was to smack it from his hand, but then she tried to calm herself. She may not get the offer of drink again. Taking the cup, she drank greedily of the strong spirits, coughing and sputtering as the liquid burned its way down her throat and to her stomach.

She swiped a hand over her wet lips. "Why are you taking me back to my father's?"

"To marry you."

"I'm already married," she screamed.

"Not much longer." He tweaked her nose. "I've left four of my knights there to help the nasty Scot kill your filthy husband when he returns from visiting the soon-to-be powerless King Edward." Froste paused and looked thoughtful for a moment. Marion's mind rushed through the possibilities of escape as her heart filled with worry for Iain. "Don't look so glum, Marion. When your father is king, I'll be a baron or possibly greater. You will be respected and wealthy. And married to me. Your status will be far superior to what you hold now."

Marion pressed her fingers to her throbbing temples to keep from screaming. Iain would come for her—if he had not been killed. *No!* Her mind refused to believe the worst. He would come, but she feared he'd never defeat her father and Froste. Their knights together slightly outnumbered his clan, and she didn't think he'd be so foolish as to bring his entire clan and leave the castle vulnerable. Her father would have the advantage of his castle to protect him if Iain tried to invade, too. Would King Edward help Iain? Or would he sit back and let Iain use his own men to fight what was ultimately King Edward's battle?

Marion's heart thudded with the fear that he would use Iain to weaken her father and Froste, and then—and only then—would King Edward help Iain. Her husband would be destroyed. Marion inhaled a shaky breath. So many in his clan would be killed.

She dug her nails into her palms to keep from crying out. "What did you offer Archibald in return for his betrayal?"

"Why do you care?" Froste snarled.

"I would like to know what price it takes to turn a Scot dishonorable," she replied, choosing her words with care to bait Froste into telling her.

Froste shrugged. "A low one. All I have to do in return is have one of my men kill the MacLean laird and make sure it cannot be traced to Archibald so he can easily take his cousin's place. Quite simple, really."

"My father is mad! You're mad! He'll never take the throne, and you'll never become a baron and get the lands you desire. Iain will triumph," she shouted, feeling her control slipping away.

Froste whipped his hand out and jerked her to him by the chin. Her skin stung where he gripped her, and pain shot through her jaw. "You will call him the MacLeod. Understand?"

She nodded, her heart hammering.

"When he's dead, I will marry you and you will lawfully be my wife."

The idea of being this vile man's wife made her want to crawl out of her skin. "I will never be your wife because you are no match for Iain."

Froste released her chin and slapped her. The force of the blow sent her head sideways, and the throbbing in her cheek now matched the throbbing of her skull. He gave her a mirthless smile. "You *will* be my wife, and you'll be pleased to know I find I'm quite taken with you. So much so that I have dreamed about you every night." The lust shining in his eyes sent her skittering to the edge of her seat.

Froste caught her by the elbow and yanked her over the rough wood until she was firmly against his side. "I will join with you when we reach London so you will know a *real* man. I don't need to be married to you to take you, my dear."

She had to swallow repeatedly not to lose her accounts. She prayed to God for an idea of how to escape or how to put off Froste, because one thing she knew for certain was that Iain would never reach her in time to save her from Froste's intentions.

Twenty-Three

Iain knew something was wrong at Dunvegan when the castle came into sight, but no one appeared on the seagate stairs—or anywhere, for that matter—to greet him. He and Neil exchanged a wary look, and as they stepped off the birlinn, the first thing Iain heard was hundreds of voices raised in a song for the dying. Fear for Marion rushed through his veins as he took off across the rocky land and raced up the stairs, Iain close behind him. When he reached the courtyard he came to a shuddering halt. It appeared that more than half his clan was gathered there, torches blazing. Spotting Father Murdoch, Iain shoved his way through the crowd. Lachlan stood beside the priest, and as Iain scanned the crowd, he saw the faces of those who mattered most to him—except for Marion and Graham.

By the time he reached Lachlan, icy fear had twisted around his heart.

"Where's Marion?" he demanded without greeting his brother. When Lachlan flinched, Iain's heart tightened. He clasped his brother's forearm. "Where is she?" he growled, refusing to believe she was dead.

The wariness in Lachlan's eyes was unmistakable, but something else flickered there—guilt? "Taken," Lachlan finally answered. "Archibald betrayed us and Marion was seized. Graham is upstairs dying, and all I can do is join the singing prayers that he lives."

Red filled Iain's vision. "Froste?"

Lachlan nodded.

"Where is Archibald?" Iain was going to rip out the man's heart.

"Dead," Lachlan replied, indifferent. "I killed him."

The momentary shock Iain felt yielded to black fury. "Ye should have left that to me. It is my right!"

"Graham is dying because I failed as laird in yer stead. The right to kill Archibald was mine," Lachlan spat.

Iain's fury did not ebb but turned, the tide flowing across the water to England and Froste and, undoubtedly, Marion's father. He motioned Lachlan to follow him. "Ye will tell me all as I see Graham."

Iain didn't wait for Lachlan to reply. He spun around, ignoring his now silent clan, and went into the castle.

He'd seen death too many times, and he knew the pain to come if his brother died. When he saw Graham lying in the middle of his bed, Iain had to grip the side not to fall to his knees and scream his rage and grief. Pale, Graham's brown hair was slicked back from fever sweats, his cheeks were hollow, and bloody linens were wrapped around his abdomen. But Iain was laird and leaders did not fall apart, not even when death came to his family.

He put his hand on Bridgette's shoulder as she sat by Graham's side, and she flinched before gazing dazedly up at him. Her red, swollen eyes told him she'd been crying for some time.

"What happened?" he asked her.

Bridgette swiped at her tears. "He sacrificed himself to save my life," she said, her voice full of sadness. "If he dies, I'm accountable." She started crying so hard that Fiona, who Iain blinked to realize was there and hovering in a corner, came rushing out of the shadows. Without a word, Fiona enfolded Bridgette in her arms, helped her to stand, and then led her out of the room.

For a moment, stark silence engulfed the room, then Lachlan spoke. He told Iain of Archibald's betrayal; of Marion, Graham, and Bridgette going to help an ailing bairn; their being ambushed; and Bridgette escaping back to the castle to get help.

Lachlan tugged a hand through his hair. "By the time we reached Graham, he was like this, but I killed Archibald and two of Froste's men, and Rory Mac killed the other two knights."

Iain stared down at his youngest brother, who would likely die having been shot by an arrow near his heart and gutted with an English sword. He curled his hands into fists, blood roaring through his veins with such force his body throbbed.

"I will bring Marion home. Nothing will stop me."

"*We* will bring her home," Lachlan replied and clasped Iain's forearm. "We will have vengeance."

"Aye," Iain said in a voice of steel. "Vengeance will be ours. Put out the call for the clan to ready for battle."

Lachlan's eyes widened. "Think, brother. They have greater numbers in their forces."

"Aye. We will send word to the MacLeans and the MacDonalds to join us."

Lachlan nodded. "Iain," he started, his voice hesitant, "what if...what if Marion has been ravished? What if she has a bairn in her belly come a month from now? Would ye want her back nae knowing if the bairn was yers?"

Unblinking, Iain stared at Lachlan. "I'd want her back blind, disfigured, mute, and with a belly heavy with a bairn that I could nae be sure was mine. I will want her back always. I will want her back nay matter what. She is my life. Do ye ken?"

Lachlan's eyes sharpened with understanding. "Aye, I do. We need to determine our course carefully."

"I ken," Iain replied. As much as he wanted to charge directly to Marion, none of them would return alive if he did that. He needed time to gather his allies, who he prayed truly included King Edward now that the terms of David's release had been set to scroll and made official. The king would never get the money he was demanding for David's release if Iain was killed and unable to sway the other clans to pay to see him freed, so Iain felt confident that King Edward would help. It made sense. Together, they could fell de Lacy and Froste. Yet Edward would need time to summon his knights and ride toward de Lacy's home to attack.

"Gather the council in the great hall. I'll be there in a moment."

Lachlan nodded and hastily left the room. Iain kneeled by Graham's bed and said a prayer for his brother's recovery, then made his way down to the great hall where the council sat waiting. He strode up to the dais and stood facing Lachlan, Rory Mac, Angus, and the rest of the council. "Rory Mac, ye will go to the MacLeans and gain their agreement to help us, so they will have time to prepare to depart before we arrive." Iain had no doubt that Alex would join him. "We will join ye at the MacLean hold before departing for England. Angus, go to the MacDonalds to do the same. When ye return, ye will join me. I will be training the men and readying our ships."

Rory Mac and Angus nodded, fierce determination blazing in their eyes.

Iain stared hard at Lachlan. "And ye, Lachlan…ye will journey to England to see King Edward. Go with King Edward to de Lacy's home. We will meet ye there."

"Aye, brother."

Iain paced in front of the dais continuing to speak. "I will depart in seven days for the MacLean hold." He loathed the thought of waiting so long, but they had to have all the clans and King Edward to ensure the defeat of their enemies.

"Godspeed," he said. "Now go!"

*

For once Froste was true to his word, Marion thought, distraught, as she eyed the man who stood at the opposite side of her bed. The moment they'd arrived at her father's castle, Froste had dragged her upstairs to a bedchamber. He'd not spoken yet, but she had no doubt what he intended.

"Unclothe," Froste commanded.

Marion scanned the room for any object she could use to dispatch him, and her gaze fastened on the dagger he had just removed and laid on the floor in front of the bed. She quickly looked away so he would not realize her intent. When he curled his finger in a command for her to come to him, she complied, walking toward the bed and stopping in front of him, her foot brushing the dagger. Her heart increased its pace tenfold.

When he stared at her expectantly, she raised her trembling hands to her gown and struggled to unlace it. When she feared he would try to help her, she tugged until the material ripped and the gown loosened. She then kneeled in the pretense of lowering her gown to the ground. The material fell over the dagger, and she grasped it, keeping her eyes on him. *He* had his gaze on her breasts, *the fool.* She smiled, brushing the material aside just enough to grasp the dagger, and she scrambled back a step to unsheathe it.

But he was quick—much quicker than she had expected—and with an angry roar, he knocked the dagger out of her hand and gripped her neck.

"I grow weary of you trying to kill me, Marion." He flung her onto the bed and started to lower himself atop her.

"Wait!" she cried, her mind searching for a way to stall him. She could think of only one possibility. She brought her hand to her belly. "I may be with Iain's child. If you take me now, and then I begin to quicken, you will never know if the child is his or yours. Would you truly take that risk?"

She could see the fury in his burning eyes and twisted mouth. He stared down at her, hovering over her for a long silent moment. Her pulse hammered a fearful beat until he finally pushed away from her and off the bed. He strode toward his dagger, retrieved it, and then stormed toward the door. "I will wait until your flux has come and gone but not a day longer."

The door slammed on his ominous words, and Marion was left alone. She quickly dressed in the ripped gown and then sat in the middle of her bed, hugging her knees to her chest. Tears pricked her eyes, but when the door flew open, she dashed them away.

Her father stood at the door as several servants filed into the room. He looked at her dispassionately, as if he didn't know her at all. "Clear the room of anything she can use as a weapon."

She watched in stony silence as they stripped the room bare, and Marion's heart clenched. She'd never seen love from her father and never would. When they were done, they filed back out of the chamber, and the lock clicked in the door. She was left alone once more with her fervent prayer that Iain would come soon, that he would prevail without flying the Fairy Flag.

Five days after Iain had sent Angus to the MacDonalds, he returned while Iain was training with the men. "The MacDonald will join ye, and he says he presumes the favor will be returned when he needs it."

"Aye," Iain replied. "I supposed as much." He didn't like owing the man a favor, but he would sell his soul to get Marion back.

In the days that followed, Iain and his men trained constantly, honing themselves into weapons of destruction. When they were not training, they were continuing to stock the ships and fortify the castle's defenses for those who would stay behind.

Marion occupied his thoughts every moment. During the day, the need for vengeance drove him, and at night, the stabbing yearning for her in his bed, pressed so close he could feel her heat and smell the heather that surrounded her, tortured him. He spent more time pacing the ramparts than sleeping.

When the time came for them to depart, he said fare-well to Graham, who was much improved, and bid him how to proceed as laird in Iain's absence, with Angus as his guide. Angus had wanted to come to England, but Iain had to know that if he died, or God forbid, he, Lachlan, or

Cameron—who was still on his journey to take Elspeth away—didn't return, that Graham would have a strong, trusted advisor by his side to rebuild the MacLeod legacy.

Iain walked down the seagate stairs and beheld the line of his and the MacDonald's men waiting to set sail, hope filling his chest.

Lachlan set his hand on Iain's shoulder from above him on the stairs. "We will triumph."

Iain nodded. "We must."

Froste's fetid breath fanned Marion's face as he pulled her roughly to him. She was acutely aware that only the thin material of her léine separated her skin from his bare chest.

I'm going to be sick! her mind screamed, as he captured the edge of her léine and started pulling it up. Her mind flashed to the time when she had tried to teach Iain to dance, and the lesson had ended with him stripping her of her léine. That had been like Heaven while this…this was Hell.

Her ruse to keep Froste from joining with her had finally run its course. His watchwoman had reported Marion's flux had come and gone, and he'd appeared like a nightmare. Froste's mouth found her neck as he roughly tugged her clothing higher and higher. There was no fear in her, only a deep disgust and fierce boiling anger. She tried to buck away, but he crushed her between the wall and his body. Frantically, her gaze darted around the room, praying there was something to kill the man with that her father's knights had left behind.

Her heart lurched with excitement. The maid who'd come in with Froste not long ago had left a tree branch by the fire that she must have used to tend to it! If Marion could reach it, she could hit him in the head and flee.

The man pressed a slobbery kiss to her neck again, and she flinched, in spite of knowing she had to feign to like it long enough to get him to release her. "Be at ease, Marion. This can be pleasurable, I assure you."

That was it! She'd play up to his arrogance and pride!

"I don't want to fight you, but I'm afraid," she whispered. "It was never pleasurable with my husband," she added, trying to instill a sense of shame into her tone. "And I've never seen a man's body. He always joined with me in darkness."

Froste pulled backward and stared at her with astonishment, then his mouth curved into a smirk. "I should have known a filthy Scot would not know how to please a lady. And what a fool the MacLeod was not to see your body clearly by a blazing fire—or better still the daylight," Froste added while running his gaze over her. She clenched her jaw against her revulsion. "Tomorrow, I'll join with you in the daylight, but tonight"—he looked around the room—"go tend the fire."

She had to bite down on her cheek to stop herself from showing any relief as he released her. This dim man was used to giving orders, and this time was no exception.

Nodding, she stepped around him and ambled to the hearth, thinking on how to take him unawares. She grimaced as she realized unclothing was the best way to distract him, but she was prepared to do anything to escape that man joining with her. She slowly turned in a languid motion, met Froste's stare, and pulled her clothing up over her head. She let the garment drop in a puddle at her feet, her stomach roiling violently.

"Do you like what you see, William?" she asked, using

his Christian name. Her voice didn't hold the slightest tremble. Iain would have been proud.

A lecherous look came to Froste's face. "Very much." He started toward her, and as he did, she bent down, picked up the thick branch, and stuck the tip of it into the fire as if she meant to tend to it. Her pulse raced as she heard him draw near.

She gripped the wood tightly. If she didn't kill him, or at least cause him to swoon, he'd surely kill her, but she could not—*could not*—stand meekly by and let him take her.

"Marion, face me so I can see you again," he said in a low voice that made her stomach churn. She stood and turned toward him, swinging the branch hard. It smacked him in the face. He howled as the fire singed his flesh and the wood made a deep gouge across his cheekbone. Blood poured from the wound, but when his feral gaze locked on her, she knew with terrifying clarity that she'd not hit near hard enough to kill this man. Bellowing his rage, he raised a hand to hit her, and she scrambled to lift the wood once again to defend herself but he swatted the branch away from her. The branch fell to the floor at her feet.

His hand clamped like a vise around her neck. "You bitch," he snarled, spittle flying from his mouth. "You will pay for that dearly." His grip became tighter and tighter until specks dotted her vision and the room spun. He was going to kill her, but still she wondered if death would not be better than his touch. Sluggishly, she remembered Iain. She would live for him. She began clawing at Froste's hands, even as someone pounded on the door.

"Froste, open the damn door! The Scots are here!" her father roared.

Froste released her, and she fell to the floor in a heap,

so close to the fire that heat consumed her. Instinctively she shoved her body away and curled into a ball, holding her neck as she gasped for air. His hard footsteps pounded across the room, and then the sound of the door banging open reverberated around her.

"We've a problem," her father said, but Froste's reply was muffled by their footsteps as they walked away…leaving the door open!

Marion didn't waste a second. She crawled to her gown and jerked it on as she ran to the window that pointed out to sea. Like spots in the ocean, ships peppered the water, and hope and fear both bloomed within her. She was sure it was Iain, but she was also sure that she had to do something to help him win the battle. She hurried out the door, paused to make sure there was no one to see her, and then continued down the stairs toward the front entrance. If she could somehow get to the drawbridge, perchance she could lower it.

The main keep was deserted, which didn't surprise her as everyone would have been ordered to take up arms. As she burst outside, the sounds of men and horns filled the twilight. As far out as she could see, the moat and the bailey below teemed with knights. She started to make her way to the stairs that led to the bailey, but a hand clamped on her arm.

"Lady Marion, get back inside to safety. The Scots are already winning the battle!"

"What?" Marion gasped turning to look in Peter's face.

"Don't worry!" he rushed out. "We will triumph!"

He'd misunderstood her. She jerked out of his hold. "You'll not triumph, Peter," she said, raising her voice over the deafening noise. "My father is trying to take the throne from King Edward, and the king is my husband's ally. Even if Father wins now, King Edward will come for him. You must take me to my husband and join with him."

Peter gaped at her. "Baron de Lacy means to overthrow the king?"

Marion nodded. "With Froste's help. Please, Peter. Feign that you've captured me and help me find my husband. I love him!"

Peter was a good man, and she could see him battling between his vow to her father and his duty to the king. "Edward is your king," she nudged. "Your duty to him comes before any vow of fealty to my father."

Peter nodded. "Come."

He took her by the arm, and they made their way down the stairs and through the crowds of knights and servants. No one questioned them, presuming, she was sure, that Peter had her in hand.

Her heart raced as they came to the inner bailey, where chaos reigned. Everywhere she looked, knights fought Scots, sword to sword. The drawbridge had been lowered, and Scots poured forward into the bailey. Yet there was something else—or rather someone else—coming to their aid. She squinted but could not make out the banner, until Peter exclaimed, "It's the king's men!"

Iain did not let anyone who got in his way slow him down. He cut Froste's and de Lacy's men down as they came toward him. Most men fell with one easy blow, but a few of his enemies required two. Lachlan was by his side, and Lachlan ended as many lives as Iain did. Around them, Scots from the MacDonald and MacLean clans, along with King Edward's knights, fought alongside Iain to destroy the potential usurpers and rescue Marion.

Iain battled his way into the bailey, searching the sea of faces for Marion. Was she out here? Or was she locked in her room or worse, the dungeon? All Iain wanted was to find her, and as he finished fighting yet another knight, he turned in a circle, trying to determine where Marion might be in this melee. And as he did, he caught sight of the one man he was certain would know—Froste.

Froste strode directly toward him, sword in hand and a snarl on his face. Blood covered one side where a deep gash was. Froste sneered at Iain. "You've proven to be a worthy opponent."

"Ye've nae," Iain responded. "Where is my wife?"

Froste circled his sword in readiness to fight, and when Iain saw one of his men move toward Froste, Iain ordered him back.

"Where is Marion?" Iain demanded again, his rage flowing through him like a river.

Froste's mouth twisted into a lecherous smile. "Your wife is naked in my bedchamber where I left her after enjoying her body and killing her."

Reason left Iain in a blinding flash of red. He charged Froste, as if he'd waited a thousand lifetimes to kill the man. Their swords met in a loud clash, swiveled down in an arc, and then drew upward once more. As Iain surged forward and then was driven back, he had to fight not only Froste but himself. He could not let his anguish consume him and defeat him. Froste drove him back ten paces before a deadly calm finally descended and Marion's face faded in his mind, along with all noise. He defended every strike Froste offered and then turned the tide and unleashed his rage with one brutal blow after another.

Marion could not see Iain anywhere in the crush of bodies, and then suddenly, there he was. To her right, near the newly built stables, Iain battled Froste.

"Peter, come!" She grabbed his hand, and they dashed around fighting men as they made their way toward Iain. Marion gasped at the sight of her husband in a frenzy of fury, delivering repeated blows to Froste. Her breath caught in her chest in horror and relief as Froste staggered and then fell to his knees after Iain sliced through the man's chest plate with his sword. Froste's sword clattered from his hands, and as the man looked up at Iain, Iain lifted his sword.

"For Marion," he shouted, bringing his sword swiftly back down and ending the man's life with a clean cut.

When Iain dropped his own sword and fell to the ground, looking up at the sky with his eyes shut, Marion called out. She ran to him and fell at his knees as the battle continued around them.

He gazed at her in clear wonder and reached out a shaking hand to touch her cheek. "Are ye real?"

Tears filled her eyes and spilled down her face. "Yes," she choked out.

Iain crushed her to him, and she could feel the violent thundering of his heart and trembling of his body.

"Watch out," Peter shouted, and Iain jerked up, bringing her with him. He shoved her behind him, withdrew a dagger, and killed the knight attempting to kill him. Wordlessly, he bent down, retrieved his sword, and looked at her. "Stay by my side."

"I will," she replied as he pressed through the battle, Peter beside him, until they got to the wall.

"Dunnae move from the wall. I will nae leave ye," he promised.

She nodded and pressed her back against the wall, then watched in almost fascinated horror as King Edward's banner was raised and cheers erupted from the Scots, Edward's knights, and even some of her father's. Yet the battle raged on until bodies lay thick across the bailey, Iain defending her all the while, alongside his brother Lachlan, who had joined him and Peter.

Finally, a trumpet sounded and cheers rose again. Iain turned, dropped his sword, and strode toward her. As he helped her to her feet and she looked out at the castle grounds, she saw her father with his head hanging, kneeling before the king.

"It's over," she whispered.

"Aye," Iain said. Then his brow furrowed and he reached out to touch her bruised neck. "What did he do to you?"

"It doesn't matter now," she replied through her tears, and then she remembered about the Fairy Flag. Had he flown it? Surely, there had been no need.

"Iain," she said, "the Fairy Flag... You didn't fly it, did you?"

He frowned at her as several of his men came to surround them. "Nay. I did nae even bring it. I had nae a doubt I would triumph." With those words, he pressed his lips to hers and kissed her deeply to the cheering of his men.

Twenty-Four

It was a long time before Marion was alone with Iain. When daylight had dawned and silence had finally mostly descended over the knights and Scots camped in her father's—or what had been her father's—inner bailey, and Iain's talks with King Edward and the other lairds finally ended, Iain came for her. She'd elected to sleep in the stables rather than in the keep in her old bedchamber. She never wanted to go in the keep that held so many bad memories again.

Clutching Iain's plaid around her, she sat alone with Lachlan, their backs against a stall and the stable door open wide. A breeze blew strands of her hair across her face, and she pushed them away as she watched Iain approach. Her heart swelled with happiness that he was alive, but a sadness dulled the joy. Her father was to be put to death, and though he'd not loved her, he had been her father.

With the darkness gone, she could clearly see myriad cuts on Iain's face, arms, and parts of his chest. He'd pulled his hair back and tied it at the base of his neck, making him appear even more foreboding with the hard lines of his face and the way he'd set his mouth in a grimace.

She searched his gaze as he neared, and while she saw the gentleness she knew there, something else dwelled in the blue depths. It appeared to be wariness, and the idea made her breath catch in her throat. Whatever could be wrong?

"Brother," Lachlan said, as if a silent command had been given and understood. Lachlan rose quickly and departed without a word, shutting the stable door behind him.

Marion's heart pounded nervously as Iain kneeled down before her. He started to reach for her hands and then stilled, as if unsure. What was this strangeness in him?

"Will ye let me touch ye?" he asked.

She frowned, her heart tripping in her chest. "Why would I not? I've longed for nothing but you since the day I was taken from Dunvegan."

He scrubbed a hand across his face. "Then ye're nae fearful?"

"Not of your touch, but I am worried about this strangeness between us."

"Ah, *a ghràidh*," he choked out as he gently enfolded her in his arms.

She pressed her cheek to his chest and listened to the frenzied beating of his heart. Something was troubling him greatly. She pushed away from him until he loosened his arms so she could look up at him.

His eyes filled with an odd understanding and sadness. "It's too much, then? To be held?"

"No." She shook her head. "Is it too much for you to hold me?"

"Of course nae!" he said, his tone forceful. "It does nae matter to me. I want ye to ken that. All that matters is that I have ye back alive. We'll take what's to come together. If'—he inhaled sharply—"if ye have Froste's bairn in yer belly, I'll raise the child as my own. I swear it. The bairn would be a part of ye, as well."

Shock ran through her, followed swiftly by overwhelming love. "Iain." She grasped his hand and pressed her cheek against it. "I didn't think I could ever love you more than I already do, but you've proven me wrong."

"I feel the same, *a ghràidh*. I—"

She set her finger to his lips. "Froste never joined with me, Iain."

He brushed her hand away. "But—"

"No." She stopped his words yet again. She could only imagine how Froste must have taunted and lied to Iain before they had fought. "I don't know what he said to you, but it was a lie. He wanted to take me, but I pointed out to him that if he did before I'd gotten my flux and then I had a bairn, he'd not know if it was his or yours."

A dark look of rage swept over Iain's face. "If he was nae already dead I'd kill him."

Marion wrapped her arms around her husband's waist, and this time, when he enveloped her, it was in a crushing embrace.

"He tried to force me right before you came," she said, "and I hit him with a tree branch. Then Father came to tell Froste you'd arrived and they left me alone. When I next saw you and you asked me what he'd done, I thought you meant had he tortured or hurt me. I would not have said it didn't matter had I known. I'm so sor—"

Her apology was smothered under the hot assault of Iain's mouth on hers. His lips parted hers in a soul-reaching message: *mine*. And she was. Each slant of his mouth over hers demanded an answer, and soon they were running their hands frantically over each other's bodies, ripping at the meager clothing between them. When his hands touched her bare skin, he branded her with every touch, every caress down her belly and swirl over her breasts. He kissed a path across her neck and over each shoulder, whispering his love and need for her between each kiss. He kneaded her back as his mouth burned a trail down her stomach to press a kiss on each trembling leg. She wanted him to take her. She needed him inside her, to feel him as she'd not felt him in so long.

"Iain," she gasped as her desire became almost unbearable with each slide of his finger into her body. When he didn't answer, she grasped his hair and tugged.

He gazed up at her, his eyes dazed with his own fierce need.

"Take me!" she demanded, passion pounding the blood through her veins to her heart.

"Gladly, *a ghràidh*," he growled, and in one sweeping motion, he laid her back on the straw and plunged inside her.

Their joining was unlike anything she had experienced before. It was raw and primitive, fueled by the exhilaration of surviving battle and laced with a potent need to assure each other that the connection between them could never be broken. They reached their climax together, their screams likely putting smiles on many Scots' faces. When their frenzied joining was over, Iain took her again, slowly and gently. This time, they came together in calmness and gently explored each other, bringing each other to slow, torturous climaxes. When they were both utterly spent, they lay on Iain's plaid and simply stared into each other's eyes until they fell asleep.

Hours later, Marion awoke to find Iain was gazing at her in awe. She smiled at him. "Have you slept at all?"

"Nay."

"Why not?"

"I was listening to yer breath and watching yer face. Ye

smile when ye sleep, and ye do this little thing with yer lips where ye suck on the lower one." He rolled toward her and brought her into the cradle of his arm.

She laid her ear against his heart and traced a finger over his ribs. "I can hear your heart beating."

"I imagine it's loud," he said with a chuckle.

She tilted her head back and looked at him. "Why would you imagine that?"

A wistful smile pulled at the corners of his mouth. "Because ye've made my heart grow, Marion. I thought I could never open it up again but ye helped me to do so, and with as much as I love ye, it must be a verra big thing beating in my chest now. I am verra fortunate."

Marion laid her palm over his heart. "I'm the fortunate one. You've given me what I always wanted—to be loved and to feel like I'm part of a family."

He kissed her on the forehead. "We are both fortunate, aye?"

She pressed her lips to his. "Aye," she replied, mimicking his burr.

"Ye're no longer a Sassenach at all," he said with a chuckle.

"Nay," she replied, grinning. "I'm a MacLeod."

Epilogue

Two months later

After supper had ended and the entertainment had begun, Marion sat beside Iain on the dais and watched Cameron, Graham, and Lachlan each dance a jig for the honor of being declared the champion, allowing them to pick the maiden he wished to dance with for the rest of the night. Cheers erupted after each man finished his jig, and when the competition came to an end, everyone in the great hall looked to Iain to announce the winner.

He held up a hand for patience and turned to Marion. "Who should I choose?" he whispered in her ear.

She cast a surreptitious glance from under her lashes at each brother and then to Bridgette, who sat at the table just below Marion. Bridgette stared at Lachlan with thinly veiled longing. When Graham turned to give Bridgette a wink, she ripped her gaze off Lachlan and blushed furiously at Graham. Marion sighed. Graham would think the blush was for him, but Marion knew Bridgette's pink cheeks were from having been caught gaping at Lachlan, who had seemed to have done his best to avoid Bridgette altogether upon their return from England, which told Marion he felt something for Bridgette.

"Marion," Iain urged softly.

She sighed again and pressed her mouth close to his

ear. "I think Bridgette likes Lachlan but feels she owes Graham since he almost died to save her."

"Aye, and Graham has eyes only for Bridgette. What shall we do?" he asked in a low voice.

"Pick Cameron."

"But was it nae plain to see that he was the worst at the jig?"

Marion giggled. "Undoubtedly, but we can tell them our secret to distract anyone who may wish to object."

Iain cocked an eyebrow at her. "We've a secret?"

"Aye, laird," she purred, fairly bursting with joy. "We've a bairn on the way."

Iain's jaw dropped open, and then he grinned and gathered her into his arms to give her a passionate kiss.

Cheers erupted in the hall once again.

"Who's the winner?" Graham demanded.

"Aye," Lachlan added. "Which of us has triumphed?"

"I'm certain I'm the winner," Cameron said, crowing with laughter.

"Nay, I'm the winner," Iain announced. "I've a bairn on the way!"

With that, Iain leaped over the table and attempted to dance a jig, the likes of which Marion had never seen.

She laughed as she watched her husband, secretly thinking that she was the biggest winner of them all.

Dear Readers,

I invite you to try Wicked Highland Wishes (Highlander Vows: Entangled Hearts Book 2)

Prologue

Isle of Mull, Scotland
Duart Castle
1354

Bridgette MacLean was beginning to suspect that God had erred when he had made her a girl. Standing in the courtyard of her home, she tapped her foot as she watched her brother, Alex, laird of the MacLean Clan, ride out of the keep. A dozen of his men followed, including the MacLeod laird and his three younger brothers.

"This is a girl's fate in life," she grumbled. "Staying behind while the men have all the merriment. *They* leave to hunt while we"—she poked herself in the chest—"are ordered to remain at the castle because clot-heid men suppose all girls are helpless creatures. Oh, but men are so braw," she said with a roll of her eyes. "I'm a better shot at sixteen than half the men out there hunting!" She kicked the ground in frustration. A puff of dirt rose up, causing a cloud of dust to swirl around her feet.

"Ye're nae usually in the habit of talking to yerself, lass," came the jovial voice of Father Ferguson from behind her.

A blush heated her cheeks as she turned to face the portly, older man. Amused, faded blue eyes met her stare.

Father Ferguson raised his bushy gray eyebrows expectant-ly, and Bridgette cleared her throat.

"I'm nae, 'tis true enough," she admitted. She inclined her head the direction in which Alex had ridden off. "Alex refused to listen to me any longer, so I was left to grumble to myself."

Father Ferguson chuckled a deep belly laugh that made Bridgette smile despite her ire. "What's vexing ye, lass?"

She quirked her mouth, unsure if she should tell him. She didn't particularly feel like being lectured, and Father Ferguson truly loved to lecture. Yet, the priest was the best man to help her resolve her doubts about God. "I fear God dunnae ken what he was doing when he made me."

Father Ferguson's mouth dropped open.

"Never ye mind," Bridgette rushed out. "I'm being a clot-heid."

"Nay, lass. Ye surprised me, 'tis all. What's put such a thought in yer head?"

She took a deep, shuddering breath. "Alex will nae let me hunt with him and the men. He says I'm a woman, and God dunnae fashion women to do such things." When the priest looked as though he was going to agree with her brother, she went on. "Ye always say God has a divine purpose for each of us," she said, her tone accusatory.

Father Ferguson gave her a wary look. "Aye, I do."

"Well God gave me perfect aim with an arrow." An excited grin pulled at her lips. Why had she not thought of this argument sooner? It was brilliant, and she was fairly certain it was true. "At only fifteen years, he's made me—a mere woman—a better shot than most grown men." Father Ferguson backed up a step, as if her words might cause them both to be struck by a bolt of lightning, but she continued. "If God has given me this gift, is it nae a sin nae to use it? Who am I, or even my brother, the great, mighty laird that he is"—she struggled to keep the sarcasm out of her voice—"to refute our Creator's intention for me?" She was panting with the newfound righteous indignation coursing through her.

"Well I—" Father Ferguson started, but she was far too incensed to allow him to continue.

Words the priest had once proclaimed came to her in a flash. "Ye said we must always abide by what the Lord wants for us."

Father Ferguson's shoulders slumped. "Aye, lass," he grumbled. "I did."

Triumph flared in her chest. Setting her hands on her hips, she swooped in to finish her argument. "Then, unless ye mean to tell me now that God made an error when he gave me my gift, I should do all in my power to use it."

The priest gave her a beleaguered look. "God dunnae make errors."

Impulsively, she rose up on her tiptoes and kissed the priest's warm, chubby cheek. "Excellent!" she exclaimed and turned away to run to her bedchamber and fetch her bow and arrows.

"Where are ye going, lass?"

She had one foot inside the castle door, but she turned around and looked at the priest. "To hunt, of course!"

Father Ferguson's eyes grew wide, and he shook his head. "The laird will nae like that."

"The laird," she retorted boldly, "will be committing a sin if he denies me my right to do as God wishes me to do. I may be a great many things, but I'm nae a sinner."

Father Ferguson looked at her dubiously.

"Nae much of one, anyway," she corrected, her cheeks flaming.

The priest threw up his hands in defeat, and a giggle escaped her as she dashed into the castle, to her bedchamber, and back outside. She was relieved to find Father Ferguson had not stayed to try to stop her. Knowing the priest as she did, he'd probably gone to fetch one of the councilmen to convince her to stay, but the stout priest was slow, and she'd be well away before he returned.

She grinned as she strode across the courtyard, nodding dismissively to the guards. One opened his mouth to speak—likely to try to stop her—but she narrowed her eyes and shook her head at him. His face turned red as he clamped his mouth shut and turned his head away. Emboldened by her second triumph of the day, she straightened her shoulders and marched through the entrance between the high walls that enclosed the courtyard like the future warrior maiden she knew she was.

She carefully picked her way down the steep embankment upon which her home sat, and she hummed to herself. It was nice to have confirmation that she did not need to change, despite her brother demanding she do so last night. Her steps faltered a bit when she imagined how angry Alex would be that she had disobeyed him. Not only had he plainly denied her request to hunt but with the fighting between their clan and the MacKinnon clan these last few months, Alex had given strict orders that no women were to leave castle grounds without a male escort.

She made a derisive noise from deep in her throat as she strode across the grassy, rolling land that led to the woods in the distance.

Let some MacKinnon try to put his hands on me. I'll shoot him straight between the eyes.

Today she would prove to her brother that she could

take care of herself as well as any of his men could. Once she did that, surely he'd finally allow her to go on hunts and train with his archers. Maybe he would even teach her how to wield a sword. It wasn't as if she was asking to *be* an archer—not yet, anyway. She knew well it would be difficult, if possible at all, to convince her brother she was truly equal to his men and that he should let her fight in battles, but she could train with them. She could teach others to be better archers and become a contributing member of the clan. No longer would she be the burden her brother was left to watch over since their parents had died.

The best way she knew to show her brother and his men that she was capable was to track and kill her own wild boar, just as Alex, his men, and the MacLeods were out trying to do now. For six winters she'd been begging to participate in the Winter Wild Boar Hunt, and for six years she'd been unreasonably denied. This was going to be the winter that *she* won the hunt. Then let her brother try to tell her that her place was in the kitchens.

Pulling the hood of her cloak up to cut the wind, she hastened her steps over the sharp rocks. As she moved down the old familiar paths, she pushed branches out of the way while also scanning the area for signs of the wild boar. She knew her brother and his party were headed for the shores of Loch na Keal. He was certain he would find one of the beasts there. Though the triangular loch gave way to the sea, it was surrounded on two sides by steep cliffs, while leading into the loch was a great plain of flatland. Many crofters had been built there, and Alex was certain it was where the boar had come from and where it would return. If her brother had listened to her, however, he would know that she'd spotted a boar last week in the woods near their castle. But Alex had refused to heed her.

She'd prove she was right.

She walked along a stream for a long spell, crossing it at one point by jumping from rock to rock. In the distance, the woods were a thick, green outline against the sky. By the time she reached the edge of the tall trees, she was warm from the walk and loosened her hold on her cloak.

The muscles of her legs burned as she climbed the gentle hills, and the wind whistled in her ear as rain drizzled down from the suddenly cloudy sky. She climbed over and around stones, scraping her hands as she went, and passed several small waterfalls that hummed in her ears. Heather swirled in the air, and every time she took a deep breath it filled her lungs and left a sweet taste in her mouth. The path she tread was worn, and it led her up a hill into a thick blanket of trees.

She followed the trail deep into the cover of the forest, where the trees blocked out the little bit of sun in the sky and caused shadows to grow around her. The temperature was cooler in the woods, and she pulled her cloak tight around her once again. The normal calls of birds talking died away, replaced with a quiet that sent a shiver down her spine.

She wasn't easily scared, but there had been talk all her life of these woods being haunted. She glanced all around, seeing nothing suspicious, yet the sense that something was watching her blossomed in her belly and made gooseflesh rise up on her arms and legs. Though she had yet to see the boar, she withdrew her bow, almost instantly feeling better with it in her hands. Dead leaves crunched under her feet as she walked, and she paused where the path split in two. She tried to recollect which way she'd seen the boar, and she thought she heard the distinct sound of another crunch. But she was no longer moving.

She drew her bow back in the same instant that she sucked in a sharp breath. Swinging around, her entire body grew rigid at the thought of what she might face, yet the path was empty. She stared into the dancing shadows and had the oddest feeling that someone was staring back.

"Show yerself, ye coward."

Her voice echoed around her, seeming overly loud in the utter silence. She drew in four, long, measured breaths to calm herself, yet the hairs on the back of her neck prickled, and her stomach clenched. "Quit being so scairt," she admonished herself. "Ye're alone, ye wee clot-heid."

With that reproach, she swung back around and nearly screamed. A man with the height of a tree and the width of a thick trunk stared down at her. He smiled, displaying a mouth full of rotten teeth. The skin over his cheekbones and nose was stretched thin, as if there was hardly enough of it to cover his bones. His nose had a crooked twist to it, and a bone that protruded up under the tight skin, making it appear white in the spot where the sharp bone was. A wave of disgust rolled through her.

"Move out of my way," she commanded in as firm a voice as she could manage. When he didn't budge, she pulled back the string of her bow. "Move now, or I'll shoot ye between yer beady brown eyes."

"Ye can try," he answered, his voice deep and abrasive. "But ye'll find it hard without a bow."

"What foolishness do ye—"

The sentence died on her lips as someone grabbed her arm from behind, jerked it upward and caused the bow to snap and the arrow to fly toward the sky. She made a grab for her bow, but it was snatched out of her hands before she could get a firm grip. The weapon left a slit in her hand as it slid away from her. Dismay filled her as the arrow landed uselessly some distance away. The realization that she had been rendered weaponless caused her heart to explode, unleashing fear in her chest. She gulped it back, swung around to face her other enemy, and felt her knees weaken when she beheld the angular, grim face of Hugh MacKinnon, cousin to the MacKinnon laird and her brother's greatest enemy. The fool was trying to steal Alex's land.

When Bridgette's gaze locked with Hugh's, he lunged for her, and she stumbled backward, barely out of his reach. Outrunning them was her only chance. She turned to dash through the thicket of trees, and just as she made it to the hill and started to climb, Hugh clasped her by the waist and yanked her down the hill again. She threw her head back, and it connected with something hard. Hugh released her, and she lurched forward, tripping and going down on her knees.

He grabbed her by the leg and tugged her belly-first over gnarled tree roots and twigs before she was flipped over. He loomed over her, his greasy hair swinging on either side of his face. She bucked upward, but he knocked her back to the ground with one palm, then pinned her to the earth with a knee over her legs and his hands on her shoulders.

"Yer brother took land from us, and now I'm going to take from him. Yer innocence is the first thing I'll be taking."

As Hugh lowered his face to hers and kissed her, invading her mouth, Bridgette let out a muffled scream of pure rage and disgust. When he pulled back with a chuckle, his face still very near hers, she didn't hesitate. She drove her forehead into his, their skulls cracking loudly and sending a stab of sharp pain down the sides of her face. Hugh fell off her and to the side, where he sat cradling his head.

She scrambled up to run, and just as she was about to make her escape, a fearful war cry rent the air. Lachlan MacLeod came charging through the woods wielding his arrow and wearing an expression of menace that stole her breath and froze her in awe.

At the terror-filled scream of a woman, Lachlan MacLeod had abandoned his hunt for the wild boar and made his way quickly toward the sounds of distress. He wasn't sure what he'd expected to find, but as he charged into the thick woods and spotted Bridgette MacLean, eyes wide, with two large men closing in on her, he had to shake off his shock at finding her out of the castle.

Dismissing the surprise from his mind, he charged toward the men, raising his sword high.

He met his first opponent blade to blade, and the clash of steel echoed in his ears. He advanced swiftly, bringing his foe's blade low and exposing his belly. Lachlan was swifter and stronger than his enemy. As the man struggled to lift his sword, Lachlan knocked it out of the man's hands, caught it with his foot, and propelled it into the air so he could grasp it. The man gaped at Lachlan with fearful eyes.

"Away with ye," Lachlan snarled, giving the man a slice across the chest that drew blood but was not fatal. "The next strike will fell ye if ye remain here."

As the man scurried away, Lachlan sensed movement behind him.

"Lachlan!" Bridgette screamed.

He swung around and stilled at the sight of Hugh MacKinnon holding Bridgette, who was fighting like a rabid dog, in front of him like a human shield. Hugh's show of cowardice surprised Lachlan, but Bridgette's fiery resistance did not. The appearance of the scruffy girl he remembered from the last visit he and his brothers had made to the MacLean hold two winters ago may have been gone and replaced by a beautiful young woman, but inwardly Bridgette still appeared to be unlike any other. She had a will to match any man's and an almost palpable dislike for her role as a woman. Lachlan searched Bridgette's face to see if she was frightened and was pleased when rage-filled eyes met his.

"Ye're a coward to use a lass as a shield, Hugh," Lachlan said to draw the man's attention as much as to give himself time to decide how to strike.

"I'm wise, nae a coward," the man snarled.

"Dispense with yer talking, will ye?" Bridgette demanded, her blazing green gaze piercing Lachlan. With that command, she suddenly drove her foot backward and up into Hugh's groin, causing him to howl in pain and release her.

Lachlan admired the expertly placed maneuver for one brief moment before he darted to Hugh's side and sent his sword down into the burly man's foot, gave it a twist, and then jerked it out. Hugh drew his own sword upward, and when he did, Lachlan rammed the hilt of his dagger into the man's nose. A crack resounded in the air, and Hugh let out a howl as he doubled over in pain, dropping his sword. Lachlan quickly knocked him over the head with the hilt of his sword and watched with pleasure as Hugh crumpled to the ground in a forced sleep.

Bridgette stepped to Lachlan's side, staring at Hugh for

a long spell. Clucking her tongue, she bent down, picked up the man's sword with some effort, and dragged it away from him. When she turned back to Lachlan, he was surprised at the accusatory, angry look she gave him. "Ye should have let me gut him. 'Twas my right. But I kinnae gut a defenseless man."

"Is it nae traditional to thank a man who saves yer life?" Lachlan asked, half-amused at her anger and half-curious at her reaction.

A scowl swept across her face. "Och!" She pressed her lips together. "I escaped him myself, if ye did nae notice," she snapped.

With a shake of his head, Lachlan kneeled down, took out his rope, and secured Hugh's hands and feet before he stood once more. "What I noticed is that he had ye in his clutches until I appeared."

She narrowed her eyes. "I'd already escaped him once, but when ye charged into the woods screaming like a loon, ye distracted me and he got his filthy hands on me once again."

"I saved ye," he insisted, though he felt sure she could have saved herself as she claimed. But the lovely, mutinous look her face took on when she argued did make it rather entertaining to keep goading her.

She snorted. "Ye men are all so cocky. I saved myself," she repeated.

"If that's what ye wish to believe," he teased.

Bridgette blew out an irritated breath. "What shall we do with him?" She nodded toward Hugh.

Lachlan thought for a moment, glancing toward the woods that led to the castle. "I'm nae going to carry him on my horse back to yer brother. Alex can come for him." When she didn't respond, he turned to her.

She was bent over collecting her bow and arrows, but when she stood, she did not look at him. She sheathed her weapon and kept her face turned away, but he could see her pulse beating rapidly against the alabaster skin of her delicate neck. "I suppose I dunnae need to ask if ye're fine," he said, even as an uneasy feeling that he'd not reached her soon enough rose in him.

"Nay, ye dunnae need to fash yerself about me," she replied, still not looking at him.

Lachlan frowned. Her voice had a tremor in it that had not been there moments before. "Bridgette?"

"Away with ye," she demanded, wrapping her arms around her waist. "I'll walk back to the castle alone."

His gut clenched. Had he been too late? Had she been defiled? Fresh rage enveloped him. "Bridgette, did Hugh take ye?" he asked, bending down to retrieve his dagger, which he may well need to use to gut the man.

She wrenched her gaze to his. The tears that swam in her green eyes made his chest tighten. He was never without easy banter for a lass, especially a beautiful one like the woman Bridgette undeniably now was, even if she was only but fifteen, yet he found himself unable to think of the proper words for innocence lost.

He struggled for a moment, then blurted, "I'll cut his heart out for ye."

Bridgette MacLean, who he'd known since she had toddled around in a nappy but had never seen cry, burst into tears.

Lachlan shook off his disbelief, quickly drew her to his side, and slid his arm around her shaking shoulders. While she wept, he led her to a rock some distance away from Hugh, gently guided her down, and then sat beside her. He held her and ran a soothing hand through her hair. "I'm sorry I did nae hear ye sooner, lass. Dunnae cry. All will be well. Nae a soul need ken yer innocence has been stolen."

She pulled back from him and gave him a look of amazement. "Lachlan MacLeod," she mumbled through fresh sobs, "that's the most foolish thing I've ever heard ye say, and I've heard ye say many a clot-heid things." She sniffed loudly and swiped at the tears coursing down her cheeks. "Any man with sense would ken if his new wife's innocence was gone. I ken enough about relations between men and women to ken *that*."

Lachlan felt his neck turn hot and his lips pinch together into a frown. "And just how do ye ken about relations between men and women when ye're nae married?" he demanded, knowing her brother would not be pleased if she had given away her charms willingly. Lachlan tugged a hand through his hair. She was not even his sister and he wasn't pleased to hear this news. But he had known her all her life, and he had thought her the sort of lass who would only give her body to her husband.

"Are ye married?" she growled, standing and marching away.

"Ye ken I'm nae," he retorted, hurrying to follow her.

"Aye, I do. Yet I'd hazard my life that ye ken about relations between men and women." She gave him a contemptuous look. "How can *that* be, Lachlan MacLeod?"

"Och! Ye ken very well it's different for men than for women."

She glared at him. "Oh, I ken it, for certain. It's hardly fair. And nae that it's any of yer concern, but my mother told me afore she passed what happened between a man and a woman once they were married."

The knots in his shoulders loosened, and he smiled. "Well then, that's good." When she started to climb the hill, a rip showed in the shoulder of her gown and he remembered his original question. "So were ye crying over yer lost innocence, lass?" he asked in the most delicate tone he could manage.

"Och, nay," she replied, waving a hand at him. "I'd have carved out Hugh's heart myself if he'd taken my innocence." She quirked her mouth. "Though Alex may well decide to carve it out anyway when he hears of this." She gave a parting glance toward where they had left the man tied and continued on.

The last of what troubled him eased away, yet he was confused. "Then why the tears? Were ye scairt?"

"Of course nae, ye eedjit!" she snapped and faced him. The tears that had dried up filled her large eyes once again. She blinked and her russet lashes fanned her cheeks, causing tears to leak out of her eyes and slide down her face.

Lachlan watched as they trailed over the slope of her high cheekbones, fighting the urge to wipe them away. They trickled to her chin, and he could resist no longer. He brushed a finger over one cheek and then the other, meaning only to comfort her, yet when he touched her, desire stirred within him. He jerked his hand away, cursing his body for responding to his friend's sister like that. Bridgette was not a willing and experienced lass with whom to dally. Beyond that, she was too young.

He folded his arms across his chest, where he'd keep them no matter what. "If ye were nae scairt and yer innocence was nae stolen, then why are ye crying?"

She raised her gaze to his, her brows dipping together and a frown coming to her face. "I hardly ken why," she mumbled. They stood in silence for a short time and then she spoke again. "I suppose 'tis because I never imagined my first kiss—and certainly nae like this. I presumed it would happen only when I married."

"Why nae till then? Ye're certainly bonny." It had always been his habit to speak plainly, but he saw by the widening of her eyes and the parting of her mouth that he likely should have kept his thoughts to himself.

Pink infused her cheeks, but her gaze held his. "Because I am odd. I wish to fight in battles."

He nodded. Her brother had often lamented Bridgette's desire to be treated as a man, and giving it thought now, Lachlan could recall her pleading to be trained to use a sword and her brother refusing her. "So," he said, choosing his words with care, "ye believe that a woman who wishes to fight battles is undesirable to men?"

Her cheeks turned a deeper shade of pink and traveled swiftly to her neck. "Aye."

"Ye're desirable," he assured her, though it was surely foolish for him to do so.

She stared at him as if he'd just sprouted wings, and then a smile twitched at her lips. "Ye're verra kind," she murmured and started to look away.

He caught her chin, then cursed himself for breaking his promise not to touch her, yet he did not release her. "I'm nae being kind. I'm being truthful." God's bones, his tongue was spouting words his brain knew better than to release.

Her eyes widened again, and her tongue darted out to lick her full upper lip and then lower lip. "I feel foolish," she blurted, her blush turning the tips of her ears red. "I'd nae dreamed of being kissed, but now that I have been, I'm sore that my first kiss was so awful, and that will be a memory I keep always. And that is why I was blubbering. I dunnae usually cry. 'Tis weak."

"I vow to ye," he said, his voice coming out rougher than he'd meant it to. The desire coursing through him was affecting every part of him. "Ye will receive a kiss someday that will destroy the memory of the one just forced upon ye."

"I dunnae see how. I'll nae have a great love. I'll marry because the men will clamor for my hand so as to make an alliance with my brother."

He stared at her in wonder. She truly had no notion of her loveliness, nor how enticing her spirited behavior.

"I can taste his sourness," she continued as she started walking ahead, her hips gently swaying and making his desire grow hotter. She let out a disgruntled sigh. "His kiss was rough," she said with a shiver.

Ah, God above! The thought in his head now was one that he was certain he should ignore, yet how could he let her only memory of being kissed be such a terrible one when God alone knew when she'd make the next memory. He could not. One simple kiss would harm neither of them. One kiss, done well, would show her what she had to look forward to with a good and honorable man.

"Bridgette." He clenched his jaw on his husky tone and strove harder to beat back the desire that was battering him. He cleared his throat. "Bridgette," he tried again, pleased with his now-strong tone. "I'd like to kiss ye to give ye a better memory."

She stopped and turned to him, doubt flickering in her gaze. She was going to need some convincing, which made him want to laugh. His thoughts were normally sinfully wicked for the lasses, and they all responded eagerly; now that his intentions were pure, he was met with resistance. Determination hardened his resolve. He had to sway her. He was certain it would help her.

Bridgette blinked and stared into Lachlan's green eyes as they held hers. She had often dreamed of battles but never of being kissed. But she had fancied herself in love with Lachlan for near a sennight when she was but eight summers and he had rescued her dog after it had fallen into a ravine. The infatuation had been quickly forgotten when Lachlan's family had departed from their visit and she had taken it into her head to become a warrior. All her thoughts had been for that, and no man had caused her to ponder anything different—nothing more intimate and female—until now.

She had to admit, now that she was presented with the opportunity to kiss Lachlan, she found herself eager. Lachlan was, after all, a fierce, honorable Scot, whom she had long admired and who also happened to be very pleasing to look upon. Muscle carved every part of his powerful body, but the easy smile he often wore tempered the ferocious picture he presented. Even so, she had doubts that a kiss from him—or any man—could wipe away the memory replaying in her mind.

"I dunnae think—"

Lachlan set a calloused finger gently to Bridgette's lips, and a slow smile spread across his face. "Let me be the one to do the thinking for a spell."

She snorted at that, even as her heart pounded. "How many lasses have ye said that to?"

To her dismay, he cocked his head and appeared to be thinking, but then a chuckle rumbled from him. "Nae a one. Ye're the first lass who's ever hesitated when I asked to kiss them."

She smacked him on the chest. "It's sinful to be so

proud, ye ken?"

He caught her small hand with his big one and pressed it to his heart. The thump against her fingertips made them tingle. At least she thought that's what it was. Her mind felt a tad fuzzy as his open stare bore into her. "I ken it's sinful," he said, his voice velvety and strong. "I'll repent later. Now let me help ye."

"A kiss kinnae have that much power, Lachlan Mac—"

His mouth covered hers, stealing the last of her protests and all of her doubts.

She eagerly let the words go, consumed by the searing heat of his kiss and the way her own body flamed in response to his demanding mastery. The peculiar pulsing at the juncture of her thighs and the tightening of her insides, which felt much like the string of her bow when she pulled it taut, made her moan and wiggle closer to him. A low growl emanated from him before his hand delved into her hair and he tugged her nearer. His tongue traced her upper and lower lips, then slipped between the two to explore her mouth. She welcomed him, tasting his saltiness and the slick slide of his tongue against hers.

He retreated slightly, and she groaned in disappointment only to be silenced by his lips once again taking hers with a savage intensity that made her blood roar in her ears, sing through her body, and pound in her head. Aching, unrelenting need consumed her as she moved her hands up the hard planes of his chest to cling to his shoulders. Her wounded hand pained her a bit, but she ignored it. Under her fingertips, his muscles bunched and twitched, as if her touch filled him with as much yearning as his did her.

Feeling emboldened, she pressed her chest against his, and the contact of his hard body to her soft one yanked a hiss from her and a guttural cry from him. Her eyes flew open as he shoved her away, panting. They didn't speak but stood unmoving in the shadows, their short, sharp breaths filling the silence between them. After a time, Lachlan gave her a probing look. "Do ye think ye'll forget the other kiss now?"

She stared at the rugged yet gentle warrior. The concern swimming in his eyes made her body tremble. The only thing she'd remember about this day was him and the way he had just made her feel, yet she could not say that. The man surely already knew too well how he affected women.

She tossed her hair over her shoulder as she started to walk back to the castle. "Aye, yer kiss was pleasing enough that I'll nae remember the other. What about ye? Was my kiss pleasing enough that ye'll forget the thousands that came before mine?" Her heartbeat stilled as she waited for his response.

His gaze met hers and held her prisoner. "Aye," he said, his voice breaking with huskiness. "But Bridgette—"

"Nay," she said, not wanting him to ruin the moment. "I ken what ye're going to say."

He arched an eyebrow at her. "Do ye now? Ye're a seer, then, are ye?"

"Of course I'm nae a seer," she grumbled, though she firmly believed in them and their powers. "I dunnae need to be a seer to ken that ye all think of me as a young girl with odd ideas."

He frowned. "That's nae what I was thinking. I was recalling how yer brother intends to wed ye to the Campbell laird's son when ye reach eighteen years."

She pursed her lips. "He'll nae proceed with it when the time comes. He vowed to our mother on her deathbed to let me choose my husband."

"Three years is a long time," he replied before reaching out and surprising her by tucking a few strands of her loose hair behind her ear. She stilled as he trailed his fingers to her cheek and brushed them across her skin. An almost wistful expression came to his face. Her breath caught in her chest. Was he going to ask her to consider him in the future?

"Make sure when the time comes ye choose yer husband wisely," he said, his tone impassive.

Disappointment sliced through her, making her feel foolish. She knew that up until the kiss of moments before, Lachlan had thought of her as no more than Alex's bothersome sister. Perhaps he still thought of her that way. And in truth, before he'd kissed her, she had not really thought of him since her brief infatuation long ago had faded. Well, she *had* noticed he was handsome since then. And she *had* thought he was honorable, albeit slightly dangerous. Now she *knew* he was both of those things, but he also had a caring heart and he seemed to understand her in a way no one else ever had. That last bit of newfound knowledge drew her to him. Well, that and the extraordinary kiss. She didn't think any kiss from any other man would ever compare to his. But as Lachlan had said, three years was a long time. Still…

"What sort of man would ye say I'd need to pick?"

"One who will always put ye first," he said, matter-of-fact, before clamping a hand on her shoulder and pushing her to the ground.

"What are ye doing?" she demanded.

His answer was to cut his gaze to her while withdrawing his bow and arrow. "Killing the wild boar to win the hunt."

Bridgette sucked in a sharp breath. "That's what I had intended to do. I came to the woods to kill the boar and finally prove to my brother that women can be equal to men."

She expected him to scoff at her. Instead, he used his bow to motion to hers before quickly aiming at the boar again. "Then be quick about it."

Her jaw dropped open at his invitation. "Ye're going to let me take the shot?"

He chuckled as he stole a quick glance at her. "Nae if ye dunnae hurry."

She quickly withdrew her bow and arrow, readied the shot, and fired. Her arrow whistled through the air before piercing the boar in the head. He went down with a thud. Grinning, she turned to Lachlan, who had already stood and held out his hand to help her up. She set her hand in his, the contact making her stomach clench. He pulled her to a stand and then released her. When he started to walk toward the boar, she grabbed his arm. He turned to her, eyebrows raised in question.

"Why did ye let me have yer shot? she asked. "Ye'll lose the contest now." The winner received a nice purse of coin, but more importantly, the victor would receive great respect.

He unsheathed his dagger and then looked at her. "Do ye happen to have rope? I used all of mine on Hugh."

She nodded. "I'm always ready."

"I dunnae doubt that," he said on a chuckle and took the rope she handed to him. "I let ye have the shot because I judged it of greater importance for ye to prove to yerself and yer brother what I suspected was so than for me to win the contest."

For the second time in a brief span, her lips parted in

shock. "Ye mean to say that ye suspected I was equal to ye men?"

He offered a grin that made her dizzy. "I may be arrogant, but I'm nae a clot-heid. In truth," he continued as he strode toward the boar, "I like to think I'm a wee bit smarter than most men." He glanced back at her and winked. "At least when it comes to the lasses. And I learned long ago to have sufficient regard for lasses."

She pursed her lips. "Which of the many lasses that ye have joined with taught ye that?"

"My mother taught me that," he shot back in a chiding tone, "with a few smacks to the head and by beating me soundly in sword-to-sword combat when I was fifteen."

"Yer mother was a warrior?" She could not keep the surprise from her tone.

He nodded as he tied the boar's legs together. "She was a fierce one who defended her father's castle and his life by picking up his sword and killing his enemies when he was too injured to do so. Ye made me think of my mother when ye told me ye wanted to be seen as an equal." He stood and faced her. "Come then. Let's find the others."

She nodded, followed Lachlan to the horse he had tied some distance away, and swung up behind him.

"Hold tight," he ordered.

She circled her hands around his waist, feeling the hardness of his body. Her insides turned like swirling water. She'd long heard the whispers that the high, sweet singing of the fairies floated on the wind the day Lachlan had been born. People—well, *lasses*—said he'd been blessed by the fairies. She'd scoffed at that, but now, as she stared at his broad back and thick burnished hair tied at the nape of his neck, she wondered if it was true. She wanted to reach up, let loose his hair, and slide her fingers into it. Oh, she was wicked! He had to have some sort of magic within him because he had captured her heart with a kiss. Now all she had to do was capture his.

***

Lachlan had watched Bridgette from a distance throughout the feast to celebrate her victory, considering if he should go talk to her. Had he imagined her response to his kiss? He didn't think he had, yet she'd not looked at him once all night. In truth, it almost seemed she was avoiding his gaze. Just as the thought filled his mind, his younger brother Graham sat down next to him at the same instant Bridgette's gaze turned Lachlan's way.

The hum of voices around him disappeared as his eyes clung to hers, analyzing her reaction. Her lashes didn't lower to conceal a thing. Yearning—he was almost certain—smoldered in her bright-green eyes. Intent on learning the truth, he stood, but Graham's hand clamped on Lachlan's arm.

"Did ye hear me?" Graham asked.

Distracted, Lachlan shook his head but glanced down at his brother. "Nay. Can this wait?"

"A lass has my heart," Graham announced.

Lachlan frowned, torn between the wish to go to Bridgette and the desire to stay and speak with his brother, who rarely sought him out for advice or confidences. He glanced across the room to where Bridgette had stood, but she had moved away and was speaking with his older brother Iain. Lachlan looked down at his brother who stared up at him with a face full of expectancy.

Family first, he thought, sitting once more.

"What lass has yer heart?" he asked.

Graham offered a grin. "Bridgette MacLean. I'm going to marry her someday."

Before Lachlan could control his astonishment enough to gather his wits and form a reply, Bridgette's voice rose in anger over the dull roar in the great hall. Silence suddenly fell, and Lachlan glanced to where she stood facing her brother.

Forgetting Graham for the moment, Lachlan stood and made his way across the great hall to the men gathered around her and Alex.

Her head was tilted back to look up at Alex, and Lachlan could see the beat of her heart under the creamy skin of her neck. One look at her hard expression and fiery eyes told him she was angry, and a protective instinct, greater than any he'd known before, flared in him.

"It was nae luck that I killed the boar!" she snapped.

Alex stared down at her with unconcealed disbelief. "'Twas luck," he replied with the obstinacy of a leader who was not used to being questioned. "I'll nae chance ye being killed by allowing ye to hunt with us again. Yer request is denied."

Frustration flashed across Bridgette's face. "But Alex—"

"Nay!" her brother interrupted in a sharp, unyielding tone.

Bridgette's gaze circled the men around her, and Lachlan suspected she was searching for help from her clansmen. No one stepped forward, though Lachlan was certain the men knew she was the superior archer. It was not his place as he was not part of her clan and she was not his woman, yet he found himself moving toward her as if pulled by some invisible thread.

He stepped to her side and faced her brother. "I was with her, ye ken."

Alex nodded, his gaze wary yet not closed to hearing what Lachlan had to say.

"It was nae luck. Yer sister is a better shot than any man I've ever seen. Ye'd be a fool nae to allow her to hunt with ye and yer men."

"Lachlan," Alex spoke, his voice tinged with anger. "Ye overstep."

"Perchance I do," Lachlan agreed. "But I'd rather overstep than stand by and watch an injustice."

Alex's gaze narrowed, but a hint of amusement danced in his eyes. "Are ye saying I'm serving my sister an injustice?"

"Aye. Her shot was nae luck. If there was a woman in our clan that could shoot as yer sister can, I'm certain Iain would allow her to hunt," Lachlan said, flicking his gaze to his brother and hoping he'd not misjudged.

"Lachlan speaks the truth," Iain said.

Alex nodded thoughtfully. "So be it." He glanced to Bridgette. "Ye may hunt with us."

Bridgette flew into her brother's arms and gave him a fierce hug. "Thank ye, Alex!"

Her brother returned Bridgette's hug, then set her away and pinned Lachlan with an unblinking stare. "If anything should ever happen to my sister on a hunt, I'll nae forget that ye're the one who convinced me to allow this."

"I'll nae forget, either!" Bridgette said happily as she gave her brother a reproachful look.

Alex turned away with a snort, and the men who were gathered around disbanded, but Lachlan stood unmoving, as did Bridgette. They stared at each other for a long spell, and the air between them felt as it did right before a lightning storm—charged with a great tension. She moved toward him, and he felt an eagerness akin to the anticipation of a great battle. It built within him as she paused so near that her heather scent swirled around him.

"Do ye like to dance?" she asked.

It was only then that he realized the minstrels were singing and playing the lute and that people had started to dance. He was about to tell her that he'd like to dance with her when Graham came up behind her and tapped her on the shoulder. His eyes locked with Lachlan's and pleaded. Lachlan swallowed and called upon the will that had seen him through many battles and tournaments. Deliberately, he set his awareness of her and his newfound desire for her aside.

"I dunnae dance." He looked past her to Graham. He heard Graham's earlier admission in his head, and he recalled in a flash the countless times he'd hoped his relationship with his brother would improve. Now was his chance to make that happen. "But Graham dances," he said simply.

With that, he offered a hasty incline of his head and turned to depart the great hall. *Family first,* he repeated to himself as he strode out of the room, all the while fighting the desire to turn back to Bridgette, take her in his arms, and think only of himself and the yearning that was spreading through him like a fast-growing vine.

Dear Readers,

I invite you to try My Fair Duchess (A Once Upon a Rogue Novel, Book 1)

Prologue

The Year of Our Lord 1795
St. Ives, Cambridgeshire, England

The day Colin Sinclair, the Marquess of Nortingham and the future Duke of Aversley, entered the world, he brought nothing but havoc with him.

The Duchess of Aversley's birthing screams filled Waverly House, accompanied by the relentless pattering of rain that beat against the large glass window of Alexander Sinclair's study. The current Duke of Aversley gripped the edge of his desk, the wood digging into his palms. He did not know how much more he could take or how much longer he could acquiesce to his wife's refusal of his request to be present in the birthing room. He knew his wish was unusual and that she feared what he saw would dampen his desire for her, but nothing would ever do that.

Camilla's hoarse voice sliced through the silence again and fed the festering fear that filled him. She might die from this.

The possibility made him tremble. Why hadn't he controlled his lust? After six failed attempts to give him a child, Camilla's body was weak. He'd known the truth but had chosen to ignore it. Moisture dampened his silk shirt, and Camilla screeched once more. He shook his head, trying to ward off the sound.

He reached across his desk, and with a pounding heart and trembling hand, he slid the crystal decanter toward him. If he did not do something to calm his nerves, he would bolt straight out of this room and barge into their bedchamber. The last thing he wanted to do was cause Camilla undue anxiety. The Scotch lapped over the edge of the tumbler as he poured it, dripping small droplets of liquor on the contracts he had been blindly staring at for the last four hours.

He did not make a move to rescue the papers as the ink blurred. He did not give a goddamn about the papers. All he cared about was Camilla. The physician's previous words of warning that the duchess should not try for an heir again played repeatedly through Alexander's mind. The words grew in volume as the storm raged outside and his wife's shrieks tore through the mansion.

Alexander could have lived a thousand lifetimes without an heir, but he was a weak fool. He craved Camilla, body and soul. His desire, along with his pompous certainty that everything would eventually turn out all right for them because he was the duke, had caused him to ignore the physician and eagerly yield to his wife's fervent wish to have a child.

As Camilla's high, keening wails vibrated the air around him, he gripped his glass a fraction harder. The crystal cracked, cutting his hand with razor-like precision. He yanked off his cravat and wrapped it around his bleeding hand. Lightning split the shadows in the room with bright, blinding light, followed by his study door crashing open and Camilla's sister, Jane, flying through the entrance. Her red hair streamed out behind her, tears running down her face.

"The physician says come now. Camilla's—" Jane's voice cracked. She dashed a hand across her wet cheeks and moved across the room and around the desk to stand behind his chair. She placed a hand on his shoulder. "Camilla is dying. The doctor needs you to tell him whether to try to save her or the baby."

Pain, the likes of which the duke had never experienced, sliced through his chest and curled in his belly. A fierce cramp immediately seized him. "What sort of choice is that?" he cried as he stood.

Jane nodded sympathetically, then simply turned and motioned him to follow her. With effort, he forced his numb legs to move up the stairs toward his wife's moans. With every step, his heartbeat increased until he was certain it would pound out of his chest. He could not live without her, yet he knew she would not want to live without the babe. If he told the doctor to save her over their child, she would hate him, and misery would continue to plague her and chafe as it had done every time she had lost a babe these past six years.

He could not cause her such pain, but he could not pick the child over her. Outside the bedchamber door, Jane paused and turned to him, her face splotchy. "What are you going to do? I must know to prepare myself."

Alexander had never been a praying man, despite the fact that his mother had been a devout believer and had tried to get him to be one, as well. His father and grandfather had always said Aversley dukes made their own fates and only weak men looked to a higher power to grant them favors and exceptions. Alexander stiffened. He was a stupid fool who had thought himself more powerful than God. The day his mother had died, she had told him that one day, he would have to pay for this sin.

Was today the day? Alexander drew in a long, shuddering breath, mind racing. What could he do? He would renounce every conviction he held dear to keep his wife and child.

Squeezing his eyes shut, he made a vow to God. If He would save Camilla and the babe, he would pray every day and seek God's wisdom in all things. Surely, this penance would suffice.

A blood-curdling scream split the silence. Alexander's heart exploded as he shoved past Jane and threw the door open. The cream-colored sheets of their bed, now soaked crimson, lay scattered on the dark hardwood floor. Camilla, appearing incredibly small, twisted and whimpered in the center of the gigantic four-poster. Her once-white lacy gown was bunched at her waist to expose her slender legs, and Alexander winced at the blood smeared across her normally olive skin.

Moving toward her, his world tilted. His wife, his Camilla, stared at him with glazed eyes and cracked lips. A deathly pallor had replaced the healthy flush her face usually held. Blue veins pulsed along the base of her neck, giving her skin a thin, papery appearance. The sour stench of death filled the heavy air.

Only seconds had passed, yet it seemed like much longer. The physician swung toward Alexander. He appeared aged since coming through the door hours before; deep lines marked his forehead, the sides of his eyes, and around his mouth. Normally an impeccably kept man, his hair dangled over his right eye, and his shirt, stained dark red, hung out from his trousers. Shoving his hair out of his eye, the physician asked, "Who do you want me to try to save, Your Grace?"

Alexander curled his hands into fists by his sides, hissing at the throbbing pain the movement caused his cut palm. His mother's last words echoed in his head: *Great sins require great penance.*

The duke glanced at his wife's face, then slowly slid his gaze to her swollen belly. "Both of them," he responded. Fresh sweat broke out across his forehead as the doctor shook his head.

"The babe is twisted the wrong way. Even if I can get it out, Her Grace will be ripped beyond repair. She'll likely bleed out."

Anger coursed through Alexander's veins. "Both of them," he repeated, his voice shaking.

"If she lives, I'm certain she'll be barren. You are sure?"

"Positive," he snapped, seized by a wave of nausea and a certainty that he had failed to give up enough to save them both. Rushing to Camilla's side, he kneeled and gripped her hand as her back formed a perfect arch and another cry broke past her lips—the loudest scream yet.

Alexander closed his eyes and fervently vowed to God never to touch his wife again if only she and his babe would be allowed to live. He would do this and would keep his sacrifice between God and himself for as long as he drew breath and never tell a living soul of his penance. This time he would heed his mother's warnings. Her threadbare voice filled his head as he murmured her words. "True atonement is between the sinner and God or else it is not true, and the day of reckoning will come more terrible and shattering than imaginable."

Alexander repeated the oath, coldness gripping him and burrowing into his bones.

Moments later, his throat burned, and he could not stop the tears of happiness and relief that rolled down his face as he cradled his healthy son in his arms.

Then in a faint but happy voice Camilla called out to him. "Alex, come to me," Camilla murmured, gazing at him with shining eyes and raising a willowy arm to beckon him. He froze where he stood and curled his fingers tighter around his swaddled son, desperate to hold on to the joy of seconds ago, and yet the elation slipped away when realizing the promise he had made to God.

That vow had saved his wife and child. As much as he wanted to tell Camilla of it now, as her forehead wrinkled and uncertainty filled her eyes, fear stilled his tongue. What if he told her, and then she died? Or the babe died?

"You've done well, Camilla," he said in a cool tone. The words felt ripped from his gut. Inside, he throbbed, raw and broken.

He handed the babe to Jane and then turned on his heel and quit the room. At the stairs, he gripped the banister for support as he summoned the butler and gave the orders to remove his belongings from the bedchamber he had shared with Camilla since the day they had married.

As he feared, as soon as Camilla was able to, she came to him, desperate and pleading for explanations. Her words seared his heart and branded him with misery. He trembled every time he sent her away from him, and her broken-hearted sobs rang through the halls. The pain that stole her smile and the gleam that had once filled her eyes made him fear for her and for them, but the dreams that dogged him of her death or their son's death should the vow be broken frightened him more. Sleeplessness plagued him, and he took to creeping into his son's nursery, where he would send the nanny away and rock his boy until the wee hours of the morning, pouring all his love into his child.

Days slid into months that turned to the first year and then the second. As his bond with Camilla weakened, his tie to his heir strengthened. Laughter filled Waverly House, but it was only the child's laughter and Alexander's. It seemed to him, the closer he became to his child and the more attention he lavished on him, the larger the wall became between him and Camilla until she reminded him of an angry queen reigning in her mountainous tower of ice. Yet, it was his fault she was there with no hope of rescue.

The night she quit coming to his bedchamber, Alexander thanked God and prayed she would now turn the love he knew was in her to their son, whom she seemed to blame for Alexander's abandonment. He awoke in the morning, and when the nanny brought Colin to Alexander, he decided to carry his son with him to break his fast, in hopes that Camilla would want to hold him. As he entered the room with Colin, she did not smile. Her lips thinned with obvious anger as she excused herself, and he was caught between the wish to cry and the urge to rage at her.

Still, his fingers burned to hold her hand and itched to caress the gentle slope of her cheekbone. Eventually, his skin became cold. His fingers curiously numb. Then one day, sitting across from him at dinner in the silent dining room, Camilla looked at him and he recoiled at the sharp thorns of revenge shining in her eyes.

The following week the Season began, and he dutifully escorted her to the first ball. Knots of tension made his shoulders ache as they walked down the staircase, side by side, so close yet a thousand ballrooms apart. After they were announced, she turned to him and he prepared himself to decline her request to dance.

She raised one eyebrow, her lips curling into a thinly veiled smile of contempt. "Quit cringing, Alexander. You may go to the card room. My dances are all taken, I assure you."

Within moments, she twirled onto the dance floor, first with one gentleman and then another and another until the night faded near to morning. Alexander stood in the shadows, leaning against a column and never moving, aware of the curious looks people cast his way. He was helplessly sure his wife was trying to hurt him, and he silently started to pray she would finally turn all her wrath at how he had changed to him and begin to love the child she had longed for…and for whom she had almost died.

Series by Julie Johnstone

Scottish Medieval Romance Books:

Highlander Vows: Entangled Hearts Series

Regency Romance Books:

A Whisper of Scandal Series

A Once Upon A Rogue Series

Lords of Deception Series

Danby Regency Christmas Novellas
The Redemption of a Dissolute Earl, Book 1
Season For Surrender, Book 2
It's in the Duke's Kiss, Book 3

Regency Anthologies
A Summons from the Duke of Danby (Regency Christmas Summons Book 2)
Thwarting the Duke (When the Duke Comes to Town, Book 2)

Regency Romance Box Sets
Dukes, Duchesses & Dashing Noblemen (A Once Upon a Rogue Regency Novels, Books 1-3)

Paranormal Books:

The Siren Saga
Echoes in the Silence, Book 1

About the Author

As a little girl I loved to create fantasy worlds and then give all my friends roles to play. Of course, I was always the heroine! Books have always been an escape for me and brought me so much pleasure, but it didn't occur to me that I could possibly be a writer for a living until I was in a career that was not my passion. One day, I decided I wanted to craft stories like the ones I loved, and with a great leap of faith I quit my day job and decided to try to make my dream come true. I discovered my passion, and I have never looked back. I feel incredibly blessed and fortunate that I have been able to make a career out of sharing the stories that are in my head! I write Scottish Medieval Romance, Regency Romance, and I have even written a Paranormal Romance book. And because I have the best readers in the world, I have hit the USA Today bestseller list several times.

If you love me, I hope you do!, you can follow me on Bookbub, and they will send you notices whenever I have a sale or a new release. You can follow me here: bookbub.com/authors/julie-johnstone

You can also join my newsletter to get great prizes and inside scoops!

Join here:
www.juliejohnstoneauthor.com

I really want to hear from you! It makes my day!
Email me here:
juliejohnstoneauthor@gmail.com

I'm on Facebook a great deal chatting about books and life.
If you want to follow me, you can do so here:
facebook.com/authorjuliejohnstone

Can't get enough of me? Well, good! Come see me here:
Twitter:
@juliejohnstone
Goodreads:
https://goo.gl/T57MTA

Made in the USA
Las Vegas, NV
27 May 2022

49423259R00249